CW01510637

Resisting Mr. Rich

Elle Nicoll

Rose Hope Publishing Ltd.

Author's Note

CW—This book is intended for adult readers only and contains profanities, detailed sexual acts, Dubcon, and mentions of illness and parental death.

This book takes place in the UK, with a cast of British characters.

But for continuity with the rest of the Men Series, it has been edited with mostly American English spelling conventions.

Contents

Dear Reader,
Your smile is beautiful,
wear it.

(For content warnings and author's note, please turn back to copyright page.)

Chapter 1
Logan

"I DON'T UNDERSTAND WHY Cole can't just let Keira have it in pink as well. Of course she's going to need more than one color. Who has just one wedding gown?"

I lean back in my chair and listen to my latest swipe right date, *FlirtyGirl99*, tell me all about the latest episode of some reality TV show she's into.

"You'd let me have as many colors as I wanted, wouldn't you?" She flutters her eyelashes and places her hand on top of mine on the white tablecloth. "You're generous, I can tell. You like to spoil, don't you."

I'd fucking ruin those delicious tits of yours.

I lift my gaze back from where it's dropped to her cleavage.

"I'd treat my girlfriend like a princess, Cindy." I flash her a charming grin. It has the desired effect of making her giggle.

"It's Sandy," she muses, not bothered at my slipup.

Her hand goes to the heart necklace around her neck, and she plays with it, drawing my eyes back down.

"Do you want to touch one?"

"Excuse me?"

She bites her lower lip and gives me a coy look. "They're really soft."

My fingers flex against the tabletop beneath hers. She squeezes my hand and then lifts it, guiding it toward her tit.

I avert my eyes long enough to glance around the intimate restaurant we're dining in. We're in a private booth near the back. Tucked away into a dimly lit corner. Nothing at all stopping me from touching the tits of a woman I just met in person this evening after talking on a dating app for a few days.

Game on.

Sandy places my hand over her tit, beaming at me as she pushes on my fingers until I squeeze a handful.

"You like them?"

She drops her hand from mine, brushing her hair over her shoulder, me with my hand spread over her tit like it's the most natural thing to do on a first date.

"They're nice." I give it another squeeze, not one to waste an opportunity. "Really something."

I draw my hand back while she beams.

"I went bigger, six hundred CC."

"They look good on you."

I know some guys don't like the fake ones. But I've learned to appreciate both natural and enhanced.

I just like breasts, what can I say?

"Thank you," she gushes. "I wasn't going to go bigger, but then Humpy added to my account as a surprise." She sighs happily. "He says seventy-five percent is his share. He's so funny."

I look up from the full rounded curves of bare skin.

"Humpy?"

"Yeah." Her eyes light up. "Ooh! Can you get a picture for me? This is a new dress; he'd love to see me in it."

She shoves her phone into my hand and pulls her dress lower with a jiggle, pushing her breasts up at the same time until her nipples are almost spilling out.

I snap a picture of her and hand her phone back.

"Thank you." She looks at the screen and taps in something. "There. All uploaded." Her phone chimes almost instantly, and she giggles. "He likes it. Thank you, Logan."

She slides her phone into her purse and blinks at me innocently like she didn't send a picture of her tits in her new dress to another guy when she's on a date with me.

"Oh." She bats a hand in the air with a giggle as she takes in my frown. "He's not a boyfriend or anything. Don't worry. Humpy's just a friend."

"Is he like a camel you sponsor from the zoo or something?"

Sandy giggles more, oblivious to my souring mood as I take a sip of my wine.

"Humphrey." She rolls her eyes before her gaze homes in on the gleaming Rolex on my wrist as I lower my glass back to the table.

"He's one of my sponsors," she adds as I look at her blankly. "You know... from BuyMyBreasts?"

"Buy my—?"

"Breasts." She smiles at me and gives her chest a little shimmy. "I would have been saving months to pay for surgery myself. My sponsors got me to target in six weeks. Can you believe it?"

I stare at her as she bounces in her seat.

"Strangers bought you your breasts?"

Pride brings a blush to her cheeks as she nods.

"Amazing, isn't it? People are so generous." Her eyes cast down over my suit as she reaches for my hand on the table again.

I sit, stunned, as she entwines her fingers with mine.

"You don't mind, do you?" She rubs a long nail over my skin, making the hairs on the back of my neck stand up. "I know I said Humpy owns seventy-five percent. But I was teasing. He knows only my boyfriends get to touch them."

Except me, a virtual stranger who you invited to squeeze them in public.

"Right." I take a slow breath, rolling my lips and glancing around for the server.

"He's happy as long as I still send photos. All my sponsors are. You're okay with that though, aren't you? I mean, that's kind of how we met. You liked those photos I sent you, didn't you?" She bats her eyelashes, and I tug at my shirt collar.

When the fuck did it get so stuffy in here?

A stiletto glides up my calf, and I jump in my seat before clearing my throat.

Sandy smiles. "Shall we get going? Maybe I can come back to your place and you can show me your designs for Vick?"

My jaw clenches and I slide my hand away from beneath hers.

"Vex. It's called Vex."

"I've never seen a rocket engine before. I thought they'd be, like, solar powered or something. You know, to be echo-friendly."

"Eco-friendly," I grit and look for a server to settle the bill.

Sandy chatters incessantly as I pay, help her into her coat, and guide her outside.

She only stops when I hold a cab door open for her to slide into and stay standing on the street.

"Aren't you coming?"

"Can't." I feign utter regret, holding her gaze. "I have an early meeting."

"About Vix?" She brightens like a puppy expecting a treat for pissing in the correct spot.

"Vex." A muscle in my jaw ticks.

"Oh." She sinks back into the seat. "Maybe another time?"

I don't answer, because that would mean lying, and I hate lying.

I hand the driver a fold of notes.

"Please make sure this beautiful woman gets home safely."

Sandy giggles behind her hand as I flash her a charming smile.

I close the door before she can say anything else. My phone is out of my pocket and to my ear before the cab even pulls away.

"All right, fucker? Why you calling me? Thought you were on a date?"

I chuckle at Drew's greeting. "Nice way to talk to your best mate."

"So, what happened? Does she have brains as well as tits?"

"If she did, then Humpy's probably a shareholder."

"What? You had too much to drink? Listen, I've had one too, but if you need a ride home, I can ask Maddy."

"No, I'm fine," I say as I walk toward my Aston Martin. "I've had half a glass of wine. Besides, you know your sister would rather leave me to crawl over hot coals to get home than give me a lift."

Drew chuckles. It's always been a source of amusement how much his sister, Maddy, dislikes me. I could help my cause, but it's far too fun playing with her when I see her. It's become a compulsion to see how deep I can make the frown line that appears between her eyebrows when she sees me. Maybe it's the lack of any siblings of my own to mess with.

"Did you know there are websites where girls can get their boob jobs paid for by guys with names like Humphrey?"

I unlock my car and sink into the driver's seat.

"Yeah, didn't you?"

"I do now," I groan and tip my head back into the headrest.

"FlirtyGirl99? Really?"

"Yep."

Drew breaks out into a booming laugh. "Jesus Christ. Why wasn't this a double date? I'd have paid to see your face."

"Fuck off."

I drag a hand down my face. Maybe I need a break from the dating apps. Vex is going to need all my energy anyway. It's a gigantic project. I'm heading to Italy soon for a month-long business trip to secure funding for it.

My mind flashes to Sandy's tit as I squeezed it. Humpy has a good investment at least. They were nice tits.

"You sure know how to pick them," Drew interrupts my thoughts.

"Am I that shallow? Don't fucking answer that."

He breaks out into laughter as I curse at him with a half-smile on my lips and end our call.

I exhale as I sit, watching a couple wander along the street. He has his arm around her and she's smiling at something he's saying.

Just then, my phone chimes.

Treena2000 wants to send you a message.

My brows quirk with interest as my thumb hovers over the screen. I hesitate as I read the notification again.

"Fuck."

I throw my phone into the center console, the message unopened.

I want a hot shower and my own bed.

It can wait.

Chapter 2
Maddy

"YOU ARE EVERYTHING I'VE been searching for all this time. I love you, and I'm an idiot for not seeing it sooner. Don't marry him, marry me."

A swoony sigh leaves my lips at the deep rumble of his voice. *Sexual healing straight to my ears.*

I prop my chin in one hand and scroll up the screen with my mouse. I squint as I spot a typo.

"Hey!"

Cold air hits my ear as my friend and colleague, Chloe, whips my earbud out and holds it up to her ear.

"Again?" She rolls her eyes and clicks her tongue. "You'll turn into one of those voice recognition AIs. Able to identify him from one syllable."

I pull my other earbud out and hit pause on my audiobook. Nate Black's voice disappears, and my stomach sinks at the loss.

"I bet he's old and bald. Probably wears crocs too... *with* those clip decoration things on them." Chloe shudders, making me laugh as I retrieve the earbud from her outstretched palm.

"He's not, and he wouldn't."

"You don't know that," she sings, raising her brows as she leans against my desk.

I glance around the open plan office of In Sync, the online magazine I've worked at since graduating from university with a degree in English Literature two years ago. Everyone else is working with earbuds in or chatting in small groups around their desks.

"I do. A voice like that..." I drift off, a goofy smile spreading across my face before Chloe snaps her fingers, bringing me out of my head. "A voice like that," I continue, "most definitely has a body to match."

"You hope?"

I bite my lower lip. "Plus, I might have, you know... seen his new narrator headshot that Eve got through."

"You didn't?" Chloe's eyes widen. "Was he—?"

"Completely gorgeous with eyes that penetrate your soul? Yes." I sigh, conjuring up the mental image I've safely stored away. Short, dark hair, warm brown eyes, an open smile... and the deepest, smoothest voice in the history of all human voices...

Nate Black is perfection.

"Fuck." She blows out a breath before eyeing up my earbuds. "Maybe I should listen to these books. It'd drown out the ogre."

I scoop them off the desk and drop them into my purse on the floor. "Frankie's back on the scene, then?"

She drops her head back to groan at the ceiling at the mention of her housemate's on-and-off boyfriend, whose snores are loud enough to make the walls vibrate. "Yeah, and he's sleeping over again. Until the next time he fucks up, anyway."

I click back into the document in front of me. "You staying at mine again tonight, then?"

She presses her hands into a prayer sign. "Yes! God, you're a lifesaver... well, a sleep-saver. I hate not getting eight hours. I need my sleep."

I laugh as she leans down and hugs me.

"Thanks, Maddy."

"Anytime."

Chloe glances at the literary roundup I'm working on. She's a features writer. And at two years my senior, her extra experience gets her the juicy stuff like politics, which isn't my thing. But I'm still jealous that she gets to write full length feature pieces. It's what I'm working toward. I love the literary column I have control over, where I get to share all the latest book releases. But I want more. I want to interview authors and publishers, and the teams behind the audiobooks that I love listening to. I want to delve deeper into the industry. See behind the scenes. But so far, our editor, Eve, hasn't given me any more online space, despite lobbying for it at every team meeting.

But I'm not giving up.

"Um, breaking news entering at two o'clock."

I turn to see what's gotten Chloe's expression resembling a dog that's been thrown a prime rib-eye steak.

"Ugh. You have got to be kidding me!" I drop my head into my hands, raking my fingers back through my hair before raising my eyes and plastering a fake smile onto my face.

"You all right, Mads? Your face looks weird."

I abandon my forced smile for the glare that comes naturally in his company.

I flick my gaze up and down his immaculate, over-priced, designer suit. "And you look one hundred per-cent buffoon, as per usual."

Chloe's quiet, watching our exchange. This happens whenever Drew's best friend appears. *Logan Rich.* Ugh. Even his name gives me the ick. But women get awestruck and silent as is the situation with Chloe right now when he's around. Or they get all flirty and start swishing their hair around.

Logan smirks, causing two dimples to pop either side of his cosmetically perfect smile. No braces for him as a teen. Logan bypassed teenage awkwardness that every normal person endures. He went straight from cute kid that grandmas would coo over to apparently a devastat-ingly handsome man, judging by the way even the sanest of women react in his company.

It baffles me. This is the guy who told all the boys in my class at school I had crabs.

I didn't get asked out for two years... and I had to go to the prom without a date.

He thought it was funny.

I didn't. I still don't.

His eyes cast over the piles of wrapped packages on my desk, and I shift in my seat so he can't read the labels.

He smirks as I narrow my eyes at him. "You checking me out, Mads?"

"As if," I scoff. "I'm swallowing back my lunch that's threatening to reappear. And what the hell is with the mud-colored tie?" I study the deep brown fabric against his crisp white shirt. It's nice. Like the spine of a classic book. But I'd rather eat my own tongue than admit as much to Logan.

He glances down at it, and his green eyes glow with mischief as he brings them back up to meet mine. "I don't mind a bit of dirt, Mads. Maybe you should try it sometime. Live a little."

I snort. I'm not falling for it. He does this. Makes little jabs about the fact that I'm not out every night of the week living this extravagant, glamorous lifestyle like him. He thinks I'm boring. But I couldn't care less.

He's Drew's friend, not mine. And since my brother finds it amusing that I hate Logan so much, and he just shakes his head when I ask him why he's friends with him, I guess I'm stuck with him being around.

"Hang on. Why are you here?" The only other time Logan's ever been to my workplace is to drop something off from Drew for me. "Is Drew okay? Is he—?"

Drew's working on some skyscraper project with his business partner, Tanner Grayson, in San Francisco. Together, they run a multi-billion-pound design and building company that has its head office in London. The two are due to land home today. Drew called me before they took off, but I haven't heard from him since.

"He's fine. I'm here for a meeting."

"Oh, thank god."

I let out the breath I'm holding. Drew might be five years older than me, but we've always been close. He's a good guy, despite getting in with a bad crowd and ending up in a juvenile detention center for six months when he was sixteen.

Logan was in that stolen car, joyriding too. But he got off with a slap on the wrist and community service. The benefits of Daddy's money.

Those were the loneliest months of my life. A prime example of Logan being an asshole. He followed me home from school every day like a creeper. It was enough to scare off the three boys in my class who lived in my road, who I could have befriended and walked with.

Instead, I walked alone.

Logan Rich has never, and will never, be my friend.

"Hold on. You said meeting." I frown up at Logan, towering above my desk chair. "You work with engines and tinker with weird eco-fuel stuff. What are you doing here? Is it about Project Vex?"

"You listen to me as well as take interest in my wardrobe choices now, then?" He grins.

I shake my head and turn back to my screen, but Logan spins my chair back around. My eyes are level with his tie. It's nicer than I first noticed. It's got a fine copper thread running through it. I doubt he picked it himself. He's probably got a personal stylist that does that for him. That's what rich people have, right? And a personal chef and trainer.

He runs his hand down his tie, then puts both hands in his pockets, which causes his suit pants to pull across his groin area, and... oh god... dick outline. I choke back a gag and avert my gaze.

"I'm here to talk to Eve about the eco-fuel *stuff* I tinker with."

"So, you mean you're not here to finally sell your story?"

His brow furrows.

"About what it's like to be the first human trial patient for a personality transplant with a baboon?" I smile sweetly.

The corners of his lips twitch. "Oh, Smiles. Your investigative powers need some work... It's a walrus."

His green eyes hold mine as if he's daring me to continue our little spat, or whatever this is. I don't know why, but I get drawn into them whenever he's around. It's like he gets a perverse pleasure out of trying to push my buttons.

But not today.

Logan Rich is not winning today.

Chloe's shrill laugh cuts between us, and Logan turns to her. She flicks her blonde hair over her shoulder.

Here we go.

"I can show you to Eve's office and let her know you're here?" Chloe offers with an over-enthusiastic smile.

I don't point out that Logan will have checked in at reception and been offered to be shown to Eve's office. And he likely declined because he already knows his way around from his previous visit.

Chloe knows this.

"That's really kind, Chloe. Thank you." Logan smiles at her, and she lights up like a Christmas tree.

I rein in my disgusted grunt. Even my intelligent, political correspondent friend isn't immune.

Logan looks at my phone on the desk faster than I can bat him away or cover it. His lips twitch and one eyebrow quirks as he reads the title of the audiobook I was listening to—*My Hot Billionaire Daddy.*

I bite back the excuse on the tip of my tongue about it being the story of a father/daughter relationship during a freak tropical heatwave. I will not allow Logan Rich or anyone else to make me feel embarrassed about what I read or listen to. This is a modern female right of empowerment. Besides, it's an amazing book.

I arch a challenging brow at him, waiting for his smart retort. But instead, he winks at me.

"See you later, Smiles."

He walks away with Chloe, leaving some fresh and spicy smelling expensive cologne lingering behind him. Her giggle rings out around the office as they stop in front of Eve's door. Eve opens it with a flourish and sweeps Logan inside after a kiss on each cheek like she's greeting a lifelong friend.

I glance around the office. All eyes are on Eve's office doorway. They drop away the minute the door clicks closed.

Ridiculous.

I pull my earbuds from my purse and put them back in again.

"Don't marry him. Marry me. I'm nothing without you. I'll trade every dollar I have to see you look at me again the way you once did."

I sigh, a smile settling on my face as I get back to work.

Chapter 3
Logan

"Do you want me to pick you up a scarf while I'm in Rome, Mum?" I ask as I flick the coffee machine on in her kitchen.

Despite having my own house, I like coming back here for breakfast. Dad suggested that their housekeeper start earlier, but Mum insists that she likes to make Dad breakfast herself before he goes to work each morning.

I lean against the marble counter as she whisks eggs in a bowl. Forty years of marriage and they're still the most in love couple I've ever seen. I've never known them to argue. It's the classic rags to riches story. Dad met Mum at a local dance hall at seventeen, spent months courting her, then they married when they turned eighteen. Not a penny to either of their names. But Dad's stubborn, and he promised my mother he would build her a palace and treat her like a queen. And that's exactly what he did.

Long hours working two jobs so he could fund his degree in design and engineering, plus some dumb luck when he landed a job with a big car engine manufacturer has led him to this—the owner of the country's largest luxury engine design company. The business produces modern engines for sports cars, super yachts, and private jets. And now, the new project I'm working on with him is for an environmentally friendly bio-fuel rocket engine. Most engines can only operate with a partial biofuel mix rather than one hundred percent biofuel. But we've designed aircraft engines that use it at one hundred percent. And now we're working on one for rockets, aiming to work with NASA once we have a tested prototype. It's ground-breaking.

I have to pinch myself, because even living and breathing it every day as we've been doing the past six months, it still sounds damn cool.

"No." Mum laughs. "Your father keeps buying them. I told him I only have one neck. I can't wear twenty at once."

"Can't wear twenty what?" Dad walks into the room, fastening his tie. "All right, son?" He pats me on the back, then walks over to Mum.

She places the whisk down in the bowl and fixes his tie for him and folds his collar down. "You don't look so good. How much sleep did you get?"

Dad sighs before kissing her on the forehead. "I'm fine."

"Len."

Dad runs a hand around the back of his neck and his shoulders sag. Today, he looks downtrodden, beaten... drained.

"I woke up at two AM and you still weren't in bed," Mum continues.

Dad's eyes lack their usual glint. "I came to bed late. Work. You know how it is."

Mum holds his eyes. "Tell me."

"Dad?" I ask, ignoring the flashing green light on the coffee machine indicating that it's ready.

I've spent time in and out of the family business over the years. My friend, Dax, who runs a distillery, needed my help. And I persuaded Dad it was a good idea for me to experience working with other companies before joining him permanently. But now I'm firmly back in the family business. If something is going on, then I should know about it.

"Sit down. Both of you."

Mum's worried expression matches the increasing tightness in my chest.

"What's wrong? Are you sick?" I sit at the shiny glass kitchen table and wait for him to say something.

"No. Not sick." Dad laughs, even though nothing about the sudden tension in the air tells me that what he's about to say is funny.

"Len?" Mum's questioning gaze from the seat next to his matches my own as we stare at my father, the most capable man I've ever known.

Dad exhales slowly as he looks around the room. "This." He holds his palms up and gestures at the luxury marble kitchen they had designed and installed last year.

"We built this. Our family, the Riches. Years of hard graft. But what we have, the business, the houses, the jet... Everything... It's ours. We built this together as a family. I couldn't have done it without you both."

His eyes shine as he reaches out and clasps Mum's hand.

Fuck, he is sick. He must be. This is a dying man's speech.

"And we must do whatever it takes to protect it." His eyes meet mine, a new determination filling in them. "*Whatever* it takes."

"Of course we will, Dad. This new project, it's—"

"A drain on resources." He drops his gaze to the side like he can't bring himself to meet my eyes.

My head spins. "It's just getting started. We have investors. I'm going to Italy to secure more funding. You're worrying over nothing. We've got this. We—"

"We haven't got anything," he snaps with an uncharacteristic anger that makes Mum gasp. "This project, brilliant as it might be on paper, son, could ruin us. It *is* ruining us."

"Dad." I can't help the laugh that fires from my chest at the bizarreness of this conversation. He's a multi-billionaire. My family owns houses around the world, a fleet of luxury cars and a private jet. My thirtieth birthday present was my own private fucking island.

"This isn't a laughing matter," Dad bellows.

Mum clasps a hand over her mouth and weeps.

Leonard Rich never shouts. Not when a tree crashed into our house during a storm last year and caused half a million pounds of damage. Not when Mum lost her six-carat engagement ring while swimming in the sea on vacation, and he had to replace it. Not when I was caught joyriding in a stolen car with Drew when we were sixteen.

But now he looks like his head might explode from the mix of rage and fear in his eyes.

He takes a deep breath, threading his fingers together on the table in front of him and fixating on them. "We need to ensure the future success of the business... of the family."

"I'll get more investors on my trip. Get them to bring higher buy-ins," I say.

I know I can do it. I've already brought in millions from investors.

"It's not enough." Dad hangs his head. "It's time we made choices for the family."

Why are the hairs on the back of my neck pricking to attention at the sound of where this is headed?

"You're thirty-four in six months, son."

"And?"

He raises his eyes to meet mine and the look in them makes my mouth dry up.

"You need to do things for the family. The same as I have over the years. A union that strengthens the business, strengthens our family."

A union?

Oh.

"You want me to get married? Hey, I'm working on it."

I've been using dating apps for months. Work is so busy that I'll never meet anyone without them. I mean, sure it's been more for random hook-ups. A guy has needs. But in the long-term, I always saw myself getting married and having kids. One day.

"I'll take dating a little more seriously, I'll—"

Dad snorts, and even Mum's weeping halts as she gives me a pointed look.

Okay, so my track record isn't great. Most people don't meet and fall in love at seventeen like my parents did. You've got to experience what life has to offer, and the right one comes along when they're good and ready. Tanner and Dax are living examples. Neither were saints growing up, and yet both are now pussy-whipped and grinning all the time. Although Drew is like me and hasn't joined that camp yet. But I know he has his eye on some hot-shot lawyer he met ages ago. She was my blind date from a double date I went on with Drew. But it was obvious there was no connection there. Drew's blind date was much more my type... Incredible tits.

"I saw Spencer last week. His manufacturing business is doing well. But he's still undercut by overseas labor sometimes," Dad says.

"That's his company's strength, though. That it's all British designed and manufactured," I say.

Dad's friend, Spencer North, has a similar story. Both are self-made men. Both built their businesses from the ground up. Both are strong family men.

"Being the best isn't enough anymore, son. You have a thousand wolves snapping at your heels, ready to take what's yours given the chance." His chest sags as though it pains him to say it. "Strong business unions are what's needed. Exclusive contracts will give Spencer's company an edge. Something competitors won't have. He's going to talk with Gabrielle about it. I'm confident she'll see that this is what's best for both families."

"Gabrielle? Dad—?"

Gabrielle is Spencer's only daughter. We know one another from all the time our parents spent together as we were growing up. But I haven't seen her in a few years. Last I heard, she was in Nigeria, working as a UN aid doctor. She's worked overseas ever since her mother passed away. She didn't want to take over the family business, which caused a lot of upset for Spencer. I recall him spending many late nights here, talking with my father in his office about it.

"Len, what have you done?" Mum gasps.

"I did what was needed."

My eyes flick between the two as realization dawns, settling low in my gut before my father's words reach my ears.

"You're marrying Gabrielle, son."

"Fuck." Dax exhales, leaning back in his seat and clasping the back of his head between his hands. The dark ink of the tattoos covering both of his arms seems even darker in the corner of the bar we're sat in to dissect the shitstorm that is my life. I stare at the flowered vines wrapping around his forearms and wish they could slap me around the face. Wake me up from this nightmare.

"He's got it all planned, huh?" Drew runs a hand around his jaw.

"Hell, man," Tanner agrees, swirling the deep amber whiskey in his glass and frowning at it.

"Gabrielle North," Drew muses, brushing his hair out of his eyes as he tilts his head to the side and meets my eyes. "She's a nice girl."

I shrug. What can I say? She's smart and beautiful, and stood up to her father about becoming a doctor and not working for him. So I expect she'll stand up to him regarding this ludicrous notion of the two of us getting married. Dad told me that she's planning to come back to the UK permanently. Spencer sees it as a sign of her being ready to settle down and thinks it's divine timing from the universe or some shit.

When I left, Mum was still weeping and pleading with Dad to think about what he was asking. He thinks I'll come around. He's betting on it. Leonard Rich is stubborn. But unfortunately for him, I inherited all his stubbornness... and then some.

"Beautiful too," Drew adds, watching me carefully.

I glare at him.

"I practically grew up with her. It'd be like..." I knock my drink back, savoring the burn in my throat as I cast my eyes around the table. "It'd be like me marrying Mads."

"Maddy," Drew corrects. "You know she hates you calling her Mads."

I ignore him and look at Tanner. He's the married one. He married his soulmate, Rachel. They've got two kids and a third on the way, and the fucker looks an equal mix of exhausted and deliriously happy each time I see him.

He lifts a shoulder. "You can't force it. But maybe, you know, if you spent more time with her, then things might develop, they might—"

"Fuck off, man."

"Ease up. He's only thinking like that because Rachel hated his guts when they first met," Dax says.

"When they second met, you mean?" Drew snorts. "She can barely remember the first time they met. Tan left that much of an impression on her."

"Wankers," Tanner fires out as the two throw back their heads and roar with laughter.

"I'm glad you bastards can find things to laugh about while my life is being torn to shreds." I reach for the whiskey and refill my glass.

The table falls silent.

"He's worried about money, right?" Tanner says thoughtfully.

Out of all the guys, he's the second richest out of us. Like Dad, he built his company from nothing except his own blood, sweat, and determination. If anyone can understand my father's logic behind this decision, then it's Tanner.

"Yeah." I eye him over my glass.

"Then get it from elsewhere. Do whatever the fuck magic it is that you do that's gotten you all the funding in the past. And do it tenfold. No, make that a billion-fold."

"Yeah. Talk the shit out of the investors on your trip and come back with money pouring from your ears. You won't need any company merging crap then," Drew says.

This is my thought process. But something about Dad's finality in the way he told me we can discuss wedding venues upon my return has doubt clawing at me. Niggling like an old sore that hasn't healed. One scratch and it'll bleed once more. Weak to infection.

I'm missing something. I must be.

"Better delete the dating apps," Dax throws in with a raised brow. "No more choosing your next date based upon the size of her rack. Jasmin will be impressed."

I flip him the middle finger. Dax's sister, Jasmin, has been going on at me for months to delete the app, saying I'm wasting my time. We grew close when Dax went to jail and I helped her keep their business running. Helping out friends' sisters seems to be my calling. Maybe because I have no siblings of my own. I don't know. Where Jasmin and I became friends, Maddy and I are more like... sparring partners.

The thought of her getting all worked up at her office when she saw me is almost enough to thaw my mood. I made that line between her brows deep.

The guys continue laughing around me, so I turn my palms up, tuning back into our conversation.

"I like tits, so what? It's ingrained into humans. It's a basic survival instinct that a baby knows how to suck a nipple. I'm human. Which is more than I can say for you assholes."

Their eyes all cast around the table between one another before they throw their heads back and laugh again. This time, Tanner joins in.

"Yeah, laugh at the poor sucker who's having their life dictated to them," I grumble.

But despite the earlier shock of Dad's bombshell, my spirits lift. The guys are right. I can bring more money into the company. It's only the Vex project that needs extra funding. Our other lines are running like usual, bringing in huge revenue. Our airline contracts being the largest. Those alone keep our company in billions of profits per year. The rest could all go to shit, and they would keep us afloat. Project Vex is ambitious. But it's not impossible. Dad and I knew it wouldn't be easy, but that it'd be worth it.

It was only when I came back to work with Dad full time that we put plans into motion. I respect Dad for having complete faith in what started as merely a spark of an idea. He's been behind me every step of the way, working on the design with me, bringing in specialists, project managers, a whole team of the best minds to develop it. And we are so close. We need more funding and then we can begin testing the prototype. The amount it'll cost is huge. But it'll be worth it. Once this engine works, even a hundred billion pounds will seem like a speck compared to what we'll make.

Drew wraps an arm around my shoulders, and I manage a smile and soft jab to his middle as he ruffles my hair.

Dad's overreacting. Our company is worth billions, for fuck's sake. And our reputation will bring in the extra investors we need to uphold the project.

I don't need to marry Gabrielle North any more than a bear needs to stop shitting in the woods.

It just won't happen.

Chapter 4
Maddy

"I CAN'T BELIEVE IT!" I howl as I try to make sense of what's happened.

"Are you sure that's what Eve meant?" Chloe eyes me from her perch on the sink countertop.

I've pulled her into the ladies' room for a crisis meeting.

"I'm pretty sure, 'You're going to Italy to follow Mr. Rich and write a feature on project Vex,' only has one interpretation." I slouch against the wall, dropping my head to stare at my shoes. "I'm not a feature writer. I do the book recommendations."

"You're *head of literary news*." Chloe fixes me with a stern look as she crosses her arms. "Who has been begging Eve at every team meeting for the past seven months for an opportunity to write a feature length piece. It's a step closer to the promotion you want. Your own column, remember?"

"Yeah." I scrub a hand over my face, probably ruining my make-up, but right now I don't care what I look like. If I look a mess, then at least it'll match the despair growing in my gut. "But I meant a feature related to *books*. Like an interview with the head of a publishing house or something. Or an indie author feature. Not a…" I fight back a shudder. "Not a month-long trip with Logan Rich."

"At least he's nice to look at. And fills out his suit pants well."

I lift my eyes to meet Chloe's and she smiles at me before rolling her eyes.

"Look. Eve chose you for a reason. She's placing her trust in you to write an engaging article that will draw people in and make them excited. This new project of Logan's is ground-breaking stuff, Maddy. It's literally world-changing. You've been given a massive opportunity to get the first exclusive behind-the-scenes look at it. You're going to see who's funding it and speak to them and get quotes. You can write a candid delve into the inner workings of Logan's mind."

I snort.

"Look, you might not like the guy, but you need to forget that. He's a genius in his field. Like a hot nerd, but not nerdy. Okay, he can come across a little… playful," she adds as she catches my disgusted expression. "But you can't let him get to you. Be professional. Let your words shine through in your article. This is huge for you. It could be career-changing. Nail this and Eve might give you another feature on a subject that you do want to write about."

I straighten against the wall, sucking in a determined breath. "You're right. This isn't about him. This is about me showing Eve what I can do."

Eve was so excited to call me into her office after Logan left. She was buzzing with more energy than a new vibrator as she told me he'd agreed to an exclusive behind-the-scenes interview. Vex is making waves in the science world. Even I can't deny that he's gotten people excited at the prospect of a rocket engine that works on one hundred percent biofuel.

I'm stumped as to why she was adamant I write it. She's aware of my disdain for the man and knows Logan has a reputation as a serial-dater. Maybe she didn't want to subject one of her staff to that and thought I would be immune. She's onto a winner because there is no way I'll be spending more time with him on this trip than is necessary. No way in hell.

I've always wanted to visit Italy. The architecture, the history. It's all so beautiful and romantic. I'll get free time to explore.

Count the positives, Maddy.

"That's the spirit." Chloe grins as she hops down from the counter and looks at my softening expression.

"Wait." I dig around in my purse and pull out my keychain. "Here." I hand her my spare key. "Use my place as much as you like while I'm gone. Get your sleep."

Chloe's eyes light up. "Really? I'll pay you rent."

"Don't you dare even try. You'll be helping me out. You can water the plants."

"Are you sure?" Chloe pulls me into a hug.

"Yeah, we're all winners this way," I say, hugging her back. Although I'd pick having to endure other people's snoring over having a month in close proximity with Logan Rich.

Still, count the positives. Italy... Sightseeing.

I follow her back into the office, feeling lighter. Eve said we leave in two days. And she's given me tomorrow off to pack. The thought of seeing the Vatican has me giddy with anticipation. I'm going to download some guidebooks. And I'll be able to finish my audiobook while I'm there, or on the plane over, because, well... I need to know how it all works out with the billionaire daddy.

This trip will be fun. I can visit places I've been dreaming of and take lots of photos to show Drew when I get home. And I can avoid Logan as much as possible. When we aren't in meetings, he'll probably be on those dating apps he uses all the time anyway. And all my expenses are paid for by the magazine. I'll have my own hotel room. I'll probably be with Logan a few hours a day max. All I'll need to do is record the meetings and take notes to write up in the feature later.

Simple.

"Dad!" I screw my face up in exasperation as he presses the credit card into my palm. I've come to their house to say goodbye before I leave.

"Look, I'm not having my princess in a foreign country without some backups in place." He kisses my forehead and the skin around his eyes crinkles as he pulls back.

I look at his proud face, then think better of upsetting him by protesting again. He's just being a protective parent. I grab him into a hug, sinking my nose into his shirt collar below his salt and pepper hair, and inhale his musky cologne. It's the one I bought him for his birthday when I was eleven. Drew and Mum have both bought him other ones since, but they all sit unopened in the bathroom cabinet. Instead, he asks me to buy him a new bottle of the same one every year for his birthday. It's become our thing.

"Thank you," I whisper.

I kiss his cheek and then deposit the card into my purse. It won't have a limit, despite him being on a modest police sergeants' salary. He's always tried to give me anything I want, even if I'm reluctant to accept it and he likely can't afford it. Pony riding lessons and piano lessons as a kid. Neither of which I was any good at. Then there were driving lessons. I took three attempts to pass my test. But I guess his confidence in me finally paid off when he put me through university and my degree, and I got my job at the magazine.

I'm saving to pay him back, despite him insisting he won't accept it. But it makes me feel better. I'm getting there slowly, one month at a time. It's a world away from the billions Logan makes. He told me he'll pick me up from my house to go to the airport. *Told.* He didn't ask if I had my own transport arranged before informing me that he'd collect me. This will be a long-ass month if he thinks he will be in charge.

"Hey." I grin as Mum comes into the kitchen, followed by Drew.

I run over and into Drew's outstretched arms, squeezing him hard. "All right, sis. Packed enough?"

He laughs at my giant stuffed suitcase.

"Half of it is work stuff."

"Sure."

Even knowing Logan will be here any second can't affect my delight at seeing my brother. I'll never understand why someone as great as Drew is friends with someone who used his father's money to weasel his way out of punishment. Says a lot about a person's character. I'm not naïve enough to think my dad doesn't spoil me. But I appreciate it, and I'm working to pay him back.

I can't say the same for Logan. He might be smart and talented. But he's still had everything handed to him and had privileges that weren't extended to people like Drew. Privileges that took my brother away from me for six months.

"This one is the next big features editor, just you watch," Dad says, walking over to clasp my shoulder.

"Yeah." Drew smiles at me proudly as the doorbell rings and Mum goes to answer it.

"And seeing Logan in action's going to be exciting," Dad continues. "That boy has done great things, the way he runs that business with Len. And Tanner, how is he?" Dad looks at Drew, acknowledging him for the first time since he walked in.

Drew clears his throat. "Tan's good. He's—"

"Always been a hard worker. Built that company from nothing. Outstanding, it really is," Dad muses.

He strides off into the hallway after Mum as I open my mouth to correct him. Tanner might have built his company from nothing. But Drew was there by his side. They're more like business partners than boss and employee. He's great with people. The entire staff respect him.

Just not Dad.

"Leave it." Drew's eyes pinch at the corners before he slings an arm around my shoulders and steers me into the hallway and toward the front door. "I expect Dad already gave you enough emergency cash to fund a small country."

He laughs as I wiggle my wallet with the new credit card inside in response. "Busted."

"Good. So, all that's left for me to do is tell you to be careful."

"Drew." I slide my arm around his waist and squeeze. "You know I will."

"I know. But I also know how men think, Maddy. We're pigs. Don't go letting any of these wannabe Italian studs sweet talk you into anything you aren't comfortable with."

"As if," I snort. I'm hardly the girl who gets guys falling at her feet. That was always my friends at school. And even if all the boys didn't think I had crabs, courtesy of Logan, then I doubt things would have been much different. I'm the quiet girl that studied hard and liked books. And I'm good with that.

"I'm just saying," Drew continues. "Never place your worth in a man or the way he treats you."

"Thanks." This is his brotherly love talking. He hates to see me hurt. He gave my first boyfriend a bloody nose after he kissed me and then told all his mates about it at school.

We walk outside, and I fight not to roll my eyes at the over-the-top flashy car with a driver that's pulled up at the curb. Logan's leaning against it in a deep charcoal suit, arms crossed over his broad chest, eyes full of mirth, and a smug smile.

My hand aches to smack it off his face.

The curtains two doors down twitch. Logan doesn't miss it, puffing his chest out and waving to our neighbor, Mrs. Templeton. She's going to have fuel for neighborhood gossip for the rest of the month at this rate. He loves the attention. He usually comes over in one of his noisy-engine supercars. But today, he's stepped it up one notch further.

I give his driver a polite smile as he takes my suitcase and places it in the trunk of the car.

"Your chariot awaits, Princess," Logan says with a smirk as he opens the back door for me.

"Who does that make you? Prince Charming?"

Logan chuckles, and I narrow my eyes at him before I turn and hug Mum, Dad, and Drew goodbye again. Then I walk past him to climb into the car.

"This next month is going to be fun, Mads." He grins through the doorway at me as I sink into the cool leather seat.

Drew walks over, and Logan straightens up, clapping his palm on my brother's back as they hug, exchanging words in lowered voices. All I catch is, *'Look after her'* from Drew, and the end of Logan's response, something about not needing to worry, and then the final words of *'When have I not?'*

They look thick as thieves, and I bite my tongue from commenting how I don't need to be looked after, especially by a man-child who struggles to be serious.

Logan slides into the car next to me and grins. "Hope you know Italian."

"I'll manage." I cross my arms, wishing I'd downloaded a translation app. I've been so busy packing I forgot. It can wait until we get there now. There's no way I'm giving Logan any more reasons to be smug if he sees me do it now.

His thigh presses up against mine as he settles into his seat. I scoot away, giving us both more room, and turn to wave out of the back window at Mum, Dad, and Drew's shrinking forms.

When I turn back around, Logan is watching me, his green eyes bright. "Do you want to start now? Ask me questions for your article?"

I'd rather clean out a rat's cage with my tongue. But instead, I take a breath and plaster what I hope is a professional expression on my face as I pull my voice recorder from my purse and press record. Might as well get the basics down. I can write the intro up when we get to Milan, which is our first stop. That way, I might get some time off tomorrow after Logan's first meeting.

"Sure. Why don't you start by telling me how you came up with the idea for the new engine? Some people will think it's your father's idea and you're taking the credit."

Logan laughs. His eyes crease at the corners and he sweeps a hand back through his thick, light brown hair. I thought he'd be pissed at my suggestion, which I literally just thought of this second to rile him. But he's amused.

He looks at me, his eyes glowing.

"Oh, Smiles. I can see we're going to have lots of fun together, you and me. You'll not go easy on me, huh?"

"Like you'd ever deserve me going easy on you."

He laughs again, missing the hostility in my tone. "Write it was all my dad's idea if you like. It doesn't matter."

I eye him curiously. Maybe he isn't always such a big-headed jerk.

"What matters is that it's going to be the greatest engine that was ever designed," he says, stretching his hands behind his head, his signature smug smile firmly back in place.

Okay, that hope was short-lived.

I roll my eyes as I move onto the next question.

Chapter 5
Logan

I ANSWER ALL MADDY'S questions as best I can on the drive to the airport, unable to resist the urge to mess with her once or twice. She gets this deep, angry line between her brows when she's annoyed, and making it into a game of how many times I get that line to appear brings me a perverse sense of enjoyment.

I especially enjoy the way she bites down on her bottom lip and her eyes grow wide as we sail through the private entrance of the airport and over to the hangar the jet is kept in. I forget that it's Drew who's seen my family's wealth more than she ever has. But if she thinks this is impressive, then she might pass out when we get to Rome. The thought pleases me, and I grin as we board the jet and I greet the pilots and two flight attendants.

Maddy's watching me but snaps her eyes away with a small huff as I catch her looking.

"Sit where you like," I say, walking in behind her and placing my briefcase down on a shiny table set up between four giant, cream leather seats.

She glances at me before her eyes return to their previous assessment of the cabin interior. Dad bought this jet last year. It can get us to Milan in under an hour and a half. Faster than any other jet in existence. It makes business sense. Every minute saved is an extra minute I have in Italy to drum up excitement from the list of investors I'm meeting with. And with any luck, some extra ones I might secure.

The back of my neck grows hot, and I tip my chin at the flight attendant. I offer Maddy a drink, then ask for an iced water for myself. Every trip for investors has a lot riding on it. The stakes are always high.

But there's even more counting on this one being successful. The small issue of an organized marriage that I have no intention of entering into. I thought Dad would have caved by now. That he would have realized that I'll get the funding on this trip and chalk his suggestion up to momentary panic at the fact we're taking on our biggest project to date. That, or a mid-life crisis about his ticking clock for becoming a grandfather or something.

But he hasn't. And judging by the fact the housekeeper changed the guest room bedding when I was at their house earlier, I'd say he isn't any closer to taking back what he said. If anything would have made him think more clearly, then it would be Mum banishing him from the master suite. They've never spent a night apart, bar one before their wedding.

He really is hellbent on me marrying Gabrielle. And I would bet my left kidney that Gabrielle won't want this either. I tried to reach her as soon as Dad dropped the bombshell. But she's flown to help at an earthquake site in Turkey, so it could be days before she replies to my message. Still, even knowing that she will never agree to it either hasn't eased the lingering tension that's knotted my gut since the conversation with Dad. He said Spencer was waiting to talk with Gabrielle too, so she's probably still oblivious to their crazy scheme.

Ignorance is bliss, indeed.

I wipe at my brow and then loosen my tie and undo the top button of my shirt, thanking the flight attendant for my water as she returns. I down the contents of the crystal tumbler and place the glass down and look at Maddy, who's settled herself into one of the seats on the opposite side of the aisle. She's typing furiously into her phone.

I get up and move toward her. She's so engrossed she doesn't notice.

"What Maddy's reading?"

She jumps as I drop into the seat next to her, reading over her shoulder.

"It's the social media account I run for the magazine." She tilts the screen away as a dude with a rippling six pack fills it. "I post book teasers and give reading recommendations."

"Never said a word." I hold my hands up in the air, biting back my smile.

She turns her attention back to her phone, side-eyeing me after a few minutes. "Don't you have to strap in for take-off?" Her gaze moves to the seat across the aisle.

"How could I forget?" I slap my palm against my forehead and start to stand. She exhales with a relieved-sounding sigh. But it's cut short as I fall back into the seat next to hers and click my seatbelt fastened. I even add a little wink as I pull the strap tight.

Her eyes drop to my crotch before the deep line appears between her brows. Her lips curl down like she's tasted something gross.

"I like the view from this side on take-off." I lean closer to her and gesture out of the window. "You'll see Buckingham Palace once we get up in the air."

She huffs. "Will I also see my escape pod? Because I'm thinking it might get used once we're airborne."

I close my eyes as I relax into my seat. "Yeah, it's a special one I had installed when I knew you were coming on this trip. It's got British Retreat Aero Tank printed on the side. Can't miss it."

She's silent for a beat, and I peel one eye open. She's glaring at me.

"British Retreat Aero Tank?" She arches a brow.

"BRAT for short. Thought you'd appreciate it, feel at home."

"You're such a jerk," she mutters, pulling a set of earpods from her purse and pushing them into her ears.

"A handsome jerk though, right?" I grin at her, and she points at her ears with a mock apologetic smile, indicating she can no longer hear me.

I reach over and gently take one from her ear, before whispering, "Enjoy your billionaire daddy."

She bristles as I carefully slide the pod back into her ear, my fingers brushing her dark curls.

"I'm going to get some work done," I say, getting up from the seat once we're in the air.

I easily catch her muttered words. "Italy... So romantic... And I'm going there with Logan Rich."

A chuckle vibrates my chest as I move to the other side of the cabin and fire up my laptop. Maddy's eyes are on me as I sit. I pretend not to notice, cracking my knuckles before I begin typing.

When I look again, she's staring out of the window.

"I'll keep the room my office booked for me, thanks." Maddy folds her arms and gives me a challenging look.

The receptionist at the Milan hotel remains patient and polite as she continues to wait for us to sort the matter out. So far, we've been arguing for five minutes and gotten nowhere.

"I have a three bedroomed penthouse," I grit.

I'm usually easy-going, but the fact she's pushing back over this has rubbed me up the wrong way. I promised Drew I'd look out for her, and that would be a lot simpler if she stayed in the penthouse with me. If she has her own room, she can go out anywhere at any time without me knowing. She could bring a guy back. Some idiot interested in nothing more than getting his dick wet for the night.

I know the type because a lot of people would say that *I am* the type.

My blood pressure soars even more. Drew would hate Mads with a guy like that.

"Good for you." She sniffs. "Your ego needs the extra room. Please, may I have my key." She turns and smiles at the receptionist.

"You'll have more space to work. You could use one of the bedrooms as an office."

Maddy pauses for a moment, and I hold my breath. But then she shrugs.

"Nah, I'm good."

I curse inwardly as the receptionist taps away on her keyboard, checking Maddy in.

"Is it okay to have the Wi-Fi password, please? I need to download some apps," Maddy asks her.

The receptionist slides a card over the counter.

"*Grazie*." Maddy smiles apologetically, seeming embarrassed at her pronunciation. But she said it perfectly.

"That was good."

"Don't be a jerk," she mutters.

"I wasn't."

Her voice brightens as she leans across the counter toward the receptionist. "Can you help me with one more thing? How do you say, 'You are the biggest jerk I've ever had the displeasure of meeting?'"

The young woman looks over Maddy's shoulder at me, then parts her lips.

"*Hai un cazzo squisito, princepe del piacere*," I say before she can answer.

Maddy turns and her eyes narrow. "I should have known you'd speak Italian." She huffs before glancing back at the receptionist.

"Could you please repeat what he said for me?" Maddy holds out her voice recorder to the receptionist.

She's planning on practicing it. I can see the steely determination in her eyes. The receptionist obliges with a curious smile and Maddy drops the recorder back into her purse and thanks her.

I check in, then insist on escorting Maddy to her room even though she makes a huge fuss about it and chews my ear off about how women are independent, and that Chloe would have my balls for insinuating that they're weak and need protecting.

I never said a word about being weak or needing protection. But I let Maddy chatter on because if nothing else, she seems happy to be educating me. She even has a gleeful smile on her face as we step into the busy elevator.

She whips the voice recorder out of her purse as I select our floors. She presses play and the confined space makes the recording echo.

"Hai un cazzo squisito, princepe del piacere."

An older lady on the other side of the elevator mumbles something to her husband. Maddy's too busy looking pleased with herself and continuing her chatter to notice.

The husband's eyes flick between me and Maddy, and he chuckles, looking at me. *"Giovane Amore." Young Love.*

I laugh along as we stop, and they leave the elevator.

"Don't think about coming in and checking for creepers. I can do that myself," Maddy calls over her shoulder as we get to her room. She props the door open with her suitcase before walking inside.

I stand in the doorway and peer in. I don't need to go inside to check for creepers. I can see every inch of the cramped space from here. This must be one of the hotel's more compact rooms. Maddy's office obviously doesn't stretch far when it comes to traveling expenses. She should have accepted my offer to stay in the penthouse.

"This is amazing! Look at that view." She whips the drapes at the window open and stares out at the city. Then she whirls around and takes the five steps back to the main door to retrieve her suitcase.

"I'll come down for you at seven," I say, turning away.

"Why?" She sticks her head out of the door to look at me.

"To take you for dinner."

She waves a hand in the air. "Don't worry about it. The office gave me an allowance. I can sort myself out."

I bite back my retort about her office's 'allowance' likely only stretching to a greasy fast-food burger if her room is anything to go by.

"Maybe so. But I told Drew I'd take you to the same restaurant he liked when he came here with me."

Her mouth opens and then closes again. She won't want to tell Drew she didn't go. And I know she'll be curious. They have similar tastes in food.

She gives me a brief nod. "Sure. That sounds... nice. Thanks."

I nod back and turn to leave, my footsteps remaining slow until her door clicks shut, and the lock is turned.

Chapter 6
Maddy

I'M IN LOVE.

With Milan.

With Italy. With all of it.

The past three days have been a dream. The first night here, Logan took me to this beautiful family-owned restaurant that served the most mouth-watering fresh pasta with shaved truffles. I had to talk to him all evening, but every time he asked about me, I steered the conversation back onto Vex. The last thing I need is more of his disapproval over my choice in reading material or lack of extravagant socializing. And I'm sure that's what I would have gotten if I'd indulged him in answering the questions about me that he kept trying to ask.

I've managed to squeeze some sightseeing in around accompanying Logan to meetings. I've been to the cathedral, Il Duomo, went to see Leonardo da Vinci's *Last Supper*, wandered around the shops in Galleria Vittorio Emanuele 11, and stood staring at the Teatro alla Scala. It's considered the greatest opera house in the world, and I'd have loved to have gotten tickets to watch an opera, but they were sold out.

Most of Logan's meetings stretch through lunches and even some dinners. He wins the support of the investors with an easy charm that I've never noticed before. I knew he must be able to function as an intelligent, even likeable human, otherwise he wouldn't be as successful as he is. But I've never seen it with my own eyes before.

It's... interesting.

I've been recording the meetings to help me write my article. But when it's got to the money part, I've turned off my recorder while Logan and whoever he's meeting with, sometimes one person, other times three or four at once, talk figures. He never seems fazed whether he's up against one person or four. He maintains this calm, confident air. He has faith in the project. That much is clear. Faith and passion that make his green eyes light up as he talks about the environmental benefits of Vex. But he also answers their questions honestly and listens to their concerns and suggestions.

Businessman Logan Rich is a different man to my brother's irritating best friend, Logan Rich.

Some meetings are conducted in Italian, so despite me recording, I haven't been able to write up notes from those. I will have to spend an evening with him so he can translate. The idea is about as appealing as having a verruca dug out with a spoon. Because despite being able to admit he's impressive in work mode, he's still Logan.

I reach out for my recorder, preparing to turn it off as today's meeting wraps up. It's been with Trent Forde, a Hollywood special effects director who agreed to a meeting while he and his wife, Shona, are here on vacation. Apparently, Shona has an interest in rockets and space, hence his agreement to invest.

I knock the recorder as I pick it up, and it starts playing at full volume.

I mouth, *Sorry,* to Trent and Logan as the words *"Hai un cazzo squisito, princepe del piacere"* ring out around the restaurant we're in, attracting glances from the other diners.

"Spiacente," I apologize, gesturing to Logan with a shrug and half smile. I don't want the other customers thinking I'm calling Trent Forde the most annoying man I've ever met. *That* would be embarrassing.

I throw the recorder into my purse and rise from my seat along with Logan and Trent. Trent extends a hand. "Pleasure to meet you, Maddy."

"The pleasure's all mine."

Trent's grin widens as he shakes Logan's hand and pats him on the upper arm at the same time. "Nice doing business with you, Prince."

We say goodbye to Trent outside where Logan's driver is waiting for us patiently with the car. He opens the rear door as we approach.

"Prince?"

"Just a nickname." Logan shrugs, gesturing for me to get in first.

I pause. "Actually, I think I'll walk. It's a nice night." I look up the street at all the fairy-lit restaurants with tables out on the street. Each filled with a mix of families, couples, and friends out for a meal together.

"Okay." Logan nods to his driver.

I swallow down the burst of irritation in my gut as he closes the door before rounding the hood and climbing back in behind the wheel, leaving Logan standing beside me.

Logan holds out a hand, indicating for me to lead the way. He falls into an easy pace beside me as we walk up the street.

"Are you getting close to how much you need to fund the project?" I ask to fill the silence and prevent the conversation from turning to personal topics.

"Slowly but surely." Logan thrusts his hands deep into his pant pockets as we turn up a small alleyway with a set of stone steps at the end.

"What will you do if you don't get enough?"

"That can't happen."

The sudden seriousness his voice has taken on surprises me.

"It must be a possibility, though? I mean, I don't know a lot about how much these things cost, but I'm guessing it's a lot."

The deepening scowl on his face makes me regret asking. I know he takes his work seriously. But I've never seen him this *worried* before.

"One hundred and fifty million."

"What?" I stop walking and turn to face him.

"That's how much we need to fund the project, give or take. Finish developing the prototype, run test flights. Pay the team involved."

"Wow, that's... a lot of paper rounds."

Logan's expression softens and he laughs as we walk again. "Sure is. But it's something that has people excited. I'll get the funding."

I don't ask again what will happen if he can't. Because as much as I don't like him, I don't want to upset him on purpose, either.

As we reach the top of the stone steps, the area opens into a square. It's filled with people cheering as a newly married couple walk from a building, the bride holding a giant bouquet of calla lilies up in the air.

"Wow, it's stunning." I stop and take in the scene as their guests envelop them in hugs and kisses. The bride is wearing the most incredible lace wedding dress I've ever seen. And as the groom accepts the well-wishes, he looks back at his bride every few seconds with a look of complete adoration on his face.

I wrap my arms around myself, pulling my cardigan around my dress.

"Getting soppy on me, Smiles?" Logan bumps shoulders with me.

"I don't expect a man with the emotional maturity of a rock to understand," I breathe absentmindedly as I immerse myself in the magic of the moment taking place in front of us.

The wedding party moves up the street together, a ball of happy, buzzing energy, and we trail behind, heading in the same direction. I still can't take my eyes off the bride and how happy she looks.

"Try me," Logan says.

I'd rather give my full attention to the wedding group than indulge him in whatever 'make Maddy look stupid' game he's got in mind.

I follow the bride's movements. She's laughing, her head tipped back to the evening air as her long hair flows down her back in waves. She's the epitome of joy right now. Carefree... In the moment... In love.

I blink and wipe under my eyes. "You wouldn't get it."

"Probably not. But I'll try... for you."

I side-eye him, waiting for the smirk. But it never comes.

"Fine." I blow out a breath.. "It's love. It's beautiful and simple all at once. And it gives hope."

For once, Logan's quiet and listening with a thoughtful expression instead of a smug one. He nods at me to continue.

I pull my cardigan tighter across my chest. "It's why I love reading. It's about escaping somewhere safe, forgetting real life and whatever drama or conflict might be going on in the world. And just... being in a safe place, I guess."

"I think I understand that." He frowns as we walk, his eyes on his feet, hands still in his pockets. And he'd probably look adorable to someone else. The tall billionaire, clothed in his designer suit, all powerful, but with an uncharacteristic vulnerability on his face as he tries to see something in a way he never has before.

But I'm not someone else.

"Reading can make a hard day a little easier. It's powerful. I know lots of people who read to leave their worries behind, even if only while they're lost between the pages."

"Maybe I should try it," Logan says softly.

I turn and study his furrowed brow as he keeps his eyes cast down. His eyelashes fan out around his eyes, dark and thick. This version of Logan—the one with a heart—is not one I'm accustomed to. It's unnerving enough to make my words dry up.

We walk a little further and the wedding party soon disappears in another direction, leaving us alone. I can't stop glancing at Logan. He's deep in thought, his lips in a firm line and creases worrying the edges of his eyes. His hair is swept back from his face and he's no longer freshly shaven. The early start we had has left a dusting of a shadow on his strong jaw. It stands out against his stark white collar. He swallows, and the motion contracts the muscles in his thick neck, but he remains silent.

"What do you worry about?" The words spill out before I can stop them. I mentally curse myself for sounding like I care and opening myself up to his ridicule.

I learned years ago not to show weakness around Logan. Like when Drew was sent away. Logan following me home from school made me notice Drew's absence more. And made me hate Logan for the unfairness of it all. Him telling half the school I had crabs was nothing in comparison. He should have been with Drew. They were both as guilty as each other. Drew wouldn't have been alone if Logan hadn't squirmed his way out of it.

Some people might argue that Leonard Rich did that, using his money and power, and not Logan. But I still can't bring myself not to hate Logan for it. He walked free while Drew didn't. I was the one who lost my brother. Left with a boy who made sure I felt loneliness in a way I would never wish upon anyone.

I doubt Logan worries about the choices he made. Not speaking up. Living under the protection of his dad and the family money. Unless he has a conscience, after all?

I study him as his eyes meet mine, both of us caught in a rare moment of looking at each other. The hairs on the back of my arms prick up as his eyes sweep over my face. There's a tension in them that makes his green irises burn a darker shade of emerald.

"I worry about disappointing my dad," he says finally.

I drop my eyes away, disgust washing through me. For a second, I hoped he would say something else. Logan's always been a daddy's boy. I bet there's a long list of times he's been bailed out by his family fortune.

I increase my pace, eager to get back to the hotel and into my room. Alone. The magic impregnated in the air that the wedding party created is long gone. Now the streets are as empty as the old memories are making me feel. I tug my cardigan tighter around me.

"Here." Logan unbuttons his jacket.

"I'm not cold. Just... tired," I say quickly.

I breathe out in relief as he keeps his jacket on. I can't deal with him being chivalrous. Not when I'm tired and my guard is down. I'm still processing these new facets of him that keep popping through.

"I doubt your dad will be disappointed. Like you said, you'll get the funding for this project. He'll be pleased. You can go home and work on it together. Make new history. Make more money," I mutter.

Logan walks along beside me, his eyes darting to me every few minutes. The side of my face heats with the attention he's giving it.

"What?" I snap, unable to take anymore.

He shakes his head, a joyless smile lifting his lips. "Nothing."

We get to the hotel and he walks me to my room. I've given up telling him it's unnecessary. He does it every time regardless of what I say.

"See you in the morning. We're leaving at ten, yeah? I'll meet you in the lobby."

Logan hovers in the doorway. *Surely, he isn't expecting an invitation in.*

"I'll be here before that to take your suitcase down."

"I'm a grown-ass woman," I protest.

"I promised Drew I'd take care of you," Logan says, the smug smile back on his face. He knows if he throws Drew's name into things, then I'll comply.

I begin to close the door, but he sticks his foot into it and raises his brows at me.

"Fine," I mumble.

His smile grows and he removes his foot. "Sweet dreams, Smiles."

I hold onto the delight I get from watching the door shut in his face and walk over to my bed, falling back onto it. I pull out my phone and text Chloe.

Me: How many years would I serve for killing Logan as a matter of my own preservation of sanity?

Chloe: I don't know... twenty-five? I don't think the defense of 'he annoyed me so much, it was either him or me' would stand up in court.

Me: Shame. Tell me something that'll make me smile.

Chloe: A baboon's dick is only 5.5 inches long. But a walrus's is 22 inches.

Me: Why would that make me smile?

Chloe: If you can't kill him, there's something else you could take your energy out on ;)

Ugh! Realization dawns that she's talking about when Logan came in for his meeting with Eve, and I commented about the personality transplant.

Me: You're sick!

Chloe: Just saying...

Me: Don't. I've already exceeded my usual annual quota of time spent with him. I DO NOT want to see any more of him than necessary to write this piece, thank you.

Chloe: Well, I don't mind. Feel free to send pics of the sexy walrus.

Me: You and I are no longer friends.

Chloe: Lol. Miss you.

Me: I missed you as well until three minutes ago.

I put my phone down and roll onto my front on the bed, then pull my recorder out and press play. Logan and Trent discuss the project and how revolutionary it is. Trent has a friendly American accent. And he uses mine and Logan's names a lot. Logan's voice is deeper, each word deliberate and confident as he talks. And it has a rough timbre when he laughs. He laughs a lot. Trent says something that has him laughing again, and I stop the recording, abandoning writing up any notes tonight. It's late, and we have the flight to Rome in the morning, followed by a meeting after we arrive.

I open my audiobook instead, taking my phone with me to the bathroom and placing it on the side of the sink as I remove my makeup. Nate Black's smooth voice plays from the speaker and my shoulders relax. But he doesn't sound like he usually does. Not as rich, not as deep. It must be because I usually listen with my earbuds in, not through the phone's speaker.

I pause the audio. I'll listen on the plane tomorrow with my earbuds so I can enjoy his voice. It'll mean I won't have to talk to Logan on the flight either.

Double win.

Chapter 7
Maddy

"It's going well... Yes, I'm eating, Mum." Logan talks on his phone as he gazes out the car's window, one elbow resting on the doorframe and his hand rubbing back and forth over his jaw.

He's freshly shaven. I noticed it when he collected my suitcase for me in Milan. And that... bothers me. It bothers me that my first reaction to him when I opened the door to him this morning wasn't my usual frown. This time my frown had a companion—my eyes. And they were intent on tracing the smooth line of Logan's newly shaven jaw like it deserved my attention.

I know what this is. My mind is playing tricks on me, trying to fill the void that reading and listening to books gives me. I haven't had my daily escape I treasure so much today. I tried on the private jet over to Rome this morning. But there must be something wrong with my earbuds because my audiobook sounds funny. Nate Black's voice deserves earbuds that portray his smooth tone perfectly. Instead, I listened to music as I worked. Then when I switched that off, I kept my earbuds in and sat watching the view from the window as we landed. Logan didn't speak to me, probably thinking I was still listening to something and couldn't hear him.

They're the perfect Logan deterrent.

It's why I'm sitting in the back of the car as we're being driven through Rome with them in my ears, even though they're not playing anything.

"She's enjoying seeing the sights when she gets the chance." Logan glances at me, and I pretend I'm fascinated by something outside.

"Yeah, I'll tell her." He pauses and then laughs softly. "How's Dad?"

A change in the air makes me sneak another look over at Logan. His brow is furrowed, much like last night on the walk back to the hotel. He clears his throat and his jaw ticks as he listens to his mum.

"I know. I thought he would as well. I don't understand why he's so hellbent on it. It doesn't make sense."

He sighs and the heaviness in it makes me twitch.

"I don't..." Logan lowers his voice and inclines his head toward the window, away from me. "I can't do that. She's not... Exactly. I doubt she will either."

Are they talking about me? This is why it's a bad idea to eavesdrop. I can't ask Logan what she said because then he'll know, and it'll give him more ammo to ridicule me with.

He makes a few more sounds of agreement and then ends the call, his gaze remaining outside the car until we come to a stop.

"Where are we? This doesn't look like a hotel." I pull my earbuds out and stare at the giant building in front of us.

"Because it isn't." He smirks, back in full-asshole mode as he exits the car and holds his hand out to help me.

I climb out without his help and look around. We've driven up a long sweeping driveway and through metal gates to get here. That should have been my first clue. But I was too busy listening to his private phone call to pay attention.

"This is a palace," I gasp.

I gaze up at the giant cream building. It has large archways forming a cover over the main entrance. They're held up by giant pillars. So thick I couldn't fit my arms around if I tried. Each window in the building is curved, stone architraves above each one. There are even two rounded walls, one on either end of the building with turreted roofs, like a fairy-tale castle.

"No. Just one of our properties." Logan shrugs as I turn and gape at him. "Speechless, Smiles? That's not like you."

I close my mouth, fighting the urge to smack him in his smooth jaw.

"Am I being taken to my hotel after our first meeting?" I resist the urge to feed Logan's ego further by checking out the mansion again and instead keep my eyes fixed firmly on his face.

Instead of answering me, he helps the driver get our suitcases from the trunk.

"Can you put Ms. Harper's suitcase in the East wing guest suite, please."

The driver nods and takes our suitcases in through the front door.

I shake my head so fast I'm surprised my brain doesn't rattle. "No. No, no, no. I'm not staying here with you. The office has booked me a hotel room."

"A closet, you mean?" Logan's expression is unreadable as he looks at me. "You're not staying in any other places the office has booked for you. You're with me from now on."

"Like hell I am," I hiss. "I don't want to see your naked ass when you get out the shower or walk around in your underwear drinking coffee in the mornings." My mind chooses this moment to flash the image of Logan's suit-panted dick outline from that day in the office. I take a deep breath before bile can rise from my stomach.

He shrugs one shoulder. "I don't think you'd be saying that if you saw the size of my—"

"Stop!" I throw my palm up in front of his face. "I don't want to be sick."

He uses his pointer finger to slowly nudge my hand out of the way so he can look into my eyes.

"—the size of my coffee machine." He raises his brows. "Finest Italian beans from our neighbor's personal supply." He sweeps his arm toward where his nearest neighbor must live, but it must be miles away. This isn't a palace; it's an estate with manicured lawns and flowering gardens as far as the eye can see.

It's nothing short of spectacular.

I look up at the house again. Anything not to look at Logan.

"I'm glad my discomfort in this situation amuses you," I huff.

His voice deepens. "Mads?"

I still don't look at him.

He places his hand on my lower back, and I jump as electricity sparks through my skin. Logan takes his hand away, likely warned by my body's natural reaction to him. My built-in defense mechanism.

"Your room has its own bathroom. And if it makes you more comfortable, I'll make sure to wear multiple layers of clothing around the house in your presence, okay? Maybe ten. I can sweat out toxins at the same time and call it a cleanse."

I purse my lips and chance a look up at him. He's not smirking anymore. His mouth is relaxed. But his eyes still hold the shine of mischief they always do.

"You could do with a cleanse." He's in a navy suit today—Italian leather shoes and belt, another crisp white shirt, and expensive, fresh cologne. "Will it sweat out a bad attitude as well?"

"I don't know. But we could try it on you first and then we'd know," he answers without missing a beat.

I bite back my smart retort because that would only prove his point.

"Come on. I'll show you around before the meeting."

This time, he doesn't try and lead me with a hand on my lower back. He lets me walk ahead, the heels of my black patent pumps clicking on the shiny marble floor as we walk into the entry hall.

"Logan," I breathe in awe.

"You like it? Drew and Tanner organized the re-model when we first bought it."

I recall Drew saying he was working on something for Leonard Rich once. But that was years ago when Tanner's company was a lot smaller than it is now. It was only a few months after Drew had joined him to work together. They were barely out of their teens. This must have been a huge project for them to have won the bid when the business was still so small.

I chew my bottom lip as I look around the lavish cream marble interior. The sweeping staircase is like the one Cinderella walks down to enter the ballroom. *Were Drew and Tanner given this job by Leonard out of guilt?* Guilt at Drew being sent away when Logan wasn't?

"It's beautiful," I admit as he takes me on a tour. It's like walking into a glamorous Italian film set. The kitchen is giant and overlooks the swimming pool and gardens at the rear of the house, and there's a seating area by the floor-to-ceiling doors that lead outside. It's the perfect spot to read in the morning sun.

Logan shows me from room to room. Including his home office for when he works here, which he tells me he does often because being in the business of luxury engines used in super cars and yachts, amongst other things, he has a lot of business to take care of in Italy. Now I get why he speaks fluent Italian. I don't know why I didn't know this already.

The more he shows me around the property and tells me about its history and what he does when he stays here, the more holes appear in that knowledge. And the realization that there's a lot more to discover about him has an uneasy tightness growing in my chest.

I've hated Logan Rich for years. It's the way it's always been. It's the way it always will be. It's as certain as the sun rising each day.

"This is Mum's dressing room." Logan walks into the huge space. The walls are lined with shelves of designer shoes and purses and racks upon racks of clothes.

In the center is a giant island of glass-topped drawers with a huge vase of lilies on top. I peer through the glass at the rows of watches, jewelry, belts, and purses. There's an entire section of intricately detailed silk scarves down one side, each more beautiful than the last.

"If you see something you like, Mum said to help yourself."

"What?" I drag my eyes away from the scarves and look at Logan.

"Most of it hasn't been worn. The staff keep it stocked in case Mum visits. But they rarely come to this house anymore. They use the one in Florence. This one's mine now."

Logan's face doesn't hold the delight in it that I would expect when you're telling someone that you own a palatial Italian estate all to yourself. But the closest I've ever come is buying my own small apartment, which is hardly comparable. Still, I cracked open multiple champagne bottles when the sale went through a few years ago.

"We need to leave for the meeting in twenty minutes. Let me show you your room."

One and a half hours later, I'm smoothing down the deep red pencil skirt that I've tucked my blouse into as we exit the car. I run a hand through my curls as I look at the yacht moored in Ostia Marina. Logan said we're fortunate to have secured a meeting. Apparently, this man is harder to pin down than a first edition copy of The Gutenberg Bible.

I look at Logan. He's changed into a deep gray suit that makes his eyes glow a brighter green.

Today's meeting is with a man called Sterling Beaufort. Logan said he's never met him, but Sterling knows Leonard from business they did years ago. He's American, so I'll be able to follow along what's being said. Logan briefed me before we left Milan. Apparently, as well as owning a multi-billion-dollar jewelry business, Sterling runs a collection of elite members-only clubs around the world. The types of places that don't exist to you unless your bank account has infinite zeros after the first figure. Logan's hoping Sterling will invest a sizeable amount, and I get the feeling he's nervous about this meeting.

"Ready?"

He looks at me and gives me a tight smile. "Always."

We head along the walkway toward a man in navy slacks and a white shirt—one of the crew from the yacht—who welcomes us onboard. I step on and we follow the man to the top deck where a table is set up, covered in platters of fruit, and a bottle of something chilling in an ice bucket.

I try not to make it obvious I'm looking around. I should be used to the luxury that goes along with obscene amounts of wealth by now. Especially after Logan's marble palace. But my eyes still widen at the sheer beauty of the yacht.

"Mr. Rich?" A handsome man with silver hair stands from the table to greet us. His eyes land on mine and he gives me a warm smile, his blue eyes twinkling. "I can see you brought beautiful company."

He shakes Logan's hand and then takes my hand, never breaking eye contact. The devilish glint in his eye, paired with a wolfish smile, works for him, making it charming, albeit in an intense way.

This man screams power and doesn't care to hide it.

"I'm Maddy. Nice to meet you."

He invites us both to sit and pulls out a chair for me, pushing it in for me as I sit.

"Short for Madeleine?"

"Maddox, actually," Logan interjects, clearing his throat as he takes the seat next to mine.

"How unique." Sterling's eyes stay on mine, and I shiver in my thin silk blouse under his scorching gaze. I've never been into older men, he must be around my father's age, but he's helping me to understand the appeal.

I swallow, aware of his eyes tracking my every move with interest. They stay on my face as he motions for a member of staff to come over and pour us drinks. Then he lifts a crystal champagne flute and hands it to me.

"To new beginnings and exciting ventures."

Sterling clinks my glass first and then Logan's. Logan thrusts his glass a little too hard and some of Sterling's champagne slips over the side, spilling onto his hand. Sterling's lips quirk into a smile as he places his glass down and dries his hand on a linen napkin before giving Logan his full attention.

"So, you want forty million?"

I accidentally swallow a huge mouthful of champagne and a bubble lodges itself in my throat. Logan said Sterling's time was precious. He's obviously a man who likes to get straight to the point.

Logan hands me his napkin, his eyes meeting mine for a second before he looks back at Sterling. I take it gratefully and cover my mouth to cough quietly.

"You've read the proposal I sent. Sixty is more in line," Logan says, his voice deep and confident.

I pat my lips with the napkin before placing it down on the table.

Sterling's eyes narrow, the corner of his lips curling up. He turns his eyes onto me as he speaks to Logan. "You said forty."

"Plans change," Logan snaps.

Sterling's eyes twinkle with amusement as I turn away and stare at Logan. He's being so rude. I want to kick him under the table and ask what the hell he's playing at.

"Fifty," Sterling says.

"No deal." Logan stands to leave and fastens his suit jacket with one hand. "Mads, we're leaving."

A deep chuckle breaks free. "Is he always like this?" Sterling asks me.

I open my mouth, wondering if I should apologize on Logan's behalf. But I'm not his minder. He's a grown man and if he wants to stuff up this deal by being a rude jerk, that's up to him.

"Mads," Logan growls.

I smile politely at Sterling as I push my chair back. "It was nice meeting you."

Sterling dips his chin and smiles. Then he looks back at Logan. "Sit back down and have a drink with me and I'll give you the sixty."

"You want us both to sit again, then the price just went to sixty-five," Logan growls.

I bite back my gasp as I look between the two men.

There's silence for a few seconds, then Sterling throws his head back and laughs, slapping a hand on his thigh. "You're like your father."

"Thank you."

Logan places his hand on my lower back, ready to lead me away. Electricity fires across my skin.

"Sixty-five," Sterling muses, his eyes twinkling as he watches Logan's stiff posture. "Okay... We've got a deal."

I let out the breath I'm holding. He's talking about six-ty-five *million*. And judging from the absence of sweat on his brow, it's mere pocket change to him.

Wow.

Logan's fingers flex against my lower back, and I gulp as he stares at Sterling, now on his feet, standing and waiting.

Take the deal. I wish I could slap Logan around the head for being such a rude jerk. Here he is, being given the opportunity to boost Vex's fund, and he's deathly still, except for the subtle movement of his thumb smoothing over my blouse at the base of my spine.

I swear they must be able to hear my pulse thundering in my veins from the tension swirling around us.

After a long pause, Logan turns back to the table and tips his chin at my abandoned chair. "Sit."

I comply, my eyes shifting back and forth between the two men. He pushes the chair in for me, his eyes fixed on Sterling.

He takes his seat next to me as Sterling sits back down too, his eyes staying on Logan.

Then the meeting continues. Logan slips back into business mode, relaxing more as they discuss the project. He no longer looks like he's about to burst a blood vessel. And Sterling seems genuinely excited about it. He's a nice guy. He asks me about sightseeing in Milan, and I tell him where I went and what was my favorite—Teatro alla Scala.

By the time we leave, it's as if nothing ever happened.

Chapter 8
Logan

I ROLL MY NECK, groaning as it cracks and brings some release to the stirrings of a headache threatening to form. The meeting with Sterling was a success. But I can't enjoy the moment. My mind keeps skipping back to Dad. I spoke to him this morning before we checked out in Milan. He's still adamant that Gabrielle and I marry. She's back in London now. And Mum's still arguing with Dad and sounding angrier with him each time I speak to her. Now, I'm equal parts scared that Dad's going mad and equal parts hoping that he is, because it will explain what the hell's going on.

At least if this headache does come, I have no more meetings today. I can relax at the house and try and get hold of Gabrielle. Sort this out once and for all. Spencer won't push her into a marriage she doesn't want when she tells him it's a no, right?

It'll all be sorted by the end of the week.

"Why did you put the price up?" Maddy eyes me across the backseat.

"Sterling can afford it. He wouldn't have paid if he couldn't."

Her lips part, and she stares at me, wide-eyed. "That doesn't answer my question. Twenty-five million is a hell of a lot of money to increase the offer by on a whim."

She's right, it doesn't answer her question. But I can't answer it. I don't know why I put the price up on the spot. Gut instinct maybe? My subconscious must have tapped into something.

"It is," I agree. "But the project's worth it and Beaufort knows that. He'll get back over ten times what he invests." She's still staring at me, so I add, "It's just business."

"Yeah." She rolls her eyes. "Just business. Like I'd ever be able to understand."

"That's not what I meant."

She leans forward to our driver and asks him to pull over to let her out.

"Where are you going?" I snap my head in her direction as she climbs out of the car.

"Sightseeing," she replies as I jump out behind her.

"On your own?"

She rolls her eyes again. She does it a lot in my company and it's starting to grate on me. She views spending time with me with the same amount of enthusiasm as someone who's about to have a rectal examination.

"There are things I want to see, and I've booked a Vatican tour at four o'clock."

"I told Drew I'd—"

"Ugh. Leave my brother out of this. I went alone in Milan, didn't I?"

Yeah, and you had one of my security team following you discreetly the whole time.

"Rome's busier," I argue.

Maddy screws her face up. "You're being ridiculous. I'm going and that's that. Instead of worrying about what I'm doing all the time, why don't you do something for you? *Live a little.*" She smirks. "That was the advice you gave me before this trip. Now it's your turn." She cocks a brow at me and then rummages inside her purse. "Go on your dating apps. I've not seen you use them since we arrived. Find a beautiful Italian woman to stroke your ego for a while."

When I don't reply, she glances up at me. "What? Lost the thrill of bedding a woman purely based upon looks?"

"Not now, Mads!" I snap with more force than I intend.

Her brows pull together, the line between them cutting deep into her skin. Only I don't feel any delight in seeing it there this time.

Here comes the fucking headache.

"You can't sightsee in those, anyway." I look at the black stilettos on her feet. She'll have to come back to the house to change them, and that'll give me enough time to arrange a member of the security team to keep an eye on her for the rest of the day. Problem solved.

"Oh, darn it. You're right." She bats her eyelashes at me in mock sweetness as she rests one hand on the roof of the car. She pulls a pair of flat sandals from her purse and removes her heels one at a time, swapping them for the new pair. Then she hands her heels to me.

"Mads—"

"Bye, Logan. Don't wait up!" She thanks our driver and then skips away, her head already spinning side to side as she looks up at the beautiful buildings in delight, a wide smile on her face.

"Sir?"

I glance at my driver, then at Maddy's retreating figure.

Fuck's sake.

"I'll call you if I need you. But you might as well take the rest of the day off," I mutter.

He gives me a questioning look as I hand him Maddy's shoes.

Then I race up the street after her.

"Gelato. Mm, this is good." Maddy grins and then wraps her lips around the ice cream again.

"I told you I'm a fountain of knowledge of the best places to visit in Rome. Including where to source the best gelato."

"Yeah," she scoffs and then carries on licking the cone as we walk.

After the initial eye rolls, huffs, and bursts of displeasure at me catching her up in the street, we've had an amicable time. We've been to the Spanish Steps, the Sistine Chapel, and the Colosseum. Maddy wants to see the Trevi Fountain, but it will have to wait until after the

Vatican tour. Maybe it's because we're busy and she's distracted, but her dislike for me hasn't been voiced as passionately as usual. Or maybe she's tired. Either way, I'm enjoying the reprieve.

"Such a fountain of knowledge, and yet, you've never been inside the Vatican." She smirks.

I shake my head with a smile. She took great delight in the fact I've not made time to visit it properly before. But that changes today. I booked a ticket online as Maddy was gazing at the ceiling in the Sistine Chapel.

"Maybe I was waiting for the right bitchy woman to go with. Inspiring, historical places just aren't the same if not viewed with a side of loathing. Adds to the atmosphere." I lick my mint-choc-chip cone as Maddy fights back a smile.

"I can definitely provide that for you."

"Like no other," I muse as we walk into Vatican City. We finish our cones and join the end of a long line.

"You know this is the smallest independent country in the world?" Maddy says.

"Am I expected to tip the tour guide at the end?"

She tuts. "The best thing you could give me right now would be personal space," she says, stepping away from me.

"In case you didn't notice, the rest of the world seems to be visiting the smallest independent country at the same time as us." I step closer to her again as I'm forced forward in the queue by a group of excited female students all wearing Sapienza, University of Rome sweaters and snapping selfies together.

"You can wait outside if you like? Or go back to the house?"

Her expression is hopeful as she looks at me. One of the students steps on my foot, then I look further down the queue and catch eyes with a guy whose friend is busy eye-fucking Maddy.

Heat flares across the back of my neck. "And miss tour guide Mads' private one-on-one service? I'm good."

Her face falls and she folds her arms. The movement pushes her breasts up beneath her blouse. I look back at the two guys. Eye-fuck's friend has the sense to elbow him as he sees me watching them. *Yeah, fucker. I'm onto you.* Drew would be too if he were here. But he's not, so I must be the biggest cock-blocking asshole there is for him. It's what friends do for one another.

I glare at the two guys for another few minutes, making sure they don't look our way again. When I'm satisfied that they will not carry on, I turn my attention back to Maddy. She's got her earbuds in, but frowns as she pulls them out and shoves them into her purse.

"Something up?"

She chews on her bottom lip. "No. I thought they were broken, but they're playing the guidebook I downloaded just fine."

I nod as we move ahead in the line. Eventually it's our turn and we make it inside. Maddy walks through the space in awe, her head tilted back looking at the painted ceilings. She gets this look of wonder on her face as she sucks in small gasps of delight. It's kind of cute. Makes a change from her usual glaring and retorts.

We follow the group we entered with up and through winding tunnels and staircase after staircase. Then we walk across a narrow mesh-enclosed walkway that places us high in the roof space, looking down over the tourists filing in.

Maddy stops suddenly to stare at the intricate designs on the ceiling and the group of female students from the queue bump into the back of me with a giggle.

"It's amazing." Maddy grins at me, oblivious to the pile-up, then turns and carries on.

"This is getting narrower," I say as we turn the corner and face yet another long, stone walkway that slopes upward.

"We're climbing to the roof; it's going to be narrow. And people were smaller when this was built."

"Yeah." I duck to avoid hitting my head on the low stone opening. "Fuck me, it's getting warm." I tug at my shirt collar as Maddy glances back at me, her eyes flitting over my suit.

"Wishing you'd gone back to the house?"

"Not at all. It's all counting toward my cleanse." I wink at her.

"God," she groans. "You're something else."

"That's what I'm told."

She turns back around, but the shake of her head and snort is unmistakable.

"You rolling your eyes too?" I lean forward and whisper in her ear.

"What?" She bats me away. "Stop that! You're too close, Rich. Get back."

"Ooh, we're onto surnames. You flirting with me, Harper?"

She raises her hand over her shoulder and flicks me her middle finger without looking back.

I laugh as we turn another corner and are at the bottom of a narrow spiral stone staircase with an old rope fixed to the wall as a makeshift handrail.

"Need a leg up?" I say as she pauses at the base of it, trying to peer around the older couple in front of us waiting on the steps.

"Logan, cut it out," she snaps. Then she raises her voice and jabs me in the chest with her finger as she says, in pronounced Italian, "*Hai un cazzo squisito, princepe del piacere!*"

The entire cramped hallway falls silent.

Maddy blinks.

Then one of the female students behind me coughs out a strangled giggle before her friends join her and erupt into laughter. One pulls out her phone and snaps a picture of me and Maddy.

Maddy's cheeks burn scarlet as she looks around at all the eyes on us. The group of students start chatting excitedly in Italian between giggles.

"Ooh, Prince."

"Looks rather royal to me."

"I'd do him."

"Ew, Rosa! You always go for the ancient ones."

"Yeah, he's older than this building!"

"Ancient? I'm thirty fucking three." I turn to face them, and they all stop talking and stare at me. One gives me a flirty smile, her eyes dropping to my suit pants. I'm guessing that's Rosa.

"Logan?" Maddy tugs on my sleeve.

I turn back around and open my mouth.

"Ooh, he speaks Italian."

"Even sexier."

"Yeah, I'd do him too."

"Shh, that's his girlfriend he's with."

"She's not my girlfriend," I say over my shoulder, but realize I've said it in English.

"Hell no!" Maddy peers around me at the group of girls as one pinches my ass, and I jump forward.

More giggles.

The entire corridor is watching the exchange with more interest than they have given the sights on the tour.

The older woman from the couple ahead of us turns to Maddy with a chuckle. "Maybe he should be." She gives me a once-over appreciatively. "He sounds like my husband." She smiles at the man she's with, then whispers to Maddy, "You're a lucky girl."

"Um... I'm not sure lucky is the word I have in mind," Maddy replies politely, her accusing eyes holding mine.

"Logan, what the—?" she hisses as the group start climbing the stairs again and new chatter breaks out.

No idea, I mouth, feigning ignorance.

We carry on with the tour, going out onto the roof and I suck in a breath of fresh air, despite the space still being limited.

"Thank fuck no one farted in there. We'd have all choked to death."

"Please don't talk to me," Maddy says as she snaps a picture of the view with her phone.

"Shall I take one for you?" the older woman from earlier offers.

She takes Maddy's phone out of her hand before waiting for a reply and then motions with her hands. "I can't fit you in unless you move closer."

Maddy's eyes narrow at me. "Don't even think about—"

I wrap my arm around her waist, and she bristles as I pull her into my side, my hand clasping her hip.

"Are the shudders because you're turned on?" I whisper in her ear as our picture's taken.

"God," she groans at me before thanking the lady as she takes her phone back. "More like violated. Don't mistake physical contact for a blossoming friendship. We aren't going to ride off into the sunset together now, you know?"

"Shame. I bet you're good at riding."

"Ugh, please stop." She turns and glares at me. "I preferred it when you were being a moody jerk on the yacht over this version of you."

"I wasn't moody."

She scoffs. "You were."

I purse my lips, then pluck her phone from her hands. "Would a moody jerk make you smile like that?" I turn the phone around, and Maddy snatches it, staring at the screen.

"That's not a smile." She squints at the photo of the two of us, me with my arm around her, her with the hint of a smile on her lips.

"Looks like one to me." I stand behind her and rest my chin on her shoulder to study the image.

She reaches up and pushes me away with a flick to my forehead. "Get off before I throw you off this roof."

I chuckle, resisting the urge to mess with her more.

She's still staring at the photo as I stand and take in the view over Rome, all thoughts of home, Dad, and weddings temporarily gone.

And my earlier headache has vanished.

Chapter 9
Maddy

"YOU'RE A BILLIONAIRE AND you don't have a coin?" I fish a euro out of my wallet and slap it into Logan's palm. "Here."

"It's fine. Have it back."

"Shut up." I tut, closing my wallet so he can't drop the coin back inside. "Everyone has to make a wish. It's the law of the Trevi Fountain."

"Sounds like something you just made up."

"Just throw the damn coin."

I close my eyes, silently preparing my wish. The breeze blows my hair around my face, but I ignore it, mentally conjuring up the image of Drew being happy to make it more powerful.

I throw my coin into the water with a smile, then look at Logan. He's staring at the silver and gold euro in his hand.

"Don't tell me the man that has everything can't think of a single thing to wish for?"

He glances at me before closing his fingers around the coin and bringing it to his lips, squeezing his eyes shut.

"Oh, dear wish granting fairies of the Trevi Fountain, please give the gift of laryngitis for my companion, Maddox Harper." He peels an eye open and looks at me with the beginning of a smirk. "Let her rest her sweet voice until we return to London."

"You're so annoying."

He winks at me and then whispers something against his fist. Then he flicks the coin. It spins high in the air before splashing into the fountain with perfect precision.

He looks at me with a smug smile. "Are you going to tell me what you wished for?"

"Are you?" I fire back.

He shoves his hands into his suit pants as we walk. "Well, having a big dick was already granted, so..."

"Ugh. Are you ever serious if it isn't about work?"

"I can be serious."

"No," I scoff. "You can't. Anyway, it doesn't matter."

"I wished for a happy future," Logan says.

"Okay... Not very specific, but better than I expected."

"You didn't tell me the fairies needed me to be specific. Can I have another coin? I need to go back and re-phrase it. I want a happy future for my big dick."

"For God's sake," I groan.

"Too much?"

"Yes."

"How much is too much? Like... nine inches too much?" He bumps shoulders with me, and I roll my eyes.

"Come on, Mads. I'll find something that makes you laugh one day."

"You getting hit by a meteor? Your dick falling off and everyone pointing and laughing as they whip out their magnifying glasses? You growing body hair all over and getting mistaken for a yeti and having to go into hiding high up in the Himalayas so you don't become a science project? Any will do." I beam as my step gains a bounce.

His brows rise. "You wouldn't want me ending up as a lab rat? That's sweet, Smiles. You do care."

"I—"

I slam my mouth shut, speechless.

The walk back improved ten-fold when we stopped talking. Although I had to bite back my surprise when Logan got a cab for us instead of calling his driver. Thinking about it, for a billionaire, he's as happy wandering around like a tourist and queuing for things, as he is being driven around in a luxury car and having meetings on private yachts.

I let out a sigh as I sink down in the bubbles of the giant marble tub in the guest bathroom. There was a bottle of foaming bath oil on the side and a whole load ran out faster than I could stop it when I ran the bath. The result? Bubbles up around my ears and that slippery, silkiness of oil on skin.

"Mm, bliss." I wriggle my toes underwater, my calves sliding against one another, slick with oil as I lean my head back against the side.

Nate Black's voice fills the room. It's definitely not the same through my phone speaker. His warm tone is still smooth, but something is missing. But I'm so engrossed with the story that I don't care. I want to finish it so I can start posting teasers for it on my book account.

I stare at the ceiling as all the tension in my body evaporates with the steam from the bath. Nate's character, Cameron, is arguing with someone about Frederica, the heroine. The two start fighting and Frederica screams repeatedly as she watches the other guy try and kill Cameron.

I slide down, letting the water come up over my head and the bubbles form a cloud over me as I close my eyes. The screaming muffles underwater, and I stay still for a moment, cocooned in an underwater haven of warmth.

Shouting voices. A man's. Nate?

"Oh my god!"

This book turned dramatic suddenly. I love it.

"No, no, no!"

Nate sounds panicked. What did I miss? Did Frederica get struck during the fight?

"Fuck!"

I jerk underwater as something grabs me around the torso and hauls me from the water.

God, it's a break in! Logan's mansion is a target. I'm being abducted. They probably think I'm worth something as a hostage.

"Stop!" I splutter, gasping for breath through the bubbles on my face. "You don't want me. I'm useless to you." I can't punch because my arms are crushed to my side, wrapped inside the big unforgiving arms of my attacker.

"I've got you," a deep voice booms. His chest rises and falls with sharp breaths as he holds me against him, naked and dripping wet.

"No." I wriggle, but it's useless. My feet lift from the floor as he grips me tighter with one arm around my waist.

A hand swipes the bubbles from my eyes and then clasps my cheek, turning my face.

Oh, God, no. He's going to do things to me right here.

I wriggle harder and fight to turn my face away from his, but he's too strong. And he's wearing *suit pants?* I glance down, taking in his shirt sleeves rolled up over muscly, corded forearms, and his dark suit pants. He's not wearing any shoes or socks. *What criminals break into houses in designer shirts and pants but no shoes or socks?*

"You're okay. Look at me."

I suck in a breath, readying myself to look at his face, even though I don't want to. It might be the last one I ever see.

Light brown hair. Strong jaw. Perfect cupids bow lips. Green eyes.

"What the hell? Logan!"

His eyes are wild and he's panting as he grabs the other side of my face and stares into my eyes. Then his gaze darts all around my face, checking me over. My forehead, my cheeks, my lips, and back to my eyes.

"Jesus," he hisses, his eyes pinching at the corners. He moves back enough to perform a sweep down my body. Then he pulls me close again as his thick neck contracts with a deep swallow.

"What are you doing?" My pulse is still firing blood around my body as I struggle to catch my breath. My breasts are squashed against his shirt, making the material wet.

"I heard you screaming." He cups my face in his hands again and sweeps his eyes over it as if he doesn't trust his first assessment.

"Don't even think about it," I pant, balling his shirt and pulling him closer so he can't do a second check of my body. *My naked, wet body. Oh God.*

"I thought you were drowning." His eyes have lost some of their wildness. But his hands are still firmly cupping my cheeks.

"I wasn't, you idiot. People don't scream when they're drowning. It's my audiobook. Listen..."

My lips are close to his, and he glances down at them and then back up into my eyes. My phone continues to play the audiobook on the countertop behind me. Only the story has moved on, and Cameron and Frederica are having raw, uninhibited sex, judging by the moans and heavy breathing.

"You like that? I know you've been waiting for my cock, baby."

My eyes widen as I stare into Logan's eyes. I loosen my grip on his shirt. Water runs down my back from my hair, tracing all the way down over my ass and the backs of my thighs.

I shiver.

"You need a towel. You're cold." He moves his hands from my face, but I fist his shirt, preventing him from moving away.

"No way are you going over there to get one. You'll see everything."

"I love your cock. Fuck me with it... hard," Frederica moans.

"Okay. We need to do something." My voice is shrill as I dart my eyes around. I shiver again and goosebumps prick up all over my body.

Logan wraps his arms back around me. He's seen way more than I'd ever want him to. But I need to block that out for now. I can dissect it later when I'm dressed and don't have blood heating my cheeks with embarrassment... and when Frederica's moans as she builds up to having multiple orgasms aren't echoing around the room.

Logan's eyes flick to something over my shoulder. He stiffens and clears his throat before focusing on my face again. "I'll close my eyes."

I stare back, all my senses heightened from the fact I'm naked, soapy, and dripping wet... and in Logan Rich's arms.

God, my life couldn't get any worse right now.

"You're so wet, baby. Dripping with cream for me," Nate groans.

Okay. It's worse.

I squeeze my eyes shut, closing out the burning emerald of Logan's gaze before I see him react to the audiobook. I don't want to know if he's laughing at me right now.

"No. You can't close them. The floor's too wet, you could slip."

As if to accentuate my point, my soapy foot slides underneath me, making me gasp. I wrap my arms around Logan's neck as he stops me from falling and pulls me against his body. I jerk my hips back, away from his groin. He looks down at me, his eyes darkening as he licks his lips, flashing a hint of perfect white teeth.

"Told you that you care about me, Mads. You're scared I'll get hurt."

"Get over yourself." I scoff.

The intense look in his eyes has my breathing quickening. "I just don't want to clean your brains up off the tiles. Not that it'd take long."

He chuckles, breaking the weird moment, and I sigh in relief.

"Just like that, huh? You like to be spanked?" Nate's voice rumbles.

My mouth drops open. "Now. We need to shuffle together. Now." I can't stand here a second longer listening to this with Logan. I eye the white robe hanging on the back of the door. It's calling to me like a lifeline.

Logan follows my gaze, seemingly unfazed by the sounds of slapping skin and grunts echoing around us.

"Okay."

The next couple of minutes consist of us shuffling one tiny step at a time toward the door, our feet threatening to slip out beneath us with every move we make. I grip on to Logan, and he holds me tight to stop us falling.

Frederica and Cameron fuck the entire time, and hell, I wish I'd listened to this part already, because it's one impressive hot sex scene. But now I will never be able to listen to this book again without thinking about this moment and the sheer mortification that's infiltrated every cell of my body.

We make it over to the door, and Logan reaches behind me and unhooks the robe, wrapping it around my shoulders. I stare at his strong neck and the days' worth of stubble over his jaw as he keeps his eyes averted while pulling the robe together over my breasts.

"Thank you." I exhale heavily, relief softening all the muscles in my body as I slide my arms into the sleeves and knot the robe around my waist.

Logan glances down, checking I'm covered.

Frederica and Nate's voices cry out.

"I'm coming! Oh yes! I'm cooommmiinngggg!"

"Yes, baby. Squirt that cum all over my cock!"

Logan arches a brow; the corners of his mouth twitching, and I scowl at him as the audio reaches its crescendo.

"Don't."

He closes his mouth, flattening his lips. But his eyes are sparkling. "Take care with the floor, Mads."

Then he turns and walks out of the door.

My lungs deflate as I blow out a strangled breath.

"That was amazing," Frederica mewls.

First things first, turn off my freaking phone. I glare at it on the marble countertop by the sink as Frederica continues with her post-orgasmic complimenting of Nate's character's physical prowess. I catch sight of myself in the giant mirror above the sink. My hair is plastered around my face, cheeks flushed, eyes bright and alert.

The mirror.

My tongue feels thick in my mouth. I had my back to that mirror the entire time Logan was holding me.

My naked back.

Shit, that's what the bastard was looking at.

That's what he was looking at, right before I almost slipped and he caught me. Right before he pulled me against his body... Where I felt his raging erection in his pants before moving my hips back from his.

I groan and drag a hand down my face. Not only have I spent the last five minutes naked and wet, clinging to Logan's shirt like a baby monkey as we listened to two people pretending to fuck. But he could see my naked ass the entire time.

And it made him hard. And not just hard... Solid as a rock, pressing into my stomach, wasn't lying about nine inches, hard.

Someone trade lives with me, please.

It takes fifteen minutes to mop the floor with a towel and shower the remaining bubbles and excess oil from my body. And the entire time, my stomach twists in knots.

Logan saw me naked.

I keep telling myself it's no big deal, hoping that it'll desensitize me. Make me numb to the curling ball of humiliation in my gut. Anyone... anyone but him.

"Why did it have to be him?" I groan, pulling an oversized T-shirt and shorts on.

I fix my towel-dried hair into a bun and glare at my phone, like it's to blame for playing that audio. But it's not. It's my fault. I didn't know there'd be screaming. It's so realistic. I should have kept the volume down.

Then Logan wouldn't have heard and come running like a white knight to save the helpless princess.

I snort in annoyance. Only five people have seen me naked. Mum, Dad, and Drew when I was a baby. And two ex-boyfriends. I've never had a one-night stand. Not exactly by choice, more like shyness at college and university. And before that, well, Logan made damn sure no one went near 'crab girl' at high school.

I can't believe he's number six, and he's not my boyfriend. He's—

Clarity hits me like a freight train.

"Asshole! What did you do, Logan?"

I grab my phone. Those students this afternoon thought he was my boyfriend. They thought me calling him the most irritating man I've ever met was hilarious. I mean, it's factually correct, but it's hardly prime stand-up comedy.

I jab at the phone screen, tutting impatiently as the Italian translation app opens. I don't know how to write the words, so I say them instead.

"Hai un cazzo squisito, princepe del piacere."

Then I click the translate button.

Chapter 10
Logan

"Take them."

"It's not necessary—"

Sterling Beaufort's deep baritone voice reaches down the phone. "I insist. Think of it as an apology."

"For what?" I frown, placing my phone on speakerphone and dropping it onto the bed so I can peel off my wet clothes.

My phone was ringing with Sterling's call as I walked back into my bedroom from Maddy's room. I've spent the past fifteen minutes talking to him in soaking wet clothes. I would never normally conduct a business call in my underwear, despite the fact the other person can't see me. But Sterling's spent the last five minutes trying to convince me to accept Royal box tickets to the opera in Milan, and I've been standing soaking wet the entire time.

"I didn't know you two had something going on."

"We don't." I walk into the bathroom, grab a towel, and wipe it over my chest.

Sterling chuckles. "You sure about that?"

I rub at the back of my neck where Maddy wrapped her wet arms around me, getting my hair wet. "Pretty damn sure."

I smirk as I recall how much she was blushing as she made us shuffle across the bathroom together. I'd already seen her when I pulled her from the tub and checked her over. Although, I was running on adrenaline then. Still, how the fuck did I never notice how full and perfect her tits are before? And the way her nipples hardened and pressed against my ribs when she got cold.

I bite back a groan, shoving the thought aside before my body can react. As if being in my underwear isn't bad enough, I can't get a hard-on while talking to Sterling. That's fucking weird. Almost as weird as the fact I got one in the bathroom. I mean, this is Mads. Drew's little sister. What kind of shit friend am I?

It's just a natural male reaction to a naked female pressed against you, all wet and slippery. And her tits... God her tits.

It's her tit's fault.

"I appreciate the gesture, honestly," I say to Sterling. "But we aren't going back to Milan. We're in Rome a few more days, then we're heading back to London early."

The extra boost Sterling's contribution gave means I'm a lot closer to target than I expected being at this stage. A couple more investors and we can return to

London. I can tell Dad I've got the money and finally put this ridiculous notion of his about me getting married to an end.

I think I've worked it out. He's using the business as an excuse. It's not about the money. It's about me being single. I've never taken a serious girlfriend home to meet them. Never even thought about taking any of my exes home. I've gotten Dad worried. Maybe he thinks he won't live to see grandkids.

It's a mid-life crisis.

A leather jacket or a toupee would have been preferable. But Dad went full on, choosing the ticking time bomb of procreation instead. Spencer's his oldest friend, and Gabrielle's a lovely woman. Dad's being logical in his choice, even if he is also stark raving mad if he thinks it'll happen.

"Pity," Sterling muses. "I think she'd enjoy it."

I drop the towel onto the bed next to my phone. Maybe Maddy would enjoy the opera. But I need to get the funding and get home quickly. Smooth things over with Dad. Reassure him. Get him and Mum back on speaking terms. I know it'll be killing Dad that she's still making him sleep in the guest room.

"I—"

My bedroom door flies open and bounces off the wall with a loud *bang*. Something hits me square in the chest, then drops to the floor. I glance down at the white object as something else slaps me around the side of the head with a soft *thud*.

"I bet you think you're really clever, don't you?"

I stare at the white slippers on the floor. The ones my housekeeper puts out for guests.

"At least look at me, you jerk!"

Maddy's standing in my bedroom doorway dressed in shorts and a T-shirt, her wet hair piled on top of her head as she points at me. Her finger is shaking, and her cheeks are bright red.

"What are—?"

She storms over to me like a miniature pressure cooker, ready to erupt.

"Forget baboon!" She pokes me in the chest. I look down at her finger jabbing into me, then back at her face, which only seems to rile her further. "You'd be more like a gnat, if gnats have dicks. Or..." Her crazed eyes dart side to side. "...or an animal with an inverted dick. Yes!" She barks out a laugh before scowling. "An inverted dick. A speck of dust that wouldn't even register on any scale of measurement."

I grab her by her upper arms gently. "Did you slip after I left? Hit your head on the tiles?" I lift my chin to study the top of her head for wounds.

"Stop that." She bats my arms away, then drags in a deep breath as she glares up at me. "You're ridiculous, you know that? I'd get closer to an orgasm from a sneeze than I would from you."

"Whoa." I hold my hands up with a smirk. "That's—"

"Don't whoa me." Her eyes narrow. "Did you even know women can orgasm? Or is it always about your pleasure, *Prince*?"

She folds her arms, and I fail to stop my eyes dropping to her breasts for a split second. Now that I've seen them, it's virtually impossible not to notice the way they're straining beneath the thin fabric of her T-shirt. Thankfully, Maddy's too busy going batshit crazy to notice my slip up.

"You finally translated it, then?"

"God, I want to slap that smirk off your face." She stomps her foot on the floor, her hands in fists by her side.

"You actually just stomped like a kid having a tantrum," I say, raising my brows.

Wrong fucking thing to say.

Maddy's eyes widen until there's enough white on show to make her look like she's also about to blow steam from her ears.

"Since when did you deem it acceptable for me to be walking around Italy saying the words, '*Your dick is exquisite, Pleasure Prince?*' There could have been kids around."

"I thought you'd have a translation app. I expected it to last until you checked into your room, no longer." I give her a genuine smile.

"Don't give me that. You could have told me. You let me say it in the elevator with that sweet old couple, and that crowded staircase in the Vatican, and..." Her eyes widen further, and she picks up the slipper from the floor and starts beating my abs with it. "And at Trent Forde's meeting. You asshole."

I jump side to side as she lands smack after smack to my skin. They don't hurt, but then one lands low and catches me on the dick.

"Fuck," I hiss, covering myself with both hands to prevent any more rogue shots.

She hits me a few more times and then stops, her shoulders rising and falling as she pants.

"Even if you were the last man on earth, Logan Rich, I wouldn't have sex with you. Whether you consider yourself to be a Prince of pleasure, or not. More like a Prince of how to make a girl want to sew up her vagina."

"That sounds painful." My eyes drop to her tiny shorts, and her hand holding the slippers twitches. "Okay, I'm sorry. I should have told you."

"Not good enough." She looks at me with disgust. "You're the biggest jerk I've ever met, you know that?"

"It was a joke, Mads. I'm sorry." I grit my teeth as she gives me another look of utter contempt that makes my skin crawl. Fire ignites low in my gut and heat floods my veins as she continues to look at me like I'm the biggest asshole in the world. "It was only a joke."

"Yeah? Everything's a joke to you, isn't it, Logan? And anything that's serious, you can just throw money at it to make the problem go away."

"What the hell's that supposed to mean? It was a joke, for fuck's sake. I didn't think you'd be so upset. It was a mistake; I can see that now. Hardly the worst one I've ever made, though."

Her lips curl down. "You can say that again."

"What the fuck's gotten into you? I said I'm sorry."

"You know what? Next time you think I'm drowning... Let me." She spins and storms for the doorway, shouting over her shoulder, "I'd rather die than be naked near you again."

"You know what?" I call after her as she strides into the hallway.

"I don't care what you're going to say," she yells back.

"Well, I'm going to say it anyway." I cross the room and stare at her retreating back. She holds her hand above her shoulder and gives me the middle finger. "Yeah, real mature. But you know what?" I'm yelling now too, blood pounding inside my skull. "If we fucked, you'd realize those little twitches you've felt didn't even come close. You'd realize you'd never fucking come before until you had an orgasm that I gave you... With my fingers... My tongue... My *cock*." I'm on a roll. A herd of wild bulls couldn't stop me from this train wreck now.

"Don't flatter yourself," Maddy snaps without breaking stride, still not turning around.

"I'd make you fucking scream louder than Frederica!"

She slams to a halt, then twists, looking like a woman possessed as she moves closer and screams, "I hate you. Do you know that? I *really fucking* hate you! I always have."

Then she hurls both slippers at me.

I walk back into my room, pinching my nose to stop the bleeding. Stupid fucking slippers and their hard soles. She probably expected me to move out the way fast enough. Then again, she said she hates me, so maybe she was aiming for an artery. Either could be true.

She hates me.

I sit down on the bed, grabbing the towel and blotting beneath my nose. The blood flow is easing already.

"Fuck," I groan, resting my forearms on my thighs and dropping my head into my hands.

"So, you'll take the tickets, then?"

I snap my head up and stare at my phone. Sterling's deep voice rings out. I open my mouth to apologize about what he witnessed, but his accompanying laugh tells me he isn't offended in the slightest.

"Did you not hear her?" A smile pulls at my lips as I wipe the final drops of blood away from my nose. "Not if I was the last man on earth."

"I heard." Sterling chuckles.

"And she hates me," I add as my smile slides off my face. No one's ever told me they hate me before. It kind of... stings.

Sterling's voice softens. "There's a fine line between love and hate. And you know what both need?"

"What?" I ask, dropping my towel onto the bed next to me.

"Passion."

I swallow the metallic taste in my mouth.

"I'll leave the tickets for you to collect there on the night. Enjoy the show."

Then he hangs up.

Chapter 11
Maddy

"How are you friends with him? You're you, and he's... he's..." I study the canopy above the bed as I lie on my back. It's a beautiful four poster with gilded arches beneath the four corner posts.

Everything about Logan's mansion is luxurious. Being stuck here with any other man would be paradise.

"Relax, sis. He's not that bad."

"If by not that bad you mean better than being a man and having your balls rubbed in poison ivy and then nibbled off by rabid rats, then you're right," I reply brightly, smiling at the thought of it happening to Logan.

My smile falls right away as I imagine his dick. Imagine each long, thick, hard inch that pressed into me in the bathroom earlier.

Drew laughs. "He's a good guy beneath the bad jokes. You said he apologized, right?"

"Yeah," I grumble.

"So, he gets it wrong sometimes. But he has a good heart."

I roll onto my tummy and pick a piece of fluff off the duvet. "If you say so."

I don't sound convinced because I'm not. But Drew is a good judge of character, and he's been friends with Logan for years. Maybe Logan's been a good friend to Drew since the joyriding incident. But I still can't forgive him for leaving my brother and getting his dad to bail him out.

"How is everyone?" I change the subject. "Mum and Dad?"

"Yeah, they're..." Drew pauses.

"They're what? Is everything okay?"

"It's fine." He exhales slowly and the tension laced in his breath makes me sit upright.

"Drew?"

"Mum's just..." He pauses again. "She thinks Dad's having an affair."

"What? That's ridiculous." I laugh as Drew remains silent on the other end of the phone. "He wouldn't do that."

"I know you..." Drew pauses again as if choosing his words carefully. "I know you and he are close. But he's not perfect, Maddy."

"I know. But, come on. This is Dad." I wait for Drew to agree, but he doesn't. "Why would you even think he would do that?" I whisper, my stomach knotting painfully.

"Mum found hotel charges on his credit card."

"So? He uses them for work all the time when he's working cases."

Dad's job in the police regularly takes him away.

"And condoms in his wallet."

"But—" The air leaves my lungs. Mum's gone through the menopause. We laughed about all the hormones and how men have it easier. "He wouldn't, would he?"

"I hope not. But Mum seems convinced."

"Oh, God." I rub at my temples with my free hand.

"I didn't want to tell you while you were away. Mum's not making any decisions yet. She said she wants to think it over."

"I can't even... Shall I come home? Does she need me to? I can talk to Logan, I'm sure he can help me get a flight or..."

I think about the look on his face as I screamed that I hated him. He looked shocked. Like he had no idea. I mean, how could he not? I think it's damn obvious. And I threw those slippers at him. My stomach clenches. Too far? I did go raving bitch on him.

I doubt he'll help me now even if I beg.

"No. I didn't tell you so that you'd come back early. And that's the last thing Mum wants. She's so happy that you got a full-length feature. It's what you wanted."

"Even if it's about Logan?"

"Especially because it's about Logan."

"Don't tell me Mum's part of his fan club too?"

Drew chuckles. "She's seen the kid she fed chocolate spread sandwiches to on play dates become a world-leader in his field of expertise. She's just excited for him."

The thought makes my heart clench. Mum's always been the first to tell us she's proud of us. And growing up, she was always looking out for our friends, too.

"Are you sure she's okay?"

I don't want to believe Dad would cheat. There's got to be an explanation. People don't do that to someone they love. And he loves Mum.

"She will be." Drew sighs. "Mum's been unhappy awhile. This isn't the first time she's suspected Dad. This might be the start of something better for both of them."

"What? She hasn't. She's never told me that."

"She wouldn't." Drew's voice is heavy. "She wouldn't want either of us worrying about her. She's made it work for the family."

My stomach sinks. How have I been blind for so long? I thought they were happy. They were never into public displays of affection. But they never seemed *unhappy*.

"Look, don't worry about it. Nothing's going to change overnight. Mum said to tell you to enjoy the rest of your trip. She's loving the photos you've been sending."

"I'm glad." I smile weakly. "I'll send her some of Rome. We did some sightseeing today." I can't muster the same usual joy about the wonderful places I've visited.

"Great, do it. She'll love them. Listen, sis, I've got to go. Tan's about to start one of his end of the day boring-ass roundups."

Tanner quips some smart comeback to my brother that includes the words *jack* and *ass* in the background as Drew laughs.

Drew doesn't sound concerned, so I shouldn't be. It's probably a misunderstanding. I hope it is. I can't imagine

Dad having an affair. Working for the police means his life is about right and wrong. But maybe I'm being naïve. Nothing's black and white. There're all shades of gray in-between.

I open my phone's camera roll to select images to send to Mum. I include the photo of me and Logan at The Vatican. The one where I'm definitely *not* smiling. Mum will like it. I haven't sent any with Logan to her. Plus, it'll be evidence I haven't murdered him yet.

I drop my phone onto the bed as there's a soft knock on the door.

"Come in." I sigh.

Logan's lucky the call from Drew has sucked all the energy from me and left me feeling numb. Because otherwise I'm sure I could go for round two if he makes any smartass comments.

The door cracks open and something white is stuck through it, attached to a coat hanger.

Logan waves it like a truce flag.

"I thought your feet might be cold." He steps inside, pulling the slipper from the coat hanger and handing it to me, along with the second one in his other hand. "I'd prefer it if you didn't throw them at me this time."

I take both from his hands and nod, my throat thick as I keep my eyes cast down. "I shouldn't have done that."

"Is that an apology?"

"It's an acknowledgment of potentially un guest-like behavior," I say.

"Then I accept. On the condition that you accept this as my acknowledgment of un host-like behavior." He holds his phone out in front of me and I lift my head to look at it.

"Why are you showing me a red room? I don't want to know about Walrus kinks."

His lips curl into a gentle smile. "It's the royal box at Teatro alla Scala. Sterling gave us tickets to see a show."

"He did?" Despite Drew's phone call, my stomach flutters as I give the phone screen my full attention. The red velvet seats are lined up facing the stage in the private viewing box beneath beautiful golden architraves.

"It's a love story. Right up your street," Logan adds.

I wait for him to comment about the audiobook again. But he's silent.

My eyes flick to his face and back to the phone screen. "But that's in Milan. We aren't going back there."

"We can if you want to. I can move some of the Rome meetings around, have some when we come back here after Milan. It'd mean extending our trip, though. Your call." He slides his phone back into the black joggers he's put on.

One day extra with Logan.

Before our fight, nothing could have persuaded me to consider it. But now? It's like the release of all the shouting, combined with the complete dragging sensation in my gut from Drew's phone call, has gotten me needing to cling to something positive. To escape the real world.

"Would *you* like to go?" I ask.

"Yes." His eyes hold mine as he answers without hesitation.

I remain silent for a few beats.

"But we don't have—"

"Okay." I swallow. "Thank you. I'd like to go."

"Great. I'll make the arrangements. You okay?" Logan's brow knots.

I'm not trying to kill him with a slipper, of course he thinks something's wrong. The atmosphere is a world apart from an hour ago when we were yelling at each other. But suddenly, I'm exhausted. The emotion of the whole day is weighing on my shoulders, making my stomach sore and my heart heavy.

"Just tired."

"You know where I am if you need anything."

My eyes snap back to his. "I told you I hated you and you're not worried I'm going to smother you in your sleep?"

His eyes pinch at the corners briefly before his signature smirk pulls at his lips. "You also called me a Walrus when I came in. And not a gnat or another animal with an inverted dick. So I'd say we're one degree away from murder now."

"I'd say half a degree, but whatever."

"Just to be on the safe side." He takes the slippers from my hands gently, his thumb brushing over the top of my hand as he does. "I'd better keep these fluffy assassins."

He walks over to the door, then leans one shoulder against the frame. "Good night, Smiles."

My voice sounds as drained of energy as my body feels, but I still manage a quiet, "Goodnight, *Prince*."

But it's loud enough for Logan to hear, and he chuckles as he walks away.

When I wake the next morning, Logan's gone. He's left a note in the kitchen saying he's moved some meetings around to allow for Milan and that I should get some rest.

I spend the day listening to my recordings and writing up notes, setting out a basic outline for the feature. I email Eve to keep her updated and speak to Chloe on the phone. I've no idea how long Logan will be, so I have a swim in the outdoor pool, take a shower, unable to even look at the bathtub, and then settle into the plush seating area in the kitchen to read a new book.

Two hours pass before the sound of shoes moving on the marble floor toward the kitchen pulls my attention away from my book. Logan walks in wearing a black suit, white shirt, and an emerald tie that makes his eyes stand out across the room.

I drop my gaze back to my e-reader. "I heard you coming from the front door. You know what would work if you were wanting to sneak up on someone?"

"What's that?"

I glance up as he walks over to the coffee machine.

"Slippers."

His shoulders stiffen before he chuckles.

"You want one?" He looks at me over his shoulder and our eyes meet. The sunlight from the window catches his hair, highlighting streaks of dark gold in the light brown.

"Had one already."

He turns back around.

"Thanks, though," I add.

I abandon my reading and watch the fluid way he moves around the kitchen, fetching a mug and getting the milk from the refrigerator as he reads messages on his phone.

"How was the meeting? Is there anything I should know for the feature?"

He frowns at whatever he's reading before glancing up at me. "No. Straightforward. She invested the amount I told you."

I nod as Logan's attention returns to his phone. He was meeting a female entrepreneur today who developed a dating app that pairs people by matching their vibrations. It's made her millions. And some high-profile couples swear by her method.

"Good. What was Halliday like? She's young, isn't she?"

"Mid-twenties, I think," Logan replies absentmindedly as he stands in front of the coffee machine waiting for it to fill his mug.

"She looks nice in the photos."

Logan smiles at something on his phone, his shoulders relaxing. "Sorry." He glances at me apologetically, giving me his attention. "Yes, she's beautiful. I just have to make a call." He heads toward the door, coffee in hand, before turning as if forgetting something. "Did you have a good day?"

"Yeah. Did some work. Went for a swim. Been reading." I lift my e-reader, and Logan looks at it and then smiles at me.

"Same book?"

I shake my head. "The next one in the series."

He tips his head and winks at me. "I hope it's as exciting as the last one." Then he walks out and calls, "Happy reading."

I stare at the rows of beautiful gowns lining the walls of the dressing room as I tug at the sleeves of my sweatshirt. This is... overwhelming. But Logan said his mum won't mind.

My hand skims along the silks, cashmere, and tulle as I walk along. *Where do I even start?*

I take down a hanger with a long cream dress on. It's got a high halter neck. I turn it around. *Backless.* I hang it back on the rack. I need something with in-built support if I can't wear a bra.

I pull down another long dress. This one's red with wide straps that lead to a scooped neckline, and it's a thicker material. I lay it on the giant round velvet stool and pull my sweatshirt over my head to try it on.

Forty minutes later, and enough dresses that I've lost count, I give up, slumping onto the velvet stool with a groan. It's no use. All these beautiful dresses and none fit. It's not like my breasts are massive. Maybe on the larger side for my frame, but I inherited that from Mum. Chloe's always said I should show them off more. But the rate this is going, I'll have to wear my sweatshirt to the opera.

I stare glumly at all the brand-new designer shoes displayed in neat rows on the opposite wall. We aren't even the same shoe size, so I've no luck there either.

"There aren't any slippers in here. No matter how hard you stare, trying to find a pair."

Logan's standing in the doorway, his eyes glinting. He's changed into his black joggers and T-shirt again.

"Destroy my dreams, why don't you?"

He comes and drops next to me on the giant stool. He smells incredible. I should ask him what it is. I might get it for Drew. But then, why would I want my brother to smell like Logan? Why would I want anyone to smell like the man I can't stand? Maybe I did hit my head in the bathroom yesterday.

"What's with the frown?"

"I'm not frowning."

Logan chuckles.

"I'm not." I side-eye him, crossing my arms with a huff.

"All right, Mads. You aren't."

He falls into a happy silence next to me, his face relaxed as he looks around the dressing room.

"Why do you call me Mads? Everyone else calls me Maddy."

He lifts one shoulder. "You don't look mad when everyone else speaks to you. You save that face for me. Told you that you think I'm special."

"Ugh, please."

Logan lies on the stool, stretching his arms above his head with his usual smirk on his face. His t-shirt rides up showing off sculpted abs and muscular hipbones where his joggers hang low.

"My retinas are getting burned." I tut and look away as he laughs.

He's a lot happier since he came back from his meeting this morning. Less distracted. Maybe that's got to do with the phone call he went off to make. Maybe he was calling Halliday to thank her for meeting him. He did say he thought she was beautiful.

I swallow, tracing circles in the plush carpet with my toe. "I was looking to see if there was a dress I could borrow for the opera."

"And is there?"

Logan's got his hands behind his head, his shoulders lifted as he looks at me. How can he look so comfortable? He's holding a goddamn sit up position like he finds it relaxing.

"No."

He sits all the way up, his brows pulling low. "Oh." His eyes scan the racks full of clothes.

"I'm not being picky," I huff. "They're all beautiful."

"Okay." He rests his forearms on his thighs and turns his head to the side to look at me. His eyes soften, creasing at the corners as I chew on my lower lip.

"Don't laugh."

"Would I laugh at you?"

"Um, yes." I snort and turn away. "Forget it."

"Mads."

I bring my eyes back to his. His face is serious.

"Fine." I roll my eyes. "I can't fasten any of them."

"None?" Logan's brows shoot up.

"God, I wish there was a slipper here right now because I'd beat your ass."

"I didn't mean it like that."

"Like what?" I arch a brow at him, challenging him. It's obvious to anyone with eyes I would never fit into any of his mum's dresses. She's tall and slim. And I'm smaller and curvy. Not only did I inherit my mum's boobs, but I inherited her hips too. I don't know why I even came in here to try dresses on. Stupid idea.

"Come on, Mads." Logan smiles, his perfect, straight white teeth flashing as he avoids meeting my eyes. "Don't make me say it."

"Say what?" I bait him. I wonder what word he'll use. *A little bigger? Softer?*

His eyes flick to my breasts beneath my sweatshirt, and he swallows making his Adam's apple bob in his neck. "Your curves, they're too, well, you know."

"Enlighten me," I grit.

"They're..." Logan runs a hand around his jaw. "Sexy," he says thickly. "*Fucking* sexy."

Heat fires over my cheeks and I gape as he stands.

"We'll go shopping tomorrow in Milan." He smiles at me as though he did not just say the words that have set an unwelcome heat blazing a trail though my body.

"I thought you had a meeting here first. You said we were flying after lunch?" My voice comes out normal even though my heart is beating unnaturally fast.

I study his face for any sign of a smirk or cocky remark to tell me he was messing with me. But he's already walking out of the door.

"I'll sort it, Mads. Don't worry. The prince won't let you go to the ball without a dress."

"Quit with the prince crap." I fight the unexpected smile that's trying to form on my face.

He grins and I stare after him as he leaves.

What the hell was that?

Sexy. Not just sexy. *Fucking* sexy.

The usual urge to vomit at the thought of Logan and the word sexy being used in the same sentence doesn't hit me as it usually would.

But it's still there. I swear it is.

I wrap my fingers around the edge of the stool centering myself.

I swear it is.

Chapter 12
Logan

"How about the blue, sir?" The sales assistant sweeps over to me, draping another long gown over her arm for me to inspect as she speaks to me in English.

"Like I said before." I smile politely. "Whatever Ms. Harper likes."

She leans closer to where I'm sitting in the waiting area, my laptop set up on the low table in front of me. I clear my throat as she lingers and her perfume surrounds me, tickling my windpipe.

"This one is very forgiving." She lowers her voice. "I'd also suggest some of our control garments."

"Control what?"

She licks her lips and bats her eyelashes at me. "Special lingerie, very popular with women carrying some excess wei—"

"Don't finish that sentence." I slam my laptop shut.

Her eyes widen as I glare at her.

"Mia?" Another woman rushes over to us. "Take your lunch."

"But—"

"Take your lunch," the new woman repeats with a tight smile.

Mia's eyes dart toward the changing room Maddy is in. She looks back at me, her eyes roaming over my suit and then my face before she purses her lips. "I was only trying to help."

"Your help isn't required any longer," the new woman says, effectively dismissing Mia, who then stalks off.

"I'm Elena. I manage this store. Please accept my apologies, Mr. Rich. Mia hasn't been working with us long."

I doubt it'll be much longer if that's how she talks to her customers. I stand and shake her hand.

"It's lovely to meet you in person." Her smile grows. "Our store has supplied many of the designer gowns for your mother."

"So you have." It's why I brought Maddy here. And because the staff all speak English fluently. I wanted Maddy to feel comfortable.

"Your mother has exceptional taste. So elegant." Elena's eyes narrow as she thinks, one finger tapping against her lips. "But for Ms. Harper, I think we should try something a little more..." She tilts her head with a smile. "Alluring. I'll pull some gowns and see what she thinks."

"I appreciate it, thank you."

I sit back down and open my laptop. Elena enlists the help of two other staff members who begin whirling around the seating area I'm in. A rainbow of gowns swish past, held in one girl's arms as another carries a pile of shoe boxes.

I settle down to work, firing off a quick text to Mum first. We spoke yesterday and she seemed relieved to tell me that Gabrielle laughed in Spencer's face when he suggested the idea of us marrying. Mum's update quelled some of the unease hanging around in my gut.

"I don't think it's the one. But at least it fits."

I look up as Maddy walks from the changing rooms in a long blue dress. The material's floaty and she's frowning and fidgeting with it as she walks closer to look in the giant mirror on the wall.

"It's nice." I stand and shove my hands into my pant pockets as I step closer to her, meeting her eyes in the reflection.

She shakes her head.

I nod. "Okay. It's a no."

She turns to face me. "You don't have to stay if you've got work to do." Her eyes travel to my laptop on the table.

"It's fine. I can do it here."

Her brow creases as she frowns. "Okay. I'll try the next one, then."

She glances back at me before she disappears back into the changing room. Elena follows her.

I abandon my laptop and stroll toward a display of crystal figurines. I pick up a large one; an undistinguishable lump shaped like a dildo.

"That one's said to bring harmony in the form of physical love. Each one is unique. These are signed by the artist."

I arch a brow at the sales assistant who is unboxing a pair of shoes nearby before bringing my eyes back to the crystal dildo.

"We have one that just came in that's a little smaller. It symbolizes truth and union." She begins to stand. "I can fetch it for you if you'd like to see."

"No, thank you. That's all right." I turn to place the ugly dildo back on the shelf.

"What do you think?"

I turn my head toward Maddy's voice.

And drop the giant crystal dildo.

The fucker cracks me on the foot and then bounces onto the floor where it smashes into a million pieces like a sheet of ice.

"Logan." Maddy rushes over, her eyes round.

I ignore the throbbing in my foot as she stops in front of me and looks at the shattered crystal all over the floor.

"I've got it." A sales assistant swoops in with a brush and pan and bends to retrieve the glittering pieces.

"My apologies. Let me help." I crouch, but she shakes her head fiercely.

"No, Mr. Rich. I insist." She sweeps fast, gathering all the pieces in seconds.

"Please add it to my tab."

The pan full of crystal shards clinks as she stands. "It's seventy thousand euros."

I nod.

I turn my attention back to Maddy.

She looks uneasy as the sales assistant carries the broken crystal away. "Seventy thousand," she whispers.

"Who cares about an overpriced dildo? Show me the back."

She looks unsure for a moment, then slowly spins.

I can't tear my eyes away from her. "Green suits you."

"You think?" Her face lights up as she moves to the mirror and looks at her reflection.

The dress has two pieces of silk that cover each breast and then wrap around her waist. And it has this long skirt that glides over Maddy's curvy hips and then spreads out wider at the bottom. I'm a guy, I don't know what the hell a woman's dress like this is called. But in my language it's called an inappropriate sexual fucking fantasy, starring your friend's little sister as the main character.

I swallow, my throat thick. "I do. What do you think? Nice?"

Her eyes meet mine in the mirror as I stand behind her. She bites her bottom lip and then turns side to side, looking at herself with a small blush on her cheeks.

"Nice," she agrees. "I can't believe we're going to the opera, and I can wear this." She looks at her reflection like she's seeing herself for the first time.

"Okay. Then we'll take it." I turn to call the sales assistant.

"Wait." Maddy grabs onto the lapel of my suit jacket with one hand and lowers her voice, her eyes flicking around the store. "Check the tag for me."

"Why?"

She lets go of my jacket and holds her long dark hair up, turning so the neckline of the dress at the back is exposed.

"Just do it."

I pull the tag out and she's holding her breath. "Well?"

"Well what?"

"How much is it?" she whispers.

I tuck the tag back inside the dress, my fingers brushing the base of her neck before she drops her hair, and the long curls tumble down her shoulders.

"Why does it matter?"

She huffs, turning to face me. "Just tell me."

"Nine."

Her eyes widen and then she looks down, mumbling something.

"Okay." She smiles. "And if it's nine hundred I can probably get some shoes too and keep it all under a thousand."

The sales assistant shuffles nervously near us. "I'm afraid the dress is actually—"

"The last one you have? Yes, we're aware. Thank you. She'll take it." I keep my eyes on Maddy. "And whatever shoes and things she needs. Just put it on my tab."

"Of course, Mr. Rich." The sales assistant leaves as Elena walks back over.

"Stunning." She assesses Maddy, walking around her in a circle. This dress was made for your figure, Ms. Harper. You look sensational."

Maddy blushes, meeting my eyes for a second and then looking away.

"Of course, you'll need the correct lingerie." Elena holds up a finger. "One moment."

She glides across the store. She better not be bringing those control garments Mia mentioned or I will lose it. And it won't be an ugly dildo getting smashed.

"How much is it really?"

"What?" My jaw tenses as Elena pulls open some giant drawers in the center of the store and pulls out something black.

"Logan," Maddy hisses. "The dress?"

"I forgot."

"Bullshit."

I turn to her after Elena pulls another small scrap of black material from a different drawer.

"Nine thousand."

"What?" she shrieks, spinning in front of me. "Unfasten it. I need to get it off."

"No. You're getting the dress, Mads." I fix her with a look in the mirror and to my surprise she snaps her mouth shut. But she glares at me.

Elena reappears as the two of us are having a staring match. If Maddy thinks she will win, then she's mistaken. Like I said, I inherited Dad's stubbornness, and then some.

"Here," Elena sings brightly. "These will be perfect." She holds up the black silk bra and matching G-string proudly in the gap between us. "There's a matching garter belt if you'd like?"

"No, thank you."

"She'll take it."

We both reply at the same time.

Maddy's glare intensifies, and Elena looks between the two of us.

"They're beautiful." Maddy breaks eye contact with me to stare longingly at the fabric. "But I only came to look for a dress."

"Do they come in any other colors?" I ask Elena, my eyes staying on Maddy's face. A muscle in her jaw twitches as she looks back into my eyes.

"This set comes in the black as well as red, cream, and green," Elena says.

"We'll take them all. And the dress."

"Logan," Maddy hisses.

"Very well, Mr. Rich." Elena smiles professionally, ignoring the tension seeping from Maddy's pores. "I'll go and box these up."

"What are you doing?"

I step closer to Maddy. She has to tilt her head back to continue her glaring at me.

"You want to go to the opera, don't you?"

She pouts.

"Don't you?" I press.

She rolls her eyes. "Yes. But that doesn't mean you should be—"

I lean close so I can whisper in her ear. "Then let me buy you the fucking dress."

She stills and her breath hitches. Her throat contracts as she swallows slowly and then nods.

"Fine. But not the panties."

I lower my voice further, playing with fire. "Especially the panties."

She shivers but says nothing.

"Good girl."

I stand tall. She meets my eyes, her usual fire still there, but muted by what looks like confusion as her brows pull together.

I call across to Elena, keeping my eyes firmly on Maddy's. "Ms. Harper would like to know if you also sell slippers?"

A sharp jab lands in my gut.

"Asshole," she mutters.

I chuckle as she walks back into the changing rooms, a fired-up vision in green.

Chapter 13
Logan

I WALK ACROSS THE penthouse's bedroom, phone to my ear as it tries to connect.

"Come on, come, on," I urge.

I close the door, even though there's no sign of Maddy in the hallway. To say she was less than pleased that I checked her into the hotel's penthouse with me would be an understatement. But I won the argument because her office wasn't expecting us to return to Milan, so they hadn't booked her a room. Plus, I told her they were all booked out. Which could be true. I never bothered to find out. If she stays with me, I can keep an eye on her, like I promised Drew.

"Hello?"

"Gabrielle?"

"Logan." There's a warmth in her voice. "It's been a while. How are you?"

"Good. All good." I walk over to the floor-to-ceiling windows and move the thin drapes so I can look out at the city. The evening lights are making the streets glow a warm yellow. "How are you?"

She blows out a breath with a soft laugh. "Getting used to being back in London."

"I guess it's a change from field hospitals."

"You can say that again. It's nice to spend more time with Dad, though. I can't get this crazy idea about you and me out of his head."

I drop my head back and look at the ceiling. The muscles in my shoulders and back loosen with my relieved laugh. "Yeah. What the hell is that all about?"

"I know." Gabrielle laughs too. "You think our dads had a weird age-related epiphany and decided to drag us into it? They should have gotten a new sports car or something."

"Or something."

"You're not worried about it, are you?"

I reach up and tug at the collar of my tuxedo shirt. "No, I mean, not really."

"Good, there's no need. I bet it was my father's idea. He comes up with these hair-brained schemes all the time. Remember when we were kids and he sent me to those boring finishing classes, convinced I was going to marry into the royal family one day?"

"I thought there was something wrong with your pinkie whenever you drank."

"Exactly." She sighs. "It's just another silly idea. I think Dad has it in his head since losing Mum that he needs to make sure I'm settled. He worries about the future more than he used to."

"Mm." Gabrielle lost her Mum to cancer a few of years ago, and I've noticed when Spencer visits Dad, he's a lot more reserved than he used to be. Lacking some of the energy he once had.

"Dad said you're in Italy?"

"Yeah. Meeting with investors."

"This new project sounds exciting. Let's meet up when you get back. We can make a united front and crush our fathers' matchmaking dreams together." Gabrielle laughs.

"That's a meeting I'm looking forward to."

Gabrielle is right. This stupid wedding idea would never happen, and hearing her say it out loud, and being so unfazed settles the niggle of unease that's been lurking in my gut since leaving London.

She's not worried. So I am no longer even the tiniest bit concerned.

My smile widens as she says goodbye.

Another call comes through my phone within seconds.

"Hey."

"You sound even happier than usual. You've not got company, have you?"

My lips curls down as I sit on the end of the bed. "Like I'd answer a call and speak to you if I did. Way to make a guy's dick shrivel."

"I don't want to think about your dick," Drew says.

"You were the one asking about it."

"Shut up, fucker."

We both laugh.

"So, how's it going?" Drew asks.

"Good. Great, actually. I just got off a call with Gabrielle. She's shot the idea down with Spencer. And we're going to meet when I'm back and make sure it's skinned and bled out too."

"Knew the idea of you getting married was never going to happen." Drew chuckles. "You been using the dating apps there, then? Making the most of the local *sights?*"

I groan. "I wish. I've been too busy with meetings. And I went sightseeing with Mads the one day I had some downtime."

"Sounds like she's keeping you out of trouble as much as you are her. She going easy on you?" Drew's voice is laced with amusement. He knows damn well when Maddy and I are in a room together, sparks of the sarcastic comment kind fly. Usually from her.

"Like hell she is."

My mind still flicks back to our fight. It's been good the past day, but...

I hate you. I've always hated you.

"We're going to the opera tonight. One of the investors gave us tickets." I smooth a hand down over my shirt, then check my watch. We are due to leave in ten minutes.

"Yeah, I just called her. She's really excited," Drew says.

"I get it. I'm second choice."

"Fourth. I rang Tan and Dax before you."

"Jerk," I mutter with a grin. "How is everyone? Tanner, Dax? Jasmin?"

"They're good. Really good."

"Good," I echo.

Regret settles in my gut like a lead weight. I've always tried to help my friends when they've needed me. Only with Maddy I screwed it up. I was young and stupid. I didn't know what I was doing. I made Drew a promise to look after her. The same promise I made Dax when he got sent to jail. Only with Jasmin I got it right. Me and her are friends. She likes me.

Maddy *hates* me.

"Just..." Drew's voice drops. "Keep an eye on her?"

"You know I will. I always have, haven't I?"

"I know, I know." Drew pauses. "It's just Dad..."

"What about him?" I curse under my breath at the mention of Drew's father. The tension I happily shed with Gabrielle's call wraps itself back around my back and shoulders like a cloak.

"Mum thinks he's having an affair."

"Another one?"

"Yep." Drew snorts in disgust.

"And Mads—?"

"I told her when we spoke a couple of nights ago. She was oblivious. I don't think she wants to believe it. I didn't tell her it probably isn't the first one."

"Uh-huh."

Two nights ago was the night of our fight. I thought Maddy caved easily when I went to apologize. I'd mentally prepared for another round of insults to be launched at me. Once she gets going, she lets loose. Although, I was no better. The way she looked at me fired up something inside me. I thought what we had was banter. But in her eyes, all I could see was pure hatred.

"She knows he's not a saint though," I say. "I mean after what—"

"She doesn't know."

"What?" I pace around the room, rubbing my chin with one hand as my grip on the phone tightens. "But you said—"

"I know. But I couldn't tell her. She has a closer relationship with him than me. I didn't know what it would do to her. I kept putting it off and..." His groan is heavy. "Fuck, then we get to now. When I have to tell her not only does Dad cheat on Mum like it's an Olympic sport, but that he—"

"She deserves to know. You said you were going to tell her when you found out. How do you think she's going to feel knowing you've known about this for—"

"I know," Drew snaps. "Fuck, I know." He sighs. "Sorry. I just... I'll tell her, okay. When she gets home. She's got enough to digest right now."

I nod, helpless to the turmoil in my friend's voice. Drew wants to protect Maddy. It's what family does for one another. It's what friends do.

"Just, look after her, yeah? She might not show it. But I know she'll be thinking about Mum and Dad and stuff at home."

"Okay."

Now I understand why Maddy hates me so much, or at least, I'm starting to.

"Thanks, man," Drew says. "I know she's safe with you."

"Yeah." I try and fail to clear my throat.

So safe that I got a fucking hard-on when she was wet and clinging to me in the bathroom. So safe that I told her that her curves are sexy as I fought not to imagine her naked tits pressed against my chest again. So safe that I took great delight in the way she shivered as I whispered in her ear to buy the damn panties. Panties that I spent my earlier shower thinking about, wondering what they'd look like on her.

"Yeah." I don't even bother trying to move the lump again. "She's safe."

"This is so amazing!" Maddy squeals.

Squeals.

I've never seen her excited about anything before. Her usual setting around me is a notch above hit me in the dick and one below rip my head off.

"Look at the stage." She points over the balcony of the royal box, before gazing around in wonder at all the occupied seats below us.

I've got to hand it to Sterling Beaufort, this is impressive.

"Best view in the house. Royal box for the prince." I grin.

Maddy looks at me and rolls her eyes. "Even the company can't ruin tonight for me." She turns back toward the stage and leans forward resting her arms on the low wall in front of us, then lets out a happy sigh. "It's magical."

My eyes skim over her. Her hair is tied up. There are a few loose tendrils slipping free, which she keeps tutting at, but she seems to have forgotten about them since we sat down in the royal box. And the green silk dress that hugs her curves is... hugging her curves.

I swallow, flexing and straightening my hands in and out of fists against my tuxedo pants as I spot a hint of black fabric peeking out above the neckline of her dress as she leans forward.

She's wearing the bra. Which means she's also wearing the black G-string. And perhaps the garter belt? My eyes drop to her legs and the thigh-high split in the dress.

Black silk.

Fuck.

I clear my throat, dragging my eyes away, but that fucker of a ball has taken up permanent residence near my vocal cords, making my voice deep and gravelly when I speak.

"Show's about to start, Mads."

The lights dim, and she looks at me, her eyes glittering with delight. A spotlight falls on the stage and music begins to play.

I don't have the first fucking clue what the story is about. A load of singing, which is impressive, accompanied by a lot of wailing and stricken looks between the characters on the stage.

"It's so beautifully sad," Maddy whispers, leaning close so I can hear her over the music. "She's desperately in love with Pinkerton. She's waited years for him to return to her."

"You can tell that from the singing?"

"By the way she looks at him." She lays a hand over my arm and points with her free one. "See? But he's re-married while they were apart without telling her."

I squint at the stage. The actress looks hopeful, in love, I guess, like Maddy says. But I can't read his face.

"Oh my god!" Maddy brings a hand to her mouth as the music builds. Then grabs my thigh with her other hand and squeezes it. "She's going to do something."

She lets out a gasp as the female character acts out killing herself.

"No." Maddy wipes tears from her eyes, enthralled by the stage as the story ends. "Logan, it's... Oh my god, it's so sad. But so utterly beautiful too." She sniffs, wiping the tears from her cheeks as she smiles through them.

My mouth goes dry.

"It is," I agree, my voice thick. "Beautiful."

Her breath hitches and she blinks at me. "You enjoyed it?"

"Never felt anything like it," I reply with complete honesty.

Her dark curls fall around her face, and her hazel eyes shine with tears, but sparkle with energy at the same time. Her lips are a deep pink from where she's biting the bottom one, bringing more blood to the soft surface.

She breaks eye contact with me and leans down to rub her foot.

"Is it okay if we go now? These shoes are killing me."

I look down at the high heels she's wearing that I also insisted on buying her.

"Of course, my driver will be waiting outside."

"Good," she groans, continuing to rub her foot.

I stand and offer her my hand to help her up. She takes it and bites her lip, her eyes glittering.

"You know, I can't wait to get the stupid things off and put some slippers on."

My lips twitch.

I place a hand on her lower back to guide her to the exit.

"All slippers have been removed from our penthouse. In fact, I'll pay to see them banned from Italy altogether. I want to live to see thirty-four."

She giggles. Fucking *giggles*. And it takes every ounce of strength I have not to do anything that could taint this moment and make it something other than it is... *Magic*.

I promised Maddy I would make her laugh one day, but as I lead her out, I acknowledge a simple fact.

I never expected it to feel this good.

Chapter 14
Maddy

My smile hasn't left my face since walking out of Teatro alla Scala. Being there, feeling the emotions running through the opera house from every person in there is the experience I've only dreamed about.

Logan swipes his key card, and the penthouse level lights up on the elevator display panel. I sink back against the wall with a sigh as it begins to climb.

"You glad we came back to Milan now?" Logan asks.

"Yes."

"Even if you have to share a penthouse with me?" He cocks one thick brow, his signature smirk playing on his lips.

"I'd share a cardboard box with you after that show." I sigh again as Logan chuckles. "It's what I love. The story, the passion, the heartbreak."

"The woman killing herself," Logan says.

I shake my head, straightening my back away from the wall. "She died because of her love for him. Pinkerton married someone else and it broke Butterfly."

Logan smiles. "Ah, that's what I've been doing wrong. Forget the dating apps. The best way to find a woman is to marry someone else."

A clouded expression passes over his face as though he's just processed what he's said.

"I don't think that's the moral of the story." I shrug a shoulder, still riding my high.

My smile slips on one side as Logan meets my gaze, an unfamiliar look in his eyes.

"I thought you went on those apps for fun?" I narrow my eyes and study him.

He looks away from me.

"Logan?" I move to face him and see the seriousness taking over his face. "Oh my god!" I laugh in delight. "Seriously? The billionaire playboy actually wants to find love? And here's me thinking you have those apps because you're shallow and think with your dick. Tell me..." I tease, "... What's wrong with them all? Why is no one perfect enough for Mr. Perfect himself, huh?"

"Leave it, Mads."

"Do they not laugh at your bad jokes?" I smirk, tapping a finger against my lips. "Or maybe they have better jokes than you and you don't like it."

"Mads," Logan snaps. "I said leave it."

The atmosphere in the elevator plummets to icy. What's gotten into him? We were having a great time when we left the opera. I was actually enjoying his company instead of enduring it. And now he's acting all weird.

The elevator stops and Logan strides out when the doors open, heading to the penthouse. He opens the door, standing back so I can go inside first.

I step through and whirl to face him, a strange giddiness inside that I have something to toy with him about. I doubt he really has been a closet romantic all these years, but whatever it is, I'm getting to him, and it makes me feel strong, in control. I'm the one poking fun at his weakness for once. This is minor payback for the loneliness he made me feel years ago and all the jibes he's made since.

"I'm not going to leave it," I sing playfully. "I'm having way too much fun."

I walk backward into the open living space as Logan follows, his eyes cast down, pulling off his bowtie as he walks.

"Can dish it out but can't take it, eh?"

His eyes meet mine, flashing with something, before he walks over to the minibar, taking out two miniature bottles of something dark and pouring two glasses. He walks over to me and holds one out. I take it, knocking it back in one, the heat from the liquid fueling the manic fire that's ignited in my gut, burning with years of frustration. *Years of hatred.*

Logan schools his features as I place the empty glass onto the sideboard before he's even taken a sip from his.

I poke out my bottom lip, unable to resist goading him further. This is... fun. *This is what we do.* Me and him.

"Aww." I pout. "Does the prince of pleasure get lonely at night, waiting for his princess to find him? Empty sex losing its shine?"

"Stop," he growls in warning, his jaw tightening as he raises his glass to his lips. He sucks in sharply through his nose before knocking back his drink in one.

I laugh, my hands wrapping around the edges of the sideboard as I lean against it.

"Come on. Tonight's been a great night. Give me something back. Where's the asshole Logan that's always ready to bring me down and put me in my place, huh?"

"You want me to be an asshole?" He steps closer, his fingers flexing around his empty glass.

"Why not? You're so good at it." I do a good job of mimicking his signature smirk as I look at him. But I'm met with a frown and stormy eyes.

He takes another step closer. A vein is pulsing wildly in his neck. I zero in on it, fascinated that tonight I'm getting to him. I'm making him as mad as he makes me.

It's oddly thrilling, and yet, something else too. I shake off the hint of empathy trying to poke at me. He's not really mad. This is how we are together. Only it's usually him winding me up and me taking it.

He should play fair and let me have a go for a change.

"I guess growing up being protected gives you the freedom to be whatever you want." My eyes flick up and down his broad body in his tuxedo. It's radiating heat as he stands rigid mere inches from me. "And you chose to be... *you*," I deliver the last word clipped and precise in a sickly-sweet tone.

"And who exactly am I seeing as you know so fucking well?"

The venom in his tone surprises me, but I conceal my shock as my hands tighten around the wooden edge of the sideboard. It digs into my back as Logan moves closer still, forcing me to push backward unless I want our chests to touch.

"Well?" he presses, a glinting challenge in his eyes.

I stare into intense green eyes. He's never asked me why I hate him before. Never given me that opportunity. If I've ever plucked up the courage in the past to say something, he's stolen it from me with his jokes and teasing. I gave up trying to talk to Logan years ago. But now he's laying himself bare and asking what I think. It could be a trap that he will turn back onto me somehow. But regardless, my skin pricks with adrenaline at the chance to finally tell him.

I intend to savor every second.

I let my eyes convey everything I've ever felt in his presence as I open my veins and let the words bleed out.

"You're the guy who got away with it and watched as his friend took all the punishment. The guy who followed his sister home from school when all she wanted was her brother. The reason she walked alone every day. The guy who made sure she didn't have a date to prom because everyone thought she had crabs. The guy who laughed about it. Laughed at her."

I jab a finger into his chest, but he doesn't even flinch. He just holds my eyes with a cold stare.

"You're the guy who, for whatever reason, decided he hated her first, before she hated you," I spit finally, dragging in a deep breath that makes my lungs burn like they're on fire.

It's the first time I've ever said those words out loud to him.

And I want it to hurt.

I want it to rip him up deep inside. To feel like someone has crawled inside him and is destroying him from the inside out. The way he made me feel all those years ago.

And now that it's out, I feel... better? At least, I should. But the only sensation I'm aware of is the bottoming out of my gut as Logan stares at me without a trace of regret on his face.

Why isn't he reacting? Doing something? Anything?

He just continues to stand painfully close to me, his green eyes scorching in their intensity as he stares into mine, his mouth set in a grim line.

His lack of reaction makes my heart pound painfully in my chest. He made my life hell for six whole months while Drew was gone. And he hasn't stopped since. We've just grown up, and I've gained distance from him. Reprieve.

The least he can do is say something.

I rake my gaze over him in disgust. The mood in the room is toxic. I lost exactly where our banter changed to something dark and ugly. But now the truth is laid bare, in all its messed-up glory.

"Maybe it was all a game to you," I choke, my voice catching. "But it was my fucking *life* you were playing with. Mine and Drew's. He didn't have Daddy's money to protect him."

Logan grimaces, but his eyes maintain the intensity that's penetrating my skin and ravaging through me like acid.

When he finally speaks, his voice is low and jagged.

"No. Drew didn't have anyone protecting him. But if you think my dad bought my way out, then you're wrong. You don't know shit, Mads."

I snort.

"And you're a bigger spoiled Daddy's princess than I thought."

My arms shake with rage by my sides. "I hate you."

He leans close enough that our foreheads almost touch as he spits, "So you keep telling me."

"So get out of my face."

He leans closer. My chest rises and falls in labored breaths as his body presses up against mine and his hips push into me.

I feel his arousal instantly, hard and thick between us. I refuse to move away and show weakness, so I stay with it pressed against me.

"Get the fuck out of my head and I will," he growls.

Both of us stare at the other with a mix of fury and something else swirling in the thin slice of space that still exists between us.

There's a soft thud as Logan drops his glass onto the thick carpet.

"I said..." His lips hover above mine.

He smells like brandy. Warm and dangerous.

"Get. The. Fuck. Out. Of. My. Head."

He reaches up and holds my face between his palms. I'm too stunned to move.

Until he smashes his lips against mine.

A searing kiss.

It's rough, commanding, and entitled. Like he has every right to do it. *Like I'm his.*

His tongue finds mine, and someone moans.

Me.

"What are you doing?" I gasp, ripping my lips from his.

His eyes are dark, lust entwined with anger.

"Giving us both a release."

"What—?"

He cuts me off by swiping his thumb over my bottom lip, before pushing it into my mouth. He runs the pad over the tip of my tongue, narrowing his eyes as he watches it.

A small whimper escapes my throat, and Logan smirks.

I wrench my mouth away.

"I don't want anything from you," I hiss.

He looks at the shining wetness coating his thumb. Something dangerous flickers in his gaze as he brings his hand to his mouth and swipes his thumb over his tongue, tasting it. *Tasting me.*

A deep rumble fills the back of his throat as his eyes drop back to my mouth.

"You don't want anything from me?" he rasps.

"God, no." I grimace.

"You sure about that?"

He rolls his hips and his erection presses against me. Instinctively, I part my legs, my heartrate spiking as my breath catches in my throat.

Another tiny moan slips free.

"I don't want you," I repeat as he brings his signature smirk so close to my mouth that my breath becomes his.

"You don't?" he breathes.

"No."

"Then kiss me because you hate me. And because it's what we both need."

His lips brush mine, leaving them tingling.

"I don't need you. I'll never need you."

He licks the seam of my mouth, making me shudder.

"Okay," he whispers.

He moves away, leaving me cold. My cheeks flare with heat and my lips thrum with energy.

I blink as he holds my eyes, a million thoughts running through my mind over why I hate this man. Why I've hated him for years. I want to hit him. Pound his chest with my fists until he begs me to stop. Give myself what I so desperately need.

A release.

It's overwhelming, the desire to affect him, to do something, to...

"You're an asshole."

My words are instantly buried, working their way down his throat as I grab his shirt with both hands and yank him toward me.

He comes without hesitation.

He curls one hand around the back of my neck and slides the other inside the thigh-high split of my dress.

"You know what kind of asshole I am?"

"I can think of a few kinds."

I don't stifle my gasp in time, and it breaks free as he runs his thumb beneath the garter belt, pulling it back, then letting it snap against my skin, leaving goosebumps in its wake.

"An asshole that's thought about nothing other than touching you since the moment I saw you in this dress." He grabs a handful of my thigh.

"So be the asshole that touches me," I taunt.

Time pauses for one heartbeat.

And as it re-starts, we crash together spectacularly.

I gasp into Logan's mouth as he kisses me back with the ferocity to match mine. Tongues, teeth, lips, all clash and take from the other. A never-ending duel with no clear winner. I bite his bottom lip and he repays me by sliding his hand to the front of my drenched silk panties and balling them inside his fist.

"Fuck, you're soaking. Don't lie and say it's because you haven't thought about this."

"I haven't."

"Liar."

"Fuck—"

He rips my panties, the delicate silk a weak opponent. Then he slips two fingers inside me without hesitation.

"—off," I gasp, pulling my lips from his so I'm able to breathe.

Logan chuckles. And it's as dark as his eyes as he stares at me, twisting his wrist until he's stroking my G-spot arrogantly, confident in his ability to make me unravel.

I drop my hand to grip his wrist, keeping him in the perfect spot. The tendons in his forearm flex as he finger-fucks me with the precision of someone who knows my body like he's studied it daily.

"Try lying again and telling me you don't like this." His eyes roam over my face and come to rest on my parted lips. "Your cream's filling my palm," he sneers.

I tighten my hold on his wrist, unable to reply as his movements draw more wetness from me.

"I—"

He pulls his fingers back.

My body sags forward at the loss, and I lift my eyes to his.

He licks his lips, then sucks his fingers. His breath catches as he cleans my arousal off them, making a wet sound as he pops them free.

"You know what you taste like, Mads?"

"Pretty sure you're about to tell me," I snipe.

"You taste like you enjoy being fingered by the guy you insist is an asshole—warm and sweet. I bet your pussy will be throwing orgasms at him like fucking confetti, given the chance."

"Don't flatter yourself."

His eyes narrow at the corners, and he drops a hand to the zipper of his pants like he's still considering his next move.

I glance down. The dark fabric is straining against the bulge of his erection.

I look back into his eyes in challenge, holding my breath.

He swallows, unblinking as he returns my stare.

Then the sound of his zipper being slowly dragged down slices through the air.

My clit throbs painfully and all sane thoughts evaporate, fueled by lust.

I push his hand away and grab his zipper, yanking it all the way down. His pupils blow wide and then he starts moving, helping me to rid him of his tuxedo's cummerbund. I tear his shirt from his pants and together we force his pants and underwear out of the way.

He grabs my thighs, wrapping them around his hips as he lifts me on top of the sideboard.

Then he sinks his cock inside me.

I feel every thick inch as he pushes inside me, stretching me to take him. His eyes don't lose mine for a second. I have every opportunity to stop him. Enough time to say no.

But my choice was made before he even kissed me.

I've hated Logan Rich for years. And in a sick, twisted way, this is exactly what I need. So instead, I stare into his eyes, silent except for my hitched breath passing through my lips as he melds our bodies into one.

He curses as he pushes the final inch inside me until his balls meet my skin. My body throbs.

"This what you wanted?" he grits, his palms spread over my hips. "To be stuffed full of my cock."

"Don't kid yourself." I gather my breath as I get used to his size. He's bigger than anyone else I've ever known. "I've felt better."

"Really?" His fingers dig into my hips, and he holds himself still like he's fighting to maintain control.

"Really."

My pussy clenches around him before I can stop it.

He draws back and then thrusts back inside, making the air whoosh from my lungs as I cry out.

"You sure about that?"

He pulls back and drives inside me again with a deep hiss. My eyes fall closed as I succumb to the pleasure rippling through me.

"Look at the guy you hate while he fucks you, Mads," he growls.

My mouth parts as Logan fucks me with punishing thrusts. My ass gets thrown further back on the sideboard with each one, and each time he drags me back onto his cock, burying himself deeper inside me.

We move together, making the sideboard bang against the wall. Silent hatred burns between us as our foreheads press together and our breath mingles, sharing pants and groans of pure physical pleasure.

Nothing more.

He attacks my mouth with a kiss, making my chest clench and my heart race. I grab fistfuls of his hair in both of my hands, and I moan around his tongue as something shifts inside my mind that I refuse to acknowledge.

Thinking in this moment is dangerous.

I break away, my lips tingling. A flash of something passes through Logan's eyes as we stare at each other, panting. I ball up the bottom edges of his shirt and pull him back, crashing my lips back onto his.

He drives his hips faster to meet me with more force.

I thought he was fucking me hard before, but his thrusts grow fiercer, wilder, accompanied by deep, rough groans that sound like they're being dragged from deep inside his chest. The sound of them only makes me wetter.

He kisses me again, nipping at my bottom lip, and then he draws back, casting his eyes down to where his cock is driving inside my body.

"Fuck," he breathes.

His grip tightens on one of my hips as he slides his other hand between my legs, using his thumb to rub my clit in deliberate circles.

My eyes dart from his thumb to his face and back again.

And the bastard smirks.

"You can admit it feels good."

He knows I'm about to come. And he's the one who's giving it to me.

"Get that smirk off your face," I say through a whimper of pleasure. "This means nothing. I hate you, remember?"

Logan presses his thumb harder against my clit, and my back arches as pleasure singes between my thighs.

"There's nothing hateful about the way your pussy's gripping onto my cock right now though, is there? Desperate for me to make you come all over it."

"You're insufferable," I pant as the pressure builds, making my vision blur.

Logan cants his hips, and the movement makes me gasp. His eyes glitter with arrogance.

"Suffer through how hard I make you come for me." He leans closer so his lips graze my ear. "You can even scream out my name if you like. Because I know you'll be screaming it inside your head."

"Fuck y—" The words die in my throat as the orgasm hits me, stealing my air, my vision, and my mind at the same time as it ravages my body.

And in this moment, I hate Logan Rich even more.

Because I scream his name. I scream it inside my head. I scream it out loud. A confused, emotional shout. A gasp. Then a curse. Then another gasp. And finally, a whimpered cry as surge after surge of pure electric bliss rips through my body, stripping it of all its bones, until I'm putty inside his strong hands.

I tear my eyes open and watch him watching me. He's still thrusting into me, his cock sliding with ease now that my body has released and opened up to him, covering him in more wetness.

I expect words. Taunting. Instead, he looks at me in silent lust.

Just that smug, arrogant smirk on his face.

I shudder as he fucks me through my orgasm to the other side. Except there is no other side. I'm suspended inside it, the pleasure refusing to leave my body, hanging on tight for the ride, the feel of him inside me too goddamn good to give up.

I look down. My body is stretched obscenely to take him.

He tuts to bring my eyes back to his face. "When you're still feeling me inside you tomorrow..." He thrusts deep. "You can say thank you."

My eyes widen as the reality of what's about to happen sinks in.

"No!" I shake my head. "Don't you dare. I don't want it."

"Yet you're the one pulling me deeper," he tsks.

My hands are gripping his ass cheeks so hard that my nails must be puncturing his skin. But I can't move them.

"Just let go, Mads. And I'll stop," he groans as his cock thickens inside me.

But I can't. Despite the horror of what's coming, I can't let go. My head is screaming no. But my hands are tightening their grip on Logan's muscular ass as my lips whimper and moan sounds of encouragement. *Traitors.*

He dips his head, leaning down to whisper in my ear, "Last chance."

I shake my head, fury in my eyes as his pupils blow wide. Every muscle in his body seems to tense at once.

"Too. Late. Now," he grits.

Then he groans, and I swear heat fires into every space inside me as he comes. His eyes glow with a menacing darkness, his lips curling into the smirk I hate so much as his cock pumps out inside me, his release burning me inside.

He digs his fingers deep into the skin around my hips and growls my name.

"Mads, fuck, take it, baby."

"You asshole..."

My words of disgust shrivel as my body decides that the sensation of Logan's cock thickening and pulsing inside me is too much.

I explode into another orgasm around him, even bigger than the first one.

"No," I cry, my entire body quivering as sweat beads along my hairline, and a drop rolls between my breasts.

"I don't want it. I—" I gasp as another surge hits me. "Oh my god... *Yes.*"

"There it is," Logan growls with a sinful smile. He leans forward and drives inside me with more determination, like he's trying to push everything he's released deeper inside my body.

My mouth falls slack as I continue coming in helpless waves around him.

"There it fucking is," he grunts. And then he wraps a hand around my throat, pulling my face to his to kiss me.

All I can do is breathe through the pulses searing through my body as Logan growls and curses, his orgasm stretching on, and spilling inside me.

And I hate that I love it so much. Because I'd never have dreamed of doing this with Logan before this trip. I'd never have let my guard slip and gotten close to him. All the watching Italian weddings together, making wishes in fountains, opening up about why I love books so much... I've let him get close, see the real me. I shouldn't have put myself in a position of being vulnerable with him. Not again.

I let him kiss me long after I've whimpered the remnants of my second orgasm against his lips. He swallowed every moan down like it belonged to him.

We kiss long after the final pulses of his dick can no longer be felt inside me, until his kisses turn gentle and he sucks on my bottom lip, his fingers caressing my neck in sweeping, tender strokes.

"Better?" he whispers.

I breathe, not knowing what else to do. The second I say something, or move, the moment will be over. He'll pull out of my body. Some of his cum will be dragged out with his cock. The rest will remain lodged deep inside me.

And I'll be left alone.

With a part of him inside me. Still feeling him.

Never the same.

Left to face the consequences.

"We didn't use a condom."

Logan flexes deep inside me with a grin. "I know. It felt incredible."

I make a sound of disgust, and he grabs my chin, bringing my eyes to his. His eyes burn like green flames, his grin gone.

"You said 'we', but your tone implied you think I was the only one in this." His pupils dilate with the anger in his clipped voice. Something about it re-ignites a spark of my own. I don't know how to do anything with Logan other than fight.

It's what we do.

"Well, I'm sorry for being upset about the fact that I've never had a man come inside me before. And yet, stupidity allowed me to lose all sense of reason, and I let *you*, of all people, be the first. I'm on birth control, thank God. But do you even know if you're clean?" I glare at him, appalled with my body as it flutters deep in my core when he shifts inside me.

"'Course I'm fucking clean. You think I'd touch you if I wasn't? I've never not used one before... Jesus. I know you think I'm an asshole, Mads. You tell me often enough. But I'm not a sadist."

My lips part before I snap them closed again, something twisted blossoming in my chest as he confirms I'm his first. A first for both of us.

"I'm surprised, that's all."

"Surprised?"

Hurt laces Logan's voice. I can't bring myself to meet his eyes, so I stare to the side as he withdraws out of me and fastens his pants.

"Well, I'm pretty sure I have your nail marks in my ass proving that you wanted it as much as me," he hisses, dragging a hand down his face before turning away.

I bring my legs together, ignoring the throb between them and my torn panties hanging around my hips as I stand and smooth down my dress. My legs tremble.

Logan's back tenses beneath his tuxedo jacket. I'm not being fair. I might be confused as hell over what happened. But I can't blame him for all of it. I can't imply for a second that he took something from me that I didn't give freely.

We both must accept the gravity of what happened between us.

"You're right," I croak. "It's my fault too. In fact, it's all my fault. I should never have—"

"Don't—" He inclines his chin over his shoulder but doesn't look at me. "Just don't."

I step toward him, then think better of it. What can I say? I can't undo what happened, even if we are both regretting it already. I don't even understand it or where it came from.

But I can't stand here and watch the waves of anger and regret roll from him in front of my eyes.

It's too much.

"I...I'm going to bed." I pause, but he doesn't look at me. "Thank you for the opera."

As I leave, he curses softly, barely loud enough for me to hear. My step falters, but I keep walking.

Chapter 15
Logan

IT'S EARLY WHEN I wake. Although to say I slept much would be a lie. Maddy didn't either. I heard her in the hallway during the night, outside my bedroom door. But when I opened it, she was already walking back into her own room down the hall.

I've fucked everything up.

I touched the one girl I have no right to even think about touching. One of my best friend's little sisters. I'd punch myself in the face if I could. I've never overstepped that mark before. Ever. I'm a loyal friend. One who can be trusted to look out for someone. Keep other guys away. Make sure she's safe. I'm not the snake that goes behind someone's back.

Only now, it seems I am.

I throw back the duvet and pull on a pair of joggers. I open my bedroom door and almost walk into Maddy.

"The machine made too much. I couldn't figure it out." She thrusts the coffee into my hand and then casts her eyes down to the floor.

It's a lie. She used the penthouse coffee machine fine yesterday. But I don't call her bluff. This is the nearest to an olive branch I've ever received from Maddox Harper in my life. I'm too stunned to question it.

"Thanks."

She glances up at me, then turns away.

"Mads, wait."

She pauses, inclining her head over her shoulder toward me before turning back to face me with a small sigh. She's wearing a thin cotton nightdress that does nothing to hide the hardness of her nipples beneath.

I drag my eyes up to her face. "We need to talk about last night."

"Nothing to talk about." Her eyes hold mine and I place the mug down on a table near my door.

"That's how you want to play this?"

Her expression closes off as she frowns. "Play this? There is no this." She stalks over to me. "I don't want you," she says, as though saying the words out loud makes them true. "I didn't want anything to do with you last night. And I don't want anything to do with you now, either."

"Doesn't change the fact it happened."

Her mouth opens, then closes and she glares. "Nothing happened."

"Seriously?" Anger pricks at my veins.

"Nothing that I'd ever want to happen again, at least." She lets out a frustrated sigh and crosses her arms. The movement pulls the neckline of her nightdress lower until one strap slides off her shoulder. I reach up and smooth it back into place. She sucks in a breath, her eyes dropping to my lips.

"You sure about that?"

I curse inwardly. *What am I doing?* Everything about this screams at me to shut my mouth. If Maddy wants to forget it, then so should I. It's best for everyone. Yet, the idea has my blood heating in my veins.

I smirk at my own stupidity. You don't forget nights like last night, no matter how hard you might wish you can.

"God, you're so sure of yourself," she spits. "Drew told me to give you a chance. I said I'd make an effort, but I don't know why I bothered."

My brows shoot up my forehead. "Having sex with me last night was because you told Drew you'd make an effort?"

Saying his name has guilt gnawing away at my insides.

"What? No. I didn't say that."

"Well, what was it then?"

Her mouth flaps. "It was... a mistake. A huge, enormous, gigantic, stupid regret I'll carry for the rest of my life. We're clear about that, right?" Defiance glitters in her eyes.

I don't know what's gotten into me since coming to Italy, but my patience has been sucked away day by day by this girl.

"Oh yeah. We're clear." My voice booms. "Real crystal fucking clear! But just to set things straight, you didn't get off, did you? You weren't grinding down onto my cock like you needed it more than fucking air? You didn't scream out *my name*?" I jab a finger into my chest angrily. "When you came so hard your whole body shook."

"I—"

"Twice!"

"That's not what—"

"You don't think I know it shouldn't have happened, either?" I continue. "You don't think I know I can't take you home and say, 'Here you go, Drew, here's your little sister. I looked after her, she's in one piece, but oh yeah, she's full of my cum! We're good though, yeah? Still mates? What's a little betrayal and sibling fucking between friends?'"

"You're gross."

"Yeah?" I bark out an empty laugh. "Seems gross is what makes you come so hard you scream."

"I can't..." She holds a hand up. "I can't do this with you." She stalks away down the hall.

I should leave her be. Not fan the flames. But I'm already racing after her as I disregard all sense of reason.

"Mads."

I catch up with her in the kitchen, reaching for her elbow. She whirls around. I expected fire in her eyes. Anger. But they're shimmering with unconcealed lust.

"I don't want you, Logan. Not then, not now, not ever," she says, her chest rising and falling.

I step closer, dancing with the devil on my shoulder as I move into her space until her body heat rolls into mine.

"I haven't fucking slept because I've been thinking about you. Why were you outside my bedroom door in the night?"

"I wasn't." Her cheeks flush.

"Liar."

"I wasn't coming to demand a replay if that's what you're thinking. I still hate you."

A swell of arousal rushes to my dick as her eyes drop to my lips.

She's thinking about when we kissed. She must be. How can she not think about it when it was like that moment on a rollercoaster as you reach the top of the highest drop. The ultimate thrill, the anticipation, and then the stomach lifting exhilaration when you roll over that peak.

And fall.

"I know you do. You hate me all the time. It's like you have to say it out loud to remind yourself."

"Shut up," she snaps.

I move closer, logic and reason being blown out of my head as desire takes over. I'm a shit friend. I'm already going to hell. Does it make it worse if the betrayal is more than one time? I know the answer, but it doesn't stop me from taking Maddy's hand in mine and pressing it onto my rock-hard dick.

I dip my head until my lips graze her ear. "And yet you still do this to me. Imagine what would happen if you told me you like me."

She stills, and I wait for her to rip her hand away. To slap me. To yell at me. To hammer some sense back into me. Because it all seems to desert me when she's around.

But instead, she wraps her fingers around me as I grunt in response.

"I *tolerated* your dick last night, Logan. Don't get it confused for anything else."

The hairs on the back of my neck stand up and my cock swells with more urgency.

"Fuck," I hiss as she slides her hand beneath the waistband of my joggers. When she wraps it around my dick again, skin to skin, I thicken more in her palm.

"Just tolerated it, that's all," she breathes.

Then she starts to jerk me off.

I fight not to fall back onto the tiled kitchen floor as I groan. Maddy stares at me, a mesmerized expression on her face, her brows pulling together in question like she isn't the one controlling her hand. But she doesn't stop. She slides it up, using her thumb to smear pre-cum around the crown, before sliding back down again.

She watches me the entire time, and faster than I expect, I'm tensing and groaning, my balls pulling close to my body with the need to come.

"Mads," I hiss in warning.

"Logan," she counters.

Her grip tightens and she drops her eyes to my cock as the first spurt fires out, hitting her nightdress and sinking into it. Drop after drop fires out, spraying a pattern all over the light gray material until it's ruined by patches of darkness. Each one is a glaring mark of how far past the line we've stepped.

I shudder as my balls empty all over her. The final pulse leaves me and before I can give it any rational thought, I slide my hands under the ruined material, curving them over Maddy's bare hips.

She lifts her arms in silence, letting me pull the night-dress over her head.

I stand back to look at her. My throat tightens as I take in her naked body. Curves and soft skin. Inches and inches of it I want to run my tongue over.

And her breasts.

I stifle a groan as I step forward, cupping each one. I rub my thumbs over her puckered nipples. Maddy freezes, and I hold her eyes as I bend to take one into my mouth.

"I've never seen a body as beautiful as yours." I let my eyes flutter closed as I wrap my lips around her and suck with a deep moan of appreciation. "So fucking sexy."

"Logan." Her hands sink into my hair and tug.

"Please don't stop me."

I drop to my knees on the tiled floor in front of her and run a hand up from her ankle to her inner thigh, encouraging her to part her thighs.

"Tell me you hate me if you want to. But do it while my tongue's buried in you, tasting you."

I press my tongue to her, teasing her lips apart and finding her entrance. I slide inside, unable to fight the pull in my gut to taste her repeatedly and make her mine.

"I don't... I don't—"

I pull back.

"You don't what? Want to come on my tongue?" I groan as I dive back into her, smiling against her as she gasps and twists her fingers in my hair until my scalp stings. "Is it worse than coming on my cock, Mads? Because we're way beyond that."

"I don't want you to talk," she gasps. "Just… stop… talking." Her words morph into a moan as I replace my tongue with two fingers and suck on her clit instead.

I fuck her with my fingers in the exact way she liked last night, tracing my tongue over her clit. I drink up everything she gives me until her inner thighs shake around my head.

"I hate you," she cries as I hit her G-spot and she comes with a force that has her legs buckling.

I grip one hip with my free hand and guide her to lean against the kitchen counter as I growl against her swollen flesh. "Hate me again. This time around my tongue." I switch my fingers to her clit and sink my tongue back inside her again, taking full advantage of her heightened senses as her orgasm still pulses on. If I can catch her before she's down and keep the pressure on her clit, then maybe—

"Fuck." She pulls my hair as her pussy erupts around my tongue, clenching down onto it as she comes again.

"Good girl," I groan. It's muffled, but the extra yank of my hair means she heard me.

"Stop." She grinds on my face as her orgasm continues. "I'm not doing this with you again," she pants.

I wait until the last pulse leaves her and then slide my tongue from inside her, kissing my way up her body until I'm standing. "And yet you are."

Her eyes are bright, her lips and cheeks a deep pink.

"Don't read anything more into this than it is."

I curl a hand around her waist and stroke the skin there as I wait for her to catch her breath.

166

"You and me, we're... never going to happen. You know that." She swallows, then takes more deep breaths as she waves a finger back and forth in the gap between our naked torsos. "This is... marginally better than fighting with you, that's all."

"Marginally better?" I cock a brow, desperate to kiss her again.

"Only just." The deep line I like to tempt out between her brows appears. "I don't get a headache with this."

"That's what this is? Avoiding a headache?"

"It's choosing not to fight with you for a change."

She gathers up her nightdress from the floor and clutches it to the front of her as her eyes scan up and down my body.

"Right," I murmur.

Her eyes snap to mine, her usual fire back in them. "Don't be an asshole."

"I said one word. But just so we're clear, you don't want to fight with me anymore?"

She purses her lips, then jerks her head side to side quickly like a stubborn toddler.

"But you fight with me every day. Multiple times."

Her eyes rake over my body, and I twist subtly to make my abs flex.

"Then I guess this could happen again." She frowns, her attention glued to my stomach. "But it's only until we get back to London. No one can know, and if you tell anyone, I'll deny it."

"Mads."

"Logan." Her eyes meet mine, a steely determination in them.

I've just been told she's up for no strings sex for the rest of this trip. I can't deny the idea is a hell of a lot more appealing than her usual hatred toward me. But as I nod back at her, my lips set in a firm line, I know this is probably the worst deal I've ever agreed to in my life.

I don't even fucking negotiate.

I glance at Maddy as I make us both a coffee. She's sitting in my kitchen window seat, tapping away on her laptop in the sun, her legs folded underneath her on the seat. It's day one back in Rome and she's barely spoken since we left Milan. She hasn't mentioned a thing about what happened.

"You working on the article?"

"I was."

"You going to let me read it?"

Her head snaps up and something passes over her face before she schools her features. "No. It's... No."

"Okay. So, what are you working on?"

She looks up and her eyes brighten. "Book fairy mail."

I screw my face up in confusion.

"I send out books from people's wish lists to them." She spins her laptop screen toward me. There's a list of books as she scrolls down.

"Is this part of what you do, then? At work? Send them out as a marketing thing?"

"No." She turns the screen back to face her. "It's just something I like to do myself."

"You gift people all those books yourself?" I hold out her coffee mug and she closes her laptop and takes the mug from me. "When I came for the meeting with Eve, your desk was covered in boxes. Was that—?"

"Yep. More fairy mail." She shrugs as she blows the steam from the top of her mug. "Books give people—"

"A safe place. An escape." I smile as I take a seat next to her and sip my coffee.

Her eyes narrow, accompanied by an impressed smile, rather than her usual frown. "You do listen."

"To you, Smiles? Always."

She snorts and looks into her mug. "It makes me feel like I'm helping a little. It sounds stupid."

"It doesn't," I interject, but she rolls her eyes.

"I'm not a doctor. I can't heal people. I'm not a teacher with the skills to help someone learn. I'm not an engineering genius who designs world-changing rocket engines." She side-eyes, her lips twitching. "I'm not anything like that. My imprint in the world is a small one. But this makes me feel like I'm making a small difference. Even if it's only to one person at a time through words. It's still... something."

I rest my head against the back of the seat. "I'd say it's everything to that one person. Don't underestimate how much of an impact you can have on someone, Mads."

Her eyes drop to my lips. And mine drop to hers.

My phone rings on the table in front of us and her face lights up. "It's Drew."

"Go ahead." I gesture to my phone, and she scoops it up with the biggest smile I've seen on her face since we were at the opera. She pauses, swiping something off the screen before she connects the call.

"Drew," she answers with undisguised delight. Her eyes flick to me, then away. "Yeah, he's here. I was just closer to the phone."

I drink my coffee as I listen to the easy way they chat. I always wondered what having a sibling would be like. Growing up with Drew is the closest I have.

"I can't wait to tell you all about it," Maddy muses, stroking the book stickers that decorate the lid of her laptop. "Oh, Chloe's staying longer at my place now. So those things you and Tan were going to help fix for me, maybe wait until I'm home? Or at least, check she's okay with you doing it while she's there. Thank you." Maddy pauses. "How are Mum and Dad?"

She gnaws on her bottom lip, mumbling the odd "yeah", and "I know". Then she says, "Love you too," and holds the phone out to me.

I take it and walk over to the rear doors, staring out over the formal gardens and pool. Guilt twists at my gut before I even get my first word out.

"Hey."

"All right?" Drew asks.

"All good here." *I had sex with your sister.*

"How's funding going?"

"Nearly there." *Then I ate her out in the kitchen.*

"That's great. Be good to have your ugly face back."

My eyes dart to Maddy, but she's typing on her laptop again.

"Missed me, have you?" *But that's all, I swear. I haven't touched her since. And I won't again. I can't.*

"Like you'd miss an infection in your dick. But you make me look better. And I need that lucky charm. It's time we had another double date. It's been too long."

I chuckle. "You're full of shit."

Drew laughs. We've always made a good duo when it comes to women. He's dark and broody, with an air of danger about him, which women seem to go mad for. Even though he and I both know his bad boy days are way behind him. Behind both of us. And I'm fairer and can break out the charm when I need it.

"I thought we weren't dating together again. What happened to the lawyer?"

Maddy's eyes snap to mine, then away just as fast. I clear my throat and turn away, looking back at the garden.

"She's dating someone."

"Since when did that stop you?" I resist looking back at Maddy and instead step to the side so I can make out her reflection in the glass of the doors. She's closed her laptop and is drinking her coffee.

"Since she threatened me with a restraining order, remember?"

I swallow my laugh and cough instead.

"She was joking," Drew adds. "Obviously."

"Obviously." I smirk. Drew's been hung up on this lawyer since he met her. And when he wants something, he goes for it. Only, where persistence has paid off for him in the past, this woman's having none of it. It's like the harder Drew tries, the more she resists.

"I need a distraction. We should set something up. And since you're no longer getting married..."

"Thank God." I drag a hand down my face with a groan. "Gabrielle ripped that thought out of Spencer's head. I'm hoping he'll have already spoken to Dad before I get back. Make the blow less of a surprise when I confirm it."

"I don't know. Your dad's a stubborn bastard."

"Lucky for me that I'm one too."

Since talking to Gabrielle all thoughts of the wedding that never was, have been pushed to the back of my mind. Apart from that one reaction to the comment Maddy made after the opera about Pinkerton marrying someone else. That one comment that got me all fired up and fucking my friend's sister on a piece of furniture.

I stop laughing and look at Maddy. She looks away and takes another sip of her coffee.

"Right. Better leave you to it. I've got a load of Tan's work to do."

"Where's he gone?"

"Rachel called," Drew says, not needing to explain further.

Tanner's wife is pregnant with their third kid and horny as hell. Poor fucker can't keep up. She phones him mid-day, insisting he sorts out the problem he caused, and the lucky bastard drives home, does the job, then comes back to work. Drew says the record is three times in one day. Tanner likes to seek our sympathy over how exhausted he is. He's the only one with kids. But he also has a horny wife demanding sex multiple times a day. So yeah, we're real sympathetic.

"Lucky bastard," I say.

"Yeah, fucker." Drew snorts.

"You can get him back when it's your turn."

Drew sucks in a breath. "Yeah, pregnancy sex."

Maddy shuffles on the sofa. I doubt she knows that her brother is obsessed with pregnancy sex. I've never thought about it. With the right girl, I can see its appeal. But Drew is mad for it. Despite seeing how drained Tanner is, he still looks at him like he's discovered the meaning of life every time he comes back from answering one of Rachel's calls.

"Go. I'm not talking about it with you again. Not now." *Not when your sister is sitting behind me and all I can think about is that I've tasted the inside of her body.*

I swallow the guilt down from re-surfacing as I hang up.

"Why's my brother asking you to double date with him?"

I turn to face Maddy. She's scowling.

"You don't like that idea?" I step closer to her, but she stands in a rush and gathers up her laptop.

"You can do what you like. I just don't see why you need to double date with my brother when you have that dating app you're usually addicted to on your phone. When do you find time to sleep?"

Tension knots my brow as I look at my phone screen. There's a notification from the app. *Looking for fun26 wants to send you a private message.* Maddy must have seen it when she answered Drew's call.

"I haven't been on here in weeks," I answer honestly.

"You don't need to explain to me."

"Yet somehow it sounds like you want me to."

"Get over yourself, Logan." She stomps to the other side of the kitchen.

I follow her, my fingers tapping fast on the phone screen at the same time. "Here." I thrust it at her so the button confirming I want to delete the app is at eye-level.

She shoves it aside. "What are you doing?"

I touch the button and watch as the app disappears. All my old contacts. My random call ups I had in my back pocket. *Gone.*

"I don't know. Losing my fucking mind, it seems."

Maddy scrunches her nose up. "I'm going to my room until it's time to leave for the meeting. Thanks for the coffee."

She leaves without looking back, and I drop my phone onto the counter, placing my palms down and leaning forward as tension creeps through my shoulders. Mads is impossible to work out. She hates me, but then acts jealous.

Maddox Harper is getting under my skin. And rather than keeping her out, I'm welcoming her with open arms.

I screw my eyes shut. I'm the worst fucking friend.

Chapter 16
Maddy

THE AFTERNOON'S MEETING GOES by without a hitch. It's with two male investors. And between them and Logan, the conversation flows so fast I don't need to participate. I'm glad because everything I want to say in Logan's presence seems wrong. I don't know why him double dating with Drew irked me so much. They've always done it and I'm used to hearing the two talk about it. I've even been their lift home once or twice. I know what they get up to.

I just don't want it shoved in my face with my morning coffee, that's all.

By the time we get back to the house, it's getting dark. I mumble a good night to Logan and head to my room, pulling my high heels off on the way through my door. A pair of white slippers are waiting for me. They weren't there before we left. I pick them up, running my fingertip over the stitching on the fabric. A smile tugs at my lips. *MH.*

The bastard got me my own personalized pair.

I slip them onto my feet and walk quickly to Logan's room before I can overthink what I'm doing. I knock lightly on the door. The shower is running inside.

I ignore the energy dancing in my stomach and open the door, walking straight into his ensuite purposefully.

His eyes are closed, head facing the shower head, letting the water run over him as he rests both palms against the tiles. His ensuite is a wet room, so there's nothing between us. No glass screen, no wall. Nothing to hide the magnificence that is Logan Rich in his full naked glory.

I stand in the doorway as he rolls his neck side to side, moaning deeply when it cracks. He drops one hand to his dick, gripping it tight and giving it a hard tug. He curses out something that's muffled by the sound of the water dropping around him, then shakes his head and lets it go. The muscles across his shoulders all ripple beneath his skin as he pushes away from the wall and turns. I'm gifted with a full frontal of him before he leans back under the spray again, his eyes still closed.

I knew he was ripped. I've seen it enough times when he's working out with Drew. And in the kitchen yesterday morning. But seeing him like this when he's unaware of my presence is different. There's no joking about, no smirks. It's just Logan in his physical fineness. And that's something I can appreciate.

My eyes drop to his dick again and the short, neat hair at its base. He hasn't got any hair on his chest, so it draws my attention. Or maybe it's the fact that his dick is long and thick, and attractive. *And it feels good inside me.*

I shake the thought from my head as my feet carry me closer to the shower. Logan's smoothing his hands back through his hair, his biceps bulging as he rolls his shoulders back with a deep sigh.

I reach around and unzip my dress at the exact moment Logan opens his eyes. I'm pinned in place by a questioning green gaze. I don't falter. I push my dress from my shoulders and let it fall to the floor. His eyes darken as I step out of my slippers, then peel off the red set of lingerie he bought me in Milan. His gaze drops over my body as I join him under the hot spray.

"Something wrong with your shower, Smiles?"

"Mm."

His eyes tighten at the corners as I place my palms against his wet chest. I have no idea how I ended up here. Only that the thrumming deep in my core is happy that I did.

"What happened yesterday—"

I place a finger to his lips and shake my head gently. "Stop thinking. When we think, we fight."

He pulls my hand away, his fingers closing gently around my wrist over my deepening pulse.

"You're not mine, Mads. Not mine to touch like this," he says, his voice a gravelly whisper.

I move close enough that my nipple grazes the back of the hand holding my wrist.

"That didn't stop you before."

His eyes drop to my breasts.

"This is just misplaced dislike. We don't have to make it anything more. It *isn't* anything more." My eyes scan over his face and the water droplets running along his strong jaw.

"Misplaced hate, you mean?" he murmurs.

I pause, waiting for him to do something. But he just stares at me, his brows drawn low like he's battling with his conscience inside his head.

"I like my slippers." I bat my eyelashes playfully.

A gleam enters his eyes. "Yeah?"

"Yeah," I breathe.

With a skilled flex of the hand that's holding my wrist, he pulls me to him, spinning us at the same time so my back is pinned against the tiles and my front is pressed up along the wet length of his body. The heat radiating from him is hotter than the shower water and I bite down a moan as he reaches up and strokes one of my breasts lightly.

"I like giving you things." His voice is husky as he stares into my eyes.

"What else do you like?"

He smiles, flashing perfect white teeth.

"I like these." He pinches my nipple, and I yelp. "And I like these." He presses his lips to mine but doesn't kiss me. "And I like the way you hold your breath when I do this." He drags the back of his knuckles across my clit. "But mostly, I like what's in here." He places a hand over my heart, but being Logan, it involves him fondling my breast with a groan. "And in here." He presses a kiss on my forehead.

I stiffen.

"Touch my breasts again," I say, needing to diffuse the sudden display of tenderness threatening to creep in.

This is just misplaced dislike. Better than fighting. Marginally better. That's all.

His familiar smirk touches his lips. "You like my hands on you here?" He places both hands on my breasts, rubbing them together and teasing my nipples, making me moan loudly. I don't care how needy I sound. Not anymore. Because when he does that, there's not much else better.

He bends, sucking a nipple between his lips and then circling it with his tongue. *Okay, that's better.*

"We aren't friends," I murmur as his lips travel up and he kisses and sucks his way over my collarbone and to my ear.

"I don't want to be your friend." His breath is warm against my ear, then he spins me fast, pressing my front into the tiles so that I'm sandwiched between him and the wall.

"Good."

He rubs the head of his weeping cock between my legs.

"I'd hate that." My voice falters as he uses his cock to spread my lips and tease my entrance.

"As much as you hate me?"

He bends, hitching one of my legs up with his hand behind my knee. Then he thrusts up inside me with one confident stroke that makes me cry out. My cheek presses against the tiles as he flattens his chest to my back.

"More, I'd hate it more," I say as he pulls back and pushes inside me again, sliding one hand between my body and the wall until he's caressing my breast and rolling my nipple between his finger and thumb.

"How are you so wet? So fucking perfect," he rasps as he increases his pace, nailing me into the wall.

"What is that? What are you—?" My eyes roll back in my head on a whimper as he angles his hips so he's dragging over my G-spot with each thrust.

He slides his hand down until his fingers roll over my clit. He grunts when he feels how swollen I am and drops his lips to my shoulder, kissing my wet skin.

"We just fit, Mads. Your pussy loves my cock, even if you hate me."

"Fuck off," I murmur. But Logan's chuckle makes me smile as I say it.

I arch my ass toward him, and he lowers my leg, stepping back and pulling me with him. Then he grasps my hip with one hand as he drives inside me with a grunt. His other hand stays between my legs, playing with my clit.

He pumps into me, setting a steady pace as he whips my clit into a frenzy, and I moan, all care deserting me over how loud I'm being. All I care about is that he doesn't stop. It feels too good.

"Shit, Mads," he growls as I clench around him.

"That feel good?"

"Keep doing it and I'm going to explode." He sounds like he's barely holding it together. His fingers press harder against my clit, and it makes me clench involuntarily around him this time. "Jesus." He groans, and his cock thickens more inside me. "Where do you want me?"

The sound of his deep voice growling those words and knowing he's almost there releases a trigger inside me. *I came so hard last time, knowing he was filling me.* The memory bursts through my mind, and I shudder around him, calling his name as I come in a rush.

I squeeze my eyes shut as the waves overtake me, making my stomach clench and every muscle in my body hum with warm vibrations.

"Inside," I pant as my orgasm stretches on. I put my hand on top of Logan's, circling my clit with him to keep my orgasm going.

"You sure?"

"Inside," I beg, knowing a second orgasm is on its way as my core begins winding tightly again.

Logan's hand flexes on my hip and the knuckles turn white. "There's something about knowing you have my cum inside you, Mads. It makes me fucking crazy."

I whimper as his cock swells inside me.

"Make it deep," I moan.

For the second time in two days, we've passed the point of no return. If we're doing this again, I'm going all in.

Logan groans and thrusts hard, his fingers playing my clit with perfect precision. My legs shake, signaling a second, even stronger orgasm is imminent.

"Yes, Logan."

I throw my head back and come again. Logan thrusts twice more, cursing before the breath rushes from his lungs and he comes.

We're a mix of groans, panted curses, and stuttered breaths. He drops his mouth to my neck and bites me.

"You're so tight, you're milking my cock," he grits, sucking the tender skin on my neck as he empties everything he has inside me.

I can't respond. I'm speechless as my orgasm tails off and my body relaxes into a sated calmness with him nestled snugly inside it. I drop my head back and rest it on his shoulder. His lips find my temple, kissing me as his breathing slows.

"Stay with me tonight," he murmurs.

Maybe it's a question, maybe it's a request. I'm too breathless to do anything other than nod. His chest relaxes against my back, and he takes hold of my chin, turning it to him. Then he kisses me on the lips for the first time since we came back to Rome. And I kiss him back with one thing swirling in my head as his tongue seeks mine.

It's better than fighting.

That's all this is. Kissing Logan Rich, having him buried deep inside my body. Coming harder with him than I ever have in my life. It's the lesser of two evils.

Nothing more.

Logan's body is warm against mine as I lie naked on my side, cocooned in his strong arms. I should have left. Gone back to my room. I shouldn't be spooning with him like I've forgotten everything he's ever done and the way he made me feel growing up.

"I still hate you," I whisper into the darkness of the room.

"I know," he says softly.

"It's who we are," I add as his arms tighten around me and he presses a kiss to my shoulder blade.

"I know."

"Do you know everything?" I turn to face him.

"I know we shouldn't be doing this. But I also know I can't stop now even if I wanted to." His fingers trail down my side, over the bare skin to my hip. He splays his fingers out and holds me there. "I never knew you hated me so much."

I'm glad it's dark because I don't think I'd like what I'd see in his eyes if the heaviness in his voice is any indication of how he's feeling right now.

"You walked away while Drew got sent away. It wasn't fair."

"My dad didn't buy my freedom, Mads."

"I knew you'd say that."

He strokes my hips, his voice firm. "He didn't. I swear to you. I asked him myself, more than once. I didn't understand it, either. He said maybe the police went harder on Drew because he was driving. I told them I was the one who had the idea. I told them I broke into the car and hotwired it. I tried. I swear, I tried."

He squeezes my hip and I hold my breath. My chest is not only tight but burning too.

"I know you lost your brother. But I lost my friend."

Hearing Logan say it out loud hits me like a sledge-hammer. He suffered as well. I never allowed myself to acknowledge that before. I was too focused on my own heartache and pain to consider his. I blamed him and disregarded any feelings he might have had.

He was the cause. The enemy.

"That doesn't make up for what you did when he was gone." My voice sounds strong, but inside, I'm trembling with the loneliness of memories.

"I promised Drew I'd look out for you. I'd do anything for him."

"Except get locked up with him," I snort.

Logan's silent. He can't argue with history.

"You followed me home and scared off any friends I could have made." My strength wavers and my voice cracks.

Logan's hand stills on my hip. "They were teenage boys with one agenda."

"You don't know that." I push his hand away and immediately hate myself because I miss the warmth of his skin on mine.

"I didn't know how to be a big brother, Mads. I just promised Drew I'd keep you safe. I did what I thought I needed to."

"You weren't supposed to be my big brother. You weren't supposed to replace him. You were supposed to be my friend. And if you couldn't have done that, then you should have just left me alone."

Logan's darkened silhouette rolls in the bed so he's on his back. He brings his hands to his face and scrubs it with a pained sigh. "I'm sorry. For all of it. You were always so ready to fight me. I thought you got a kick out of it. I thought it was harmless."

"You told half the school I had crabs," I hiss. "And that was after Drew came home. You had no right to be acting like that. Whether you thought you were protecting me in some piss-poor fake big brother way or not. You laughed about it."

Logan lies in silence next to me as the sound of my angry breaths fill the air.

"I deserve you to hate me. It's the least I deserve. I was young and stupid. I went about everything the wrong way. I can see that now," he whispers finally. "But I *am* sorry."

A million emotions hurtle around my body and weigh me down. If I accept his apology, it's like admitting that all these years, hating him have been for nothing. That it's been nothing more than a waste of my time and energy because nothing has come from it. I have nothing to show. And that would mean he gets away with it. He gets to rid himself of any guilt he might have and leave me alone to be the only one in this.

On my own. Again.

I've spent years hating Logan. I don't know how to do anything else.

A strange sound leaves my throat, and I shiver, overcome with memories that still haunt me.

"Don't," Logan says softly.

"Don't what?"

"Leave."

He tentatively places his arm above my head on the pillow. I accept his silent invitation and shuffle into his side, resting my head on his chest as he wraps his arm around me and holds me close.

We don't say anything else. There are no words to convey what we're both thinking. We're two people stuck together, away from home. Both thinking about the past and wishing we could re-write it.

We're choosing something other than fighting for a change. Because it's marginally better. Because fighting is exhausting.

Nothing more.

Chapter 17
Logan

MADDY'S LAUGH CARRIES UP the hallway as I walk down the stairs fixing my tie. She was gone when I woke up and her side of the bed was cold.

"Seriously? Eve said I could interview him?"

Her eyes meet mine briefly as I walk into the kitchen and motion to the coffee machine. She nods, leaning against the counter. I feel her eyes follow me as I move around fixing our drinks.

"It's amazing. I can't believe it. Yeah, I will. Bye."

"That was Chloe," she says as she places her phone on the counter.

"She okay?" I place her cup underneath the machine first and wait for it to fill.

"Yeah. She's enjoying my apartment. I think I'll have to give her an eviction notice when we get home."

"She's got one more night there. What if she's changed the locks when you get back?"

Maddy shrugs as I hand her the cup. "Then I guess I'll have a roomie on my couch. At least for two more days. That's when Frankie leaves."

"The housemate's boyfriend?"

"That's the one." She sips her coffee. "You know what else?"

She's glowing as I look at her and she finally meets my eyes properly.

"What else?" I can't help smiling at the excitement on her face.

"Eve's been so happy with the updates and drafts of the article I've been sending her that she's lined me up another interview next week."

"Oh yeah?" I lift one brow.

"Yeah." She's almost breathless with giddiness as she bites her bottom lip. "It's with a narrator, Nate Black. Eve wants me to do a whole behind-the-scenes interview with him."

"Is he the audiobook guy with Frederica that—?"

"That's him." Maddy blushes.

"That's great. Congratulations."

"Thank you." She sips her coffee, glancing up at me from beneath her lashes.

"Mads—"

She turns and gazes across the room and out of the back doors to the pool. "I can't believe you have an amazing pool and I've swam in it once."

This is becoming our norm. Sex, heavy talk. Or heavy talk and then sex. And then pretending nothing happened. If I push her to talk about it when she doesn't want to, she'll shut down, and it'll end in a fight.

"I've got a beach too. And you've never even seen that," I say.

"Right." She rolls her eyes. "The thirtieth birthday present. Everyone else gets a watch or a weekend away. You get an island."

I take my now full cup of coffee and lean against the opposite counter, crossing my legs at the ankle. "It's an investment."

She laughs. "Are you going to build a rocket launcher there like a Bond villain?"

I smirk. "Do I detect some jealousy there, Ms. Harper? Don't tell me you always wanted your own launch pad?"

She shakes her head with a sarcastic snort as she drinks her coffee.

"Do you want to see it?"

Her head jerks back. "Your island?"

"Yeah." I shrug. "It's just off the coast. We could stop off on the way back home. Spend a day there. It might stop you needing to kick Chloe out early."

Her brow furrows as she stares at me. I wait for her knockback. She's made no secret of looking forward to getting home since the minute we boarded the jet in London. I know she can't wait to get away from me.

"Do you... Does it have somewhere to sleep?"

I mask my amusement. "Don't worry about that. We'll manage."

"You asshole." Maddy shoves me in the chest as she walks inside the island's main house.

I grin as she gazes around the open foyer. I love this house. It's become my place for a retreat if I've ever needed one over the past couple of years. It's designed like a small hotel with twenty rooms, all curving around a central open-air hallway. Each room is its own self-contained apartment, but it's also got a main kitchen and a large dining hall on the ground floor for when guests want to dine together. My housekeeping team comes by boat from the mainland. But unless I ask them to be here overnight, they leave each day, and the place is monitored by a security system.

And it's private. It's what I love about it most. It's away from the world. But as much as I love it, I haven't been here in over six months.

"I can't believe this." Maddy spins around in a circle, her head tilted back as she looks up at the clear blue sky overhead the open entryway. "Why don't you live here all the time?"

"You hate me that much you want me out of the country now too?"

She snaps her gaze to mine, her shoulders softening when she sees the smirk on my face. "Very funny."

"You want a tour before dinner?" I incline my head toward the main staircase.

"Dinner?" She frowns as she gazes around the space again, noticing the large double doors that lead to the dining hall.

"I have a chef who comes over from the mainland when I visit."

"I thought when the guy dropped us off on the boat that..." Maddy's frown deepens. "He'd come over here tonight, just to cook for us?"

I lift one shoulder. "If I ask him to. Unless you'd rather it just be you and me? The kitchen will have been stocked when I said we were coming."

Maddy looks between me and the double doors again. "Um. I..."

I step closer to her and take a gamble, reaching out and placing a finger underneath her chin to bring her eyes back to mine.

"I can cook, you know," I say softly as she looks into my eyes, a hint of uncharacteristic nervousness held in her gaze.

"Okay." She swallows, her pulse fluttering in her neck.

I let my eyes linger on her face a moment longer than I should, considering she's trying to avoid eye contact with me again. But I can't stop myself. She's either fighting with me, clawing at me, or clamming up. I can't work out what's going on in her head. And fuck if I understand what's going on in mine either.

I pick up our suitcases before I lead her to the stairs. She's quiet as I show her around, except for the odd gasp as she looks out of the window and sees the view. Deep blue sea and a small stretch of sandy beach.

And no one else.

"I bet the girls you've brought here loved it," she muses as she trails her fingertips over the white voiles of the four-poster bed in my master apartment. She looks at the plush, white bedding and then diverts her eyes around the room.

I place both suitcases down on a trunk at the end of the bed.

"I've never brought a girl here."

"None?"

"None," I confirm.

She glances at me and then at her suitcase. "Do I have my own room?"

"No."

Her brows shoot up at my quick answer.

"I want you in here with me."

I expect a fight, a look of defiance, a protest.

Nothing.

She walks over to me and unzips her suitcase. "One night. Then we go home to London." She purses her lips. "And we carry on like before."

"With you hating me?"

She stalls, her eyes flicking to mine. Then she rummages around in her suitcase and pulls something out. "We carry on," she repeats as she drops the items onto the floor.

She steps into the monogrammed slippers, then unpacks her suitcase.

I fight away the urge to grab her and force her to look at me, to acknowledge that there's no way in hell we can go home and just carry on like before. Like it's no big deal. There's no way I can go back to seeing the look of disgust in her eyes every time she sees me. I never realized just how deep her hate for me ran. Not until I've been gifted rare moments of it lifting like a veil this past week. Lifting for long enough for me to see her. To see the girl I hurt all those years ago. The girl I swore to my friend I would look out for. The girl who was never meant to be mine. Despite the way she fit inside my arms like no one else ever has as she slept last night.

I unzip my suitcase, unpacking in silence next to her, and when I go for a shower, I'm tense with anticipation, waiting to see if she follows me.

She doesn't.

When I come out of the bathroom, she's gone.

Chapter 18
Maddy

"Okay, fine. I'll admit you can cook."

Logan chuckles as I drop my fork into the pasta bowl and pick up my napkin, blotting away any lingering seafood linguine sauce from my lips.

The island is beautiful, the house, the beach... all of it. I took a walk by the water earlier while Logan showered. I needed air. Space. I called Chloe, but even listening to what she's been up to couldn't clear my head. It's been full of the same one thing for days now.

Logan.

"I'm not just a pretty face, Mads." He smirks.

I sigh. I gave up asking him to call me Maddy a long time ago. But now I know he calls me Mads because I always look angry when I see him, I kind of wish he'd listen. It reminds me every time he says it that he knows how deeply I've hated him over the years. How deeply I've blamed him for so much.

He stares up at the night sky, a glass of white wine balanced between his fingers. He's wearing cream slacks and a white shirt with the top three buttons undone. It's the most relaxed I've seen him since we left London. And I think I understand why. He had a video call meeting with the final investor earlier. It was a success. He has the funding now. Our trip's over.

Back to London. Back to our lives.

Separately.

"Has your dad ever used money to manipulate a situation that you know of?" I ask suddenly.

Sourness creeps over my tongue. I don't know how those words came out. But now they have, I can't take them back. The thought has been plaguing me. I'm afraid to know the answer. Logan swears his dad didn't interfere years ago. And I'm starting to believe him. Drew has always told me the same. It's like they both know something. Yet, they won't give me any evidence to prove it. They expect me to take their word for it.

Can I change everything I've based so many decisions on? What if I've been wrong all these years? I still would have wanted nothing to do with Logan after the way he scared people away from me and was an immature asshole. But would I have hated him so much? Would I have wasted so much energy?

Mum says hate is like drinking poison yourself and expecting the other person to die. It's an emotion that only takes. Strips you of happiness, of peace.

I never realized that hating Logan Rich all these years meant that I was at war with myself.

"You want the truth, full disclosure?" Logan's green eyes blaze into mine, the flames from the candles on the outdoor dining table sending shadows cascading over the planes of his freshly shaven face.

"I wouldn't ask if I didn't," I say, less sure of my words than I sound.

"He's never used money as far as I know. And I'm pretty damn certain." Logan's jaw tenses. "But recently, he's... been pushing for certain things. He's telling me it's for the good of the business and the family. For our future. He's implied we'll be ruined if I don't agree. But—"

"But?" I whisper, a sickness clawing up my windpipe at the guarded expression taking over his face.

"But I don't believe him." He groans, dropping his head back to stare at the sky again. "My family are multi-billionaires, Mads. You don't lose that kind of money from one failed project. Even if I couldn't secure the funding on this trip, we'd still have the other parts of the business running. All the cars, the yachts, the jets. Just one would still make us billions a year."

"Wow." I gulp a large mouthful of my wine, welcoming the warmth it brings to my chest and the lightness to my head. I can't fathom that kind of money. My family do well, especially Drew. But this is billions.

"I know he's not telling me something." Logan drags his head back up and his eyes meet mine in a penetrating gaze. "He's never not told me everything. That's why when I tell you he didn't bail me out years ago, I know he didn't, because he'd have admitted it when I asked him."

"But you think he's hiding something now?"

He looks away as he drains his wine glass, then immediately refills it.

"What is it? What's he pushing for?" I ask.

"A company merger."

"Oh. Isn't that a normal thing to consider? I thought you had lots of partnerships with different manufacturers and—"

"By marriage."

I recoil instantly, my tongue seeming too big for my mouth and preventing me from speaking.

"He wants me to marry Gabrielle."

I stare at him. I've met Gabrielle twice growing up at various parties the Riches have thrown. Her dad owns a large manufacturing company.

"I thought she was a doctor?" My voice comes out hoarse, and I frown at the wine in my glass like it's the culprit before placing it down on the table.

"She is." Logan swirls the remaining wine in his glass around in a circle, watching it. "She was working abroad, but now she's back to stay."

"What does she think about your dad's idea?"

Logan's still focused on his glass. "Same as me. She laughed. Then told her dad not to be ridiculous."

"You don't want to marry her, then?"

He shakes his head with a humorless laugh.

"Why are you laughing?" I knock back the rest of my wine, my skin prickling as irritation spikes in my core.

His laugh trails off. "I wouldn't be fucking about with you if I wanted to marry someone else."

"*Fucking about with me?* That's what you call it?" There's a sting in my tone as his darkened eyes meet mine.

"All right, what would *you* call this?" He lifts a finger from his wine glass and motions it between us.

"Fucking about?" I hiss. "God, you're disgusting."

"And she's back to hating me." He chuckles. It's an empty sound that sends my stomach plummeting to my feet.

"Is that what this is? All a joke to you?" I jump to my feet, knocking the table. My wineglass topples over, smashing.

I hesitate, looking at the broken shards. I should clean them up.

Logan jumps to his feet and the table rattles, making the pieces of glass scatter.

"Why don't you tell me what *this* is, Mads? Because I haven't got a fucking clue!" His eyes rain green fire.

There are so many words on the tip of my tongue that I want to hurl at him.

But none answer his question.

I don't know what this is.

But I know that I'm not going to stand here while he laughs at me.

I spin and storm into the house to escape his heated glare. The bottle of wine we've shared makes my head swim as I race through the kitchen and into the open-air hallway.

"Don't run from me!" His voice bellows behind me, making me startle.

My heart races, adrenaline gripping me as I push forward, running toward the staircase.

"Leave me alone!" I kick my heels off so I can race barefoot over the cool marble tiles.

"Mads! We need to fucking talk about this!"

My hand curls around the staircase handrail as my foot hits the bottom step. Refuge calls to me in the form of a guest room, any room. One with a locked door where he can't see me. Where I don't have to look into his emerald eyes. *And feel.*

His chest slams into my back, startling me enough to cry out. His hand curls over mine on the handrail. And then his lips are at my ear, his deep, labored breaths warm against my skin as he presses our bodies together.

"You can't keep running and ignoring this."

The deep gravel of his voice has goosebumps peppering up my spine.

"There is no *this*," I whisper. "I hate you."

An arm slides around from behind me, encasing my waist and pulling me back against him with a gentle but controlling force.

His erection digs into my ass cheeks as his breath dusts the shell of my ear.

"No, you don't."

I struggle against him, but his grip around my waist is too tight and all I achieve is wriggling enough that I rub myself against his cock until a needy whimper springs from my throat.

"I do," I croak.

"You don't," he growls.

He flexes his arm around my waist, and I still.

"You're a liar," he clips. "A fucking liar, Mads."

"Stop," I whisper. But it's weak. *I'm weak.*

"You don't fucking know what you are. But I bet if I put my hand inside your panties now, you'll drip all over my fingers."

"Lo—"

"Shall we find out?" He runs the tip of his nose down my neck to my shoulder and nips the skin there.

I draw in a sharp breath as he yanks my dress up around my waist and then slams his palm on top of my panties.

"See. Fucking soaking," he tsks.

He bites my neck. "You love me fucking you. Admit it. You say you hate me, but you love my cock. You love the way I make you scream when you come. No one else has ever done that for you, have they?"

I whimper out a pathetic, strangled noise as he slowly drags my panties to one side and slides his fingers through my slick skin like it belongs to him. "Have they?"

He pushes two fingers inside me.

I fall forward, my body clenching around him as I almost come on the spot. He grunts and pulls me back up so my back is pressed against his chest and my breasts are forced forward.

"I'm going to fuck you right here on these stairs, Smiles. And you can scream that you hate me. But we both know it'll be my cock that's really making you scream."

He leaves his fingers inside me, stroking in leisurely circles that have colors dancing behind my eyes as he takes his hand away from mine on the handrail. I could push his fingers between my legs away and run. There's nothing stopping me. But I don't. Instead, I give in to the tingles of anticipation skating over my skin as the sound of his zipper being pulled down vibrates through the air.

He draws his fingers back and reaches behind me, pulling his cock out. Precum smears across my ass cheeks as he shoves his pants down around his hips.

"You know what else?" he rasps.

"What?" I mumble, fighting the desire to grind back against him.

He lifts his arm, snaking it across my throat so he can lean over my shoulder and suck his fingers clean.

"My cock will make you scream..." he muses as he rips the front of my dress and bra down on one side so my breast is exposed to the night air.

I drag in a muffled cry as his hand closes around it possessively, tugging my nipple with the perfect amount of pressure to make more wetness flood between my legs.

"But it'll be my cum inside you that has you clamping down on me as you come."

"It won't," I cry as he spins me around and forces us both to the ground.

"Liar."

"I'm not." I glare up at him as he crawls over me, pinning me beneath his solid body.

"You are, Mads." His eyes roam over my face as the heat of his body covers me. "We both know that you come the second your pussy gets the first taste. Every. Time."

He drags my panties down my legs, throwing them to one side. Then forces my legs apart. The stairs dig into my back as he dips his head and sucks my exposed nipple into his mouth. I refuse to moan at how good it feels. I won't give him the satisfaction.

"Face it." He sucks harder until I buck. "You're a little whore for my cum. One drop of it and you're mewling all over me, desperate for that release."

"No." I fire back.

But I'm whimpering, and my pulse is throbbing between my legs as I try and fight him with words. My body wants him. Even if my head doesn't.

"Yes," he growls, teasing my nipple between his teeth until I moan.

"No."

He moves up my body, bracing himself up on his arms either side of me as he looks down at me with an anger-fueled glare.

"In that case, tell me to stop."

His eyes hold mine as he lowers his hips until the thick silky head of his cock drags over my skin.

"Tell me to stop." He rotates his hips, pushing his cock through my lips to where my body is thrumming with arousal.

"Tell me to stop!" His eyes flash as he enters me with one hard thrust.

I cry out beneath him, my back forced into the step.

"I hate you," I hiss as my body stretches around him, sucking him in like it needs him to survive.

"You don't."

"I do."

"Then. Tell. Me. To. Fucking. Stop!" he shouts as he pounds into me, fucking me without apology.

His eyes hold mine, glittering dangerously. He pumps into me, repeatedly. And I no longer care that my back is screaming out and will probably bruise. All I can do is lie, pinned beneath his hot, muscular body, as he wrings it dry of all pleasure.

And takes what he wants.

I shove my hand between my legs, seeking my clit.

"Uh-uh." Logan grabs my wrist, then pins both of my arms down on the step above my head. "You don't need to rub that swollen clit to get off, Mads. You'll come when I do."

"I won't," I snap, fighting beneath him to free my arms.

He tips his chin in arrogance and drives into me harder. "Shall we see who's right?"

I bare my teeth at him like a wild animal that's been trapped as he thrusts deeper. My body covers him in a rush of fresh arousal and the wet slapping sound of our bodies meeting crashes through the air.

"You trying to drown me?" He smirks.

"If I could hit you right now, I would!" I buck beneath him trying to throw him off, but it only makes his smirk grow.

He thrusts into me extra hard.

"You wouldn't."

"Believe me, I would!"

"You." *Thrust.* "Wouldn't." *Thrust.* "You." *Thrust.* "Know." *Thrust.* "Why?" *Thrust.*

He picks up the pace and fucks me even deeper. "Because..." He pauses, the muscles in his neck tensing, before he drives deeper with a curse. I'm thrown up the stairs. "My cum's about to make you come."

I scream with my mouth closed, filling my cheeks with rage. Logan's body blocks out the starry night sky behind him as he envelops me, looking at me like he's about to devour me.

"Open your mouth and scream my name." His pupils dilate as I writhe in pleasure beneath him.

"Fuck you!"

A groan rumbles from deep in his chest as his cock thickens inside me. I squirm and resist what I know is coming.

But control is already slipping away from me.

If I ever had it to begin with.

"Let go," he urges above me, his hips driving himself into me with perfect deep strokes.

"No!" My eyelids flutter as I fight the war raging in my core.

"Any second now and my cum will be deep inside you, Mads. Now, *let the fuck go*."

I arch beneath him, trying desperately to hold it at bay. But the tightening in my core is already reaching the point of explosion, making my whole body tremble.

"Fuuuccckkk." Logan's curse is low and drawn out as his balls hit my skin and his cock swells more.

I blink rapidly as he holds my eyes, keeping himself still inside me.

We fall silent for a heartbeat.

One.

The air shifts.

Then he moves again.

"Mads." His voice cracks like his chest is being torn in two.

Then I know he's let go.

Because the moment the first drop hits me inside, it's only a fraction of a second before I come apart beneath him. All fight deserts me.

And I scream as the most intense orgasm of my life wrecks me.

"There it is. Good girl." His eyes gleam, and he juts his chin forward. "Give me more."

I shake my head, gasping for air as moisture pricks at my eyes.

He pushes his forehead against mine.

"More," he repeats, driving into me. "I'm coming here, Mads. I'm…" He chokes out a rough groan, screwing his face up. "I'm coming so fucking hard inside you right now. Give me another."

I pant as I stare into his eyes, our lips inches from one another's. Then a second one hits me, and I come hard around him. Again.

"Logan."

His eyes pinch at the corners as he steers us both through our orgasms until I'm a whimpering, boneless mess beneath him, our clothes damp with sweat.

I turn to the side, blocking out vibrant green as the final pulses leave my body. I'm throbbing between my legs, heat and wetness coating my inner thighs where his body is still buried inside mine.

I draw in a shaky breath, the threat of tears clogging up my throat.

He lets go of my wrists, but I keep my hands where they are as he dusts the back of his knuckles down my cheek and along my jaw.

"You think saying it out loud protects you," he whispers, his breath like a caress on my face. "But it doesn't. No matter what you say you feel for me, we both know this is going to hurt like fuck when you step off my plane in London. So don't even try to lie to me and tell me it won't."

He pauses as if he's waiting for me to say something. But I screw my eyes shut and keep my face turned away.

He sighs and presses a kiss to my temple. Then he pulls out, straightening the top and bottom of my dress before fixing his pants.

I open my eyes and stare at the marble banister, tracing over the pink lines in the stone as he stands. I listen to his zipper being fastened. He's going to leave me here. Alone.

The sound of his feet moving on the stairs makes my chest cave and I swallow my sob down so hard that I think I might be sick.

Then warm arms surround me, scooping me up.

I scrunch my eyes closed even tighter as his lips lower into my hair. His chest expands as he breathes me in and then kisses my curls. I drag in a shaky breath, sinking my face into his shirt and letting him carry me. His heart beats out a steady, grounding rhythm beneath my cheek, and I focus on it as he carries us to his room.

I hold onto it like it's a lifeline stopping me from being dragged away.

Stopping me from being alone.

Chapter 19
Logan

I PLACE MADDY DOWN in the bathroom, keeping one arm around her waist to hold her up as I reach to turn the shower on. She's shaking so I turn the heat up high.

"Would you rather I leave?"

She doesn't answer me, just stares at the falling water, a sadness in her eyes that steals every drop of air from my lungs.

"Then I'll stay," I say softly.

I strip off my clothes, then unzip her dress. I run one hand down each arm as I kiss a line from her ear to her shoulder on one side. She tilts her head the tiniest amount, granting me easier access, and my entire body relaxes with that one small gesture from her.

"You're beautiful," I murmur, keeping my lips on her neck, kissing gently as I unhook her bra and let it fall away. Her panties are still somewhere in the hallway, thrown aside in a moment of whatever *this* is.

"Fucking about."

My own words ring in my ears. *Idiot.*

I step forward, bringing her with me under the hot spray, and reach for a bottle of shower gel. She's quiet as I wash her, but flinches when my hands graze her lower back. I lean around to look. There's an angry red line and quickly forming bruise at the base of her spine.

I curse quietly. "Why didn't you tell me to stop?"

She says nothing.

I drop to my knees and close my eyes, the water running over my face as I move behind her and kiss the tender skin. It's hot beneath my lips and she sucks in a breath as I dust my fingertips over it lightly.

"If I wanted you to stop, I would have told you to," she whispers, barely audible above the water.

I stand, wrapping her in my arms from behind. "I'm sorry I hurt you. I'd never do that on purpose. You know that, right?" I dip my head and kiss her shoulder, tightening my arms around her.

She shakes her head, her voice small. "It doesn't hurt. And neither will landing in London tomorrow when this ends. Don't make it more than it is, Logan."

I stiffen. Her voice is faltering. She's lying. To me. To herself. I've known her long enough to realize I can't push her. She'll only fight me.

I don't want our last night here to be spent fighting.

So I say nothing.

I continue washing her and then wash myself as she stays silent. Then I dry us both off and pull her into bed with me, wrapping her in my arms and breathing in her scent.

I've got one more night with Maddox Harper in my arms.

Then it's over.

Soft lips against my neck wake me. It's dark, only a hint of light from the moon shining in through the open drapes at the balcony doors. I left them open, so the warm night breeze could flow into the room.

"Mads?"

"Shh." Something—a finger?—presses against my mouth and is then quickly replaced with lips as she kisses me.

"Couldn't sleep?" I murmur as her kisses travel from my mouth, along my jaw to my ear.

"I just..." Her breath fans over me as she lays her chest over mine.

"Just what, Smiles?"

She laughs softly. "You call me Mads because I look mad to see you all the time. But then you call me Smiles, too. Bit of a contradiction."

She kisses me again and I breathe her in, reaching up to thread my fingers into her hair to keep her close.

"One's a challenge, the other a reward."

"I see."

My eyes adjust enough to the dark to see her small smile.

I kiss the turned-up corner of her mouth, tasting sweet victory as she parts her lips and welcomes my tongue with hers.

"You rarely give me your smiles," I say as I suck on her bottom lip.

"You've rarely deserved them," she hums as she kisses me back slowly.

"That's past tense."

She grows quiet, before whispering, "It is."

"Does that mean I get more of them in the future?" I cup the back of her neck, stroking over her fluttering pulse with my thumb.

She dusts her lips side to side over mine, her palms resting on my chest. "We have no future beyond tomorrow, Logan. We both know that. This was never about the future. This was some weird product of years of past emotions finally erupting."

I ignore the tightness in my chest and pull her to me, kissing her again. "You needed to fuck the hate from your system."

"I... maybe."

"Did it work?" I hold my breath.

She kisses me again without answering, and I stroke down her back, kissing her back slowly, matching my movements with hers. She stiffens as my hand grazes the base of her spine.

"You are hurt, Mads. Let me see." I pull up to a sitting position and reach for the bedside lamp, but she takes my hand, and places it over her naked breast, holding it in place with her own hand.

"I told you. It doesn't hurt."

"I don't believe you."

She lifts herself into my lap so she's straddling me. Then she takes my other hand and holds it against her other breast. Her nipples harden as I stroke my thumbs over them slowly.

"What are you doing?" I ask as she circles her hips, grinding gently onto me.

Her fingers find my lips again to stop me speaking, and I kiss the tips of them as she reaches between us with her other hand and strokes my hardening cock.

"Fucking about one more time before we forget any of this ever happened," she murmurs.

"That's what you want? To forget?" I stroke her nipples, and she moans. Then she wraps her hand around the base of my cock.

"That's all we both ever wanted." She slides down onto me with a gentle sigh. Then arches her breasts into my palms as she starts to ride me.

I groan as I'm buried deep inside her.

"Mads?"

"Logan," she breathes.

I push forward, wrapping my arms around her back and holding her flush against my chest as I thrust up from beneath her in leisurely strokes.

"You don't know what I want."

She shakes her head, her breath coming in soft pants as I kiss her, gripping her like it's the last time I will ever hold her like this. *Because it is.*

"I know that you don't want to be with a woman who hates you."

She gasps quietly as I pull her down onto me again, fucking her slow and deep, my heart a steady constant in my heavy chest.

"You don't hate me." I kiss her neck, and she drops her head back, her throat constricting beneath my lips as she swallows.

"I do." She whimpers as I ease back, then immediately pull her straight back down onto me. I curse softly as she stretches around me, taking every inch.

"We're way past hate now, Mads." I tilt my chin up, holding her eyes as she gazes back at me. "If this is hate, then I never need to fall in love."

She cups my face in her hands. Her eyes shine in the dark as she searches mine like she's trying to find answers.

Then she kisses me again.

She doesn't stop kissing me until I come inside her, setting off her own orgasm. She holds my gaze and whispers my name between kisses. She kisses me through all of it, through everything, until I'm hard inside her once more and we start all over again.

We spend our last night together, hating each other over and over. And every time I kiss her, I swear I taste salt on my lips.

She's wrong.

This is going to hurt like fuck.

It already does.

Chapter 20
Maddy

"ARE YOU LOOKING FORWARD to seeing your parents?"

I rest my head against the plush seat on Logan's private jet while we wait to take off and turn to where he's sitting next to me. He's wearing a navy-blue suit today with brown Italian brogues and a green tie that matches his eyes. His light brown hair touches his collar where it's grown longer during our trip.

He's every inch Logan Rich, billionaire tycoon, leaning his elbows on his knees as he frowns at his laptop screen on the table in front of us.

The man I've looked at for years, but never really seen.

After last night, we both moved on autopilot, packing, and leaving the island, catching the boat to the mainland where Logan's driver picked us up and brought us to the airport. Logan didn't kiss me again. He didn't force me to talk about what happened last night. To acknowledge the tenderness that crept between us. It feels like the blues at the end of a wonderful holiday. When you realize it's time to step back into reality.

That's all this is, this blue, sinking feeling in my stomach as I watched him effortlessly slip back into work mode when we boarded his jet. It's a blip. A tinge of bittersweetness that real life starts again today. I've spent weeks in one of the most beautiful countries on earth with a man I hated with every fiber of my being when we left London. And who I'm returning home being, not friends exactly, not... well, not anything. But not hating either.

My hate for Logan Rich stayed in Italy when I packed my suitcase this morning. When I packed the program from the opera, the green gown, the silk lingerie, and the monogrammed slippers. And in its place, there's an acceptance. I may never forget all those years I felt miserable and blamed Logan for. But I see now that it wasn't as black and white as I thought. He made mistakes. But he isn't cruel on purpose. All the times I've shouted at him, screamed that I hate him, he's never said it back once. He's never told me I had no right to feel the way I felt. He didn't dismiss it.

He apologized.

If this trip taught me something, then it's that Logan Rich isn't afraid to admit when he's wrong. And if he can do it, then I owe it to him to try too.

He glances at me with a smile. "I'm looking forward to seeing Dad now that he won't be talking about weddings."

"You two are close, aren't you?"

His smile widens, and he chuckles, looking back at his laptop. "When he isn't coming up with wild ideas, yeah."

I turn to look out of the window at the morning sun on the airstrip. I never saw Logan talking to his dad on this trip. His mum twice, but never his dad. Drew said they usually talk multiple times a day.

"Well, I hope you sort it all out. He's just acting out of misplaced love. It's what dads do."

"If only that were true in every case," he mumbles.

I look back at him with a frown but don't ask what he means. Now isn't the time to get into a heavy conversation with him. It's *never* the time to get into a heavy conversation with him. It only makes things more complicated when they don't need to be. Like me, him, and this trip. It was a release from years of built-up hatred, culminating in sex. That's all.

And I don't regret a single moment.

I left London weighed down by the past. And I'm going home freer, ready to move on with my life.

Italy shifted something. It's what I needed.

And now I need to move on and leave it behind me. We both do. Logan's got project Vex to run and things to smooth over with his dad. And I've got an article to write, and Nate Black to interview. A smile tugs at my lips. It's what I've been dreaming of for months.

Logan clears his throat. "Hey, Smiles. I got you something to listen to on the flight back. Check your email."

"What is it?"

I pull my phone out of my purse and open my emails.

"What? How did you get this? It's not out for another month. Logan?" I knock his shoulder, and he shrugs. The smirk that I always thought was smug now looks just... happy as it lifts his lips.

"I've got friends in publishing. Just don't share it with anyone, or I'll have a guy called Jaxon King after my head."

"*The* Jaxon King?" My eyes widen and Logan shrugs again as if he didn't just mention the UK's biggest name in publishing.

I catch his chuckle as I pull my earbuds from my purse. *Bastard, he knows exactly who I'm talking about.*

I grin as I open the audiobook file for the final book in Cameron and Frederica's story. Nate's character might be called Cameron. But in my head, it's Nate. Whenever I listen to his voice, it's always Nate Black I imagine, no matter what part he's reading. I can't believe I'll be meeting him face to face in a few days.

"Thank you." I put my hand on Logan's knee. Something clouds his eyes, passing quickly over his features before he places his hand on top and squeezes.

"No problem. You can tell me what happens."

"Seriously? As if you're invested?" I smile as I take my hand back and put my earbuds in.

"Just tell me if they end up together at the end." His eyes twinkle, and I roll mine in response.

"It's a romance, of course they do."

I turn to look out of the window as I press play.

"Frederica, you have to stop fighting me."

"It's not that simple."

The two grow more and more emotional, until they're kissing passionately and Cameron's murmuring her name over and over.

My eyes flick to Logan as I stop the audio. He got this for me before it's even released. I should be grateful. I should devour it, like he expects me to do. But maybe it's my earbuds playing up again, because I just... can't. Nate's voice doesn't sound right. And although I understand Frederica's hesitations, something about the way she keeps Nate's character, Cameron, at arm's length all the time has a ball tightening low in my gut. Why can't she see what's right under her nose?

Logan's oblivious to my reaction. His brows are pulled low as he reads through a document on his screen, his lips moving as he reads. Lips I spent the whole night kissing.

For the last time.

I snap my eyes away and swipe through my phone, opening a different file and pressing play.

"We're so happy to have you onboard, Trent."

I close my eyes and lean back in my seat as Logan's smooth, deep voice soothes my ears. This makes more sense. I'm technically on work time while on the flight, so I should do some actual work. Like listening to the recorded meetings for putting the final touches to the article.

I listen to Logan Rich's calm, confident tone.

I listen to it all the way back to London.

Chapter 21
Logan

"LOGAN? IS THAT YOU?" Mum calls.

"Yep." I walk up the hallway toward the kitchen.

I came straight to Mum and Dad's after dropping Maddy home. Any lingering goodbyes that might have been were thwarted by her friend, Chloe, rushing out to the car the moment we pulled up, and sweeping Maddy off inside. Probably a good thing. She's made it clear how she feels. She doesn't want anything to do with me. Yet all I've been able to think about since the second I dropped her off at her apartment is when will I see her again.

To her, we're done. We were done the moment we left Italy.

Technically, we never started. That's what Maddy insists. She doesn't want anyone to know something happened between us. But Drew's been my friend for years.

I can't lie to him. And I also can't lie to myself. Maddox Harper acts like the biggest brat most of the time with me. But she's stormed her way under my skin these past few weeks. And as much as I know I can't keep her, a part of me wants to. She at least owes me a conversation about that.

I need to give her a couple of days, then I'll hunt her down if I have to. Because we have to talk about this.

If things were good with Dad, then I'd be able to talk to him about it. But walking back into their house this morning has my stomach in knots. I'd half expected him to be gone. He and Mum never fight like this. I feel it's my fault, leaving the way I did without sorting things out first.

Mum rushes me the second I cross the threshold, pulling me into a hug. "How was your trip? How's Maddy? Did she enjoy herself? Did you look after her?"

I hug her back. "She's fine. I dropped her home with a suitcase full of souvenirs for Drew and her friend."

Mum smiles as she pulls back. "Well, that's nice."

I lock eyes across the room with Dad. He's sitting at the kitchen table, looking ten years older than when I left, deep lines etched in his forehead, and dark circles beneath his eyes.

"You two need to talk." Mum purses her lips, giving him a pointed look, and he nods.

"We do, son. Sit."

I walk over and pull a chair out, but Dad frowns, his brow wrinkling as he stands.

"What am I saying? Come here first." He draws me into a hug, slapping his hand on my back. "I've missed you.

You've done us proud, raising all those funds. I knew you would."

"Then why'd you look like you're off to a funeral?"

Mum looks at Dad from across the room, her face pinched. "You tell him. I'll make us all a drink."

I glance warily between the two. Mum's obviously been busting his balls the entire time I've been gone.

"Guest room comfy?"

Dad snorts, one side of his mouth lifting. "As much as a bed of nails in purgatory can be."

I chuckle as Mum shakes her head and turns her back on us.

Dad's face falls as he looks at me. "I didn't tell you everything before you left. I was hoping to find another way, but... the project's off, son."

"What do you mean? I got the funding. I actually got more than we need." *Thanks to Sterling.*

Dad's eyes flick to Mum's back, then he drops his gaze to his clasped hands on the table. "We owe billions. More than we can ever find."

My blood turns to ice at the finality in Dad's voice. His bloodshot eyes meet mine.

"I made bad choices, Logan. Bad investments. And I lost." He chokes on the last word, clearing his throat to conceal his emotion.

"What the hell are you talking about? You were only worried about Vex, not the rest of the business."

Dad drags his hands down his face. I've never seen him so broken. The proud, successful businessman that is my father, is sitting in front of me with gray skin and a sickly yellow sheen to his eyes.

"I thought I invested in a sure thing. It was all a scam."

"How much? You've had bad years before. This is nothing. It's ups and downs, always has been."

Growing up I recall times when funds were a little tighter. But Dad would move contracts around, re-negotiate terms. Find a way. *The Rich's always find a way, he'd say.*

He clears his throat. "Everything."

My eyes slam onto Mum who's watching us with a drained expression.

"There's a criminal investigation going on into the guy who set it all up. But it could take years. Years that we don't have. And then we might never get any of the money back. It's gone, son. And everything is connected to it. I can't afford to pay anyone as of two weeks' time. Chances are the company will fold. I need you to be prepared. We need a miracle to tide us over until it's sorted out or we will lose everything. The business, the houses, everything we've worked for."

Dad covers his mouth with his hand, his face ashen.

"Len," Mum encourages. "Tell him the rest."

"There's more? Jesus." I lean back in my chair, running my hands through my hair as my mind races a million miles per minute. *Everything. Gone.*

Dad drops his hand from his mouth, deep lines etched across his forehead as he meets my eyes.

"Spencer has offered his help. He's got access to enough funds to buy us time. To see us through while the investigation runs. I can pay the staff. Make some cutbacks. Tighten things up. But the company will survive. We'll survive."

"Okay." I lean over my forearms on the table. "That's... that's incredibly generous of him. But it's also a huge risk he's taking. What's in it for him?"

Dad glances at Mum then back at me.

"You."

"What do you mean, me?"

"Project Vex. You own the patent, son. It's in your name, not the company's. If you agree to grant sole manufacturing rights to Spencer's company, then he'll give us the money."

Every muscle in my body tenses. This has been a dream of mine for months, years. But if it means helping Dad, there's no question in my mind. This is my family.

"Fine. He can have it. I'll sign the design over to him."

Pride shines in Dad's eyes before he shakes his head. "It's worthless without you. You're the one who has the investors. People don't just buy into an idea. They buy into people. People they trust. People who excite them. Share their vision. They came onboard to work with you."

"Spencer wants me to go work for him and take the design with me?" I look between Dad and Mum again as a choking silence fills the room.

Dad shifts in his seat. "Spencer's like me. We're not getting any younger. His business is his life's work. He wants it to continue. Be a legacy. And he needs someone who knows what they're doing to carry it forward." He clears his throat. "For his future generations." He pauses as I stare at him.

Realization rains down on me like a ton of bricks.

"This is why you want me to marry Gabrielle?"

"We don't want you to do anything," Mum interjects, shooting daggers at my father, who drags a hand over his mouth with a deep exhale.

"If you agree to marry Gabrielle and run the business, keep it in Spencer's family for him, then he'll give me the money to keep us afloat. He doesn't want to be paid back. Not as long as you stay married. He wants Gabrielle provided for. He wants another generation to pass the business onto. It's all he's wanted since he lost Gabrielle's mother. A secure, comfortable future for his daughter and her children."

"Her children?" I choke out the words. Marrying Gabrielle is one thing, but having children with someone I don't love?

"These are his terms," Dad continues.

"Which you won't be agreeing to," Mum snaps, glaring at the back of Dad's head.

"We'll lose everything, Viv."

Mum presses her fingers to her lips and spins away. Her back trembles with silent sobs.

Dad looks back to me. "I know it's not an epic love story, son. But you know Gabrielle. She's a nice girl and you two get along. You could be happy together. Happy and successful."

I stare at him like he's grown a horn and told me he's identified as a unicorn that shits candy. This is Dad. The man who fell for Mum aged seventeen without a penny to his name.

And he's asking me to marry for money. *To have kids for money.*

"Gabrielle doesn't want this. She told me. Did you ever think about that? Regardless of what your own son wants, did you think about what she might want? Being told she's marrying some guy because of a business deal her father's agreed. Fuck." I stand in a rush, my chair falling over and banging loudly as it hits the floor.

"You should talk to her," Dad says, barely able to meet my eyes.

"Don't worry, I'm going to. I can't believe you'd keep this from me. What the hell, Dad." I grab the chair and throw it back onto four legs.

I stalk across the kitchen, unable to look at my father any longer. I press a rushed kiss to Mum's cheek.

"You okay, Mum?"

She nods, taking a deep breath through her weeping.

"I'll call you later, okay." My voice is soft, in direct contrast to the heated fury in my eyes as I glance at Dad. He at least has the decency to look ashamed as he stares back at me with glassy eyes.

"I'm sorry, son."

"Yeah," I snap. "Me too."

Then I storm out of the house, slamming the front door behind me.

I stand from my seat as she weaves through the people to get to me. She brushes her long blonde hair away from her face as she meets my eyes and smiles. Every man in the Knightsbridge hotel bar watches her, disappointment clear on their faces when she reaches me and kisses both of my cheeks in greeting.

"I'm sorry I'm late. I forgot what a nightmare London traffic can be. Have you been waiting long?"

"It's fine." I brush her apology away with a smile. Truth is, I'd have waited years to see Gabrielle today. To have someone to talk to who understands. Someone as baffled as me at this entire situation.

"What would you like to drink?" I signal the bartender as she takes the seat next to me.

"Something strong."

"Hell, me too." I order two Aunt Iris's gins on the rocks for us.

"You look good," Gabrielle assesses me.

I smile and say thank you. But I feel... nothing. No spark of attraction. No flare of temper because she's pushing my buttons. No spike of heartrate because she makes it race. No pulse in my dick because just hearing her voice makes it throb. None of the things I've been feeling these past few weeks in Italy.

Nothing.

"So do you," I reply sincerely.

Gabrielle is beautiful and smart. I admire her for chasing her dreams of being a doctor when Spencer made no secret of the fact he wanted her to work in the family business with him. But despite what Dad thinks, attraction doesn't always come from knowing someone for years. Not with Gabrielle, anyway.

I thank the bartender and take a large mouthful before memories of hazel eyes, dark curls, and hips that are the perfect size for me to grip onto flood my brain.

Now isn't the time to think of her. Shit's complicated enough until I wade through this mess that Dad's gotten us all into.

"How's it been? Being back?"

Gabrielle tilts her head with a smile, her eyes sparkling. "Well, I'm used to performing surgeries in a makeshift tent in the middle of disaster zones, so navigating the London traffic with a taxi driver who wanted to share his life story with me was a little different to my usual day."

"I bet."

"It's nice to be home, though... To see Dad." Her gaze drops to her glass. "I told him I was coming home to stay even though a part of me didn't truly believe it. But now I've seen him..." She blinks a few times, lifting the glass to her mouth and taking a mouthful. "I'm not leaving him, Logan. I can't be that selfish again. I've done a lot of thinking since I came back."

"What do you mean?"

She smiles sadly, pinched lines at the corners of her eyes appearing.

"After Mum died, I volunteered for the UN. I needed to get away. There were too many memories here."

"You were grieving. It makes sense you needed fresh surroundings."

"But I left Dad. He was grieving too, but I could only think about myself. Self-preservation." She sighs. "I couldn't stand to be reminded of her everywhere I looked. I left him to grieve alone. What kind of daughter does that?"

I place my hand over hers on the top of the bar. "One who was dealing with her own grief. You said it yourself, there were too many memories. You did what you needed to. He'll understand."

She places her other hand on top of mine so she's holding it between both of hers. "I can't leave him again. Not when he needs me." She strokes my hand in hers, her brow furrowing as she looks at it. "He's sick, Logan." Her eyes flick to mine, shining with unshed tears. "Maybe he hoped I wouldn't see it. But I'm a doctor, after all." She blinks rapidly, drawing in a slow breath.

"Sick?" Nausea balls inside my gut.

"I need to talk to him about it. But every time I try, he changes the subject. Changes it onto you." She continues to stroke my hand in hers. "You know he thinks us getting married is the answer to everything?"

"No wonder he and my dad are friends. They've both gone mad."

Gabrielle laughs softly, and I try to smile, but something heavy is pulling down inside my chest making breathing difficult, that way when your instincts are telling you to prepare. Because shit is about to hit the fan.

"I don't want to hurt him again. Everything he's worked for his entire life, his company, it means everything to him. Just like it does to your dad. We can make them both happy. I can make it up to him for leaving him. I can be the daughter he deserves." She looks up at me and all I can do is swallow as she furrows her brow and continues to stroke my hand.

"You don't want to marry me, Gabrielle."

I need to say it out loud. Because, fuck, whatever is happening here cannot be real. She was as adamant as me when I called her from Italy. She laughed about how ludicrous our dads were being. We both did.

"Are you in love?" Her question catches me off guard and I stare at her as she studies me, looking deep into my eyes. "Logan, are you—?"

"Why are you asking me that?"

"If you love someone else, then it's out of the question." She bites her bottom lip, her eyes shining with desperation. "But if you're not, then..."

"Then what?" I slide my hand away gently and Gabrielle picks up her glass and takes another sip.

"We know each other. We *like* each other. It could work." She lifts her shoulders, her lips pulling into a twisted line, the crease in her brow deepening as she thinks. "People marry for family reasons all the time."

My eyes almost pop out of my head. I force myself to take a slow, deep breath as I lean back in my seat. My heart fires into palpitations against my ribs.

"Your father is dangling a lifeline in front of mine and using you and I as fucking pawns in his game. That's the reason," I hiss. "He's told my dad if we divorce, he'll want all the money back with an insane amount of interest. Dad could never pay it."

Gabrielle's throat quivers as she swallows. "You're right. He is. But he's *dying*, Logan. And this is his way of doing what he thinks is best for me. He wants me to be secure. His business is doing well. And if you come and bring Vex with you, it'll thrive."

"Then why doesn't he just ask for a merger? Fuck, I'd do it to help my dad. You know I would." I shake my head, huffing out an angry breath despite my heart clenching with sympathy for her.

"Dad knows contracts are easily broken. Companies are sold all the time. He's hoping if you and I marry and have a family that...." Gabrielle looks at the ceiling before bringing her eyes back to mine. "He's hoping I'll not be alone when he dies. It's worried him ever since Mum..." She swallows, unable to finish her sentence.

"Jesus."

I rest my elbows on the bar and drop my head into my hands, tension spreading through my shoulders until I no longer feel like I can even move. I'm frozen in place. Bound by the constraints of other people's wishes and desires being forced upon me.

"I'm not sure how long he has." Her voice cracks. "But the prescriptions I've found in the house and the way his hands shake when he thinks I'm not looking..."

She fixes her eyes on mine, driving her point home.

"You're willing to sacrifice your future for your dying father's warped idealistic dream?"

"He just wants to see me happy, Logan. It's what dads want for their kids, isn't it?"

I think about Drew and his dad, sourness creeping over my tongue.

"What about what you want, what makes you happy?"

"I owe him this. And maybe we could, I don't know, be married but have our own freedoms too." She glances at me as my eyebrows shoot up my forehead.

"I'm not a fucking cheat." I lower my voice as heads around the bar turn our way. "If we're married, then there's no one else. I'm not messing around behind my wife's back."

Gabrielle's face softens like my answer comforts her. "So there's not, then?"

"Not what?"

"A girlfriend... Someone you love that you'd be giving up?"

My mouth drops open. "I-I don't have a girlfriend."

She lets out her held breath, nodding slowly. "Good. Because I couldn't even consider doing this if there was. I can't do that to you."

"You actually want to do this?" Even as I say the words, a voice inside my head is screaming at me to run. Run and never look back. Or to start hitting things. To just fuck shit up and deal with the consequences later.

"I want to make Dad happy. I want to be a better daughter." Gabrielle looks deep into my eyes, and the sickening sense of what I now recognize as dread grows in my gut. Because shining in her eyes is something I never expected to see.

Hope.

She's fucking hoping I will agree to it.

"I never thought you would... I need to think. God, I—"

"It's okay." She stands suddenly and wraps her arms around me, her hair pressing against my cheek. "It's a lot. I get it. I only just started coming round to the idea myself." She moves back, but stays close, her face hovering in front of mine. "Think about it. We'll make our fathers happy. We could be a good team."

Before I can process what's happening, she presses her lips to mine and kisses me. I sit stunned, not kissing her back, but not pushing her away either.

When she moves back, the earlier hope in her eyes has exploded into a raving parade, dancing with possibilities as she licks her lips. I still can't move as she presses another kiss to my lips, then gathers up her purse.

"I'll speak to you soon."

She lets her hand linger on my shoulder like a lover reluctant to say goodbye. She looks at me one final time, then leaves.

My frozen limbs spring into action minutes too late and I whip my head to watch her go. A man on a table nearby raises his glass. "Lucky man."

I scowl at him. I feel far from lucky right now. I feel more like I've been cursed.

What the hell happened?

Chapter 22
Maddy

"ARE YOU SURE I'M in the right hotel?" I scour the crowded bar area from the doorway, balancing my purse in one hand and phone in the other.

"Yes," Chloe confirms down the phone. "Eve said Nate will be waiting in the Grayson bar. That's where you are, right?"

I read the plaque on the wall. *Grayson Bar.* Drew and Tanner worked on the design for this hotel. I remember Drew winding Tanner up for weeks after he told the hotel they should use Tanner's last name for the bar. He wasn't amused.

"He's probably not here yet. I'm early."

I glance at my watch. Nate Black still has ten minutes until our interview. I force down the excited butterflies in my stomach as I walk into the busy bar and find a cozy booth against the back wall. I need somewhere quieter to record our interview. Ideally, we'd conduct it in his hotel suite, or some other place where the recording picks up our voices without too much background noise. But Nate suggested to Eve that I meet him here after work because he's between meetings today and doesn't have long before a dinner booking tonight. I hope I can get all of Eve's questions covered and still have time to ask some of my own as well.

The bartender comes over and I order a bottle of sparkling water and two glasses, then pull out my recorder and notebook, placing them on the table. I look around taking in the business crowd that have come in for drinks after work. They're mostly men in suits. One catches my eye and smiles at me. I look at his forest green tie and smile back politely as the color brings someone else to my mind.

I fiddle with my phone on the table. I've not seen Logan since we got back two days ago. Not that I expected to. No texts. Nothing. I told him we were forgetting anything ever happened the minute we got back to London. And he's done exactly what I asked him to. For the first time ever, Logan Rich has done what I wanted him to. And I should be happy about that.

I *am* happy about that.

"Maddox Harper?"

I startle and look up into a handsome face framed by dark hair. Warm brown eyes are waiting for a response.

"Oh. Yes. That's me."

I jump to my feet, smiling like an idiot as I shake Nate Black's hand. His are huge and mine gets lost inside warm, soft fingers as he scans my face, a smile stretching his lips.

"Thank you so much for taking the time to do this interview." My words spill fast from my mouth as we both sit. I can't believe I'm about to interview Nate Black.

"It's a pleasure. I enjoy talking about my work."

I falter at the sound of his voice as I open my notebook and place my voice recorder between us on the table.

"Well, I love to talk about it too, so that's great," I gush awkwardly.

"Great." Nate smiles, and I pick up my pen and take the cap off for something to do as confusion burrows its way into my stomach.

"Would you mind stating your name and just giving a small introduction about what you do?"

I press record on my device and wait.

Nate introduces himself, saying his age, thirty-one, and where he's originally from, Kent. And what he does for a living, a narrator or voice actor.

My stomach sinks further with each word, and my cheeks start to ache as I fight to maintain the professional, encouraging smile on my lips.

He sounds nothing like I imagined in real life. The realization is crushing. Like meeting your hero and them kicking a dog in front of you or pushing a kid over, and you realize it was all an illusion and they're a grade A asshole. Not that Nate is. He's sweet and charming as he talks. He asks me why I love books, and I tell him about the escape into another world. *The magic.* He seems genuinely interested, asking me more questions about my job at the magazine.

But every time he speaks, a voice inside my head pokes at my brain and asks, *Why isn't his voice as smooth? Since when did his laugh sound like that?*

But it's obvious. He's a voice actor. He performs in different voices.

An idea springs into my mind. I don't know why I didn't think of it before.

"Would you mind saying something in Cameron's voice? Maybe a line he says to Frederica? For our readers. They would love that."

Hope blooms in my chest. Nate looks puzzled. We have an online magazine. We have readers, not listeners.

"I can write it into the piece, maybe add a sound clip. They'll go mad for it." I nod encouragingly as I make it up on the spot. This is purely for me. So I can listen to it later with Chloe and swoon.

Nate leans over the top of the table, closer to the recorder. His eyes hold mine as he says, *"You're a smart girl, Frederica. You know you're going to choose me. Not him. We're two souls made from the same star, alike in every way."*

I swallow, waiting for the butterflies to launch an uprising in my stomach as they did when I first heard that line from book one.

Nate sits back in his chair, his broad chest rising beneath his black sweater as he looks back at me. "That okay?"

"That was incredible." I beam at him.

My stomach does nothing. The butterflies are on strike, most likely dampened down by nerves. This is Nate Black. The man I've held many fantasies about in my head as I've listened to his work. It's bound to be overwhelming. Plus, the flight back from Italy could have messed with my ears.

He smiles, accepting my compliment.

His phone vibrates in his pocket, and he pulls it out, glancing at the screen.

"I'm sorry, it's the production company. I need to call them."

We both stand, and he reaches out, curling his warm hand around mine again as his brown eyes penetrate mine.

"It was great to meet you, Maddox. I'm so sorry to cut this short."

"It's no problem," I answer truthfully, already thinking about calling Chloe and dissecting this meeting word for word with her. "Thank you so much for taking the time to meet me."

Nate lets go of my hand but keeps his eyes on mine. "It was a pleasure."

Pleasure. A ripple of something unexpected dances through me at the word, warming the blood in my veins.

I wait until Nate leaves before I fall back into my seat and turn my recorder off. I asked the questions Eve wanted and a couple of my own, too, so I'd call the interview a success. My first proper interview. Unless you count Logan. But I'm not counting him. I didn't get nervous before interviewing him like I did with Nate.

I pour another glass of sparkling water, drinking half of it before I scribble down notes in my pad. A server comes over, asking if I'd like to order any food. I decline, and as he walks away. My eyes land on a familiar suit at the bar. Navy-blue jacket leading to light brown hair, an air of what I used to think was arrogance, but the past few weeks have taught me it's really the cool confidence that comes with being brilliant at what you do and being comfortable in your own skin.

Logan.

The bubbles from the water fizz in my stomach in one giant burst of energy like flapping wings as I stand. I admire the neat trim of his hair around the sides. He's had it cut since we came back.

I gather up my recorder and notepad, tossing them into my purse, but when I look up again, Logan's been joined by a woman with long, light blonde hair.

Gabrielle.

I fall back into my seat as she kisses him on both cheeks. He smiles at her as she sits next to him at the bar. I've only met her twice, but I'd recognize her anywhere. She has an ethereal beauty. I don't think she walks anywhere. She glides. And she's a doctor, or surgeon, working for the United Nations in war zones and on aid projects. Basically, she's a saint. Her hair's probably bright blonde because there's a halo hidden beneath the strands lighting it up.

The two chat for the next few minutes. I can't move or look away. I stepped off the plane from Italy telling Logan we needed to forget about what happened between us.

Yet, I can't look away.

Why can't I look away?

From the angle I'm sitting, I can only see Gabrielle's face, not Logan's. She seems upset about something, and Logan reaches across the bar to hold her hand. I drop my eyes away like I'm interrupting a private moment and take deep breaths to quell a ball of nausea in my gut.

Less than a second passes before I'm staring at them both again.

Gabrielle stands and embraces Logan. Then she kisses him. My hand tightens around the strap of my purse. She pulls back, looking at him with a starry-eyed expression.

I jump to my feet, needing air. I've been sitting too long. I need to get out of here. His life is none of my business now. It never has been.

I stride across the bar, too far away for them to notice me. He has his back in my direction anyway, and Gabrielle is—I snap my eyes away as she kisses him again, her hand wrapped around his shoulder—pre-occupied by Logan's lips.

My pace increases until I spill out of the hotel and onto the street. I gasp, sucking in deep breaths of air. Then I snatch my phone from out of my purse and dial Chloe.

"Hey. How was the interv—?"

"I need to get drunk."

"Now?"

"Now."

I smooth down my green fitted dress, then reach up and yank out my hair clip, shaking out my curls. I'm grateful I'm wearing something that can easily go from work to bar, because God knows I need a drink.

"Say no more," Chloe sings. "Girls' cocktail night, here we come."

Chapter 23
Logan

I TOLD THE BOYS I wanted to come somewhere different tonight. Not our usual bars or clubs where I could see people I know.

"This place have good whiskey?" Tanner asks as we stretch back in a VIP booth near the dancefloor.

"Drink the proper shit," Dax pipes up, smirking at Tanner as Drew laughs.

Dax drinks Aunt Iris's gin when we're out. It's like the fucker doesn't get enough when he produces it every day at his distillery. Either that, or it's a marketing ploy so he's only seen drinking his bestselling line.

The three of them order from the waitress, then relax into a chatter as I slump back in my seat.

"Rachel let you out for the night to play then, Tan?" Drew's eyes light up.

Tanner shakes his head. "I swear my dick's in real danger of falling off."

Dax hoots with laughter, clapping Tanner on the back as Drew looks at him in envy.

"It's not funny," Tanner says. "You wait until Rose is pregnant. Then you'll know what it's like. She wakes me up twice a night for it. And it's not like lazy sex is good enough. She wants me at full power at three in the goddamn morning."

Even I manage a small smile at that. But Dax just shakes his head, stretching his arms above his head, the dark ink of his tattoos creeping up and over his neck from beneath his shirt.

"I love when Rose wakes me up in the night. Three o'clock, four o'clock. Who fucking cares? I'd happily never sleep in exchange for those wakeup calls."

Tanner looks at Dax, deadpan. "Try operating on three hours sleep a night, having one child with a bug that includes them throwing up down your back twice in one hour and another who then wakes from a nightmare because a giant smurf was chasing them. Then tell me what having a horny, pregnant wife who expects you to fuck her like it's a Magic Mike stage show when you finally collapse back into bed sounds?"

Dax throws his head back and laughs, joined by Drew.

"Hey." Drew nudges my leg with a wide grin. "See what you've got to look forward to?"

"Fuck off," I mutter.

He wraps an arm around my shoulders pulling me up from my slouch. "Come on. We're out to cheer you up. Nothing's ever that bad."

"You think?"

I smile gratefully at the waitress as she returns to our table and places two bottles and four glasses down.

Drew pours me a whiskey, ignoring Dax's snort as he reaches for the gin bottle.

"I *know*." Drew hands me the glass, then pours himself one. "Just look around this table if you want to feel better about shit." He picks up his glass and points it in Dax's direction. "We've got one fucker who went to jail and was almost killed. And he likes to cover himself in a fucking jungle."

Dax curses at Drew with a chuckle, the vines, flowers, and bird tattoo on his neck rippling as he knocks his drink back.

"Then you've got this one." Drew motions to Tanner. "Poor fucker's dick's about to fall off. It's probably been ground down to something resembling a match by now. Bump into him and it'll snap like a little twig."

Tanner mutters something into his whiskey with an exhausted smile.

"And then you've got me. Perfect as friends go, I must say." Drew puffs his chest out. "But I still can't get the hottest fucking woman I've ever met to look at me for more than two seconds, unless it's to threaten me with a restraining order. Oh, and my cheating fucker of a father hates me. So there's that. Feel better?"

Drew clinks his glass against mine as I give him a slow nod.

"I'm part of the fucked asshole gang. Yeah, comfort in company, I guess."

"That's the spirit." He pours more whiskey into my glass and I down half of it in one.

"You'll find a way." Tanner meets my eyes across the table, injecting some seriousness into the conversation.

"Unless you're coming around to the idea of marriage, pregnancy, and married sex," Drew muses.

I shake my head. "Fuck no. Nothing against Gabrielle. But this is messed up."

All evening, I've repeated her and Dad's words again and again in my head. I stayed in the hotel bar after she left, drinking alone, my gut getting heavier and heavier. I don't know what the fuck I'm going to do. I can't marry her.

"Is there someone you love that you'd be giving up?"

I didn't lie. I don't have a girlfriend. How can you give up someone who was never yours in the first place? Someone who insists she hates you. When each time you hear her say it, it only acts as another force pushing you to prove her wrong. To make her scream out your name in pleasure instead of hate.

And fuck I love the way she sounds when it's my name she screams.

I knock back the rest of my drink, sliding my glass onto the table. Drew dutifully fills it up. He wants to get me wasted. He knows I need it. Drink first and blow off some steam, then hunker the shit down and fix it. It's what we do. All of us. It's why we're all friends. Why we're all successful at what we do. We don't give up. We find a way. Like Dad always used to say before this knocked him on his ass.

The Riches always find a way.

"We'll think of something." Drew claps his hand on my back in a show of solidarity that has never wavered over years of friendship.

I look sideways at him as he drinks. He has no idea what I've been doing behind his back. What kind of friend am I? Here he is, trying to console me on what has to be one of the most epically shit days of my life bar the day he got shipped off to the juvenile detention center. And all this time, I've been banging his sister like I can't fucking control myself.

Maybe because I *can't* fucking control myself around Maddy.

She's right. I'm an asshole. And a shit friend. And now I'm going to be a shit son when I tell Dad I can't marry Gabrielle. He's going to lose everything he's ever worked for. And so is Mum. She doesn't deserve this.

I push my finger and thumb into my eye sockets as I hang my head. The guys are right. I need a drink tonight. Fuck, I need a whole bottle. Then tomorrow, I'll start searching for ways to get out of this shit. Maybe I can talk to Spencer, reason with him. Ask Gabrielle to do the same. Fuck knows, but I have to do something. I can't be responsible for people I care about losing everything. Not again. It's a disease that will grow and poison everything. Look what it did to Maddy.

Maddy.

She blamed me for losing Drew. She hates me. *She fucking hates me.* She let me inside her body, while keeping me firmly out of her heart, walking away when we got back from Italy like she said she would.

And it hurt. Just like I told her it would. But it only hurt me. Not her.

"Rachel loves this song." Tanner's tired eyes light up.

"So does Rose," Dax adds.

Drew looks at me, and I smirk. Yeah, no sympathy for either of them. The fuckers have it good and they know it.

Drew's phone vibrates in his pocket, and he pulls it out. "Just got to take this." He stands and heads toward the exit, lifting his phone to his ear.

I sit back and look at the quickly emptying whiskey bottle.

"Let's get another," I announce.

Chapter 24
Maddy

"MAYBE I NEED A new recorder as well as earbuds," I groan into my margarita as Chloe listens to Nate's voice for the millionth time with a dopey grin on her face.

"I think you need your ears tested. He sounds dreamy."

I frown and stuff the recorder back into my purse.

"He *is* dreamy. Insanely charming and good-looking in real life. Just like we knew he would be," I huff as I lift my cocktail and take a sip. I barely register the sting of alcohol after four, no, five cocktails.

We've been to a couple of bars and have ended in a new nightclub in Chelsea. Any other night and I'd be excited by the caliber of good-looking men lining the bar, and the thrum of bodies swaying on the central dancefloor to the deep bass of the music. But tonight,

I'm struggling to gather enough enthusiasm for anything. Even swallowing my cocktail seems like a chore.

Chloe reaches over and plucks my glass from my hand, sniffing at the yellowy green liquid before tasting it.

"What are you doing?"

"Just checking. And it's as I suspected." She hands my glass back and relaxes against the back of the nightclub booth.

"What is?" I ask, sensing she's about to share one of her outlandish theories.

She has one on everything, from Area 51 secretly harboring alien life forms in cryo-pods to Henry Cavill actually being a cyborg—because no real man could ever be that perfect.

I drink more of my margarita.

"You want him."

"I don't." I wrinkle my nose, the truth easily falling from my lips. "He's nice and I enjoyed interviewing him, it's definitely a career highlight. But I felt no attraction to him whatsoever."

"Not Nate." Chloe rolls her eyes. "Logan."

I spray the liquid out, coughing. Chloe grabs a napkin and hands it to me.

"Shocker, eh?" She smirks as I dry my lips.

"Oh my god. Don't. I wish I'd never told you about Italy. A bit of okay sex doesn't mean anything."

I ball up the napkin and throw it down on the table before crossing my arms. This'll teach me for not keeping my mouth shut. But Chloe was there at my apartment when Logan dropped me off. And it slipped out. I tell her everything. A fact I'm now bitterly regretting as her smirk grows, only serving as a reminder of the man I'd rather not discuss.

"Great sex."

"Huh?"

Her smirk stretches. "You said great sex."

I frown, then cast my eyes around the club, sulking. "I doubt I used that word."

"'Great sex, Chloe. The man is hung, Chloe. I came so hard I saw stars, Chloe. But I still hate him, Chloe, I promise.'"

She smiles sweetly as I turn back to her with a glare. "That was the jetlag talking."

"From Italy? Please. They're like one hour ahead."

I knock back the rest of my drink. "I don't want Logan. I never have. I don't even like him most of the time."

"Most?" Chloe lifts one brow.

"All of the time," I add. "I don't like him all of the time."

"And you especially don't like him kissing the woman his dad wants him to marry."

I seethe as she challenges my gaze without flinching.

"I didn't call you to get drunk with me so you could lecture me about things that aren't even true." I look at the crowded bar. It will take ages to get another drink. The thought has pissed off energy swirling through my body. "Let's dance." I grab her hand and pull her up with me as I sling my purse strap over my arm.

"Sounds good to me." She grins, looking at something behind me. I turn and spot the two guys on the dance-floor that have caught her attention. Both tall and broad, shirts snug around their biceps. "I'll have the blond,"

Chloe says as she leads me in their direction. "The other one looks more your type."

I narrow my eyes at her, but she ignores me and maneuvers us closer to them on the dancefloor, until I bump into the blond's friend.

Sorry, I mouth, looking up into green eyes.

He smiles, dimples popping in his cheeks as he pushes his light brown hair back from his eyes. It's longer than Logan's. And his eyes are a gray green, not an electric emerald like Logan's.

Damn it. Why am I thinking about him?

Chloe winks at me from her position in the blond's arms as she grinds against him to the music. That girl does not waste time.

I turn back to the guy in front of me. He's still smiling. It's not his fault my friend has thrown me at him with all the subtlety of a tornado.

"I'm Maddy," I shout above the loud music.

"Kent," he shouts back.

"And your friend is—?"

I glance at the other guy, who Chloe is now climbing like a tree, her arms wrapped around his neck as she grinds against one of his thick thighs.

"What was that?" Kent asks as I turn back.

I open my mouth and then close it again. It's useless trying to talk. The music is almost deafening. The song rolls into another, eliciting an excited cheer from the crowd of dancers. I'm swept along and thrown up against Kent's hard body as the crowd swells and everyone's dancing notches up a level.

His hands slide down my sides, gripping onto my hips as I roll them in a figure of eight to the music. He pulls me closer to him so we're moving together, heat from our bodies mingling as a bead of sweat runs down between my breasts.

Kent's hands flex on my hips. "You're real fucking sexy, Maddy," he murmurs in my ear, pulling me closer.

Chloe is smiling at me from her position in the guy's arms. His lips are on her neck, and she giggles at something he says, then turns and pulls his lips to hers for a kiss.

Kent spins me in his arms and gives me a sexy smile, his gaze dropping to my lips. I spin back around before he can kiss me, and he chuckles in my ear as he grasps my hips and pulls me back against his chest.

"You like to tease, baby?"

My lack of answer only feeds his interest, and he grinds his erection against my ass cheeks, his mouth dropping to my neck and kissing it.

The hairs on the back of my neck stand up and I close my eyes briefly. Kent's lips are the right mix of soft and urgent against my skin. But it's not them that have my senses heightened like I'm in a glass box being watched.

I open my eyes, searching the packed dance floor.

Kent chuckles in my ear. "Fuck, baby. You can move. I'd like to see what else you can do with these hips." He squeezes them, curling his fingers forward so they stretch closer to the inner crease of my thighs.

"You want to come back to my place and show me?" he groans at the exact same time I lock eyes with two green flames across the room, looking like they're about to rain hell on earth.

Chapter 25
Logan

I STARE AT A familiar pair of curvy hips swaying on the dance floor in a green dress. My blood heats, reaching boiling point as a pair of hands slide over them, grasping them tight and pulling them backward.

"Fucker," I hiss as the guy slides his hands forward, his fingers grazing over the sides of where her pussy is beneath the fabric. A pussy that clenched around me more times than I can count.

I'm unable to tear my eyes away as the guy leans down and whispers something in Maddy's ear. She shivers and then looks up straight into my eyes like she knew I was here the entire time.

I'm already standing, my feet carrying me over to them like a damn missile as the fucker parts his lips above her shoulder, dipping down to kiss her skin.

"Party's over, dickwad."

He pauses as my shout attracts the attention of the dancers around us.

"What?"

"You heard me, cockwaffle. Take a hike."

The stupid fucker has the audacity to look at me like I'm the prick. When he's the one whose mouth is still parted and hovering far too close to Maddy's neck.

"If you want to keep your tongue, you'll get it the fuck back in your mouth!"

I grab Maddy by the wrist, pulling her behind me and squaring up to him.

He looks past me at Maddy. "You know this asshole?"

I flick the back of my fingers against his chest. "My face is here, wankhammer. Don't look at her."

I don't know why all my old college-era insults are re-surfacing. But something about this guy is making me lose any kind of fucking decorum.

Maybe I should just punch him and get it done.

He meets my eyes, a murderous glare swirling in his. I recognize it for what it is. He isn't concerned about Maddy and whether she knows me or not. He only cares that I've spoiled his fun. He thought he was getting laid tonight.

Laid in a grave if he doesn't take the hint soon.

"Logan!" Maddy steps around me, but I sweep her back behind me again.

"You do know him then?" Prick grunts.

"Unfortunately," Maddy sighs.

"We were just about to leave. So why don't you fuck off?" Prick smiles at me as he steps closer.

He's got balls, I'll give him that. Too bad they're about to get crushed.

"She's not going anywhere with you, cuntnozzle, so back the fuck off."

"Logan!" Maddy grabs onto my bicep as I curl my hand into a fist. "You're acting like an asshole."

Prick steps closer.

"That's right. I'm an asshole." I poke him in the chest. "But guess what, wankstain... I'm the only asshole who gets to touch her."

"For god's sake," Maddy huffs.

Chloe appears with a blond guy close behind her. Her eyes ping-pong between me and prickface before she glances at Maddy.

"Why don't you and Kent go get a drink. I'll find you later," Chloe says to the blond.

Prick aka Kent glares at me as his friend moves to his side. I can tell what he's thinking. He's calculating his chances with Chloe. If he pisses her off and doesn't drag his mate away, then they'll both be going to bed with blue balls tonight and only their sad fists for company.

I stare at Kent, unblinking, as he shakes off his friend's hand on his arm, but then turns to follow him anyway.

"We're not done, asshole," he spits as he walks off.

"You are." I snort.

"What the hell?" Maddy forces her way in front of me, fixing me with a glare that could make a man wither. Except, I love that fire in her eyes. Especially when it's paired with the deep line between her brows like it is now.

"Maddy?" Chloe sidles up to her. She whispers something in her ear and Maddy nods. Then Chloe disappears through the throng of bodies dancing around us.

"Don't tell me you were going to go home and fuck that guy, Mads," I snap when her eyes come back to my face.

"Piss off, Logan. Like you aren't going to go cozy up with Gabrielle."

"What?" I reel back.

Maddy spins away from me. "Forget it."

She storms off the dancefloor, slipping through gaps in the dancers. I jostle and bump my way after her. She's halfway down a dark corridor leading to the ladies' room when I catch up.

"What was that?" I grab her wrist and spin her to face me.

Her chest heaves as she yanks her arm free and stomps further down the corridor.

I grab her again before she can disappear and pull her toward a fire exit where it's more dimly lit. But it can't dull the angry fire burning in her eyes.

"Run back to wifey, Logan. We're done. You shouldn't be following me or trying to talk to me. You can't marry me to help your business. I'm not an heiress, *Prince*." She sneers. "You and I meant nothing."

"Why are you being a bitch?"

Her eyes widen.

"I didn't mean... I... Jesus." I blow out a breath, then step closer, forcing her back against the wall. She sucks in a breath as she stares up at me, her outburst momentarily halting. "What are you doing? Are you dancing with pricks now? Going home with them?"

"Are you kissing fiancées now?" She fires back before slamming her mouth shut.

"You were at the hotel today?"

She looks to the side, her lips pressed into a firm line.

"Mads?" I turn her chin toward me, and she meets my eyes reluctantly. Her gaze drops to my mouth before she drags it up again. "You're jealous."

"I'm not." She jerks her chin out of my grip.

"You are."

"I said, I'm not, Logan. Do you need your ears tested?" Her eyes glitter with energy as she scowls. But I know that energy, I understand it now. It's like Sterling said. *It's full of passion.* Me and her together could never be muted or flat, or anything other than burning with need for each other. No matter how much she tries to deny it.

"You care."

The corners of my lips curl, and hope blooms in my chest like rain finally falling into the cracks on parched earth. And from there, it spreads, flowing, rushing, until there's a raving fucking river headed toward the sea.

She's fucking jealous.

"I don't!"

The corners of my mouth stretch wider. "Sure sounds like it."

"Get over yourself." A blush creeps over her cheeks.

"How can I? When I can't get over you?"

She gasps.

I fall serious, urgency lacing my voice. "All I've done since we got back to London is wish I could get back on that fucking plane and take you with me. Admit you want me too, Mads. Do us both a favor and *fucking admit it.*"

"You need to forget about Italy." Her eyes drop to my lips again, making blood race to my dick.

"I don't want to forget about it. Do you?"

She doesn't answer.

"I can't forget about it. You know we're good together, Mads." I lower my mouth to her ear and kiss her pulse.

She shivers as my breath fans over her neck.

"You and me are never going to happen, Logan. *Never.*"

"We already *are* happening." I press closer against her body, her resulting sharp intake of breath only fueling me to keep going. To not give up on her.

She looks at me from beneath her lashes. My guilt over Drew sails off into the fucking sunset with one look at Maddy's face. One touch of her hair. One inhale of her scent. *The sight of another guy's hands on her body.*

"You're delusional."

I press my erection into her. She moans as it makes contact, and the sound draws a primal groan from my chest.

"You still want me. Admit it. I thought you meant it when you walked away from me without looking back. But you wouldn't be getting jealous now if that were true. And your heart wouldn't be beating in your chest as hard as it is." I rest my palm over the curve of her breast.

Her heart thuds against it.

"Shut up," she breathes.

I tease the neckline of her dress down low enough that I can suck the swell of skin at the top of her breast.

She moans as I graze my teeth over her, leaving a mark, before smoothing my tongue over the tender spot.

"Logan..."

"Tell me to stop." I pull her dress lower and kiss dangerously close to her nipple.

She says nothing, so I kiss her again, over and over, working my way up past her collar bones and onto her neck. A small squeak escapes her parted lips as I place my lips by her ear.

"You want me, Mads. I bet your pussy's all swollen and wet underneath your dress now that you've seen me again."

She struggles to swallow around a small whimper. I look further down the corridor.

"Come." I take her hand and lead her to the end and around the dark corner.

The minute we're out of sight, I cage her in between my arms against the wall, reveling in the fact she doesn't push me away or object. Instead, she stares at me with lust-filled eyes.

But I'm still playing with fire as I slip a hand underneath her dress and skate my fingers up her inner thigh.

"Stop," she whispers, making no attempt to make me.

Her breath grows ragged as I move higher, and she drops her purse to the floor.

"Don't give me that shit about us meaning nothing again," I growl.

"We don't. This is nothing," she murmurs.

I slide my hand higher, and she jerks, gasping as I rip her panties to one side.

"You're a liar, Maddox Harper. You want me as much as I want you. You don't make the same mistake over and over."

"I hate you," she says with a frustrated moan as I push my fingers through her silky skin.

"Sure feels like it." My fingers glide through her arousal until I'm circling her swollen clit. She tries to hide her shudder, which only makes me smile. "See. You're fucking soaking for me."

"This isn't happening." Her hands find my shoulders, holding onto me for support. Her lips part as I move my fingers to her entrance, groaning as silkiness coats them and runs into my palm.

"This is so fucking happening." I bury my head into her neck and inhale her scent as I push two fingers inside her.

Maddy gasps, her nails biting into my skin through my jacket.

"You can't tell me Italy meant nothing to you," I say as I hold my fingers still inside her. She wriggles around them, her body urging me to move them and give her relief. But I keep them still, enjoying the rising blush creeping up her neck.

"I can," she utters.

"I spent the whole last night on the island inside you, Mads. My body joined with yours. And it was *my name* on your lips when you came. Every single time." My voice lowers to a hoarse rasp as I remember her body gripping onto me and bursting into pleasure around me that night. "You even whimpered it when you were exhausted but refused to stop. You pulled me into you again and again that night. You wanted it. Every single minute. You looked into my eyes, and you felt it. You felt *this*." My gaze burns into hers. "I know you did."

"No. We were never meant —"

"But we did! Accept it, Mads. You and me. We fit. As much as you don't want that to be true, nothing has ever been more real. What are you scared of?"

She shakes her head and her eyes pop wide as I move, pulling my soaked fingers out and sliding them back inside her slowly. Her pupils dilate as she stares at me.

"I hate you."

"Kiss me."

"I hate you," she repeats like it still means anything.

"Kiss me."

"I hate you," she whispers. But the strength has left her voice as she blinks at me, her lips parted and sucking in small inhales of breath.

I finger-fuck her slowly, as if I have all the time in the world.

"Kiss. Me." I slide my fingers deeper and curl the pads against the sweet spot inside her.

She scowls like she's thinking up a million ways to kill me and make it look like an accident. Then she grabs the back of my head and crashes her lips onto mine.

"This means nothing," she pants, drawing back and then attacking me again. "Nothing."

We kiss like a couple of sex-crazed teenagers, teeth clashing, lips bruising together, moaning far louder than is a good idea, despite hiding in shadows. I increase my speed, and my fingers piston in and out of her, my arm thrusting back and forth as I pin her to the wall.

"Fuck. You're so tight."

"Logan," she whimpers, making my dick throb painfully.

"Say my name again." I hitch one of her legs up with my free hand and wrap it around my waist. The position lets my fingers slide deeper, and Maddy mewls with pleasure.

"Logan... I want... I need—"

"You need my cock?"

Pressure builds in my balls at her whimper of agreement, and all rational thoughts leave my brain as I take my fingers back and hastily rip down my zipper, pulling my weeping dick free. It doesn't matter that we're meters away from people discovering us. I'm praying that the darkness is enough. Because I *have* to be inside her. It's an urge so strong that I can't see or hear anything else around me, except Maddy and her hot, quivering body. A body trembling with need. *For me.*

"Yes," she gasps as she grabs my cock and guides it toward her. I grasp her other leg, lifting it around my waist as I thrust up inside her with all the grace of a man desperately teetering on the edge of insanity since he was last inside her.

"Fuck," I growl as her tightness hugs me hard.

Maddy cries out as I drive into her, over and over like my life depends on it. My urgency is increased by the distant, muffled chatter of more women leaving the ladies' room around the corner.

But it doesn't stop us.

We fuck against the wall, grabbing at each other, kissing and biting, moaning and gasping, until she clenches around me and her thighs start to shake.

"I... I..."

"You need me to push you over the edge, don't you?" I hiss as my balls draw up close to my body, and I drive deeper, the head of my cock tingling.

Maddy whimpers against my lips, biting my bottom one between her teeth. I smirk. She still hates to admit it out loud.

I'll have to say it for her.

"You need my cum, don't you? You need to feel it filling up your sweet little pussy in order to get off, don't you?"

"Fuck off," she bites. But her trembling body gives her away. She's on the edge.

"I know you, Mads," I growl as the pressure increases in my balls and heat builds at the base of my dick. I glance down between our bodies to where I'm disappearing inside her. "Fuck, you look incredible stretched around me, baby."

"I'm not your baby," she moans, still balancing on the edge of her orgasm.

"You're stuffed full of my cock, Smiles. That makes you my fucking baby. No one else's. Mine." I change the angle a little, making her cry out against my mouth. "Now, do you need my cum?"

"No." She grinds down to meet each thrust, desperately trying to finish before me.

"Liar. Always fucking lying."

She whimpers, her hands clawing at my shoulders. But she still doesn't come, despite her entire body shaking in desperate need.

"Fuck!" The frustration in her voice fills the space around us, bouncing off the walls.

"You need to be quiet."

"Fuck you." She quivers, weaving her fingers through my hair and yanking at the strands.

I let go of one of her thighs and clamp my hand over her mouth. Her eyes flare as I pump up inside her, muffling her responding curse.

"So fucking noisy when you're waiting for my cum."

She glares at me as I thrust hard.

"Here it is, *baby*," I growl as my cock swells. "We both know you'll come the second you feel it inside you."

Relief flashes in her eyes.

Then she bites my hand, making me snatch it back with a hiss.

"Fuck—" Her words turn into a scream that I immediately muffle with a kiss, swallowing it down and groaning as I come deep inside her. Her entire body trembles as her pussy grips me like a vise, falling into a deep pulsating rhythm, clenching and releasing as she comes around me. Hard.

—you!" she cries.

"That's it. Good girl. Good fucking girl." I drag in a breath as I keep coming inside her, my eyes damn near rolling to the back of my head at how incredible she feels milking me.

I use my mouth to shield the rest of her cries until they abate into sated whimpers. Our kisses slow as her grip on my hair loosens, and her whimpers reduce until they're no more than deep breaths.

She drops her head against the wall, her breasts rising and falling against my chest. "We did not just fuck in a club, Logan."

I flex my cock inside her, making her bite her bottom lip. "We most definitely just fucked." I kiss her neck one final time, groaning at how good she smells. Then I pull out and set her on her feet, tucking my dick back in my pants.

Her eyes caress my face as she smooths her dress down. "I need to use the bathroom." She picks up her purse and walks off.

I follow, pulling her back the second she rounds the corner. My eyes drop to her thighs in her tight dress, and she presses them together.

"Open your legs," I rasp.

"What?" She looks into my eyes as I protect her from view with my body. I slide my hand up the front of her dress, encouraging her thighs to part.

"You've got my cum inside you, Mads. And it makes me fucking crazy. You're keeping it there." I drag her soaked panties to one side and gather a stream of warm liquid up from her skin. Then I push it back up inside her with two fingers, swirling them around for good measure.

"Logan." She grips onto my wrist.

I rub my fingers inside her, loving that she's full of me. It's everywhere, held inside her hot body.

"Smiles?" I groan.

"Yes," she whispers breathlessly as I twist my fingers and make her gasp.

"I'll be watching you for the rest of the night. And if you dance with anymore pricks, then I'll be bringing you back down here to fuck you again. Until you accept who this pussy belongs to."

She will fight back, I'm sure of it. But she must know by now that no matter how much she wants to fight this, to dismiss this... this is real. We are unavoidable. Inevitable.

Her eyes glint as I kiss her. "Pretend to hate me as much as you want. But at least admit you love my cum inside you, Mads." I curl my fingers and a grunt leaves my chest at the feel of my wet heat inside her.

She moans. "Log—"

"What the fuck?!"

Maddy's eyes snap to the side, looking over my shoulder and widening at the roar.

I pull my fingers from her body as my eyes connect with hers. Hers are round as she sucks in a sharp gasp.

"Get your fucking hands off my sister!" Fists grab my shirt, yanking me away from Maddy and throwing me into the wall opposite.

Maddy scrambles to pull her dress down over her thighs. "Drew!"

His eyes seem almost black with murderous intent as he looks between the two of us, sucking sharp breaths in through his nose like a prize-fighting bull.

Chloe races up behind him, her face pinched. "I'm sorry, Maddy. I tried to distract him."

"You fucking knew about this?" He turns to Chloe, and she shrivels under his gaze before his accusing stare slams back onto me.

"This isn't the first time?"

Tanner and Dax appear behind him. Girls pause further up the corridor, craning their necks to see what's going on.

"Nothing to see. Keep walking, ladies," Dax says to them. And they do, having more sense than to get involved in something happening in a darkened corridor of a club. A corridor I fucked Maddy in because I couldn't restrain myself long enough to take her somewhere private.

"It's not what you think," Maddy pleads with Drew.

"It's exactly what you think." I step away from the wall, ignoring the sting of pain in my back.

"Logan!" Maddy snaps.

"He deserves to know."

"Asshole," she whispers, blinking back embarrassed tears as Chloe squeezes past Drew and runs to her side, wrapping an arm around her.

"It started in Italy." I meet Drew's glare with a deep inhale.

He advances toward me, ignoring a low spoken warning of his name from Tanner.

"You've been fucking my sister for weeks? You're supposed to be my friend. You're supposed to look out for her. Keep her safe from assholes. I trusted you! My friend, the biggest asshole of the lot!"

He shoves me in the chest, but I refuse to fight him. He has every right to be angry. I lied to him. I am a shit friend.

"This is why you begged her manager to send her on that fucking Italy trip, isn't it? So you could use her as your fuck toy."

"What?" Maddy gasps behind Drew. "You asked Eve to send me?"

"Keep out of it!" Drew shouts.

"Don't yell at her." I square up to him, and he glares at me so hard his eyeballs look like they might explode in his skull.

"So what? You going to marry her now instead?" Drew's lip curls in a disgusted snarl.

"I'm not fucking marrying anyone!"

He shoves me again. "You telling me you're fingering my sister in some dark dirty hallway of a club for nothing?"

He turns to Maddy with a sneer. "Real fucking classy, sis."

Shame washes over her face as her cheeks flare.

"Hey." This time, I shove him back. "Take that the fuck back."

Drew rears back. His fist connects with my cheekbone faster than I can dive out of the way. My back hits the wall with force.

"Drew! Stop it!" Maddy screams.

My face throbs like a bitch, the taste of metal flooding my mouth as I look up. Tanner's gotten hold of Drew's arm and Dax has moved closer.

"You're right. I am an asshole." I wipe warm stickiness away from my chin with my sleeve. "But it wasn't for nothing. Not a single second. Every moment with her was everything."

I don't look at Maddy as I say it. I can't.

"Yeah," Drews snorts. "Those moments when you wanted to get your dick wet."

I snarl and step forward, but Dax places a hand on my shoulder and gives Tanner a look as he tips his head.

Tanner nods then grips Drew on the shoulder. "Come on, man. Let's go."

Drew's murderous eyes hold mine and he jerks his chin at Maddy and Chloe. "You two are getting a ride with us."

They're both frozen, looking between us.

"Now!" Drew snaps.

The two girls hold each other as they walk past me and Dax in silence.

I wipe more blood from my chin with the back of my hand as Maddy glances back at me with shining eyes. It's the first time I've ever seen her look at me with concern. Drew's fist in my face seems a small price to pay to see that confirmation. She's refused to say the words out loud until now. But that one look tells me all I need to know.

Not one part of Maddox Harper hates me anymore, not really.

Not a single one.

Whether she likes it or not.

Chapter 26
Maddy

"UGH, IF YOU'VE COME here to shout, then save your breath." I leave the door to my apartment open and walk back inside as Drew stands on the threshold. I should have ignored the buzzer and stayed in bed.

"I'm not going to fucking shout!" he shouts as he follows me inside.

I head straight to the coffee machine and flick it on, then turn and lean against the counter with my arms crossed as I look at him.

"I'm sorry that you saw what you saw last night," I say around the ball in my throat. I look to the side, heat flaring in my cheeks.

"What about what I fucking heard?"

I wince as he spits the words out like vomit. I hoped he hadn't heard it, but judging by the thundering pulse in his tense neck, he heard every word.

At least admit you love my cum inside you, Mads.

"Please don't." I cringe and turn my back to him, taking my time fixing our drinks until the heat in my face reduces. Anything to delay having to face him for more precious seconds.

"I want to kill him."

I sneak a glance over my shoulder. He's pacing up and down in his dark jeans and black T-shirt, tension stiffening his broad shoulders. I knew this was coming today. Drew barely spoke a word during the ride with Tanner and Chloe last night. I should be grateful he at least waited until the morning to pound on my door. I got to have a semi-decent amount of sleep to prepare for this. Although lying awake picturing Logan's bleeding face and split lip was hardly equal to a restful night.

"You attempted to kill him last night when you punched him so hard in the face he almost flew through the wall." I sniff, turning around and holding a mug of coffee out to him.

A hint of regret passes through his dark eyes before he closes them momentarily. We look alike. Everyone always comments on it. Drew didn't get tight curls like me. But he has the same dark as ink hair that still holds a wave despite him keeping it cut short. And the same dark brown eyes. His turn almost black when he's angry, like last night. Today they're smoldering at a shade above midnight.

"He had his hands on you." His knuckles turn white against the mug. His full height and broad build swamp my kitchen until the air is thick with tension.

"I know."

"And you wanted him to?"

His brows pull together as he studies my reaction. The underlying question in his tone makes bile rise in my throat.

"Yes."

He nods, relief softening his clenched jaw. He doesn't really think Logan would do anything without my permission. The fact he's even hinted at it has my heart seizing painfully. No matter what I've thought of Logan in the past, he doesn't deserve anyone to think that about him, even for a split second. Especially his best friend.

"Have you always had a thing for him?"

"What? Of course not."

Drew's expression is grim as he takes a large gulp from his mug. "You just decided to fuck my friend behind my back for fun, then?"

"It wasn't like that."

"You don't like Logan. That's what you've always told me."

"I didn't like him... I mean, I don't like him."

"Come on, Maddy. Lie to yourself if you must, but don't lie to me."

It's no use trying to reason with Drew when he's like this or try to explain to him. He's always been hot-headed. It's why he got in so much trouble when he was younger. He's a joker when he wants to be. But when he's serious, he's as intimidating as a gun to your temple with the safety off.

"It's bad enough that he…" His eyes drop over my body in my T-shirt and joggers before he rips them away with a hiss. "… with my *sister*. But you both lied about it."

"It was never supposed to happen again. It was a moment of madness." I stare into my cup like the answer to ending this awkward conversation immediately is held there.

"Were you both drinking one night in Italy? Is that how? Just the one time… Fuck, I don't want to know." Drew puts his cup down and tips his head back with a groan as he folds his giant biceps across his chest.

I shake my head, my voice quiet. "More than once."

"More?" Drew's eyes narrow.

I drop my eyes from his.

"Twice?" he growls.

"I lost count," I confess, squeezing my eyes shut as he curses.

"Are you in love with him?"

"What?"

"Is he in love with you?"

"No!" I put my mug down and scrub my hands down my cheeks. "God, I can't believe we're having this conversation. What's next? You going to march us down to the church and make us get married because we had sex?"

He snorts. "You'll have to join the queue. Logan's in demand. I'm almost jealous of the lying fucker."

I drop my head, pressure building behind my eyes.

"Maddy." Drew's voice softens, but he still sounds exasperated. "You're my sister. It's my job to look out for you. And he's supposed to be my friend. He has no right to touch you. He should be looking out for you too, the way he always has *for me*."

"What do you mean, *for you?*"

Guilt flickers in his eyes and he clears his throat.

"Drew?"

"It's what friends do for each other. I'd do the same for him if he had a baby sister."

"I'm not a baby."

"Not now. But back then, you were. When I was gone ... I needed to know you'd be okay. I know what assholes teenage boys are."

"Wait. You asked Logan to follow me home from school every day? Drew! No one would speak to me."

"Kept the boys away, though." A smile tugs at his lips, dropping off right away as I glare at him. He has the sense to look sheepish as he says, "Okay, Logan's methods were his own. He didn't always get them right."

"No shit."

"It made me feel better knowing you had two of us looking out for you when I came home."

I snort, crossing my arms. I'm not going to get anywhere trying to convince my brother that telling half the school I had crabs was too far. He'll just reason that the ends justified the means. Assholes, the pair of them.

"Well, now the two of you can stop. Because I am done with you both interfering with my life. I'm twenty-nine, I can live my own damn life."

I straighten up ready to fight my corner, but there's a buzzing from the intercom.

Drew turns toward it.

"It's my place, thank you," I grumble, shouldering past him before he can press it.

I buzz whoever it is without checking the screen and head down the hallway. The door is on the receiving end of my frustration as I wrench it open.

"Logan?"

"Hey." His brows lift as he locks eyes with me.

"Drew—"

"Has a mean right hook? Yeah, I know." He tries to smile, the movement curling the opposite side of his mouth to where the bloodied line of his split lip is.

My eyes scan over the developing bruise on his cheekbone.

"Don't blame him, Mads. I'd have done the same thing."

I draw in a breath through my nose. "Then you're both giant idiots."

Logan chuckles. "Can I come in?"

"As long as you don't fight with the other giant idiot who's in my kitchen."

"Drew's here?" Logan looks over my shoulder and down the hallway.

"Yeah, I am, fucker. So you better keep your hands to yourself."

I roll my eyes as his threat carries from the kitchen.

"And it's my apartment, dickhead. So you better both not be jerks or I'll kick you out on your asses," I shout over my shoulder.

I step back and let him in.

"I won't stay long. I just wanted to see if you were okay."

The sudden urge to kiss his lip better hits me square in the chest. Instead, I nod and motion up the hallway.

Tension fills the air as all three of us stand in my kitchen. I thought it seemed cramped with Drew's giant frame in it earlier, but with the two of them both here, all broad chests and giant arms, the atmosphere is so claustrophobic it's suffocating.

"What are you doing here?" Drew scowls at Logan as he positions himself next to me.

"I came to check on Mads." He holds Drew's eyes, unaffected by my brother's deathly glare.

"Her name's Maddy. She hates being called Mads," Drew snaps.

"Logan's the only one who calls me that and it's fine."

Logan looks sideways at me, a new emotion gleaming in his eyes that I can't identify. But I can't unpack it now. Not when these two brutes might kill each other in my kitchen.

"You going to kiss and make up then?" I bounce my eyes between them.

"That depends," Drew answers without breaking eye contact with Logan. "You going to keep fucking my baby sister?"

"I am not a baby," I almost yell, shaking with irritation.

"I hope so," Logan replies cockily.

"Maybe I'll split the other side of that lip then," Drew counters.

"For God's sake." I step between them like an umpire with a hand raised toward each of them. "You," I point at Drew, "need to keep your nose out and not threaten my visitors. And you," I point at Logan, "need to learn when to keep your big mouth shut."

"Sorry." Logan's smile grows as he locks eyes with me. We stare at each other for a few seconds before Drew scoffs.

"I don't fucking believe it. Stop eye-fucking her in front of me. It's bad enough knowing you went behind my back. I don't need to see it again after last night."

"Shut up, Drew," I snap before Logan can answer him with whatever stupid thing he's about to say.

My brother shakes his head. "You think I want to be here? Talking to you about who you're sleeping with? The fact it's him"—his eyes track to Logan and then back to me—"isn't the worst fucking thing about it. It's that you both lied. For weeks."

"I was going to tell you today," Logan says.

My mouth drops open. "You were?"

He at least looks guilty as he glances at me. "I wasn't going to lie now that we're home."

I tip my head back and stare at the ceiling as Drew grumbles. He knows Logan is good to his word. He isn't a liar. If he says he would tell Drew today, then he would tell him today.

"Instead, I saw you both..."

Drew doesn't need to finish. We all know what he saw. Heat flares in my cheeks again.

"I just don't... Of all the women you know," he curses. "Couldn't you have found someone on your precious dating app? Someone who isn't my fucking baby sister."

"I'm not a baby."

"I deleted that app."

Drew's brows quirk at Logan's confession.

"As soon as..." Logan's eye flick to me. "I deleted it as soon as..."

"You've not been back on it?"

"Hell no."

Drew rolls his lips with a nod. "It's a fucking start. Doesn't change the fact that she's my sister. My fucking *sister*."

Logan opens his mouth to reply.

"Look, we get it. You didn't want it to happen. We never planned for it to happen. End of the story." I slice my hands through the air like a clapperboard.

"You should have told me," he hisses at Logan like I'm not in the room.

"I was going to. I hate secrets as much as you. They're better out in the open. You get that. You feel better now that she knows, right? Well, it's the same for me. I swear I was going to tell you," Logan says.

Drew falls silent, darting his eyes to mine and then dropping them away. "Thanks, man. I haven't fucking told her yet."

Logan stiffens next to me as he exhales. "You said you were going to. You swore."

My stomach lurches. "Told me what?"

Drew shakes his head, his jaw clenched. "I know. I was waiting for a good time."

"Told me what?" I repeat.

"I thought you had. Shit, man, I'm sorry," Logan says.

"Not your fault," Drew mutters.

"Told me what?" *Just call me Maddy the parrot.*

"I just assumed... You said when she came home." Logan's voice is thick with regret.

"Told. Me. Fucking. What? I swear if one of you doesn't start talking—"

"It's about Dad." Drew drops his head, rubbing his eyes with one hand. Logan walks over and claps his shoulder—a sign of solidarity—as he lowers his voice to a reassuring tone. "Yeah," Drew agrees with whatever Logan whispers to him.

"I already know Mum suspects he's having an affair. Has she decided to throw him out?"

"No. She's still thinking about what to do. Dad has no idea she knows anything."

"Okay. So then...?"

He looks at Logan, who nods at him. "Fuck." Drew draws in a breath, then meets my eyes. "There's no easy way to tell you this, Maddy."

"Just spit it out." I stare at the two of them standing together like co-conspirators.

Drew turns his palms up in front of him. "Dad's the reason I went to juvie. He made sure I didn't get off."

I snort back my laugh. "Shut up."

Drew's face is solemn. "I'm sorry I never told you. He didn't want you or Mum to know."

"That's not what happened." I look at Logan for reassurance, but he's watching me carefully.

"It is, Maddy." Drew rolls his neck and the resulting crack echoes around the room as he curses. "He made sure I went. He *asked* the judge on our case to send me."

It's like a smack to my gut as I blink in confusion.

"N-no. You were both supposed to go. But Logan's dad paid it off somehow. Got him off the charges."

"That's not what happened." Drew runs a hand over his jaw, lines tightening across his brow. "We were both meant to get a warning, a suspended sentence, and some community service. Dad was embarrassed. He was a police sergeant with a criminal son."

"But…" A steel ball falls from my throat all the way to my feet as my mouth feels like someone has stuffed it full of sawdust. Logan nods, confirming it. "But Dad hated to talk about it while you were gone. He missed you so much."

Drew's eyes pinch and he shakes his head, looking at the floor. "He still hates to talk about it. Because I showed him up. You know he's a proud man. He had respect at work. But at home, he had a teenage son who cared for nothing more than doing whatever stupid shit he wanted. I was selfish and young. I don't blame him. Juvie taught me a thing or two. It wasn't all bad."

"You were gone for six months!" My chest burns and my eyes blur as hot tears threaten to fill them. I blink them away as I look at Logan. He stares back at me with only softness and understanding in his eyes. "It's when I started hating you," I whisper.

He gives me a sad smile. "I know."

I turn my back on them both, slamming my hand over my mouth as the urge to vomit fights to take over my body. Sweat pricks at my hairline and I force myself to take in slow, deep breaths through my nose.

"I should have told you when I found out. I'm sorry, sis."

I hold my hand out to the side, one finger extended, indicating that I can't talk right now. I'm too busy using all my energy to stay standing. How could Dad do that? Drew was only sixteen. A kid.

"I told Dad it wasn't fair that Logan got off because his family was rich," I choke out. "He *agreed* with me. He let me believe that's what happened." My lower lip trembles. "Why didn't you tell me?"

"I didn't know that Dad let you think that's the way it happened," Drew says.

"I thought Dad knew something I didn't. I thought that was him confirming it." I turn, unable to take my eyes from Logan's. His are burning bright green as he watches me.

"He's a bigger fucking liar than I thought," Drew mutters.

"Does he know that you know this?"

Drew chuckles, but it's empty. "Yeah. He knows. I found out after I got out. He told me it was my actions that got me in trouble in the first place and I should accept my punishment like a man. He was right. He said it'd only upset you and Mum if I came home and dragged it all back up again. We never spoke about it again. I caused our family enough shit back then, Maddy. You know I was no saint."

Logan remains quiet but stays close enough to Drew that his presence conveys support. I could kiss him right now for being here for my brother.

"You deserved a dad who would stand up for you." I look at Drew, my heart breaking for my sixteen-year-old brother who was let down by his own father.

"It's done. It's in the past," he says with an air of finality. "It doesn't matter now."

The air leaves my lungs in one fast rush.

"It doesn't matter now? Nothing's ever mattered more."

All these years, everything I've based my opinions on has been snatched from under my feet. Drew being sent away wasn't Logan's fault. Logan being a dick after is still his fault. But without the rest backing it up, his actions seem dulled in their menace. He was trying to help a friend he missed. Even if his methods were questionable.

"Okay." I take a deep breath to stop myself from shaking. My head is screaming out for a hot shower and solitude to process this. "Well, you haven't killed each other in my kitchen. Thank you for that. Blood's hard to clean up. But if there aren't any other bombshells you want to drop, then I'd like you both to leave now, please." My bottom lip trembles as I speak.

They both lower their brows and look at me with concern as they step forward. It's almost comical how they do it in sync with one another. Two muscular giants both stepping forward to offer comfort.

Comfort I don't deserve and can't handle right now. Not from them. *Especially Logan.*

"I'm fine," I insist before they contradict me. "I like to process things alone." I shepherd them both to the front door, holding the churning in my gut at bay. I need them out of here.

Drew exits first but lingers on the doorstep as he looks at Logan.

"He isn't staying either," I say as I place my hand on Logan's arm and guide him through the door.

Drew's expression softens as the two look back at me like a pair of puppies.

"Go," I urge. "I'm fine. I'll call you." Drew nods, and Logan's brow quirks. "*Both* of you," I croak.

I shut the door and head to the bathroom, gripping onto the sides of the sink for support as I fight to calm the hammering in my chest. I'm about to turn the shower on when there's a knock at the front door again.

"I figured you'd appreciate this." Chloe grins, brandishing a fast-food breakfast bag as I open the door. "You okay?" The grin drops from her face.

She doesn't even make it inside before my legs turn to jelly, and I throw my arms around her neck. The first sob wracks through my chest as she rubs my back.

"It's okay. Tell me what happened."

I pull back enough to let her inside.

"My dad." I hiccup. "Logan... I never knew... I was awful to him... How can he stand to look at me?"

Chapter 27
Logan

"I CAN'T MARRY A woman I'm not in love with."

And there's someone else. Someone who she says she hates me. But if she feels anything for me, then I can't give up.

I take a deep breath before raising my head.

Mum smiles, her eyes shining, while Dad wipes a hand over his forehead, a grave expression on his face. His skin is still gray. He looked like stress was making him ill before Italy. But now he looks ravaged by it.

"I know this is our family business, Dad." I wait for him to meet my eyes, but he doesn't, so I continue, "But this is my *life*. I'll build the company back up from scratch, the way you did."

Mum makes a hopeful sound and reaches to pat Dad's hand on top of the breakfast bar in their kitchen.

"You know I can do it. I'll work with Spencer like he wants. I can partner with him on Vex. I'll talk to him. Make him see that Gabrielle and the business can still be secure without us marrying. She wants to continue her work as a doctor, it's what she loves. And I'll make sure she can."

"That's a lot of work, son."

"It is. But you know I'm capable."

Understanding shines back as he sees how serious I am. But his expression clouds over almost immediately, giving way to hopelessness once again.

"It's everything. We owe billions. The company will fold before you're even close to getting a return from Vex." He sighs and rubs his eyes. "The only way it can be saved is if Spencer helps us."

"And I'll speak to him."

"It won't make a difference. He's a stubborn bastard. The fact he's even offering to help in the first place is incredibly generous of him. But he's a businessman. He knows what he wants, and he's stated his terms."

"A loveless marriage for his daughter?" I snort, falling back in my chair.

"A secure partnership for her with a good man who will respect her and give him grandchildren as soon as possible," Dad replies.

Mum rips her hand from his to wipe her eyes with a handkerchief. "This is our son's future, Len. Not one of your business deals."

She looks at me. "There's someone else, isn't there? I can see it in your eyes. Do you love her?"

"I—"

Dad grumbles. "Half of the marriages formed with love as the driving factor fail, Viv."

"Over thirty years and we're not doing so bad," she snaps at him.

I meet her eyes, and she presses her lips together and gives me a tight nod. "This is your life, Logan. Whatever choice you make is yours alone. You're the one who'll have to live with it. Think about that." She rises from the table, looking sadly at Dad before she leaves the room.

"She's right." Dad sighs. "We all must live with our choices. Even the ones we desperately wish we could change."

I stand, swallowing the lump in my throat as I clasp his shoulder and squeeze. He places his hand over mine.

"*Especially* the ones we wish we could change." He pats my hand. "The ones that hurt the people we love. The ones where we lose."

I falter, considering sitting back down. But I know Dad. He'll not want a shoulder to cry on as he thinks about the mistakes he's made. About how his actions led to him being on the cusp of losing all he's worked for. He'll want to beat himself up in private.

"Go on, son. I'll see you later."

"Yeah." I squeeze his shoulder one more time as he drops his hand from mine. "Okay."

I go hard at it in my gym as if I can solve all my problems by making my muscles scream out. All it does is make me sweat and knock my tension down by half a notch.

Seeing your father breaking is not a sight I'd wish upon anyone.

But I can't agree to marry Gabrielle. *I can't.*

I roar as I pound the bag with all my force, sweat pouring down my naked chest. *Fuck, fuck, fuck!* My internal cursing matches each hit until I'm gasping for air. I yank the gloves off and throw them on the floor, picking up my towel and dragging it down my face.

My phone dances along the bench next to me, vibrating with an incoming call. I snatch it up, answering breathlessly.

"Hi."

"Is it a good time?" She sounds different. Not like herself. Like her fire's been doused. "I don't want to inter—"

"Mads? What's wrong?"

She's silent for a beat, and I sit on the bench, throwing my soaked towel over one shoulder as I wait for her to speak.

"I-I wanted to thank you. For pushing for me to be told the truth about Dad."

I look at the floor.

"I'm sorry it took this long. I thought you'd known for years. If I'd known you didn't, I'd have... Fuck, I don't know," I admit, unsure what else to say.

She sighs.

"I get why Drew didn't want to tell you," I add softly. "He didn't want to wreck that relationship with your dad that you have. You only get one father."

"I know, and I understand that." Heaviness drags her voice down, and I wish she was here so I could see her face. Hold her. Do something. "I wish I'd been told, though. And I know you don't lie," she murmurs. "Which means you must have thought my reason for hating you was some weird jealousy thing because you're unfairly good-looking and disgustingly rich."

"I'd say unfairly *great* looking and soon to be broke, but—"

"Soon to be broke?"

She still doesn't know the whole story. Drew might be as mad as hell at me, but he's still the best friend I could ask for. Everything I've told him about Dad and the business has stayed with him. Sealed in a vault constructed from years of friendship. All Maddy knows is that Dad wants a company merger. It's what I told her in Italy.

"It's why I was meeting Gabrielle," I confess.

"Your dad still wants you to marry for the future of the company?"

"He does," I admit, nausea turning my stomach over. "But it's worse than I thought before I left. He's going to lose everything, Mads. The whole business could be at risk if we don't bail ourselves out soon."

"Oh my God, Logan..." The genuine concern in her voice brings warmth to my chest like a blanket.

"That's why he wanted..." I swallow thickly. "Gabrielle's dad, Spencer, said he'd help us. But it's not happening. I'm going to find another way."

Maddy's silent for a few seconds and I'm aching to ask her what she's thinking. But I know she'll be processing. She'll have her brows pulled together with that deep line between them. Despite the direness of our conversation, I smile at the thought.

"If you marry her, then the business is safe?"

"I'm not marrying her."

"But if you did? That's what your dad's asking of you, right?"

"I'm not—"

"What did Gabrielle say when you met with her? And remember, you don't lie," she whispers.

I run a hand around my chin with a low groan. "She wants to make her dad happy."

"She wants to marry you?" The soft intake of breath accompanying Maddy's voice is like a beacon of light in the darkness I'm in. *She hates the idea.* And something about that does more to calm the swirling chaos on my head than the last forty minutes pounding a punch bag has.

She's jealous. She doesn't want to forget we ever happened.

"It's irrelevant. I'm not marrying her. If there was even a second that I ever considered it, then you and I... I'd *never* have touched you, Mads. Can't you see that? That wouldn't be fair on anyone."

"She wants to marry you," she repeats, ignoring me.

"It's not fucking happening," I snap. "*Never.* So forget about it." I lower my voice, cursing myself internally for losing my shit.

"Last night, Drew said you asked Eve to send me to Italy," she whispers, breaking the silence. "Why?"

"Because you're an incredible writer, and you deserved the opportunity."

"And it wasn't because you'd heard me tell Drew a million times how I wanted the chance at a full feature?"

Her voice is quiet, and something tightens in my chest from hearing her doubt herself.

"You were the right choice. You've earned your chance all the years you've worked there. Don't question your abilities. Eve was going to pick you anyway. I just nudged her to decide faster, that's all."

"Uh-huh," she murmurs disbelievingly.

"Although I'm not sure you'll have an article to write now." I rotate my head, cracking my neck. "Vex might not happen. Not if we don't have a company to run it."

"It's serious, isn't it?"

I stare across the empty gym and for the first time ever I'm drowning in the emptiness of my giant house. I've never been bothered by living alone before, until now.

"Dad's still holding on to the business by a thread. But I swear I've never seen him like this before. He's... It's frightening. He looks like he could cause himself a stress-induced heart attack any second and drop dead."

"My god, Logan... What can I do to help?"

"Nothing, Mads. I'll fix it. I told him I'll find a way. Vex can bring in more than the rest of the business. It just needs to go ahead. I can't lose it. It's the only chance I've got."

There is a way. I just need to find it.

"And it's your dream," Maddy adds.

"Yeah. But that's not what matters right now."

There's a long silence as we listen to each other breathe, the comfort of knowing the other is there enough to keep the overwhelming urge to give up from winning.

"I'm so sorry, Logan," Maddy whispers. "All these years, I've been so wrong, so—"

"It's done. Don't think about it again."

I can't bear to hear her apologize to me. I was still a shit to her, something I'm beginning to understand from her point of view. But it's the lack of fire in her voice that ruins me the most. She's always been ready to fight me. Maddy without fire is like the earth without air. *Inconceivable.*

She scoffs. "How can you say that? I've been so unfair to you. I've been so *rude* to you. Over and over."

"Nah, you just kept me on my toes," I say, desperate to lighten a suffocating conversation.

"Don't try and make this any less tragic than it already is, Logan."

"Tragic? This isn't the opera, Smiles."

Her breath catches. "Maybe it should be. I can play Butterfly, and you can be Pinkerton."

"The guy who marries someone else?" My heart seizes in my chest as I use my free hand to rub my dripping hair with the towel. "I told you. I'm not—"

"Maybe you should. Gabrielle's wonderful. She's kind and smart. You look good together. And she's never told you she hates you. Never blamed you and buried her head in the sand, too *fucking* stubborn to see what's real. You'll save the business for your father. For your family."

"She's not you."

"Even better. You'll be happier."

I shake my head, tension creasing my brow. "That's bullshit."

"The universe never planned us, Logan. We were just—"

"Just what?" Anger swirls like a tornado inside me. I've heard her say we were a mistake so many times now. *She's wrong.*

"Something short and sweet, but not forever." Regret pours from her voice. "Everything comes to an end one day."

I'm unable to form the words I so desperately want to tell her. Because no matter what I say or do, she'll always push me away. Always deny what this is between us. I'm used to fighting for what I want. But I've always known I'd win. The dread balling in my gut and making sweat slide down my spine tells me this might be the first time I don't.

"Just..." She sighs like she's being crushed slowly, every last hint of breath being forced from her body. "... think about it. Think about your family. And what you deserve."

"I don't need to think about—"

"Promise me."

She's crying. The sound of it fucking rips my heart in two.

"Smiles," I choke. *Don't cry, baby.*

"Promise me," she urges. "Really think about what you deserve, Logan. Because it's more than what I can give you. It's more than what I've ever given you."

"Mads?"

"Bye, Logan."

The line goes dead.

She's gone.

Chapter 28
Logan

TALKING TO MADDY, HEARING her so despondent, has set something in motion inside me. I'm not giving up. I've got new ideas to run past Dad. I've been looking at the accounts, finding places we can reduce costs, stripping everything back as much as I can.

There *will* be another way. I just need more time to figure it out.

"What the fuck?" I stare out the windshield at the giant back loader that's blocking my parent's driveway as I pull up in my car. I roll down my window and stick my head out. "What's going on?"

A guy in cargo pants and a logoed polo shirt standing next to the vehicle looks up from his clipboard. "Won't be much longer, then we'll be on our way."

I jump out of my Aston Martin, leaving the door wide open as I crunch over the gravel toward him.

"I asked what's going on?" I stare past him to where a man in a matching polo is at the rear of the loader waving one arm in the air. Another guy drives Dad's Maclaren up onto the back of the truck, following his directions.

"Business with Mr. Rich," clipboard man says, tucking his pen behind his ear as he holds an arm out and points into the garages. "And the others," he calls to his colleagues. "We're taking the lot."

"I'm his son," I say as a guy jumps into another car and the engine purrs to life.

"Logan Rich?" Clipboard man says.

"Yes," I hiss, taking in the sight of Dad's entire collection of super cars get rounded up. He loves these cars. I grimace as one of the guys drives one too hard and gravel flies up into its paintwork.

"Is that a Vulcan?"

I follow clipboard man's eyes to my car. "Yeah, why?"

He turns back to his clipboard, flicking through the sheets of paper attached to it. "It in your name or the business's?"

"Mine."

He sniffs as though he couldn't care either way whether he's stealing another thing from us today or not. This is a job to him. But this is Dad's livelihood, Mum and Dad's things.

"It's not on the list," he says without emotion. "Think you can move it so we can get the truck out?"

I stare at him, but he just looks back at me patiently like he gets this all the time. He probably does. I imagine you need a thick skin to do his job.

"Fine," I concede, stomping back over to my car and pulling it out of the way. I get back out and stride toward the house as the man calls "thank you" after me.

"They're taking the cars," I shout as I walk straight in through the open front door.

A woman I've never seen before walks through the hallway dressed in a suit without even glancing in my direction.

"Who the fuck are you?" I ask as I follow her down the hall. We pass another man in a suit walking past with a box in his arms. "What the fuck's that?" I grab the box from him, my heart racing as I look inside at my mother's jewelry boxes.

"We have the necessary paperwork. The homeowners know we're here," the man replies politely before taking the box out of my hands and walking toward the front door.

I stumble along the hallway.

"Dad? Mum?"

"In here, son," Dad calls from the kitchen. I round the corner, tugging at my shirt collar as fire claws at my neck.

"Who the fuck are all these people?"

Mum looks up as I enter, her eyes flicking to another man in a suit. It's like they've infiltrated every part of the house. I don't care if I'm being rude. This isn't their house. Why the hell are they here?

"They're here to seize assets." Dad runs a hand over his jaw as Mum watches the suited man go through a list on a similar clipboard to the man outside with the truck.

"I thought you had enough for a few more weeks?"

Ice scatters up my spine as the woman returns with some of Mum's designer scarves draped over her arm. She shows them to clipboard man, and he nods in approval. Dad sees it too and his eyes pinch at the corners as he looks away.

"I have enough to pay the staff and keep the business afloat. But not enough to pay back all our loans." He blinks, the whites of his eyes yellow. "The cars, this house... everything in it"—he swallows hard—"they're all listed under the business. I did it years ago to fund a big investment. I've already sold the other properties we have. But this house..." Dad scrubs a hand over his face. "Nothing is safe... they can take anything they want."

"That's fucking bullshit!" I roar.

The suits ignore us, going about their business as if we aren't even here.

"Logan," Mum tuts. But her eyes dart side to side, panicked as the people tread through her house, touching her things, destroying her privacy.

"No, Mum. It is. We're going to sort this out. I'm going to find a way." I was determined before, but now I'm deadly serious. My parents will not have everything ripped away in front of their eyes in a fucking spectacle like this.

"I've got a six-carat diamond engagement ring here on the list," suited man says from across the kitchen. He looks at Mum.

"Right, right. Okay." She nods, fumbling with the ring on her finger as her hand shakes. The man in the suit watches her struggling. "Damn it, I can't—" She pulls at the ring.

"Now, just wait a minute," Dad yells, his face turning red. "That's her engagement ring. You can't take that."

"I'm afraid we can, Mr. Rich," the man replies. "We have everything else on the list. This is the last item."

I take my keys from my pocket and pull the Vulcan one off the keyring. "Here." I hold it out to the man. "Take this. It'll more than cover the ring."

"I can't accept that, sir. It needs to be the asset listed here." He taps his pen against the papers on his clip-board.

"Fuck's sake," I mutter, shoving the key back into my pocket. "What else do you have on there? Surely there's something else you can take?" I look over at my mother who's still twisting the ring on her finger, trying to get it to budge.

"After this, it's the house."

"No, we don't have anywhere else to go," Mum cries.

"But, Viv, it's your engagement ring," Dad says.

"I don't care. This is our home." She blinks back tears. "Besides, it's not the ring you proposed with."

Dad meets my eyes. The look in his makes my stomach bottom out. It's killing him seeing this happen to her.

But Mum's right. The giant custom-made ring stuck on her finger isn't the small, humble one Dad proposed with. He had no money back then.

"Here." I walk over to Mum and take her hand. I lead her to the sink where I hold her hand in mine and rub some soap over her finger. I gently work it around the ring and then slide it from her finger as she squeezes her eyes shut. I hand the ring to the suited man, and he takes it, covered in soap, without saying a word.

"You done now?" Dad scowls at him.

The man looks over his list a final time and nods. "We are. We'll show ourselves out."

Dad grunts as he leaves.

I wrap an arm around Mum as she sniffs.

"They're just things." Her voice trembles. "It's having people here in our house that I find upsetting. Not that the things are gone. We're all okay, that's the main thing."

I meet Dad's eyes over her head, and I can see from one look at him that he's thinking the same as me. They might only be things. But they're their things. Things they've worked hard for. Things that took them years to build.

"We can't lose the house too," Dad says, looking at Mum. She's holding back tears and scrubbing her hands vigorously like she can wash away the sick feeling that's no doubt crashed over her like it has me. Like it has Dad. "Not the house," he mumbles as he takes over from me and places his arm around her.

"You won't have to," I promise, swallowing down the razorblades in my throat as Mum scrubs harder until a thin line of red globules appear around her knuckle. "I'll do whatever it takes, Dad. I'll do whatever is necessary."

His eyes water as he looks at me. It's enough to tell me he understands.

This is my family, and the Riches always find a way. No matter whether they like what that way looks like or not.

I'll do whatever I have to.

Chapter 29
Maddy

I'T'S BEEN FIVE DAYS since Chloe came to my door, and I cried in her arms. Five days since I discovered the truth that Dad forced Drew away years ago. Five days since I called Logan and he told me his family will lose everything if he doesn't marry Gabrielle. And five days since I told him he should marry her. Because I don't deserve him.

That's the hard truth.

Five days feels like five decades when you don't hear from the one person whose voice you so desperately need to hear. But I can't call him. It's not fair.

Drew said Logan's been pulling all-nighters, desperately seeking a solution. Debt recovery agents turned up at his parents' house and cleared it out. He's been reeling ever since. My heart is breaking for him, wishing I could speak to him. But I'll only confuse things if I call. Distract him when he needs to focus. I need to take comfort from knowing that Drew, Dax, and Tanner have been keeping an eye on him and helping with what they can. One positive is that it's sped up Logan and Drew's truce. Drew hasn't mentioned me and Logan since.

All talk of it has been left in the past. Like it never happened.

"You sure he's doing okay?" I ask Drew as he digs around inside his toolbox in my kitchen.

"No. But he'll live." Drew pulls out a screwdriver, then pulls his phone from his back jean pocket as it buzzes. "Great, they're here."

"Who are?" I ask as he presses the button on my camera system to buzz them in.

"The boys."

I follow him to my front door.

"All right?" Drew tips his chin as he opens the door and Tanner and Dax file in dressed in paint splattered jeans and ripped t-shirts.

"What are you both doing here?" My stomach drops as Drew shuts the door and Logan doesn't appear. The four are usually together.

"Hey, Maddy." Tanner looks tired but smiles as he passes me. He goes straight into my hallway cupboard where the fuse box is.

"Morning, Maddy." Dax nods, his tattooed arms flexing around the giant box he's carrying.

"You're only supposed to be helping me fix that door that keeps jamming. What's all this?"

"Logan's idea," Tanner calls from inside the cupboard.

"Call it a gift," Dax adds as he sets the box down and opens it. He begins pulling out wires and some round white discs.

Drew pulls a measuring tape from his back pocket. "I'll mark up in the bathroom, yeah?"

"Sounds like a plan," Tanner answers.

I scramble after Drew as he strides off humming to himself.

"Are you going to tell me what's going on?"

"Logan said we ought to do this when you were out so you don't ask questions."

"What is *this*?"

Drew starts marking up the wall in my bathroom with a pencil. "It's his way of saying sorry. He said he feels bad about you and me falling out after I found out about you two."

"We didn't fall out," I say as he continues making measurements and marks.

"I know. But he feels like an asshole about it, and he's bought all the kit for us to install, so..." Drew shrugs.

God, I want to punch him. My big brother is irritatingly vague sometimes. I swear he does it on purpose because he enjoys winding me up.

"And what kit is this exactly?"

"A built-in speaker system. So you can listen to your books and shit."

"Logan said that?" I freeze, my skin prickling.

Drew writes measurements on the paintwork. "Minus the 'and shit' part, but yeah, pretty much." He places his pencil behind his ear, narrowing his eyes as he assesses the wall. "He said it had to include the bathroom because you like to listen in the tub. Although don't fucking tell me how he knows that."

In the tub? Memories of his house in Rome and being pressed against him wet and naked assault my mind. That was before we'd ever kissed. Before we'd ever... Back when I still hated him.

"I can't believe Logan asked you guys to put this in my apartment for me."

My throat goes dry and I blink furiously as Drew turns to me.

His expression softens a touch. "I'm not going to lie, Maddy. I'm still fucking pissed about you two."

"There is no us. He's better off... Never mind." I shrug and bite my bottom lip.

He stares at me unblinking like he doesn't believe a word. "Well, whatever you want to call it, Logan's got enough shit going on right now, he doesn't need more. We talked, and we're good."

"You are?"

"We've got to be. Like I said, he doesn't need any more shit right now." Drew's tone takes on a hint of warning.

I nod. It's his way of saying his friend needs him so he's stepping up and pushing his anger aside. Drew's always been fiercely loyal to his friends. Yet, it still feels like he means me. Like I cause Logan shit every time I'm near him. Maybe that's true. He'd be better far, far away from me, the girl who judged and blamed him unfairly. It's been one big fuck up since the day we first met. We were just never meant to be.

"I can't believe how serious everything's getting with his dad and the business."

"Logan's on it. He'll find a way," Drew says as he steps back, admiring the preparation work he's drawn all over my walls.

I want to ask him what he means, to dig for any clues I can get. But I'm reluctant to do anything that he might later mention to Logan, or that could result in more questions about what happened between us. I don't think I can handle any more questions that I can't answer right now.

"This shouldn't take long. If any walls or paintwork need re-touching, I'll get one of the team in to sort it next week for you," Drew says, slipping back into work mode.

"Um... Okay."

He strides past me, heading off to talk to Tanner and Dax.

I go to my bedroom and snatch up my phone. I've refrained for days, but now my fingers can't move fast enough, even if this is a bad idea.

Me: I don't know what to say. The sound system? It's so thoughtful, but I don't understand why you're the one apologizing.

My phone buzzes almost immediately and my heart clutches tightly in my chest at seeing his name light it up.

Logan: I like to see you smile. Isn't that reason enough?

Me: Not when I'm the one who was wrong.

Logan: It's all in the past.

Me: No. It should be me doing something for you, not the other way around.

Logan: You're wrong. But if it makes you feel better, then I'm sure you'll get the chance one day.

Me: Okay.

Logan: And, Smiles?

Me: Yeah.

Logan: You still haven't told me what happened with Frederica and Cameron.

My grip tightens on my phone. I haven't listened to that book he gave me on the flight back from Italy. I've been putting it off, and I'm not even sure why.

Me: I'll let you know.

Logan: Okay. I'm heading into another meeting. Say hi to the boys and go easy on them. It was my idea.

Me: Go easy? I'm not promising anything.

Logan: Just don't kill them… and happy listening, Smiles.

"I told you we are two souls made from the same star. Where you are light, I am dark. Opposites in every way, destined to come together, like magnets. It's inevitable, Frederica. There's never been any doubt for me. It's always been you."

I lift the glass of wine to my lips, leaning back and soaking in the hot water as the sounds of Frederica and Cameron's desperate words play through the speakers. I feel like I should finish it because I promised Logan I would. But I struggle every time I try. Because now I know without a doubt that it isn't my ears, or my earbuds, or anything else making Nate's voice sound different.

It's because he isn't *him*.

He isn't Logan.

I drop my head back and look at the ceiling. All I've known is hating him for something I thought was his fault when it wasn't. But I needed someone to blame because I was young and alone and hurting. Then Italy happened. Until then my feelings were safely locked in a box of hate and loathing. But now that box has been smashed to pieces. Exposed for the ugly lie it always was. And I'm left alone again. Pining after the man I don't deserve and can never have.

Even our families can't see us together. Drew's still mad, even though he's suppressed it for now. And Logan's family want him to marry Gabrielle in a union that will pave a bright future for all concerned. They couldn't be more perfect together. I saw the way she looked at him when she kissed him in the hotel bar. She sees what the world sees, an incredibly talented man with so much to give.

A man who will lose everything if I let him choose me.

That's if he even *wants* to choose me. I can't allow myself to imagine that scenario. He'd have nothing if he was with me. He'd lose his dream and ruin the relationship he has with his family.

I'd be his ruin.

My heart clenches. I dry my hand on the towel hanging over the side of the tub and pick up my phone, opening the app for the speaker system. I turn Nate's voice off and click through the files until I find what I'm looking for. I'll regret this, it'll only make me feel worse. But I'm doing it anyway. I *crave* it.

I take a slow breath and press play.

Logan's voice floats from the speaker as he talks in fluent Italian. I don't know what he's saying. Things about Vex. It doesn't matter. He could recite the periodic table and my body would still tingle from head to toe like it is now.

I take another sip of wine and slip my free hand beneath the water, inhaling sharply as my fingertips brush my swollen clit. A few words out of his mouth and I'm already aching for him. I squeeze my eyes shut as I slide my fingers over myself and imagine they're his. I rub myself, tilting my head to one side, exposing my neck, imagining his lips there, kissing, sucking, tasting, whispering words that turn me on so much.

My orgasm creeps up on me fast as Logan's voice fills my ears. My body jolts in the water, causing my glass to tilt in my hand. The wine is swallowed up by the water as it spills out. I murmur his name, my voice cracking as my cheeks burn beneath a wetness that's too salty to be bathwater.

I look at the speaker disc on the wall as he laughs. It's full and soothing. A direct contrast to the empty, painful tears spilling from my eyes.

Hearing the happiness in his voice as he talks about the project, about his dream, it's too much. I grab my phone and turn the audio off, then drop it onto the bathmat.

Silence engulfs the room.

He's so close to losing everything. It's not fair. None of it is fair.

My phone rings. I sit up in the water, hope making my stomach flutter. It could be Logan calling to say he's found a way to save the business. Something that means he won't lose his dream. I want him to have it. He deserves it and so much more.

Please.

I frown at the name on the screen before I answer.

"Nate?"

"Maddy? How are you?"

"I'm good. And you?"

"Glad to hear it. I'm great. I wanted to ask if you're free to have dinner with me?"

Chapter 30
Maddy

Nate smiles at me across the table. We've met at an Italian restaurant. I didn't have the heart to ask if we could meet somewhere else. *Anywhere else.* It would have meant having to explain to him why anything Italian might result in me crying into my purse right now.

"Maddy, I'm glad you said yes to dinner."

"Of course. Thank you for asking me." I place my napkin down, unable to stomach another mouthful of Tiramisu. It's not his fault. He's been wonderful company, but I've struggled to keep my mind from wandering away from our conversation. Wandering to Logan. To what he's doing. How he's feeling. What's happening with work. Is he getting any closer to finding a magic solution. *Is he happy.*

Nate's eyes sparkle as he rests his hand on top of the table between us. "I just knew when we met before that we—"

A flash of familiar light brown over by the bar catches the corner of my eye and I tune out from Nate once more as I glance over, searching for the source. My heart rate picks up, ever hopeful. But I'm wrong. It's not him.

"I'm sorry." I turn back to Nate, my stomach dropping. "I thought I saw someone I knew." I take a sip of my wine, but it does nothing to ease the flutters in my stomach from thinking he was here. "Could you please excuse me? I'm going to go to the ladies' room."

I stand and pick up my purse, then weave through the tables filled with couples on dates. The restaurant is beautiful. Intimate and romantic. Each white linen tablecloth is set with a single rose and candle. There's soft music playing and twinkling fairy lights strung around. They remind me of the starry night sky in the open foyer of Logan's house. That night together on the island was... I inhale deeply. I can't think about it. About what he said. *"If this is hate, then I never need to fall in love."*

I scan the bar area as I pass. But he's not there. My stomach sinks again as I leave the main room and push through the door that leads to the ladies' room.

"You enjoying your date, Smiles?"

I turn, the air leaving my lungs as I see his face.

"Logan." I rush toward him, then stop short.

The dark circles and dullness of his skin make my heart heavy. He's under so much stress. I want to reach for him. But I can't move.

His eyes roam over my face before he smiles softly. "You look beautiful."

"It's not... We're—"

"You don't have to explain, Mads. I get it." His tired eyes crease at the corners.

"Oh."

My throat burns. Does the idea of me being on a date with Nate not bother him? I search his green eyes for answers, but the swell of emotion in my chest that looking into them evokes becomes overwhelming, and I drop my gaze to his tie instead. He's wearing a light gray suit and silver tie tonight. It doesn't matter what color it is; he always looks good. Confident and in control. Ready to take on the world. Even if his eyes tell a different story tonight. One of late meetings, lack of sleep, and immense pressure at trying to save something so dear to him and his family.

"Who are you here with?"

"My parents, and Gabrielle and her father."

"Oh."

"Are you happy?" He steps closer and my lips part as heat flares across the back of my neck.

"What do you mean?"

His eyes darken as his voice lowers. "Do you feel like you can't breathe when you look at him?"

"W-what?"

"Does he make you smile? In here?" He brushes the warm pads of his fingers over my bare skin, above the low neckline of my dress, directly above my heart.

I shiver.

"That's what you do to me." His gaze intensifies until it's blinding, pinning me in place.

"Logan—"

"No, Mads. Let me say it." He steps closer, lifting his hand to my chin and tilting it up between his thumb and forefinger until our lips are inches apart. His breath dusts mine as he parts his lips. "You need to fucking hear it," he whispers.

"I can't," I choke.

I haven't seen him in days, and it's done nothing to lessen my pull to him. But what good will giving in do? I was never meant to be with him, and he was never meant to be with me. It's not our path. Recent events have proved that. We were doomed before we began.

He searches my eyes for something. Something I can't give him. So I fight to keep it locked away inside. Where it can't cause harm.

He slides his thumb over my bottom lip, his eyes tracking its movement, and I suck in a sharp breath, goosebumps scattering up my spine. It would be so easy to sink into him. To be selfish.

"I—"

"Tell me about work," I say, using all my strength to step back, breaking contact with him.

Tell me you've found a way. Tell me it's all going to be okay.

Something flashes in his eyes, making my gut churn in regret. But then he blinks, and it's gone.

"I'm working on Spencer." He runs a hand down his chin, his shoulders dropping.

It tells me all I need to know. *He's getting nowhere.*

I swallow the aching lump in my throat as he continues.

"If I can get him to agree to work on Vex with me without..."

Without marrying Gabrielle.

"Vex will bring in enough to bail out the business. I just need to get it started," he says. "We've had to tighten things... We've..." He takes a deep breath. "The business doesn't have the means to make it happen right now. I need Spencer. Once he agrees to work together, it'll all be fine. I've got the investors, I've..."

I nod, lowering my eyes to his tie again. The weariness in his voice tells me that even he is starting to doubt it will ever work.

"That's good. You're close then?" I say, unable to speak the truth that's thrown itself between us like a thunderbolt. *Hope has never been so far away.*

"Yeah."

I look into his eyes. They're shining as he sweeps his gaze over my face slowly.

I curl my fingers tightly around my purse. "I should get back. Nate's waiting. And everyone is probably wondering where you are."

I pray he walks away before my legs give out beneath me. My chest tightens as he looks at me, his lips pressed into a firm line. After what feels like a lifetime, they curl into a faint smile.

"Enjoy the rest of your evening, Smiles."

He walks past me and back into the restaurant, leaving the scent of his fresh aftershave and warm skin lingering behind him. It's only once he's gone that I realize I haven't breathed properly. I suck in a shuddering breath as I stumble into the ladies' room and lean back against the wall. I take a few minutes to compose myself and splash some cold water on my face before I walk back into the main room and back to our table.

Nate stands, waiting for me to sit so he can push my chair in for me. I look to the back of the room where a tinkling laugh has broken out. Gabrielle is sitting, like a vision, blonde hair shining, eyes lit up as she looks across the table at Logan. He doesn't make eye contact with me. His full attention is on Gabrielle, his face relaxed as he smiles at whatever story she's telling.

"Are you okay? You don't look well."

"Um. I'm—"

Nate's eyes narrow with concern. "Let me sort out the bill and I'll take you home."

I nod gratefully, fighting from looking over at their table again. Logan says he's working on Spencer. But it doesn't change the fact that they all look perfect together. Logan and his parents, Gabrielle, and Spencer. They all just... fit.

Nate pays for dinner, and I thank him as he helps me into my coat. I keep my eyes firmly fixed on his, too scared of what they might see if I let them wander. He places his hand on my lower back, keeping his body close to mine as he leads me from the restaurant carefully, probably worried I will pass out. I lean into him a little, needing the support as anxiety weaves its way through my body.

He doesn't try and draw me into a conversation as he drives me home. He glances at me with concern a couple of times, but the closer we get to my apartment, the better I begin to feel. I have space. Distance. And it allows me the clarity to see tonight for what it was. A sign of what I must do.

I thank Nate profusely as he walks me to my door. It takes a couple of assurances that I'm fine before he wishes me good night. As he drives away, the rain starts.

What do they say about rain? That it's cleansing? A symbol of new beginnings? Of re-birth?

After what I've seen tonight, it couldn't be more fitting.

Chapter 31
Logan

I LEAVE THE RESTAURANT more worked up than I've been all week.

She was there. With him. On a fucking date?

I drop the gear down in my Vulcan and step on the gas. The engine purrs and I speed toward my house.

Dinner was a disaster. Spencer's a tough old bastard. Dad's right. He's a businessman who knows what he wants, and he isn't backing down. I'm getting nowhere. My only hope now is that the extra investment I got from Sterling is enough to push Vex through without Spencer's involvement. But I've looked at the figures a hundred times and they tell me it won't work. But I'll check them again and again. A thousand times, a fucking million times if that's what it takes. If I can get this project started without Spencer, then it could solve all our problems. We won't need a merger. Or a sham marriage.

Gabrielle's been uncharacteristically quiet about the whole thing since our meeting in the hotel. I can't believe that she wants this either. She's doing it for Spencer. A loyalty which I admire and understand. But even good intentions can't make this situation any less fucked up than it is.

My jaw clenches as my wipers turn on, swiping away the fast-falling drops of rain. I didn't expect to see Maddy tonight. And I didn't expect Nate to wrap his arm around her as they left. A protective gesture. One that had my blood boiling and wanting me to storm across the room and wrench his fingers from his hand, one by one.

I flex my hands around the steering wheel, then pump the brakes, turning sharply into an empty side road and swinging the car in a one-eighty before putting it back into gear and racing in the opposite direction, one destination in mind.

My Bluetooth chimes with an incoming call. I hit answer, hiding the swelling dread in my gut as one of the investors for project Vex connects through.

"Mr. Rich?"

"Mr. Drayton, what can I do for you?"

My voice remains smooth and calm throughout our conversation. And for the investor who calls right after him. And the one after that.

It stays smooth and calm the entire time, masking the inferno raging inside me as I speed toward my destination in the hammering rain.

"I'm not leaving until you talk to me," I yell at the panel, growing more soaked by the second.

There's a click from the intercom and Maddy's voice breaks through the dark night air.

"What are you doing?" she hisses.

She sounds more like herself than she did in the restaurant. Fired up. Ready to fight.

"Do you have company?" I grit.

"What?"

"Are you fucking alone?" I tighten my hand into a fist where it's resting up against the wall, to prevent me from punching the door in.

I can't believe how stupid I've been. She's been listening to his books. I even bought her an advanced copy of his fucking audio to listen to. Does she listen to him in the bath still? In bed? Does she even need to anymore? Now that she has the real thing. Does she ask him to say the things to her he says in the books?

Does she come harder for him hearing his voice in her ear than she does for me?

"I swear to God, Mads."

I thought I was fine seeing her there with him. I acted fine. I didn't want to cause a scene for her, upset her. But then his hands were on her. *His hands. On her.*

"What do you think?" she snaps. "Of course I'm alone."

The door unlocks and I barge through, slamming it back against the wall as I rush straight to her apartment door. She's flung it open in readiness for me, her eyes blazing as she glares at my dripping form on her doorstep.

"What is it? You want white picket fences and missionary sex for the rest of your life? Because he sure looks the type."

"What?" Confusion clouds her face as I step inside, throwing the door shut behind me and backing her up against the hallway wall, panting with barely contained anger.

"With him? *Nate.*" I spit out his name like it's burning my tongue.

"He—"

"He can't give you what you need, what you want."

I'm so close that I'm dripping water onto her thin cotton tank top and the shorts she's wearing. One drop lands and makes the material darken so the tight, light brown bud of her nipple shows through. I clench my jaw to stop from biting it. To show her she's mine. I'd mark her all over her perfect body to show her if I could. She is mine. As much as she fights it.

"You don't know what I want." She looks into my eyes.

"I know you better than you think." I plant my palms against the wall either side of her head, caging her in as I press against her, my heart hammering against my ribs.

"It doesn't matter." Her eyes tighten at the corners. "We need to be serious. This... Us... It can't happen anymore. You know that, right? You must know that!"

"We need to be *serious?*" I hiss, inching closer until my lips are almost grazing hers. My wet thumb drops to her face, tracing over her cheeks.

"Yes," she breathes.

"I am serious. I am seriously fucking wrecked because of you."

A muffled sob escapes her throat. "No."

"Yes... Fuck. Yes." I relish the way her body shivers against mine. "You make my blood boil. You... Fuck, you think *I'm* infuriating? You're making me lose my goddamn mind," I growl. "Tell me you don't want him. Tell me you want me. Admit it. For once, just fucking admit it."

She pants, her body continuing to tremble where it's trapped between me and the wall. Her clothes are soaking up the rainwater from mine, making us stick together. Between that and my arms either side of her, she's sealed in with no escape.

"Did he kiss you goodnight?" Before she can answer, I tilt my head, catching her cheek with my lips. "Here?" I drop to her neck, and she draws in a breath. "Here?" I plant another kiss against her hot skin. "Or here?" I drop to her shoulder. "Or maybe here?" I kiss the dip between her collar bones. "Tell me where he fucking kissed you, Mads, because I'm going to erase every single one until you only feel my lips on you."

"He didn't," she utters, her words dying as I lift my face back to hers.

"Did you want him to?"

She presses her lips together.

"Did you want him to?" I snap.

"No."

"Why not?"

"Logan—"

"Why the fuck not?"

"Because he's not you," she chokes. "He's not you."

The breath leaves my lungs as she's finally honest with me. I crash my lips over hers, stealing the air from her lungs to feed mine. I kiss her hard. Harder than I ever have before, like I need to climb inside her and mark her with my tongue from the inside out to prove my point.

She is mine.

"Say it again." I palm her tits roughly through the damp material. Maddy's mouth drops open, and she murmurs something that sends even more blood racing to my throbbing dick. "Louder."

"He's not you," she whispers.

I pinch her nipples before pushing her top up and dropping my head to suck one.

"Louder."

"He's not you," she says again, her voice pitching as I graze her with my teeth.

"Fucking louder!"

"He's not you," she cries as I suck hard.

"No, he's fucking not." I move to suck the other side, groaning deeply as she sinks her hands into my hair and tugs.

She grabs the shoulders of my soaking jacket and pushes it down my arms. I straighten and rip it off, throwing it to the floor. I dive in to kiss her lips, groaning into her mouth as I pull my wet shirt from my pants, and she rips my belt free from the buckle.

"He's not you," she repeats as I tear my shirt off and then rid myself of the rest of my clothes, my lips diving back onto hers every available second.

I peel her wet tank up over her head and throw it onto the floor.

"He's not you," she moans as I push my hand down the front of her shorts and inside her panties.

A deep groan vibrates in my chest as I'm met with wetness, welcoming me like it's been screaming out to be spread over my fingers.

"That's right." I force her shorts and panties over her hips and hold her waist as they fall to the ground. Then I lift her, not even waiting until her legs are around my waist before I'm burying myself deep inside her, pushing her back against the wall with force. "He isn't fucking me," I growl as my balls meet her body.

She drops her head back, a satisfied moan breaking free of her lips as I pull back and then thrust inside her again.

"Bedroom," she gasps.

I pull out and hold her tight, and she snakes her arms around my neck as I carry her to her room. She's sucking on my neck, her nipples pressed tightly against my chest as my cock throbs.

"How do you want—?"

"I don't care, just fuck me," she groans into my neck.

I set us down on the bed, breaking her lips away from my neck. "Feet over my shoulders."

She does it without a word, sliding her legs over my arms, gasping as I grab her calves and force them up near my ears.

"Don't take your eyes off mine. I want to see you come apart for me. I want you to understand that you can't fucking ignore this any longer."

The rage I felt earlier has turned into pure liquid fire, heating my veins with urgency. Urgency to hear my name on her lips as she comes for me. *I need it.*

She quivers, but her eyes stay on mine as I line up and then plunge deep inside her. My wet hair drips onto her face and her mouth drops open as she cries out. It makes me move faster. Each gasp from her flushed, parted lips is like fuel to my body. Making it drive deeper inside hers.

I fuck her hard, pump after pump of all-consuming, body-hitting thrusts that make her tits bounce in the space between us.

"Logan." Her nails bite into my biceps.

I lean to kiss her, forcing her legs back and pushing my cock deeper. "Say my name again," I growl.

"God, Logan." Her lips tremble against mine.

"You ready to come for me, *baby?*" I groan, biting her bottom lip.

She moans loudly.

I thrust into her hard a few more times.

"You need me to give it to you?" I flex my cock inside her. She responds by clenching around me.

"Fuck," I groan, thrusting deep again. "I'm going to come so hard inside you."

"Yeah?" she pants.

"Fucking yes, baby." I dive into a kiss, sweeping my tongue past her lips as she whimpers.

"What are you waiting for?" she gasps as I slide in deep again, my balls pulling close to my body.

"I'm waiting for you to admit you're mine. Admit it... Because fuck, Mads. I'm yours. I've been yours since

Italy. Admit it." My jaw and neck clench as I fight to avoid spilling inside her. "I'm not giving it to you until you say it."

"Log—"

"Admit it!" I thrust hard, and she screams my name, her pussy beginning to pulse. "You're so close, tell me and you can have it. Stop fucking lying, Mads. I know you."

Her breath comes in short, sharp bursts as she screws her eyes up and then opens them again, her pupils dilating.

"I know you." I hold her eyes as she shudders beneath me.

"I know you do, and that's terrifying," she cries, her pussy gripping onto me like my cock's its lifeline.

My pace falters. "Baby."

She shakes her head. "Stop talking."

"You have no idea what I'd do for you. You're safe with me."

Her eyes shine and her fingers dig into my biceps, encouraging me to thrust hard again. I slide into her, spreading her wetness between us.

"Now fucking admit it," I growl a touch gentler as she moans.

"You know I do." She searches my eyes. "I do want you. I want you. All of you. Forever. I want *us*."

"Good girl." My voice cracks, my head feeling like it might explode as heat bursts from my balls and fire races up my dick, making my vision blur as I spill inside her.

"Good." *Thrust.* "Fucking." *Thrust.* "Girl."

My breath stalls in my throat in a pained growl as Maddy's eyelids flutter and she arches away from the bed, her body spasming around mine. I could live forever and never tire of seeing her do this. Seeing her come undone with pleasure, all set off by the feel of me inside her, the knowledge that I'm coming deep inside her. Nothing has ever been so fucking hot.

"Fuck, that feel good?" I watch her, my dick getting milked by her body. "That feel good, baby?" More cum races out of me, making the tip of my cock sear with heat as her eager body sucks it up.

"Y-yes." Her grip tightens on my arms as her orgasm rolls into another. "Logan."

"That's it. Say my name when you're coming on my cock."

She wriggles and squirms as I pin her to the bed.

"You're so good taking my cum like this. You know that?" I keep moving inside her, every muscle on high alert in my body as she comes around me, draining me of all that I have. "You've always taken it so well, ever since the first time I filled you up." The memory makes my balls send another load shooting up and out inside her as I groan in relief. I needed her so badly tonight. I needed this. To have her around me, under me. Any way I can. To have her with me.

"I want it," she whimpers. "I want you inside me all the time."

"Fuck, I'll be everywhere for you. I'll fill every sweet spot in your body you need me to, okay?" I reposition her legs around my waist so I can lean to kiss her as she rides the rest of her pulses out around me. I flex my cock, circling my hips and smiling against her lips as she gasps and then nods, unable to speak.

"I'll fill them every day. All fucking day. Mads. You know why? Because I—"

She pulls my face to hers, kissing away my words and I sink into her, soaking up every little whimper and sigh she makes as our bodies slow, until we're holding each other tight, neither wanting to let go. We kiss until our hearts slow in our chests, and I can no longer feel hers pounding against me.

"The rain tastes good on you." She runs her fingers through my wet hair as I gaze at her.

"You taste good on me." I hold myself up on my elbows and run the backs of my knuckles down one of her cheeks.

"Why did you come here tonight? Was it just seeing me with Nate?"

"I want to be with you." I let my knuckles drift lower, along her jaw, following their path with my eyes.

"Did something change? Did you get somewhere with Spencer?" Something that looks like hope blooms in her eyes, and my soul feels like it's being ripped from my body.

"No, I didn't." I exhale slowly, tension rippling through my shoulders. "In fact, it's fucking worse. Some investors called me earlier. They're pulling out of Vex."

"What?" The dread in her voice makes nausea rise in my throat.

"They've heard rumors. It was only a matter of time. I expected it after what happened at the house."

I drop my lips to her neck, inhaling her scent as I kiss her silky skin. It's the only thing that can calm my racing heart as I consider the implications of losing the funding.

"It means I've got no fucking chance of talking Spencer into helping now." I breathe in her scent more, kissing her again. "Unless I can get some more funding. Then maybe I can persuade him to add the rest himself. But it's a long shot. He's not going to be easy to convince. Not if he isn't getting everything he wants."

"Gabrielle?" Maddy whispers.

"Grandkids," I admit. I squeeze my eyes closed and press my face against her neck, shielding myself from the look on her face as she fails to hide her sharp inhale of air.

"That's what this is about? You're going to have a family with her?"

I draw back, steeling myself for the look in her eyes. But nothing can prepare me for the pain in them. It's like a dagger being twisted right through my heart.

"Of course not. There's never been a second I've even considered it. Stop thinking about it." I lean down to kiss her, but she turns her head to the side.

"Mads?"

"Don't." Her lips twist into a tight line.

I'm still inside her and she can't stand to look at me.

"Don't do this. Not again. You said you want this." Despair creeps into my voice as she slips further away. The wall behind her eyes is going back up and I can't do a fucking thing to stop it. "You said you want *us*."

"Not like this," she cries. "Not like this."

She pushes my chest. As much as I want to fight against it, keep her beneath me so she talks to me, I can't. But sliding free of her body and watching as she scrambles away and runs to her drawers to grab a T-shirt is like watching a horrific scene play out in front of me. One I should have known was coming, should have prevented.

One that was always going to be inevitable, no matter how much I wish it weren't.

"What does it matter?" I struggle not to shout as I turn to face her, naked. I get up from the bed and stride toward her. "I'm never going to marry her. I told you that. I don't love her."

"You'll lose everything." Her eyes shine as they fill with tears.

She retreats as I step closer.

"You're killing me, Mads," I whisper, staring at her as a tear breaks free and rolls down her cheek. "I want to be with you."

"We can't."

I can barely hear her because her voice is so quiet.

"We can."

"We were never meant to be."

"Stop."

"No."

A second tear joins her first as she drops her chin to her chest. Her dark curls flow around her shoulders, one falling over her cheek. I reach forward to brush it away, and she flinches. The tiny movement makes my heart crack down the center.

"How can you say that? You and I make more sense than anything. Nothing feels this good if it isn't right. And if you're worried about Drew, don't be. He wants you to be happy. He'll accept it because I'll treat you like a fucking Goddess, Mads."

She makes a small, muffled sound and it's like nails are clawing at my chest, tearing their way to my heart as she gives in and cries with shaking shoulders.

"That's not what worries me. It's... We were never meant to happen, Logan. You know that."

"That's your head talking, Mads. And it's wrong. You're hearing it. But are you listening? To what's in here?" I place my palm over her chest.

"It's not real," she utters. But she doesn't move away from my touch.

"It's never been more fucking real." *How can she not see?*

"With me, you'd have nothing. The business, the—"

"I don't care."

"You should. You're Logan Rich."

"And you know what? Since getting back from Italy, I've never felt so fucking poor. All these days and nights without you, fighting so hard to keep one thing, while knowing I'm losing another."

"With me, you'd lose it all. You'd be financially ruined."

"You think money matters to me more than you?"

She steps back again and my hand slides from her chest. "This is your family. It's not just you to think about. They'll lose everything too. Can you live with yourself knowing that? You'll resent me one day. Because without me, you could have saved it all."

334

I force down the burning lump in my windpipe. She's wrong. I could never resent her. But she's also right. My family will lose everything if I can't find another way. But that doesn't mean what she's doing is right.

"Don't do this."

"Tell Gabrielle you'll marry her," she whispers.

"What? No."

She puts her fingers over my lips and presses a kiss to the back of them while they're between us like a barrier. Her watery eyes are glistening with a million broken-hearted, unspoken words.

"Please, Logan. I want you to be okay. I want you to live your dream. For Vex to work. I..." Her voice cracks. "Tell Gabrielle. You like her. You'll love her one day too. And you'll love the beautiful children you'll both have. I don't deserve you, Logan."

I grab her wrist and pull her hand away to plead with her to stop. To tell her she's fucking crazy. But the finality in her eyes makes my stomach clench.

"Tell her. Please, Logan."

"I can't," I choke. "I'll do anything for you. But not this. Don't ask me to do this."

She looks into my eyes as I flail around for reasons to convince her to stop. For anything I can say that will talk sense into her.

"Marrying Gabrielle won't even work now. Not without the funding. If Vex is ruined, then Spencer's offer is gone. He can't fund it himself. The cost is huge."

"How much do you need?"

"What?"

"You said you can make Vex happen if you get some of the funds back, and that Spencer might be able to add the rest. How much have you lost? What do you need to make it work?"

"It's irrelevant, Mads. It's—"

"How much, Logan?"

I drag a hand around the back of my neck. "Twenty... Fifteen. I could do it with another fifteen million."

She nods gravely, then looks away. "You should go home."

"No. We need to talk about this. We need to—"

"*Please*, Logan," she whispers. "Don't make this any harder than it already is."

I freeze, staring at her as she refuses to meet my eyes. How did we go from grabbing at each other and pulling each other as deep into one another to this? How does anything so good and so right fall apart in a matter of minutes?

"Mads?"

"Please." She slaps her hand over her mouth and shakes her head hard, still not looking at me.

I search her face one last time, looking for a softening, a small sign that tells me I can convince her otherwise. But there's nothing. I won't get anywhere tonight. I know Maddy. I'll leave her to calm down. Come back tomorrow and talk to her then.

Although the sinking in my gut tells me that nothing will ever have settled. I could have lost more investors by the morning. Things could be worse than they are now. But no matter how bad they get nothing can compare to the gut-wrenching pain of seeing Maddy like this.

Hearing her tell me to go and have a life with someone else. Have a family with someone else. Someone who isn't her.

Nothing.

I trail my eyes over her tear-stained face one last time, but she won't meet my eyes. I go into the hallway, dragging on my cold, wet clothes. She doesn't come out after me.

I walk back into the bedroom and she's standing in the exact same spot. I go to her, closing my eyes as I wrap a hand around the back of her neck and press a kiss to her forehead.

"You think I'm going to be poor with no business? No money? You've got it all wrong."

She sucks in a breath as my lips leave her skin.

"You're only truly rich if you have something that no amount of money could ever buy, Smiles... And I don't have to tell you what my something is."

Then I turn and walk out.

Chapter 32
Maddy

I LET HIS CALL go to voicemail again. I've avoided him for two days. It's cowardly, I know. I've been staying with Chloe. Her housemate is on holiday with her boyfriend, so I've been using her room to lie low. Logan will only turn up at my apartment trying to talk otherwise. I can't let him. I can't let him talk me into something that will ruin him. He isn't looking at the bigger picture. I need to do that. He at least deserves that much from me after everything I've done.

My shoulders drop as I read through my article about Logan. Eve wanted scandal. She knew the way I felt about Logan. Maybe she even had an inkling about his father's business difficulties when she asked me to write it. Perhaps she expected me to write it like this. I'll never know.

A new email lands in my inbox and I close the document and open it.

"More book fairy love?" Chloe says as she appears behind me, leaning over my shoulder and reading the words on the screen.

"Yeah." I lean my chin in my hand as I read the email from a reader.

I usually gift people something from their wish list. But this girl commented on one of the videos I made. I'm not sure what it was about her comment, but she sounded like she needed something that would help lift her. Something that would give her hope that love can come again, even after tragedy. It's why I sent her one of my favorite romance stories where the heroine is a widow.

"Wow. You really changed things for her," Chloe says. "She says you've given her hope."

I read the email again. She says she was crying as she typed it.

"I didn't." I smile softly. "The story did."

Despite my heart feeling like a heavy weight since I last saw Logan, it lifts a little. The magic of words has brought something much needed to another person yet again.

Chloe shoves me on the shoulder. "Give yourself more credit."

"No." But I still smile at her as I say it because regardless of if I didn't do much, someone is still feeling better because of it. And that's worth smiling about.

"Fine." Chloe rolls her eyes dramatically. "Did you send it to Eve yet?"

"Just did." My smile falters.

Chloe's eyes widen. "How do you feel?"

"Like it's over now."

Chloe bends and wraps her arms around me in a hug. "In that case, lunch is on me. And I think we can even say that wine is acceptable today."

"I don't know," I groan.

Her face softens. She knows everything that's happened. It's all she's heard me speak about. She knows how fucked up my life is and how my sanity is holding on by a thread.

"Come on. You need it. You *deserve* it."

I let her pull me from my chair and link arms with me.

We go to one of our favorite bars across the road from the office and order paninis and a glass of Moscato each.

"You ever think there's something wrong with us?" Chloe muses after our wine arrives, lifting the glass to her lips to take a sip.

"All the time."

She laughs.

"Oh, you meant something specific?" I smile.

"Yes." She grins. "I mean, look at us. We're out for lunch and we've chosen to sit looking at the office."

I follow her gaze through the window. She's right. We have a prime location to see the office's main entrance from here.

"Can we pretend we're looking at the florist instead? Or is it too late to save ourselves from being pathetic losers?"

"It's too late." Chloe laughs.

We both gaze at the building across the street. In-Sync has one floor. The other floors house various companies, some are other publications run by the main corporation that owns the magazine, and others are independent. But the street level of the building has a florist in, *Cygnature Blooms*. They have the most incredible flowers. Not that I've ever been sent any from there.

"I think we need to own it," Chloe says.

She holds her fingers up in an 'L' shape against her forehead. I snort out a giggle and take a sip of my wine before looking around the inside of the bar at the rest of the London lunch crowd.

"You expecting a visitor?" Chloe asks, drawing my attention back to across the street.

"No." I frown as Logan walks out of Cygnature Blooms; his entire torso obscured by the giant bouquet of calla lilies in his arms.

An army of butterflies spring into action in my stomach and I place my wine glass down before I drop it. Logan pulls his phone from his suit pants and answers a call with a smile. He juggles the lilies in one arm as he speaks. I desperately wish I could lip read to see who he's talking to. To see who's got him smiling like that.

"They'll be for Gabrielle."

Chloe glances at me, her face turning sympathetic. "You don't know that."

I force my eyes away, studying my fork instead. "I hope that they are."

"Maddy—"

"They need to be." I press my lips together into a firm line. "I told him to marry her. Maybe he's finally started listening to me."

"I know you did, but..." Chloe sighs.

"I wish you'd stop looking at me like I'm losing my mind. This is the right decision. It's probably the most right decision I've ever made in my life," I huff. I might have told Logan we can never happen, but I still don't want to watch him happen with someone else in front of me.

"If it's so right, then why are you sleeping at my place and feeling like shit?"

"Who said I feel like shit?"

Chloe lifts her brows and takes another sip of wine. I exhale and move my attention back to my fork. *Calla lilies.* Like the Italian wedding we saw in Milan. That feels like a lifetime ago now.

"Has he gone yet?" I mutter.

"Not yet." Chloe's eyes narrow as she keeps her gaze fixed on a spot outside.

"Well, tell me when he does."

"Why?" she asks without turning her head.

"Just... Please."

"You should look at him, Maddy. He looks great."

"Not helping," I groan.

"I mean..." Chloe's eyes light up. "He looks really good, if a little stressed."

"I can't believe he's going through so much. I wish there was something I could do."

"Find an extra fifteen million?" Chloe suggests.

"Oh yeah. I'll just dig around the back of the couch. Get it in no time. Has he left yet?"

"No."

I'm tempted to look and see what's taking him so long, but the thought of seeing his face again is too hard. How can I look at him and not race across the street? Not run to him and beg him not to do it? Not to marry Gabrielle? Not to save his family business? How can I do that? After years of hating him and being so hurtful, how can I turn around and tell him to do something that will cause him pain?

I can't.

"Do you think Eve will give you another piece in the next issue? You've done Logan's story and Nate's interview now. You're on a roll."

I shrug as Chloe glances at me. But she quickly looks back out of the window again. Whatever Logan's doing must be interesting.

"I don't know. I hope so. The second interview at dinner the other night meant I was able to ask him some more personal questions in addition to the ones I asked at the hotel."

I chew on my bottom lip. Logan turned up in both places with Gabrielle when I was interviewing Nate. It's the universes fucked up way of making sure I saw him with Gabrielle and saw how perfect they could be together. Made sure that I do what's right for him now.

Nate called and asked for a second interview over dinner because he felt bad about cutting the first short. The thought that I used to lust over his voice seems ludicrous now. But maybe Logan needed to see me with

Nate to make him give up on us. I didn't fight hard to correct him when he thought we were on a date.

But then he came to my place and said he would erase any other kisses I'd ever had with his own.

I throw back the rest of my wine before I can get lost in self-pity at how messed up everything is. When I hated him, everything was simpler.

"You're safe now. He's gone." Chloe finally breaks her gaze from the street and looks at me cradling my empty wine glass in one hand and my phone in the other. "How is that any different than looking at the real thing?" she asks, her brow creasing as she looks at the screen and the picture of Logan and his dad that's on the news page I've brought up.

Shit. I didn't even realize what I was doing.

"I..." I look at the screen, reading the headline about their business and how it's rumored to be on the brink of collapse. My eyes blur and sickness coils in my stomach. I quickly bring up an image of Gabrielle from her LinkedIn profile and turn the screen toward Chloe.

"That's her?"

"Yeah."

"She's beautiful."

"Yeah."

"And thin."

I snort. "I know."

"But he told you he doesn't love her." Chloe sighs. "Fuck, girl. Why are you doing this to yourself?"

"I have to. I've spent so many years hating him and wishing he'd drop off the planet and leave me alone. I've been awful to him. And it wasn't even his fault."

"So... what? You punishing yourself is penance?"

"No." I close the browser and drop my phone into my purse. "He deserves better than someone who has unfairly blamed him. You get that, don't you?"

Chloe smiles at me sadly. "I get that you think that. But I don't agree." She lifts her shoulders when I shake my head at her. "I'm sorry, but I don't. I think you need to listen to what Logan wants."

"He'll lose everything," I whisper.

"Maybe he doesn't see it like that."

"I've never done anything good for him. Not once." My gut coils at the thought of the article on my laptop. "Not a single thing."

"You know what you need to do?"

"What?"

"Find fifteen million down the back of your sofa."

I try to smile. But all it does is make my jaw hurt.

We eat lunch, not talking about Logan again the entire time. Instead, Chloe talks about the piece she's working on, and I tell her about how Drew thinks Mum's going to forgive Dad. She's not confronted him about the affair and refuses to talk to either of us about it. She wants to ignore it. I can't blame her. I haven't confronted Dad about sending Drew away to the juvenile detention center either. Drew told me not to. He said it's not worth it.

I pay for lunch, despite Chloe's protests, and we head back to the office. The giant mound of white on my desk glows like a beacon the moment we step inside.

Chloe gives me a smug grin as she walks away toward her own desk. "Catch you later."

I drop into my seat and stare at the beautiful flowers, their scent filling the air with sweet perfume.

"These shouldn't be for me," I whisper as I reach for the envelope amongst the petals and pluck it free.

I take the thick manila card out and read the words.

You made me see the beauty of the story. Ours isn't over. Talk to me. L x

I blink back the burning in my eyes as I glance around the office. People are still at lunch. My chest relaxes knowing no one is close enough to see the air leaving my lungs as I read his words.

The sentimental asshole will make me cry at my desk. Chloe catches my eye from her desk, but I shake my head and give her a small smile, suggesting that I'm okay. Now I understand why Logan was taking so long. He was bringing these flowers up for me. *For me.* The wrong person.

I need him to let me go. To let us go.

I drop my head into my hands, rubbing at my temples.

"Maddy?" Eve calls from her office doorway. "Can I have a moment with you?"

"Sure." I follow her into her office, closing the door behind me.

I'm not even in my seat before she beams at me.

"The article you sent me is fantastic. Your best work yet. So raw. You didn't hold back. It digs deep into who he is. What he's going through. The way it reads is very personal."

Nausea swirls in my gut. "I've known Logan a long time. Writing about him and his family..." I drop my head, searching for the right words. "It's the story he wouldn't have expected me to tell. I hope he understands why I did."

"Well, it's certainly going to grab attention. Well done."

"Thank you."

To her, it's a story.

But to me, it's the final part of hating Logan Rich.

Now it's time to let go.

Chapter 33
Logan

"HIS SISTER STILL BUSTING your balls?" Dax asks me across the booth of the bar we've all met in after work.

"Fuck." Drew screws his face up. "Do not put my sister in the same sentence as his balls." He jabs a finger in my direction and Dax throws his hands up in mock surrender as Tanner smirks.

"And you can quit grinning, dick. Just wait until your daughter starts dating. Then you'll understand how this feels," he says to Tanner, making us all break out into laughter together.

Mine dies off quickly. As nice as it is seeing the guys for a drink, I'd rather be at Maddy's, talking to her. She hasn't been home since I was last there. I've checked. And she was out at lunch when I went to her office today. If I didn't have a meeting scheduled, I'd have waited for her. She got my flowers. Even if she won't answer my calls or texts, at least she got the message in the card.

Tanner looks between me and Drew. "It could be worse. At least you know where he lives if you want to kill him."

"Ha the fuck ha," Drew mutters.

Dax tips his empty glass at me, and I nod. He and Tanner head to the bar to get another round in.

"You know I'd do anything for her," I say.

"Doesn't change the fact you fucked my sister," Drew grunts. "Multiple times."

"I did."

"And lied about it."

"Yep."

His eyes slant over in my direction. "You look like shit."

"Thanks," I mutter, dragging my hands down over my face. I've barely slept the past two days.

"You're welcome." His lips curl the tiniest amount beneath his grimace.

I smirk in response.

"Because of the business? The funding?" He quirks a thick, dark brow at me.

My smirk falls. "It's shit. But no, that's not it."

"Do I want to fucking know?" he groans, tipping his head back and looking at the ceiling.

"Depends."

"On?"

"On whether you want to know just how fucked up I am over your sister."

He parts his lips.

"Yeah." I blow out a breath. "Guess not."

"Lay it on me." Drew straightens and brings his dark eyes to meet mine. "Just don't," his face twists, "just don't tell me anything like *that*. My sister's a virgin for the purpose of all our conversations. You hold her fucking hand and that's all, you get me?"

"Yeah, I get you."

"So, what's she done?"

"What makes you think it's her?"

Drew laughs, his face splitting into a wide-toothed grin. "This is Maddy we're talking about. Besides," his grin falters, "if it's not her and it's you, then I *will* have to come to your place and kill you like Tan said."

I snort, knowing there's both humor and seriousness in his words. "I'd never hurt her. You know that."

"Yeah." He crosses his arms. "Lucky for you I do."

"She told me we were never going to work. She wants me to marry Gabrielle."

Drew nods. "Because that way, you'll save the business?"

"Yeah. And she thinks she doesn't deserve me." I hang my head, the familiar pounding that's been in there for days rearing its ugly head again and sending a tightening across my brow that has me cursing.

"So you're telling me my sister told you to marry another woman because that way you won't lose the lot? I'm not going to mention the not deserving you part, because we fucking know my opinion on that."

"Yeah."

"Shit." He drops his head back with a groan.

"What?"

"It's worse than I fucking thought," he grumbles.

"Right? She's lost her fucking mind," I agree.

"Must have if she's in love with you."

"What?" The pounding in my head stops. I can't see, hear, or focus on anything other than Drew's eyes as he stares into mine.

He grunts, then slowly starts to chuckle, just as Tanner and Dax return with our drinks.

"What's so funny?" Tanner asks.

Dax passes me a drink, his eyes bouncing between me and Drew. He and Tanner are still on alert for Drew trying to kill me. But I think they understand that a friendship like ours that's seen so much can't be destroyed. Shaken, sure. But we're good. We will always be good. No matter what.

"Maddy told Logan to marry Gabrielle," Drew says.

They look at me without speaking. Tanner takes a drink of his whiskey, and Dax cracks his knuckles.

"She said he needs to save the business... and that she doesn't deserve him," Drew adds.

"Oh fuck." Tanner whistles.

"Shit," Dax says.

"Exactly." Drew takes his drink and knocks half back in one.

"She's in love with you," Tanner says.

"Yep," Dax agrees.

"What the fuck? How do you assholes know that?" I stare at them.

"Years of learning about women's minds from our beautiful better halves," Tanner quips, clinking his glass against Dax's.

I turn to Drew.

"Growing up with a sister who left girls' magazines lying around," he answers.

He narrows his eyes at all of us. "Don't fucking say anything. Best education in those pages. I'm telling you. Once I get the future Mrs. Harper, she's never going to want to be apart from me. I'm going to put you assholes to shame. Best fucking husband material right here." He slaps his palm on his chest.

Tanner and Dax look at each other and laugh.

"Lawyer girl doesn't know what she's in for."

"Fuck off," Drew says to Tanner.

I'm staring into space as Dax claps me on the shoulder. "Don't worry, man. The pain's worth it in the end."

I turn to him. He went through nights of sleeping outside for Rose to get her back in their early days. Pined after her like a dog. And he swears it's the best thing he ever did.

"Mads..." I look between them in bewilderment. "She said she hates me."

"You've been fucking for weeks. You still believe she hates you?" Tanner snorts.

Drew throws him a murderous look. "Holding hands," he hisses. "They've been holding hands for weeks."

Dax coughs into his glass and pulls a neutral expression to his face. "Sure. Holding hands."

"Well, all the holding hands and you really thought she still hated you?" Tanner tsks. "You have a lot to learn about women. They say one thing and mean another. All the time."

"All the fucking time," Dax agrees.

"So she doesn't want me to marry Gabrielle?"

"Oh, she does," Tanner says.

"Yeah," Dax confirms.

"Because she's in fucking love with you, you idiot." Drew knocks back the rest of his drink.

I stare between them all. Nothing makes fucking sense.

"So two nights ago when we—"

Drew glares at me.

"—held hands. And then she told me to marry Gabrielle, she was what? Telling me what she thought I wanted to hear?"

The three of them all groan at once, and Drew slaps me up the backside of the head. "Idiot."

"She's doing what she thinks is best for you," Tanner explains, taking pity on my pathetic lost ass.

"Because she loves you," Dax adds.

"God knows why," Drew mutters.

"Is it too early to say because I hold her hand harder and better than anyone else?"

Drew's hand curls into a fist and he growls at me. *Fucking growls.* I move back in my seat.

"Yeah, too early," I mumble.

Tanner chuckles, and Dax snorts into his drink, his shoulders shaking.

"What do I do?"

"What do you think you should do?" Tanner asks.

"You do what will make my sister happy," Drew cuts in.

"I do what she wants me to? I marry Gabrielle?" I stare at him. "How can I?"

"You do what will make her happy," Tanner says, fixing me with a look like there's a secret code I'm missing.

"You do the right thing. You already know what that is," Dax says.

I look at Drew again.

"You're going to hurt her either way," he says.

My eyes widen. "Then how the fuck do I—?"

"Hope I don't kill you?" He smirks.

"Not break her heart," I say.

His smirk freezes, and his eyes crinkle at the corners as he assesses me. He reaches over and squeezes my shoulder, his eyes darting to Tanner and Dax.

"Boys. There's the evidence. Lesson one is complete."

I press the bell and stand back. It takes a minute but then she opens the door.

"Logan?"

"Gabrielle." I smile. "I'm sorry I didn't call first. I thought we could talk if now's a good time?"

Her eyes roam over my face and then she nods softly as her shoulders drop. "Yes, we should talk."

I walk into her house. It's a smart, Georgian style London townhouse. Minimalist inside, but with large artwork on the walls and random artefacts specifically placed. I stop and look at a misshaped bowl on the hallway table.

"That was a gift from a little girl I helped in Nigeria. She made it." She lifts it up, running her hands over its smooth, plain sides before placing it back down with a soft smile. "Come on through. Can I get you a coffee?"

I follow her into the large, light kitchen and take a seat at the island as she walks over to the coffee machine and places a mug beneath it. She makes it without speaking, and then turns around, placing it down in front of me.

"White, no sugar, right?"

"Yeah. Thank you."

She turns back to make her own. I stare into my mug. We've seen quite a bit of each other over the years, so should it be a surprise that she knows how I take my coffee? I watch her make hers. White with one sugar. I wouldn't have known that.

Dread creeps over me as I look around the room. Could Dad imagine seeing us here? Living together? Waking up and making coffee together? Visiting us in this house, or maybe mine, if she moved in with me? Who knows. Ice inches up my spine despite taking a sip of the hot coffee.

It's wrong. Everything about this feels wrong.

"I can't marry you," I blurt.

Gabrielle drops her teaspoon on the counter and it clatters. Her shoulders tense and she takes a deep breath before she turns and faces me.

"I know." She blinks at me, her eyes glassy. "And I'm grateful to you for being honest. But also for not shooting the idea down straight away when we met at the hotel."

I shift in my seat. The idea never took flight long enough in my head to need shooting down. But telling her that is unnecessarily cruel.

"I can't do it. It's not fair on you. Or me. It's not fair on anyone."

She nods.

"You don't want to either," I say slowly, gauging her reaction. At the hotel, she said she was doing it to make her dad happy. Because Spencer is sick. She never said it's what she wanted.

She pauses before exhaling a full breath.

"No, I don't. I want to make my father happy. But... no amount of money is worth living your life as a lie. And that's what we'd both be doing. I was willing to do it, though. For my father."

"We do things for those we care about, make decisions... not always the best ones."

My thoughts flit to Maddy. *Sometimes, we get it so wrong when all we want to do is help.*

Despite thinking of how I failed all those years ago, relief floods my body as Gabrielle looks at me.

"You look happy about it," she says.

"I'm sorry."

She pauses, then laughs. "I'm not offended. Just relieved that you can still look at me after what my father's done. He's not a bad man, Logan. You know that. He's just ill and scared and..." She comes and sits next to me. "I'll do anything for him. But I can't drag you into it."

"Yeah, I know."

"I'll speak to him. Maybe there's another way. One where you can still work together, help your dad, and..." She sighs. "And he'll still be happy too."

If only it were that simple. It's what I've been working on ever since we came back from Italy. Spencer's not backing down.

"Your dad wants you to be financially secure. He wants you to have a family. A legacy for him to leave behind. He won't get both if we team up on Vex but don't..." I can't even say the word. *Marry.* Spencer won't get what he's been wanting this whole time. That's why I've gotten nowhere with him. Those are his terms. Or no deal.

Gabrielle stares at her untouched coffee in silence.

"It's irrelevant now, anyway. I've lost investors. The project's underfunded. It can't go ahead. My father will lose all he's worked for. I was hoping I could save it. It's got so much fucking potential. It could fix everything." I curl my fingers into a fist.

"I'm sorry," Gabrielle whispers. She reaches over and takes my hand, squeezing it briefly before wrapping both of her hands back around her mug.

"I told him I'd still find a way. Build everything back from scratch the way he did."

"Do you think that's possible?"

"It has to be. It might take me years but..."

She nods, then looks away blinking. Her phone pings with an incoming message on the counter and she looks at the name on the screen. Her lips lift into a pained smile.

"I admire you. Doing it for your parents. You're driven by your love for them. There's nothing stronger than a parent and child bond." She strokes the phone screen. "I left Dad alone after Mum died. And now I'm going to lose him soon too." She swipes a tear away as it rolls down her cheek. "I wish I could make him happy for what time we have left together."

"I'm sure he's happy just having you home."

She smiles but it doesn't reach her eyes. "Thank you for saying that. I love my job, and being away so much is a huge part of it. But I know he needs me right now. Only..." She picks up her phone and looks at it. "I really need to talk to him about what me staying means."

She places her phone on the counter and slides it toward me.

I glance at her and then at the image on the screen. "Who—?"

She looks at the screen, then back at me. "I should have told him the minute I got back. Earlier, in fact. But then I found his medication and everything has felt like one big mess since then." She wipes away another stray tear. "I let myself get swept along trying to make him happy. I felt I owed him because I left. But I let my guilt side-track me."

She studies the image on her phone. "This is something I've wanted for a long time. I've been making plans. Now that I'm back in London and have a fixed base, those plans can move forward. In fact, it'll work better."

I look at the image that's making her smile with devotion in her eyes.

"You love your dad, Gabrielle. There's no shame in that. We all make decisions based on what we think is better for other people sometimes. And we forget what it is that we want."

My mind drifts to Maddy again. She doesn't want me to marry Gabrielle. She wants my family to be okay.

Because she loves me. My head's still spinning on that one since last night's revelations with the boys.

She loves me.

I told her she didn't hate me anymore. But I never thought past that to what she does feel. I take a deep breath and look at Gabrielle.

"Who is he?"

"Someone Dad needs to hear about." She gives me a wobbly smile. "Would you... come with me when I tell him?"

"Me?"

"It might change the way he sees things. We can hope."

"Gabrielle, I can't do that." I look at her phone screen again. "This is for you and him to talk about. Don't give me and my father's business a second thought. This is about the two of you. Your family."

"Then come because you're my friend and I'm shaking at the thought of telling him." She laughs a little and dabs at her eyes.

I search her eyes as she looks at me anxiously.

"Please, Logan."

"Okay." I give her a soft smile.

She stands, still not having touched her coffee. "Let's take my car. Or you can follow me."

"You want to go now?"

She swipes a final tear away and straightens, taking a deep breath. "I've waited long enough."

My phone buzzes in my pocket and I pull it out.

Drew: Call me.

I slide it back into my pocket. A man of many words, as usual. I'll call him after we see Spencer. After seeing that picture on Gabrielle's phone, I think I'm going to have a lot to tell him too.

Chapter 34
Logan

I RACE DOWN THE road, throwing the Vulcan down a gear to take a bend.

Maddy.

She's all I've been able to think about since I left Spencer's house. Gabrielle's still there. They had a lot to talk about. A lot of arrangements to make. A lot to look forward to.

And everything he and I need to discuss is now scheduled into a meeting tomorrow morning. First thing tomorrow things will start changing.

The Riches always find a way.

I grin as I floor the gas. I called Dad the second I began to drive. The hope in his voice was tangible, tinting the air inside my car with white light, like snowflakes in a gray sky. We're still fifteen million short. The business could still fold. But we're closer. We're one fucking step closer, when all I feel like I've done since Italy is taken steps back, further and further away from the end of this fucking tunnel we're inside.

But now there's a light.

A small one. But it's growing. I don't have to marry a woman I don't love to find a way out.

Gabrielle was right. Spencer's way of seeing things changed the moment she showed him the photograph on her phone. He looked shocked, excited, and somehow, at peace, all at the same time. I guess knowing your time is coming makes you see things with new perspective.

I slam to a halt outside Maddy's apartment building and fly from my car. She'll have finished work. I pray she's home. I've not had any luck the past three days when coming here to look for her. But I'm here anyway. I couldn't imagine going anywhere else.

She is the first person I knew I had to be face to face with when I told them the news. Not Mum. Not Dad. Her. The girl who claims to hate me. Yet everything she does says otherwise.

"Smiles," I say as I press the intercom. "Come on, pick up, baby. Please be home."

Nothing.

I pull out my phone and bring up my call list, hitting her name. It goes straight to voicemail. I jump back into my car and start the engine. Maybe she's with her parents. I bring Drew's number up. The Bluetooth picks it up and the ringing echoes inside the car as I turn around and drive.

"Where the hell have you been?"

"Hey. Mads with you?" I swing around a bend and then reach up to tug my tie loose. I feel like stripping all my clothes off and doing a fucking victory lap around my car in the street. This is the closest that things have been to a solution in weeks.

"No. And if you'd called me back three hours ago, then you'd know she's not," Drew growls. "What the fuck did you say to her?"

"What?" I check the wing mirror as I overtake the car in front. "Nothing. I haven't seen her. She's still avoiding me."

Drew curses.

"Why? What's going on?"

"She left."

"She's what?"

"And she says she's not coming back. She told me to tell you to check your emails."

"What? Fuck!" I swerve to avoid a small fallen branch in the road. "Why?"

"I don't know."

"Fuck, okay. I'll call you back."

Unease claws its way up my spine making the back of my neck prickle as I hit the brakes and steer off the main road and into a small side street. I park at an angle, the engine still running as I pull out my phone and bring up my emails.

The latest one is from Maddy's work account.

I click into it.

I spent so long hating you when you didn't deserve it, Logan. Maybe it's time you hated me for a change. Only, I will deserve it. I'm sorry. Mads.

I open the attachment and start reading the article she's written about me.

Cold sweat gathers on my forehead, my fingers closing around my phone until my knuckles turn white.

"Logan Rich's failed launch. How this bachelor billionaire is set to lose it all."

My father, the marriage to Gabrielle, losing the investors, even the fucking seizure of goods at my parents' house. Everything I ever told her, confided in her.

It's all here in black and white.

Maddox Harper has written down just how much she's hated me all these years.

And now she's telling the world.

Chapter 35
Maddy

I SHUFFLE ALONG IN the queue. The lights above are blinding. Far too bright and unforgiving. Then again, it suits the environment. Flushing out those who aren't being honest about what they're doing here.

Am I being honest?

I move forward another step and the man behind me bumps into my suitcase.

"*Scusa.*"

I give him a small, forgiving smile. I wonder what his story is. Is he running from something? From someone? Or is he trying to help them? Or is he doing all three? Am I doing all three?

"*Sì.*" The officer at the desk lifts an arm and beckons me over. I stand in front of his desk and hand him my passport. He opens it to the photo page and looks at me. I smile because doesn't everyone smile when they do this? It feels rude not to. He doesn't smile back. But as he holds it up, something falls out, and he pauses, picking up the piece of paper and looking at it before he hands it back to me.

"Nice picture," he says in a thick Italian accent. His eyes flick to his screen as he types something in. Then he passes my passport back. "Have a nice stay." He gives me the briefest nod and dismisses me.

I move to the baggage belt and look at the photograph in my hand as I wait for my luggage. I don't know why I printed a copy. Denial? Thinking if I looked at it that I could tell myself we were nothing special. That I shouldn't feel this gut-wrenching pain when I think about him. Or maybe self-sabotage? Because I need to punish myself. I need to look at this every day and understand what I did. Who I lost. Who I never deserved.

Why I did what I did to him.

Logan's grin leaps from the image. His arm is around me on the tiny roof area of The Vatican. We're surrounded by other tourists, all taking in the breath-taking views of the world surrounding them. But him and I are in our own world. Lost in a bubble, staring at the camera. Glittering green eyes alight with mischief next to brown ones. Brown ones shining with warmth above a small but genuine smile.

A smile I never even felt touch my lips that day.

But it was there anyway. It always has been.

We look like a couple. Except we weren't. We aren't. We never will be.

I collect my suitcase and make my way out through customs, catching a cab outside. The driver asks where

I want to go, so I tell him in my best Italian, showing him the written name of the place as confirmation. He nods and we drive away.

I sink into the seat as I stare out the window. I haven't thought this through properly. It was all a whim. I asked Eve for extended leave at the last minute, with the option to work remotely for a while. I don't know how long it'll take to do what I'm planning. And I doubt it will work. But I have to try. I can't stay and watch Logan lose everything. I know I've already lost him. He'll have read the article. He'll hate me now.

It's for the best.

Things are exactly as they should be.

Who knows, maybe I'll like working remotely. I'm not the only one at In-Sync who does it. If Eve is happy with my work, then I never need to go back. I can travel to interview people and do everything online. And the agent said they have a cash buyer interested in my apartment. So it's all working out. This is a good thing.

This is a good thing.

Maybe if I repeat that in my head enough times, I'll believe it.

My phone rings and I take it from my purse.

"Drew?"

"How was your flight?"

He sounds pissed. He didn't want me to leave, tried to talk me out of it. He took my suitcase out of the car twice. It was only when I broke down in tears and told him staying would destroy me that he put it back in and drove me to the airport himself.

"It was good," I say without conviction.

We fall silent. I want to ask him so badly, but I don't know how or if I should or—

"He knows you're gone now." Drew's voice softens. "I gave him your message."

"He does?" A sob catches in my throat and my eyes burn. "What did he...? You know what? Don't tell me."

"What did you send him, Maddy? I've never seen him like this before. He's..." Drew curses softly and my heart tears in two.

"Something he had to see," I croak.

"Well, whatever it was, you need to speak to him. He went to see Spencer with Gabrielle. The three of them talked for hours. Things have happened that you don't know about, Maddy. If only you'd fucking stayed." He sighs, and the weight in his words has my heart clenching painfully in my chest.

They're moving on.

"They'll be happy, won't they?" I sniff, needing to hear it. Needing confirmation that this feeling of complete despair I have isn't for nothing.

Drew clears his throat, his voice coming out hoarse. "Logan said Spencer's the happiest he's ever seen him. Over the fucking moon about it all."

"Oh." My voice is tiny, stripped of all its strength.

I left all my strength in London.

"I need to go, we're almost there," I murmur, looking out of the cab's window.

"Wait, Maddy. You need to speak to Logan—"

I squeeze my eyes shut, my chest tightening painfully. "I don't. Everything he needs to know was in my email."

"Mad—"

"I'm sorry. I love you. I'll call again soon."

I hang up and immediately turn my phone off, ignoring all the voicemails coming through. I turned it off on the flight, too, welcoming the silence as I sat and watched London disappear from the window. Silence will be my companion from now on. A trusted one.

Logan and Gabrielle. It's what I wanted. It's what I told him to do. And after the flowers, I was scared he would never listen. But then he went quiet. Drew said he was out with them, thinking about the future. He said Logan had an epiphany, and that he knew what he had to do. A pathetic part of me hoped that meant he'd come for me, even though that would be the worst decision he's ever made.

But he didn't.

And now I understand why. He was with Gabrielle.

Logan's still only halfway there.

Something still needs to bridge that gap. That fifteen-million wide gap. The sale of my apartment is barely going to make a dent. But it'll be a start if my next move doesn't go as planned.

I sit back in my seat, my nerves growing as we approach the marina. I was convinced he wouldn't still be moored here. And according to his PA, if I'd waited until tomorrow, then he wouldn't be. Maybe the universe is on my side for once, because as we pull up, I spot the imposing, sleek white vessel sitting in the water.

I pray I have Logan's luck negotiating today.

I climb out of the cab after we stop and smooth down my skirt. I pay the driver, then take my suitcase from him and wheel it up the jetway.

A member of the yacht's crew is waiting for me as I approach and helps me onboard, taking my suitcase for me and offering me a drink.

I'm led to the familiar deck, but the table is gone. Instead, I'm shown to a cushioned seating area and told to make myself comfortable. I place my purse down by my feet and sit, inhaling the fresh sea air as I gaze out across the calm water. It's a direct contrast to the whirlpool spinning inside me.

"Ms. Harper?"

I turn and stand and am swept up in sparkling blue eyes. I can't stop the pop of heat in my cheeks. I'm not attracted to him in that way. But I can't deny that there's something about this man that makes you feel seen. *Intense.* That's probably the best word to describe his eyes when they're on you.

"Mr. Beaufort." I take his extended hand.

"My friends call me Sterling."

"Mine call me Maddy."

Tiny smile lines appear around his eyes, crinkling the skin. "Except Mr. Rich. He told me your name's Maddox."

I swallow at the mention of Logan. I knew he'd come up in conversation, but I still wasn't prepared for the wrench in my gut at hearing his name.

"It is. But he usually calls me Mads. He says it's because I look mad whenever I see him."

Sterling chuckles. "Well then, I'd say he considers himself to be a very lucky man."

I look at him, puzzled as I accept his offer to sit back down.

"I appreciate you taking the time to meet with me," I say, trying to swallow down the nerves fizzing inside my stomach.

Sterling thanks one of his staff who brings a tray of chilled drinks over. He passes one to me and I wait for him to lift his glass to clink mine before I take a grateful sip. My throat is suddenly drier than a bone in the midday sun.

"I'm intrigued to see what brings you here alone."

I shift in my seat and smile politely. He's being sincere. But the acknowledgment that last time I was here was with Logan makes my stomach sink all over again. Everything that makes me think of Logan does that now.

"But first, tell me. How was the opera? Did you enjoy it?" Sterling leans back in his seat like he has all the time in the world.

"Immensely," I answer truthfully. "It was beautiful. I can't thank you enough for your generosity."

"Then don't." He smiles. "Just tell me something good came from it and that'll make me happy."

"I... Something good came from it."

It blew the lid off years of misplaced hatred. It's the night I first started seeing Logan for who he is. And not who I thought he was. It's the first night I started to see who I've been all these years.

And who I don't want to be any longer.

Sterling watches me carefully.

"It won't be long until sunset. Being on the water for it is spectacular." His eyes glint. "Stay and have dinner. It will give us time to talk. You can tell me what made you come here."

I open my mouth to politely decline, then snap it shut. There is no way to turn down Sterling Beaufort. Especially when I'm here to ask for his help. I'm not naïve enough to think I could walk onboard, have a five-minute conversation with him, and then walk away with the answer to everything. He'll want to know why I'm here. Why I'm *really* here. And if I have any hope of getting his help, then I will have to be honest.

I'll have to tell him everything.

I look at his friendly expression and take a cleansing breath. I can pretend this is therapy. Let it all out. If he says no, I'll never see him again anyway. He's a billionaire. We don't move in the same circles. I'm safe to let it out. At least, I think I am. *I hope I am.*

"That would be lovely," I say. "But I should warn you. The truth is... messy."

He chuckles as he holds his glass around the rim between his fingertips, before bringing it to his lips with a knowing smile.

"When isn't it?"

Chapter 36
Logan

"HOW MUCH LONGER?"

"We're looking at an ETA of eighteen forty-five," the pilot replies over his shoulder.

"Fine. Good. Thank you."

I crack my knuckles as I walk out of the cockpit. The flight attendant gives me a practiced smile as I pass her and take up pacing the cabin again. She answered the same question for me ten minutes ago. I didn't want to ask her again for the fifth time this flight, so I went straight to the pilots. They probably think I'm losing it. If this were my regular crew, they'd know I was. I sit down and work on flights. I don't stalk up and down the aisle like a man possessed.

I take a deep breath and let it go slowly, but it does nothing to ease the tension that's commanded my body since reading that email. I've tried Maddy. But I can't reach her. Then I called Dad in the hope the jet hadn't been grounded yet, along with other assets. But it had. Spencer came to the rescue by chartering this one for me. I swear he's a changed fucking man since Gabrielle's talk with him. I guess it put things into perspective for him. He's getting what he wants. Just not in the way he originally planned.

I pace more as I look at my watch. I wasted time after reading her article. I sat in my car wasting precious minutes, reading it a second time.

I knew what it was the first fucking time I read it.

A lie.

Another one of her fucking lies.

"Fuck," I mutter, pushing my hands back through my hair.

Where is she? Drew told me she flew to Rome. I sped across London to her boss's house. She told me that Maddy asked to work remotely for the foreseeable future.

She isn't planning on coming back.

"Hurry up, come on."

I drop into my seat for the first time since we took off and look out of the window. I didn't even pack a suitcase. Just got on the plane as fast as I could. She's running. From me. From us. It's all she's ever done. But I can't bring myself to stop chasing her, no matter how hard she's tried to push me away.

Pushed because she *loves* me.

I pick my laptop up and read the article again.

The real one.

Eve sent it after I went to her house.

She said I get to see it first and approve it. It won't be going live for a while. But I won't change a single thing. It might be about me, but these are Maddy's words. It's her work.

"*Resisting Mr. Rich: A man with a big dream and an even bigger heart.*"

I link my fingers together on the back of my neck and lean my elbows onto my knees as I read it for the thousandth time. She can't hide behind her words.

Not her real ones.

I don't know what the fuck she was thinking. She had to have known that I'd see this eventually. Maybe she figured she'd be long gone by then and it wouldn't matter.

But everything about her matters.

Including her final words. The real ones.

She's done more than write an article about me and Project Vex. She's written an apology. In her own way. For the first time, she's been completely honest with me, in the only way she thought she could.

It's when we are on the brink of losing everything that clarity sometimes comes, sharper than ever. And we know beyond doubt what we must do. This project was never about money. To him, it's a dream, a new future. A better way of doing things. Something sustainable. Something true...

It's not what we've done in the past that matters. It's what we do now. And Logan Rich is a shining example of the future of environmentally friendly solutions to a world with a need for technology and growth. He is a pioneer... Whether this project takes off soon, or not, he's one to watch and never to underestimate. One month with him changed my outlook on life, and now he's about to change the world. It would be easy to hate him. He's successful, wealthy, and handsome. But this man and his evolutionary designs are exactly what our planet needs. It's impossible to feel anything but gratitude at the name, Logan Rich.

I pull in a slow breath as I reach the end of the article. Eve said it's Maddy's best work. Everyone in her office is talking about it, and she isn't even there. She deserves to hear it. To know just how incredible she is. I'm so damn proud of her.

"You're flapping those wings, Butterfly," I whisper. "You're fucking soaring."

But where are you, baby?

I close the laptop and press my finger and thumb into my eye sockets as I balance on the edge of my seat, ready to bolt up at the slightest movement, to the tiniest clue about where she could be. I've got the boys on high alert back home. They're all trying to find out where she is. I'd have my own security team working on it too if we hadn't had to let them take up other assignments while the shit with the business gets sorted.

That nightmare might soon be over.

But if I don't find Maddy, then I'm stepping from one straight into another. *A worse one.*

"Mr. Rich? It's time to strap in for landing." The flight attendant smiles, and I move back in my seat, scrambling to click my belt together.

My phone vibrates in my pocket, and I pull it out, clicking into Dax's message. It's a video of the sunset over the ocean posted from Maddy's book account. Nothing else. No words, no explanation of where she is. I zoom in on the silver railing at the bottom of the screen. This isn't taken from land. She's on a boat. She's near Rome, on a boat.

Hope explodes in my chest.

I know where to find her.

Chapter 37
Logan

THE YACHT IS OUT on the water when I arrive, and I'm forced to wait until it comes back in. For two hours, I pace the deserted jetway. She has to be onboard. Because if she isn't, then I'm fucking lost. Back to square one. If I thought I could swim there, I would. But it's too far. And I'm not stupid enough to think that dying before I see her face would be classed as romantic.

The vessel approaches, gliding elegantly over the water like a giant shimmering white swan.

"Mads," I yell once it's close enough for the people onboard to hear. I make out two figures up on the top deck. I wave my arms in the air like a madman. "Mads!"

"Logan?" one figure calls back.

Relief bolts into my chest like lightning, and I bend at the waist, sucking in deep lungfuls of air as her voice blankets over me, soothing something I never knew could break. *Until her.*

"What the hell?" the figure shouts.

I smile at the fire in her voice. Thank fuck it's still there. She's still her.

"What are you doing here?" she yells again.

The second figure raises a hand and waves. I straighten and raise one back in greeting. *Sterling.*

I call back as loud as I can, "I need to talk to you."

"No!"

My head jerks back. "What the fuck do you mean, no?" Irritation bubbles in my voice. "You don't get to run away and not tell me you're leaving." I jab a finger into the air, pointing in her direction.

"Why?" she snips back.

Fucking hell, this woman. Even from this distance, I can tell Sterling's amused as his faint chuckle carries. He moves away, further back along the deck, away from Maddy. Probably to give us space. But I don't care who hears us. All I care about is the fact I've chased her here and she's still being difficult.

"Why the hell do you think?" I shout and push my hands back through my hair.

"Didn't you read my email?" she calls.

The blood boils in my veins. "If you mean that ton of shit you made up, then yeah, I read it."

"It's not—"

"Don't you dare fucking lie to me again!" I drag in a deep breath until my lungs cry out. "No more, Mads. No fucking more!"

She's silent, staring in my direction.

"What is this? You think because you hated me that I have to hate you back to make us even?"

"No," she cries, the pain in her voice making my heart stall.

"Then what?"

"I-I thought if you hated me then you'd move on. Save the business. Be happy. I want you to be happy."

"I could never be happy after reading that fucking article, knowing that you hated yourself enough to write it. That you didn't think you deserved this." I jerk my arm between the giant gap between us. "This thing that's happening between us."

"Log—"

"I've read your real article. Even if I hadn't, I'd still be here. I'm not letting you push me away anymore."

She shakes her head. "What else is there? This is what we do, Logan."

She's still too far to see clearly, but something tells me that she's crying. My heart lurches.

"We change the story. We write our own fucking story. Starting right now!"

"Why would you do that? After everything?"

Fuck's sake. I spin in a circle as I tear at my hair. She's not listening to a word I'm saying.

"You know why!" I holler back until my lungs burn like they might fly out of my throat with the effort.

She freezes. "You shouldn't be here, Logan."

"No shit. Neither should you. You should be back in London. *With me*." I bang my chest with my fist.

"You're getting married." Her hands curl around the railing on the yacht's upper deck as she leans closer.

"Not unless it's to you." My chest rises and falls in desperate pants. "Can't you see? It's you or no one. Fuck, I'll get down on one knee now and prove it to you."

"Don't you dare." Panic erupts in her voice as she climbs the rail as if she wants to physically stop me. "I—"

"Don't you fucking say you hate me, Mads. I swear to God!" I clench my hand into a fist and bring it to my mouth as my blood boils.

She freezes, both of her feet on a higher rung of the railing as she stares at me across the water. "You still think I hate you?" Her face is close enough for me to see it crumple as she lets go of the railing. "I don't," she chokes out. "I don't Logan, I—"

Whatever she's about to say is ripped from her lips and replaced by a scream as the yacht lurches and she's sent hurtling over the rail headfirst.

"Mads!"

I'm diving through the surface of the water less than a second after it swallows her, breaking the surface again with burning lungs.

"Mads!" I yell.

I push through the water as fast as I can, pistoning my arms to swim to where she went under.

"Man overboard," is hollered from above, and a life ring drops into the water, followed by a crew member.

I get to where I last saw her and swing my head side to side. What if the yacht hit her after she fell? She could have been knocked out. She could have been swept under the boat. I gulp in air and dive below the surface, my eyes stinging from the saltwater as I search for her and find nothing.

"Mads?" My voice is hoarse as I take another gulp of air, preparing to dive again.

Coughing and spluttering sounds erupt behind me. I spin, my chest caving at the sight of her dark curls plastered to her face as she surfaces a distance away.

"Why are you here? You shouldn't be here." She coughs. The fire is back in her voice, no hint of concern she just fell overboard and nearly caused me a fucking heart attack.

I swim toward her, blood rushing in my ears. "I just flew all the way here for a fully clothed swim. Isn't it fucking obvious?"

She floats, staring at me as the crew member who jumped in after her calls up to the deck and tells them we're okay.

"Jesus, cut the fucking crap. I'm here for the same reason you are. Because you don't hate me anymore," I grit, swimming closer to her.

"I don't hate you anymore," she echoes, all fight leaving her voice as her bottom lip trembles and her face pales.

The boiling blood in my veins switches to ice instantly, and I swim faster. "Shit. Are you okay? Did you hit your head when you fell?"

Her lip continues to shake, followed by her voice. "L-L-Logan."

"I'm coming, baby."

I rush to close the remaining distance and pull her into my arms. She wraps her legs around my waist and clings as I reach out and grab the life ring with one hand, keeping us both afloat.

"I don't hate you anymore." Tears stream down her face. "I don't... I don't..." She cries harder, her whole body shaking with the force. I shush her, pressing my face into her hair. "Not even close. I care about you so damn much."

"Baby." My heart swells at hearing her finally admit it. Finally—

"And I hate that I do!" she sobs.

"What?" I pull back to look at her tear-stained face and she shakes her head as she looks at me.

"I hate that I care so much. Because it means I have to do what's right for you. Because I want you to be happy. I *need* you to be happy." She sniffs. "Even if it means losing you."

"You aren't losing me." I brush the wet strands back from her eyes with my free hand. "You could never lose me. No one makes me as fucking crazy as you do. And I need crazy to function."

"You'll lose everything," she whispers.

I press my forehead to hers. "If I do, it'll be worth it if I get you."

She searches my eyes as the crew member who jumped interrupts us. "It's not safe in the water here. There are too many other boats that could come past. We need to get back onboard."

I nod at him and encourage Maddy to swim over to the boat where the crew are waiting to help us up the rear steps. Suddenly we're surrounded by people, wrapping us in towels, passing us water, checking us for injuries.

Sterling waits until we're given the medical all clear before he steps closer, gripping my upper arm as he looks directly into my eyes, concern mixed with warmth in his gaze. "Way to make an entrance."

My shoulders soften, and I glance at Maddy before smiling. "Seems I like dramatic things." My eyes trace the drops of water falling from her hair and down over her cheeks and I take my towel from around my shoulders and wrap it over the top of hers, giving her an extra layer.

"You need to get out of those wet clothes. We'll get you something dry to change into," Sterling says.

Maddy looks at him. "Thank you, but—"

"I insist. The crew will show you where you can shower and change. And then when you're ready, you and I need to talk." He turns back to me.

"We do." I wrap an arm around Maddy's shoulders and pull her into my side as I nod solemnly at Sterling.

You okay? Maddy mouths.

I take her hand in mine, watching the way our fingers entwine together. I pull them up to my lips and kiss hers, one by one. "I am now."

"But..." She frowns as I tell her it doesn't matter. None of it matters.

Sterling's another investor about to pull out. I'm not surprised. But he was such a majority that his loss to the project will be the end of Vex. It's well and truly over now without him.

"I'm thinking another ten percent on my initial return might do it," Sterling says.

I whip my head toward him. "Excuse me?"

His eyes glint as he watches us both. Maddy stiffens, her fingers gripping mine tighter. "We agreed seven," she says without a hint of hesitation.

Sterling chuckles. "Just checking you were listening." He turns his attention to me. "You could have sent her alone the first time. Ruthless negotiator if ever I saw one. Now go get out of those wet clothes. We'll talk later."

"He's investing another fifteen," she says, keeping her eyes forward as he walks away.

"Why?"

She swallows slowly. "Because I told him he would be missing out on an amazing opportunity headed up by a brilliant man."

"Spencer?"

She side-eyes me, then nudges my shoulder with hers. "Idiot."

I smirk before my face settles into a frown. "You flew over here to ask him to increase his investment?"

She sighs, a sound so weighted with unhappiness that hearing it is like having broken glass forced into my ears.

"I couldn't watch you lose everything. Especially Vex, something you care so much about. I thought if you got the extra money that Spencer would still help your dad. As long as you and Gabrielle still got marr..." She swallows again, as though saying the word is too difficult for her. "And then it would be okay. At least, that's what I hoped." She shrugs.

"You wrote that article to try and make me hate you."

"I owe it to you." She meets my eyes with tears building in hers again.

My gut twists painfully at the memory of the words she'd written. They were designed to hurt me. And they did. Just not in the way she intended.

"I know you've come here to find me. But you have to go back. The funding's no good if you don't have the backing of Spencer's company to make it work. You lose if you stay."

The stirrings of defeat weigh heavy in my chest, dragging my heart down.

"I lost the second you left London, Mads. I lost the fucking second you thought that there was a reality where we could be apart and still live like we aren't just existing. *Just fucking existing.*"

She blinks through her tears and drops her head back to look at the sky.

"Why couldn't you have hated me after what I wrote?"

"I could never hate you." I reach up to cup her cheek. "Look at me. Please look at me."

She closes her eyes and gives a tiny shake of her head. "I can't."

"You can," I urge. "The heart knows when the search is over. What's yours telling you? Listen to it."

"I want you to be happy." Her lower lashes are coated in thick, wet droplets. "I *need* you to be happy."

"I'll be happy when I know that you are. Now look at me, baby."

"You need to go home, Logan," she whispers. "Without me."

She can't meet my eyes. Can't even look at me as she rips my heart to shreds.

"No. I—"

"Go!" she snaps, turning her back on me. "Get dry, get dressed, and then get back on a plane and forget you ever felt anything for me. *Please.*"

"So, that's it? This is what you really want?"

She straightens her shoulders, keeping her back to me as she remains silent.

"Fucking hell. Mads, please."

Silence.

My chest caves. Nothing I say is going to get through to her. Staring at her back makes my head spin, spots dancing in my vision.

I need to get off this yacht. I need a minute. I need...

I whirl around and stomp away, water dripping off my sodden clothes and onto the deck as I barge past a bewildered looking crew member and get off the yacht.

I storm up the wooden walkway away from the yacht.

Away from her.

I can't chase her forever when she doesn't want me. I want to... God, I want to. I don't ever want to give up on us.

But she does.

It's finally time to stop.

Chapter 38
Logan

THE LIGHTNESS IN MY head abates as my senses return.

I pat my pockets, looking for my phone. Shit, I must have lost it in the water. My pace falters. I have two choices. Go back to the yacht to ask to use one onboard. Or try to find a cab who will accept a soaking wet passenger whose world has just ended.

"Jesus," I mutter.

"Stop!"

The sound is so faint, the breeze almost carries it away.

"Stop! Please!"

I look back over my shoulder, my breath leaving my lungs.

Maddy's running.

No, she's sprinting.

"Logan! Wait! Please!"

My heart stops in the few remaining seconds it takes for her to reach me. She throws herself against me, her arms wrapping around my neck and her legs encircling my waist.

"Don't go!" she sobs into my neck, her body shaking uncontrollably. "I want the new story too." Her sobs turn into hiccups as her cries are muffled against my skin. "I want *our* story."

"Mads." I hold her to me, dragging in splintered breaths as she falls apart in my arms.

"I'm sorry I put my apartment up for sale and left without saying goodbye. I'm sorry I—"

"You did what? You're selling it?"

My stomach drops to my feet.

She was never planning on coming back.

"It's not worth anywhere near what you needed. But I thought if Sterling said no, then at least it would be something."

"You love that place. That's your home, Mads."

She clings to me harder. "I couldn't be there anymore without seeing you everywhere. Without remembering the way you kissed me there. The way I knew that I've fallen in..." She falters. "I'm sorry, Logan. You were meant to hate me. You were meant to hate me and move on."

"There's no space in my heart to hate you. Even if I'd believed for one second that your email was real, I still wouldn't have hated you."

I ease her back so I can look into her eyes.

"My heart's too full, Mads," I confess. "Too fucking full of love for you."

"No."

"Yes."

"No."

"Yes." I rest my forehead against hers. "You don't get your own way over this. I read your article," I say softly. "The real one. Every single word. I read it over and over on the flight here. It's amazing. You're so talented."

"Log—"

"I'm not marrying Gabrielle."

She tries to protest, but I slide a thumb to her lips to stop her from speaking.

"Would you still want me if I was the kind of husband who always had to borrow a coin to make a wish in fountains?"

"You do that anyway." Her voice softens but it's still joined by the line between her brows pulling deep into her skin. "Husband?"

I trace her lower lip with the pad of my thumb.

"If you swear to me you'll never run from us again, then that's where it's headed. I know you love stories, Mads. You love the fairy tale, the happy ending. Things are happening with the business. So much is changing. And I hope it's enough. But if it isn't, I need you to know that I'll fight to get it back. To get it for you. But until then, all I can promise you is the kind of love that makes me want to create our own language. Just for us. So I can write it for you. Whisper it to you. Give you something that no one else can."

My chest cracks in the center as I wait for her reaction. *Don't push me away, baby. I can't take it anymore.*

She sniffs, gifting me with a small, perfect curl of her lips. "If this is a fairy tale, then are you the prince?"

I let out the breath I'm holding, blinking back the stinging in my eyes as relief and hope thread together inside me, strengthening the parts that were weakened when she left.

"You bet I fucking am."

"*Principe*," she whispers, her lips curling a little higher before they stall their movements and form a sad smile instead. "I spent so many years hating you. I never gave myself the chance to get to know the real you."

"The real me can still be a dick."

"You still didn't deserve to be hated for something that was never your fault," she whispers.

I run my thumb over her bottom lip again. She sucks in a breath as my eyes follow its path, and I dust it back and forth.

"It doesn't matter now."

"It does." Her voice wobbles. "I hated you. I—"

"And while you were busy hating me, I was busy falling in love with you, Mads. Deeper and deeper." I bring my lips to hers. "I wouldn't change a damn thing that led me to that. Led me to you."

I curl my hand around her neck, pulling her to me. Her lips part the moment mine touch them, and she falls into me, kissing me back.

"Don't cry."

"I don't deserve you."

"Stop."

"I don't." She kisses me harder.

"You're wrong. But it doesn't matter because you've got me anyway."

"What about—?"

"I'm not marrying Gabrielle. Mum and Dad will be okay. They have the money they need to save the business."

"But Spencer was adamant. I don't understand how you convinced him."

I press my lips to her forehead.

"I didn't. Gabrielle did. She showed him a photograph of a little boy who lost his parents in the earthquake where she was working. A boy she's adopting."

Maddy frowns.

"I know. No one had any idea. She didn't know how to tell Spencer. She thought all he cared about was a son-in-law that could manage the business and about having grandkids. Which *is* what he wants. Now he's got it, mostly. Gabrielle is bringing the boy over to London to live with them."

"But how did you get the money for your dad?"

"I sold the island... and I sold the patent for Vex to Spencer. Under the condition it's to be put into the boy's name and managed by Gabrielle until he's eighteen."

"You sold it?"

"I sold it," I confirm. "It's what I was pushing for before. But Spencer wasn't interested. He was fixated on a family for Gabrielle and making her secure. A mix of his illness and losing his wife made him unable to see anything else, I guess."

I stroke Maddy's wet hair back from her face.

"We're all getting what we want."

"But Gabrielle was going to agree to marry you."

"She loves her dad. And people do crazy things for love. Even if they're hurting themselves in the process." I give her a pointed look as my voice softens. "Don't they?"

"When someone squirms their way into their heart, you mean?" She bites her bottom lip, so close to smiling I realize I'm holding my breath waiting to see it.

"Champion squirmer right here." I press a kiss to her lips.

"Do you think Drew will be happy about us? Or will we have to hold his hand through it," she murmurs as she kisses me back.

"You fucking won't be holding anyone's hands except mine," I growl, causing her to narrow her eyes at me in question. "Don't worry." I smile. "Just something he said."

"I can't believe you sold Vex. It's your dream." Her hands trace their way from my shoulders and up the sides of my neck. I groan as she slides them into my hair and strokes my scalp.

"I'll still be running it. I don't care whose name is on the paperwork. I care about seeing it happen. It's going to change the future of engineering. The way that we do things. The rest of it, having my name on it, that would just be for ego."

Maddy arches one brow.

"Yeah, fuck, okay." I smirk. "But I still get to play with rockets. I'm still cool."

"You are." She smiles.

She finally fucking smiles, and the sight steals my breath.

I pull her back and put my lips on her forehead.

"I am so in love with you, Maddox Harper. So stupidly in love with you."

"Logan..." Her voice drops to a whispered sob. "Your happiness means everything to me. I... I don't know how to tell you, to show you that. Nothing is enough, nothing is..."

The thought of her crying again makes every muscle in my body clench.

"Hey." I place my fingers beneath her chin and tilt her head so our eyes meet. "You think coming here to see Sterling and ask him for fifteen million isn't a big enough gesture? You think selling your apartment to help me, isn't?" I smile as I say the words, trying desperately to dissolve the weight she's carrying inside her.

She lets out an uneven breath and warmth fills my chest as her voice lifts.

"I was shaking the whole way here. I was sure he'd say no."

"But he didn't."

"No. He didn't. But I told him everything. About Dad and what he did to Drew, how it made me feel about you all these years. How I feel now."

"You're amazing. You know that?"

Self-doubt and guilt fill her eyes. "I wanted to do it for you. I had to do something. It'll never be enough though."

"Stop. Please stop."

The crease is back between her brows. I press my lips to it in a kiss.

"If I think of a way you can make it up to me, will you stop beating yourself up?"

"I'll try."

"Not good enough, Smiles. I want a promise."

She smiles for the second time. And once again I'm breathless. Because after everything that's happened, she must be mine.

I slant my mouth over hers and kiss her. She grips onto my collar and holds me to her as she whimpers against my mouth.

"Was that squeak a confirmation?"

She smiles as I kiss her.

"You've got to say it." I run my tongue over hers before pausing our kiss. "Say it, Smiles."

"I promise you," she breathes.

"Good girl."

I keep my hand on her face, the other cups her ass, holding her up against me. I stop myself from squeezing a handful of it, because I know where this will go if I do. I'll be making her scream my name so loud that the whole marina hears. But now she's here, in my arms again, it isn't enough to bury myself inside her again. I need more. I want everything.

I break our kiss. Her lips are pink and swollen as she blinks at me.

"Technically, I still own the island for three more days until the sale finalizes." I push a curl away from her eyes. "Come back there with me. Come back and fuck me on the staircase without telling me you hate me."

She laughs suddenly. The sound makes my heart swell so much it's in danger of exploding. But she stops abruptly when she looks into my eyes.

"You're serious?"

"Not that the hate sex isn't hot." I rest my forehead against hers and trace a finger down her throat. "But I want the loving kind. I've never had it. Not with anyone. I want it. *With you*." My finger stops over her heart, and I splay my palm over her skin.

She draws in a measured breath. "I've never had it before either."

"Then be with me without hiding, Mads. Give me all of you. *Please*."

She places her hand on my chest, mirroring my position. "You have all of me, Logan. I just didn't know how to let you before."

She smiles through a small sob, and I pull her back to me, kissing her, both of our hands firmly planted over the other's heart.

"All of me. I promise," she whispers.

Chapter 39
Maddy

I'M BAREFOOT UNDER THE moonlight as soft sand fills the gaps between my toes, and Logan's warm fingers fill the spaces between mine. I tilt my face up to the night sky and breathe deeply.

"Hurry up." Logan grins, tugging on my arm.

He pulls me toward the house, where the outdoor lights have been left on for us. His fingers grip mine tightly. I smile at the urgency communicated with his touch.

We've both waited a long time for this.

The sound of Sterling's helicopter taking off from the clearing fills the air, and I wave up at the two pilots. We could have waited until the morning. But the moment Logan and Sterling finished discussing Vex, Sterling insisted that we come here. He told us not to waste precious time.

We run the final meters to the house and spill into the open-air marble lobby, excitement swirling in the air around us. Logan drops our shoes on the floor and turns to me.

"No bruises this time." He plants a kiss to my lips and lets go of my hand, striding over to a cupboard and pulling out an armful of blankets. He spreads them on the floor and then stands to his full height.

"Come here, baby."

I slip my fingers back inside his outstretched hand and let him pull me flush to his chest. His lips seal over mine, kissing away my voice and turning it into a whimper as I sink into him.

"You're so beautiful." He kisses me again, sending warm shivers up my spine. "You and your smile, Mads. It's the only dream I'll ever need."

"Me too," I whisper, placing my fingertips to his smiling lips.

He pulls me down onto the soft blankets, and I hike my skirt up and straddle his thighs as he sits. His hands drop to grasp my hips.

"I love your curves. They're—"

"Sexy?" I smile as I remember the dressing room in his Rome house.

"Yeah." He groans as I rub myself over his erection. I roll my hips, the thin silk of my panties doing nothing to hide the heat between my legs. "Sexy and perfect," he adds huskily.

He traces his fingers up my sides beneath my top, making me shiver in anticipation as he pulls it off, then unclasps my bra and peels it away from my skin.

"You know what I saw when the cab was taking me to the marina?" I ask as Logan grabs the neck of his own T-shirt and drags it off, throwing it to the side.

"What?" His arms snake around my back, and he groans as my breasts press against his bare chest.

His skin is as hot as mine as he clasps my hips again and circles them, grinding me down onto his cock.

"A..." I swallow as he repeats the move, and my pulse flutters wildly between my legs.

"You want bare skin there too, baby?" He sucks my bottom lip, then chuckles as I'm rendered unable to let out anything other than a breathy moan of agreement.

I place my hands on his shoulders and push to my feet. I slide my skirt and panties down over my hips. His eyes are glued to each uncovered inch of my body as I step out of them and kick them away.

He pushes his own underwear down in a rush, then warm hands grasp my waist again, and he presses a scorching kiss between my legs before positioning me back to straddle him. A deep groan leaves his chest as my bare thighs meet his.

"I've missed you." I look at his thick cock, glistening with precum beneath me as I rest my hands on his shoulders.

Logan laughs. "Missed me or my cock?"

"Both," I reply, quivering, as he bends, sucking my nipple into his mouth.

"God, your tits, Mads. Fucking incredible," he moans as he switches to taste the other one.

He draws back and slides a hand between my legs, placing his thumb over my clit. I drag in a shuddery breath as his eyes glint.

"Tell me what you saw going to the marina."

"Another wedding," I moan as he circles my clit, spreading the slick arousal over my skin.

"Yeah?" His voice deepens. "What about it?" His tongue darts out, moistening his lips as he stares at my mouth, and I draw in a small gasp as he slides two fingers inside me.

"There were kids dressed up. A little boy and girl."

"Uh-huh," Logan murmurs, still staring at my lips as he curls his fingers inside me and rubs my G-spot.

"Yes," I breathe, my eyelashes fluttering as liquid heat surrounds his fingers. "It made me think…"

"What about?" His eyes stay fixed on my mouth as he takes his fingers from inside me and brings them to my lips. I part them and then wrap them around him, sucking my taste off.

"Fuck, baby."

He slides his fingers out.

"It made me think about you," I say.

"It did?" he murmurs in a gravelly voice as his hand returns to the space between my legs.

"I was thinking—" The air is pushed from my lungs in a deep moan as Logan positions his cock and then pulls me down onto it.

"You were thinking?" He grasps one hip, his other hand coming up and curling around the back of my neck as his thumb ghosts over my throbbing pulse.

"I was..." My lips part, and I whimper as he moves his hips, fucking me slowly from beneath.

Images flood my memory of our last night on the island. The way we'd stayed up all night in bed. Like this. Him sitting, and me wrapped inside his arms, straddling him. But this is different. That night I was fighting everything inside me that wanted to give in and cling to him. I was fighting against us with all I had.

Tonight, I'm finally welcoming it all.

And nothing's ever felt better.

"I was thinking about what your children would look like." I slide my hands from his shoulders and up to cup his face. "Whether they'd have your green eyes." He lifts me and pulls me back down onto him slowly and every cell in my body vibrates with desire as I clench around him. "I was thinking about whether they'd have your passion for work, your drive... your humor."

Logan chuckles, his perfect teeth flashing sinfully between his lips. "Yeah?"

"Or whether they'd be more like their mother," I whisper, blinking back the burning in my eyes. "The thought of it broke me. It's what I told you I wanted for you. But it's not what I wanted at all." The tremor in my voice matches the shake in my fingertips against his cheeks.

"Mads." Logan holds himself deep inside me. His hand on my neck burns against my skin as he smooths his thumb over my pulse point. "You know what I think?"

"What?" My thumbs ghost over his perfect high cheekbones in wonder.

"I hope they have their mother's fire, her spirit." He looks over my face, his eyes darkening with an intensity

I've never seen in them before. "Her dark curls," he rasps, his lips hovering inches from mine.

"Logan..."

"Mads, you're the only one I want that all with. Fuck, we can start now if you want?" His cock flexes inside me. "The thought of our baby inside you is..."

He looks down to where he's grasping my hip, and I follow his gaze. "It fucking does something to me. Seeing you again, finding you."

"It does something to me too." I blink furiously as warmth fills my lower lids.

I roll my hips, encouraging Logan to start moving again. He picks up the pace, maneuvering my body up and down and encouraging me to ride him.

"I've always hated the thought of anyone else touching you," he groans as we move together. My arousal coats him, enabling me to sink up and down his thick length easily. "Always. Even though I couldn't have you. I never wanted anyone else to touch you." He grips my hip harder as his thrusts deepen, stretching me around him. "Does that make me selfish?"

I press a kiss to his mouth. "It makes you honest. Something I've not been."

He looks into my eyes as we fuck, completely wrapped up in one another. Our pants begin to mingle in the warm night air. I tip my head back and look at the stars scattering the sky above us.

Logan peppers kisses over the column of my throat. "Be honest with me now. Tell me I've got you. All of you."

I take a deep breath as goosebumps cover my skin, and my body pulses around his.

"You've got me." I bring my face down and screw it up against his as tears roll down my cheeks. "You've got me." I kiss him, and he tightens his hold on me. "You've got me forever. I want you. I want us. I wouldn't know how to stop. I could *never* stop."

"Neither could I." He searches my eyes. "It's you and me now, Smiles." His fingers flex on my hips. "I love you, Maddy."

"Maddy?" It's the first time he's ever called me it.

He slides his thumb from my neck to my lips. To the smile that's on them. "Yeah. You don't look mad now," he breathes.

"How do I look?" I whisper.

He swipes his thumb over my smile, his eyes shining.

"You look happy. You look like mine."

I pull him in for a kiss. "I'm both, a million times over... Both."

I fight to keep my eyes on his. But they roll back as he changes the angle he's thrusting at and places both of his hands on my breasts and tugs on my nipples.

"God, Logan." I tremble as my core coils tightly.

"You need it, baby?"

"Please..." I can't deny it. He knows me now. *He's got all of me.*

"Deep inside you?" he murmurs as his hands continue to play with my breasts.

"Yes. Please." I'm practically crying with need as my body teeters on the edge around him.

He kisses me back with a thick growl. "For you, baby. It's all for you."

Then he lets go and curses with a thick grunt as he comes inside me.

"Oh my god." I come apart around him, gripping onto him, digging my nails into his flesh as I'm consumed by waves of blinding pleasure.

"There it is."

He fists my hair in one hand and drops the other back to my hip so he can pull me down onto him harder, burying himself deep inside me as he comes.

He thrusts over and over, not letting up until I cry out and come again. He kisses me through it, never slowing down as he rides it out with me until our combined release is coating my inner thighs. I shudder as with each deep contraction more is pushed from me, sliding over where our skin meets.

"You're so fucking pretty when you come, Smiles."

I pant through the final waves of my orgasm before I collapse, all the muscles in my body softening as I fall forward. He catches me, and I sink against his chest, snaking my arms around his neck as I rest my cheek over his thundering heart.

I clutch him, and a sob rises in my throat, catching me off guard.

"I love you."

He stops breathing.

"Mad—"

I lift my head and meet his eyes. They shine back at me, searching for truth.

I've never been so honest in my life.

"I love you," I choke out. "I love you." I sob again as he cups my face in his hands.

The confession pours from my lips as though my heart has opened and the words are falling straight out of it.

"I'm in love with you, Logan Rich."

I sniff and hiccup through every declaration, my smile growing as tears course down my cheeks.

Logan smooths my damp hair back from my forehead, tilting my face up so he can kiss me.

His warm lips dust over mine with a smile as he says, "There it fucking is."

Chapter 40
Logan

Epilogue – 3 months later

"Stop." Maddy giggles as I dip my head and kiss her neck.

"I can't help it, baby. You. That dress. Knowing you're full of my cum right now? Makes me fucking feral around you," I growl in her ear as I slide my arm around her and grasp her hip through the silky green fabric.

She snorts into another giggle. "Behave, Mr. Rich."

"Never." I grin, leading us across the ballroom to the dancefloor. "Now dance with me so I can use your body to hide what happens to my dick when you wear this dress."

Maddy smiles, and it lights up her entire face as I pull her into my arms. I'll never get tired of seeing her like this. *Happy. Smiling.*

"You've seen me wear it loads." She rolls her eyes as she snakes her arms around my neck and lets me pull her close.

"And I love you more in it each time. It reminds me of the night at the opera. And how much has changed since."

Maddy lets out a contented sigh as we dance. "Yeah. So much has changed." She casts her eyes around the packed ballroom, then brings them back to mine. "You've worked so hard to get here. You're incredible."

"I've had a pretty great cheerleader with me the entire way." I squeeze her hips, and she bites her bottom lip.

"Take the compliment, Rich." She smiles. "This was you." She looks around the room again. "This was all you," she whispers.

It's the official launch for Vex tonight. A huge, glamorous affair with more champagne than anyone can drink, and canapes made from ingredients that had to be specially flown in from around the world. Spencer insisted on it. He wanted to pull in not only Vex's investors, but also London's elite with deep pockets. The charity auction we're holding later is to raise money for victims of natural disasters. A cause that has been close to his heart ever since he first learned about Matias. Spencer's now a proud and doting grandpa, telling Dad at every opportunity how it's the best thing that's happened to him.

I don't take my eyes off Maddy as we dance to another song. When it ends, we move toward the bar. Dad catches my eye from where he's standing with Mum. He no longer looks exhausted, like the weight of the world is on his shoulders. He's made cutbacks, and since I gave him the money from selling the island and the patent, his business is getting back on track. Dad's always loved a challenge. I think he's secretly in his element. He grins and tips his glass toward me as Mum says something in his ear. I know what they're discussing. Spencer's constant grandpa talk is giving them ideas.

"What's so funny?" Maddy narrows her eyes playfully.

"Mum and Dad, mentally listing baby names in their heads."

Maddy follows my gaze to my parents, who fluster and then smile before averting their attention away.

She laughs. "They're just happy. Business is good. Your dad's back in his own bed. And they're insanely proud of their talented son. Just like I am." She grins and I press a kiss to her lips.

"Maybe so," I murmur, smiling against her mouth before drawing back. "But they still want me to get you pregnant."

"A fact I don't want to fucking think about," a voice grumbles.

Maddy laughs as she spots Drew and Tanner standing next to one another in dinner jackets.

Drew tips his chin at me, and Tanner rolls his shoulders until they click, groaning as he takes a sip from his glass. "Don't do it. Parenting is a trap."

Drew looks at Tanner with a smirk. "You've been a grumpy bastard ever since Ruby was born."

"I had three hours sleep last night. Broken into eight parts. Newborns," Tanner mutters into his glass.

"You say that now, but you'll have another on the way soon," Drew says.

"No fucking chance." But his tired eyes twinkle.

"Fucker." Drew smiles in envy before he lifts his glass to his lips, his gaze moving to someone across the room.

I follow his attention. Dax has his arm around Rose, and they're talking to two women. One I don't recognize, but the other is Sophie, the lawyer.

"How long ago did she turn you down? And you're still not over it. A decade?" I ask.

Tanner snorts into his glass as Drew's jaw tightens. "Fuck off," he snaps without taking his eyes off Sophie.

"Almost four years," Maddy says, her voice soft as she looks at her brother.

Drew's eyes flit to hers and then back to Sophie, and his gaze dials up a notch in its dark intensity. I've never seen him like this with anyone else. But the night he met Sophie, he got this look of pure fixation in his eyes. The same one that's in them now. I thought he'd let the idea go. But ever since Dax needed a lawyer last year and Sophie helped him because she'd moved to London, we suspected their paths were bound to cross again.

Tonight, it seems, is that night.

"Why don't you go and talk to her?" Maddy asks.

"Rose said she's dating someone," Drew replies flatly before draining the rest of his whiskey.

He holds his empty glass up and gestures to the bar.

I shake my head. "We need to speak to some people," I say to Maddy as I spot Sterling.

Drew nods and him and Tanner move off in the direction of the bar.

"I worry about him." She chews on her bottom lip. "He's so intense and grouchy recently. He used to laugh more."

Drew leans an elbow on the bar top, but his eyes immediately move back to Sophie. As if she can feel his gaze, she looks over at him, and then away again just as fast.

"He'll be fine," I assure her. "He's made of tough stuff."

"Because he was turned tough." Maddy sighs.

I pull her into my side, pressing a kiss to her hair. "That's all in the past now, baby."

"I know." She settles into me, melding her body against mine as she presses her palm over my heart. "But he'll never have the kind of relationship with Dad that he deserved."

"That's your dad's fault. Not Drew's."

I hold her closer. I know it still pains her to talk about what happened. She hasn't been able to confront her dad over it yet. Drew would rather she leave it altogether. But I know her. She's carried this hurt around for years from that time in her life. She needs to let it go completely. And she will... when she's ready.

Maddy's brow creases as she looks down at the floor. "I can't believe Mum's acting like everything's fine. If this wasn't going to hurt her more, then I'd have talked to Dad already. But..." She lets out a deep sigh.

I bite back the choice of words I'd like to use to describe her father. It won't help her to hear them. No words will help Maddy feel better about the fact that her mum has been confronted with further evidence about her dad having an affair but has ignored it. And the fact that his actions are holding Maddy back from healing make me despise him more.

"I want her to be happy. She deserves it." Maddy's shoulders drop. "Maybe Dad didn't do anything." There's a tiny shred of hope in her voice. She adores her father. Or at least, she did. If I could, then I'd put him back on that pedestal she had him on, just to see her look happy again when she talks about him.

But I can't.

"Let's go talk to Sterling." Maddy's voice brightens as she sees him.

"You going to make me jealous again, Smiles?"

"What?" She laughs.

"That first meeting? He couldn't hide the fact he thought you were hot."

"Shut up." She giggles.

"You know it's true," I murmur as we close the distance to him. "It's why he invested more."

"He invested more because you were a moody dick and kept increasing the buy-in."

A smirk forms on my lips. "You're good for business, baby."

"Whatever." Maddy pouts.

"And you're an incredible negotiator," I add, earning myself a flattered curl of her lips.

"Charmer."

"I love you," I whisper.

She shakes her head, her smile spreading. "I love you too."

I tighten my grip on her waist as I steer us to where Sterling is standing talking to Magnus Grant, owner of

Atlantic Airways. The two men slap each other on the backs like old buddies and part before we get there.

"Sterling?" I grasp his hand.

"Logan." He shakes it. "Maddox." He takes hers too. "Impressive turnout."

"Thank you," I reply, assessing the crowded ballroom. "All made possible by our investors."

Sterling's eyes crinkle at the corners. "Nothing to invest in if it weren't for your idea."

I nod, unable to say anything else. This wouldn't have happened without his huge investment, and he knows it. But he maintains that his involvement is nothing compared to my vision. I haven't figured him out. I know he values originality and determination highly. All the members of his exclusive clubs he owns are high performers in their chosen fields. But there's something about him he doesn't let you see. Something deeper. Painful.

"Are you staying in London long?" Maddy asks Sterling.

The smile he gives her back is a warm one. She impressed him going back to negotiate with him in Italy. My hand on her hip flexes involuntarily even though I know he isn't flirting with her.

Maddy's eyes flick up to mine, and she narrows them knowingly, then leans into my side.

"No," Sterling replies. "I'm flying back to New York in the morning. But before I go." He looks between me and Maddy. "Tell me, the name of the first Vex prototype. Who came up with it?"

"Logan did." Maddy beams at me.

"*Sorriso*," Sterling says. "Interesting, and it means—"

"Smile," I say, looking down at Maddy, my heart swelling. "It's Italian for smile."

Maddy

I step out of my heels as we walk into the hallway. The cool marble floor is like heaven to my feet after a long evening spent at the launch party.

"Why don't you go and run a bath?" Logan murmurs against my skin as he envelops me in his arms from behind and presses his lips beneath my ear.

I sink back into him. "How about I just stay here, or you carry me there?" I sigh happily.

"You get a rocket engine named after you, and suddenly you think you should be carried everywhere?" He chuckles against my neck as I elbow him lightly in the ribs.

"I could move out if I'm not valued here," I counter.

Logan stiffens behind me, his voice deepening until a small growl rolls out. "No fucking way. You live with me now. This is your home. *Our* home."

I wiggle around in his arms until I'm facing him, then reach up to trace my fingers along his jaw as I toy with him. "Yeah?" I pout.

"Yeah." He kisses me deeply, causing the breath to stall in my throat. "These are here, so this must be your home." He smirks as he lifts me around the waist and then lowers me down so my feet are over my monogrammed slippers from Rome. I slide my feet inside them, humming contentedly.

"I guess living with you has one perk. My feet are happy."

He cocks a brow and then my stomach lurches as he lifts me, throwing me over his shoulder. A firm slap lands on my ass before he strides off, carrying me up the stairs.

"I think someone needs teaching a lesson."

My slippers fall off my feet and are left behind us on the stairs. "I think someone needs to put me down. Don't you, *Princepe?*" I bite back my giggle as my 'prince' groans deep in his chest and reaches up, cupping my ass with one giant hand.

He carries us into the master bedroom and kicks open the bathroom door before placing me down inside.

He reaches up to slide my dress from my shoulders. It falls to the floor in a puddle around my feet. I lean back, one hand either side of my waist against the counter as Logan's eyes drop over my body.

"Fuck, where are your panties, baby?" he groans, his thick neck contracting as he swallows.

"Oh, those?" I look down innocently at my lingerie from Italy. I'm wearing the bra and garter, but nothing else. "They got ripped."

I look up at him through my lashes as he takes his bowtie off, his eyes intent on mine.

"So they did," he grunts. "A pussy as pretty as yours shouldn't be covered up anyway. Not when you're with me."

He steps closer, and I suck in a breath as my heartrate picks up and hot desire fires between my legs.

"I got you something," he says, his eyes dark as he unbuttons his shirt and pulls it off.

I narrow my eyes at him as he commands the voice activated speaker system to play. I swallow down my confusion as the voice talks.

"You're every fantasy I've ever had. And I'm never letting you go."

"Log—?"

He silences me with a kiss, pulling me against his bare chest as he flicks off my bra.

"You. Me. These incredible tits." He groans, his teeth pressing into his lower lip as he kneads them. "We're having a fucking happy ever after."

I arch into his touch as his voice continues playing through the speaker.

"These words?"

"The end of your book," he confirms. His thumbs roll over my nipples as his hands cup my breasts greedily. "I read it. They get their happy ending, Mads. And so do we."

"You read it?" I gasp as he bends to suck one nipple.

"Yep." His growl vibrates his lips against my skin as he closes his mouth around me again, pleasure seeping into every contour of his beautiful face as he worships my body.

I try to concentrate on the words flowing around the room as he turns me inside out with desire.

"You recorded it in your voice?" I say breathlessly as he stands tall and slides two fingers inside me.

"Yep." His moan is long and gravelly as my arousal coats his fingers easily, making them slide effortlessly as he finger-fucks me leisurely.

"I never want you getting turned on listening to a man's voice again. Not unless it's mine." He grunts, watching my eyes roll in my head as he strokes my G-spot.

I shudder as he pins me in place against the counter with his hand. The muscles in his shoulder contract as he brings me closer and closer to orgasm.

"So you recorded it?" I pant as my core coils tighter.

He smirks. "Keep listening."

I struggle to concentrate as he drops to his knees, keeping his fingers buried inside me as he rolls his hot tongue over my clit.

"Keep listening, baby," he says.

I pant again, sinking the fingers of one hand into his hair and holding tight as he eats me out like he's been starved of me for years.

We've both been starved of each other.

"Logan," I whimper, my toes dancing against the floor as his efforts increase and he pushes his face further into me.

"Listen," he growls.

I ignore the blood rushing in my ears as I fight to take in each word. Each syllable. He's no longer narrating the closing lines from the book where Cameron is telling Frederica how much she means to him. He's speaking words I've never heard from that book, or any other book before.

His words.

"I told you that if this is what hate feels like, then I never need to fall in love. Do you remember?"

"Yes," I whimper.

He stands, his lips shining with my wetness as he kisses me.

"You hating me has been the best thing that's ever happened to me," the recorded voice continues.

Tears prick at my eyes, and I cling to his shoulders as he lifts me onto the edge of the counter.

"Me too," I breathe.

His green eyes burn as he pushes forward slowly, his hands encasing my hips as he pulls me onto his cock. He sucks in a breath, holding himself still deep inside me. I quiver around him, on the edge of exploding, but not quite there.

"Logan," I whimper.

He holds my eyes as he begins to move, his thrusts slow, but achingly deep. Deep enough that my breath is pushed from my lungs in a gasp each time he buries himself inside me.

"I love you," I cry as a new wave of wetness floods him. I part my legs wider and smirk at him.

I'm not shy about it. He knows what he does to me. How hot for him I am. I always have been, ever since that first time he fucked me in this position. Even though I thought I hated him back then. Even though I couldn't see him for what he is.

The true prince of my story.

Even when I thought I hated him, I couldn't deny the effect he had on me.

"You going to show me how hard you can come on my cock, baby?" He grasps my thigh with his other hand, sliding it beneath the garter belt as he digs his fingers into my flesh. "You going to scream my name?"

"Yes," I cry as his thrusts force me back along the top of the counter with their strength. He drags me back sharply each time, pulling me back down onto his cock with a deep grunt, like he has every right to, like he did that first time.

Owning me. Controlling my pleasure. Knowing I need him.

He stares into my eyes, his jaw thickening with tension as the audio continues.

"You are all I'll ever need, Maddox Harper."

"And you're all I'll ever need too." I squeeze my eyes shut as I kiss him.

"Look at me," he urges.

I peel my eyes open and am enveloped in dazzling emerald green fire as he holds my gaze, his cock throbbing inside me with a heat so great it thrums through my entire body.

"You ready?" he rasps.

"Yes." I sink my nails into his shoulders, pretty sure I feel blood, warm against my fingertips.

Logan's pupils blow wide and his eyes flash as he groans, the sting only seeming to enhance his pleasure.

"Then get these legs wider. I want you to feel every drop going deep inside you."

I throw my legs wider so fast it makes Logan chuckle. "That's my good girl." He thrusts hard, and I scream his name. "My fucking good girl," he hisses, as his skin slaps against mine, echoing around the room, louder than the audio was before it ended.

"You ready?" he growls again.

I nod, clawing at him as I'm overcome with a need so great that I might pass out any second if he doesn't give me what I want.

"Please," I cry.

"Okay, baby." He curses under his breath. "I'm going to ruin this sweet little pussy with the amount of cum I have for it. And you're going to take it all like a good girl, aren't you?"

Nothing else exists for a moment as the two of us stare at each other.

No words needed.

He tips his chin as he explodes with a low groan.

The first drop sears me inside as it spills from him. His sinful lips curl into his signature smirk as it sets my own orgasm off and I come apart in his arms, whimpering, panting, and crying his name.

Just like the first time.

"Here it is, baby."

I struggle to breathe through the intense waves my body is clamping down onto his with. His eyes never leave mine as he growls out his own release deep inside me, sending my orgasm hurtling into another, as strong.

Just like the first time.

His smirk turns into a delicious smile as his pleasure falls over its peak.

I gaze back at him, unable to take my eyes from his.

Just like the first time.

Only this time I'm not fighting him, and I won't be pushing away the second it's done.

This time, I kiss him until we have to break apart to breathe.

This time, I give him everything as he groans out those final words, "Here it fucking is, baby."

I give him everything.

Except hate. Not hate. Never hate.

And as I do...

I smile.

The End.
(Keep reading for a bonus epilogue)

Chapter 41
Logan

Extended Epilogue

"BETTER THAN A TRAGIC story where he marries someone else and she kills herself or not?"

She giggles as she takes my arm, resting her cheek against my shoulder.

"Different. Especially the part where she gave up her voice and couldn't talk to the prince."

"Sounds like it would have some perks." I tip my head thoughtfully as Maddy nudges me in the ribs.

"You'd be lost without me."

"You and your dramatic stories. I'll be having night-mares," I tease.

She giggles more and sinks into my side. "Every great story has an element of drama to it before the happy ending. It makes it that much better once the characters finally get there. Although some operas are tragic, I'll admit."

I press a kiss to the top of her hair as we meander our way down the street away from Teatro alla Scala where we've watched Rusalka.

It's been months since we were here. Being back here with Maddy feels... right.

Every day with her feels right.

"Remember when I was being an incredible boyfriend this afternoon?"

"Mm-hm." Her eyes glitter as she looks up at me. "When you waited in line with all my parcels?"

I purse my lips. "When I partook in official book fairy business, spreading happiness globally."

She laughs and rolls her eyes. "I picked the books and packaged them up. You held the parcels... but okay."

"Packaged them up in the mailers I designed for you."

Maddy twists her lips, hiding her smile. "They are pretty mailers."

"They're a work of art."

Maddy laughs. "Okay, what about it?"

"You told me you'd thank me later." I quirk a brow.

"You have a one-track mind." She shakes her head as she strokes my bicep.

"So now, then?"

"When we get back to the hotel. I'm not getting arrested and thrown in an Italian prison for public indecency."

I slam to a halt and Maddy looks up at me in confusion.

"Ms. Harper, you're a dirty girl with a filthy mind, thinking about my cock all the time."

Her eyes widen as a blush creeps up her neck as she glances at the people walking nearby.

I love playing with her. She screamed my name so loud when she came with my head between her legs this morning that the rest of the floor in our hotel probably heard her. But now she's looking around like she's worried the whole of Milan heard me say the word cock.

"Logan." She bites her bottom lip but her eyes light up as I pull it free and press a kiss to them, groaning quietly as she kisses me back.

"You can keep that filthy mind on hold." My eyes drop to her cleavage in the green dress. "Because damn, I want to fuck your tits later."

She parts her lips as if to protest but I shush her with another kiss.

"But before that, there's somewhere we should go."

Maddy

"I guess you'll be needing this." I slap a euro into Logan's hand, smiling as he looks at me in mock outrage.

"You think I'd bring my girlfriend to the greatest wish granting fountain in the entire world and not come prepared?"

"Idiot," I snort as he winks at me.

I turn and look into the water of the Trevi Fountain. The multitude of coins, *wishes*, sparkle underneath the moonlight from their position beneath the water.

"How many do you think come true?" I muse as I wrap my arms around myself and rub them.

Warmth envelops me, along with the comforting scent of Logan's aftershave as he places his tuxedo jacket around me.

"Mine all have."

"I remember yours. You didn't let your dad down. You found a way to make Vex happen, save the business. You're a real *prince* to the rescue."

I bump his shoulder as he chuckles, then he moves behind me and wraps me inside his arms, his breath skating along the side of my neck making me shiver.

"Plus, I got a happy future for my big dick with a girl who's going to suck it again later."

I nudge his forehead with my palm as I laugh, but he catches my arm and presses a kiss to the inside of my wrist.

"In fact, I don't need to make another wish, Mads. You can have this back." He kisses my wrist again and places the coin inside my hand, curling my fingers around it.

It digs into my palm.

"What...? Logan."

I unfurl my fingers and stare at the giant marquis diamond ring in my hand.

"What is this?"

"A tiny weapon to have on hand for days you hate me. Look at the points on that thing."

I spin to look at him, but he isn't there.

"Smiles." His voice is soft, and I look down to where he's bent onto one knee.

"No," I blurt.

His face falls. "I haven't even asked you yet."

"No," I repeat, causing his brows to lock together and his eyes to bounce side to side as he searches my face. "I mean... yes... I mean... No."

"Which the fuck is it?" He stares at me with his mouth wide open.

People around us have stopped what they're doing, and I can feel their inquisitive eyes on us.

Logan drags a hand around the back of his neck as he looks up at me with a look on his face that makes my heart plummet to my feet.

"I mean, yes... yes!" I nod frantically and shove the ring into his chest.

"You said no, though." He looks at the ring like it's unstable and he shouldn't touch it.

The only thing unstable here is my heart as I fail to get my words out.

"I meant no way is this happening. Then I meant yes."

He tears his eyes away from the ring and I bring my hand back from his chest.

It looks like I'm shoving the ring back at him. And I said no. No wonder he looks confused.

"Listen." I lift the bottom of my dress and drop to my knees, facing him. "I mean yes. A million times yes."

A tear slips free as I take his hand and press the beautiful ring inside it.

"Now, ask me..."

I hold my breath as I look into his eyes. Bewilderment turns to amusement, and it dances in them like green flames as he holds my gaze.

"It's always going to be drama with you, isn't it, Smiles?"

"Yes," I breathe out in a rush as I hold my shaking hand up with my fingers outstretched. "You know you'd hate it any other way."

His face splits into a grin.

"I sure would."

He falls serious as he takes my hand and holds the ring against the tip of my finger.

"Maddox Harper, will you agree to keep my life filled with drama? And hold my hand every day." His lips twitch as I narrow my eyes at him in question. "Maddy..." He rolls the giant diamond over the tip of my finger as he smiles. "Marry me."

"Yes."

I break into my biggest smile yet.

Logan

"It feels weird having something so big there."

Maddy gazes at the ring on her finger as I open the door to our penthouse and pull her inside. She hasn't stopped staring at her hand since I put the ring on it.

"You should be used to big things, Smiles." I swoop on her from behind, sucking and kissing her neck as I press my erection into her ass.

"What do you think Drew will say?" She spins inside my arms and puts her arms around my shoulders, tugging the hair at the back of my head lightly.

I groan and lean into her touch.

"He's getting me as a brother-in-law, he basically pissed himself in excitement." I laugh.

"Shut up," Maddy snorts, but then her eyes go round. "Seriously? He knows?"

"I asked for his permission." I brush a dark curl from her eyes.

"And he gave it to you?" Her breath hitches as I skate my thumb along her jaw and then rub it over her full bottom lip.

"Practically begged me to take you on."

I smirk as she jabs me in the ribs.

"He's happy for us, Mads," I say as I tilt her chin so I can lower my lips toward hers. "But not as fucking happy as I am that you said yes. I love you, future Mrs. Rich."

Maddy's teeth sink into her lower lip, and I pull it free so I can kiss her.

The second we make contact, it's like something ignites. She pulls at my belt as I hitch her dress up and grab a handful of her thigh. We moan, nip, kiss, suck and crash our way across the room, knocking over a lamp on the way.

I lift her onto the sideboard the same time as she pulls my dick free of my pants.

We pause, chests heaving, eyes wild, as we stare at each other.

Same place. Same two people. Same passion.

New words.

"Tell me," I whisper as I pull her panties to the side and push inside her body.

She moans, clamping down onto my cock as I slide inside as deep as I can get.

"Tell me," I urge as I pick up the pace, fucking her hard enough that the sideboard bangs against the wall, the same way it did all those months ago.

She grabs onto my ass cheeks and digs her nails into my flesh. The sting has me smiling around my curse.

"I love you." She squirms in my arms, meeting me thrust for thrust. "I love you, I love you," she chants in time with our desperate movements.

"Fuck." I pull her forehead to mine. "So good, baby," I rasp.

"So good," she echoes.

"Remember I said imagine how good it would feel if you actually liked me?" I grunt as her wetness coats my cock more and she loosens a little, letting me drive deeper.

"Yeah." Her eyes hold mine as I change my angle, making her whimper.

"How's it feel now that you love me?"

"Logan..."

"How's it feel?" I push deeper.

"It feels... It feels..."

"We couldn't fight this forever, Mads. We couldn't resist this." I thrust inside her, driving my point home.

We were inevitable.

"It's everything," she cries, pulling my lips to hers as she trembles. "I love you."

"You need it, don't you?" I kiss her back, swallowing down each gasp of desire that comes from her lips.

"I *want* it." Her nails press into my skin, pulling me close. "Don't you dare stop. I want it."

"You sure?"

"Logan!" Maddy screams in frustration.

I smirk as I slam my hips against her.

"Here it is, baby."

I sink my teeth into my lower lip as I come hard.

Maddy's eyes widen, then her eyes screw shut as she shatters for me.

I growl out my release, each spasm from her body hugging my cock and drawing out my orgasm until my legs feel like they might give out.

"Tomorrow, when you're still feeling me inside you, *wife*, remember to say—"

"Thank you," Maddy whispers. She kisses me, and I taste her happiness.

"I'll smile and say thank you."

The End.

Elle's Books

Resisting Mr. Rich is book 8 in 'The Men Series', a collection of interconnected standalone stories.
They can be read in any order, however, for full enjoyment of the overlapping characters, the suggested reading order is:
Meeting Mr. Anderson – Holly and Jay
Discovering Mr. X – Rachel and Tanner
Drawn to Mr. King – Megan and Jaxon
Captured by Mr. Wild – Daisy and Blake
Pleasing Mr. Parker – Maria and Griffin
Trapped with Mr. Walker – Harley and Reed
Time with Mr. Silver – Rose and Dax
Resisting Mr. Rich – Maddy and Logan
Handling Mr. Harper – Sophie and Drew
(Also available by Elle, Forget-me-nots and Fireworks, Shona and Trent's story, a novella length prequel to The Men Series)
Get all of Elle's books here: http://author.to/elleni coll

Acknowledgements

I will start as I always do, with the lady who gave me the
courage to go on this journey...
TL Swan.
And to all the Cygnets for bringing new friends into my
life whom I adore.
Sara, my PA, for being amazingly organised and for
keeping me calm.
My beta readers; Sara, Taye, Rita, and Kelly. Thank you
for loving Logan and Maddy, despite her stubborness.
Zee, my wonderful editor. I DON'T KNOW WHAT I'D
DO WITHOUT YOUR SHOUTY CAPS.
Thank you to Abi and Sherri for nailing the covers.
Every. Single. Time.
Thank you to my ARC and street team. I couldn't do this
without you all!
Thank you bloggers, bookstagrammers, booktokkers,
and everyone who has shared my books. I am so, so
grateful.
Finally, to you, the reader.
These would just be words on a page without you.
Thank you for bringing these stories to life by reading
them.

May reading continue to bring you joy by the truckload.
If you enjoyed Resisting Mr. Rich then please leave a
review on Amazon and share it with your book besties.
It helps indie authors so much.
Until the next book...
Elle x

About Elle

Elle Nicoll is an ex long-haul flight attendant and mum of two from the UK.

After fourteen years of having her head in the clouds whilst working at 38,000ft, she is now usually found with her head between the pages of a book reading or furiously typing and making notes on another new idea for a book boyfriend who is sweet-talking her.

Elle finds it funny that she's frequently told she looks too sweet and innocent to write a steamy book, but she never wants to stop. Writing stories about people, passion, and love, what better thing is there?

Because,

Love Always Wins

xxx

To keep up to date with the latest news and releases, find Elle in the following places, and sign up for her newsletter below;

https://www.subscribepage.com/ellenicollauthorcom
Facebook Reader Group – Love always Wins – https://www.facebook.com/groups/686742179258218
Website – https://www.ellenicollauthor.com

a

http://author.to/ellenicoll

f

facebook.com/ellenicollauthor

instagram.com/ellenicollauthor

BB

bookbub.com/authors/elle-nicoll

pinterest.com/ellenicollauthor

tiktok.com/@authorellenicoll

goodreads.com/author/show/21415735.Elle_Nicoll

Printed in Great Britain
by Amazon

51283987R00260